THE THUNDER KNIGHT

BOOK THREE – LORDS OF THUNDER
THE DE SHERA BROTHERHOOD TRILOGY
A MEDIEVAL ROMANCE

BY
KATHRYN LE VEQUE

KATHRYN LE VEQUE NOVELS

Queen of Lost Stars (House of St. Hever)

Lords of Thunder: The de Shera Brotherhood Trilogy
The Thunder Lord
The Thunder Warrior
The Thunder Knight

Highland Warriors of Munro
The Red Lion

Time Travel Romance: (Saxon Lords of Hage)
The Crusader
Kingdom Come

Contemporary Romance:

Kathlyn Trent/Marcus Burton Series:
Valley of the Shadow
The Eden Factor
Canyon of the Sphinx

The American Heroes Series:
The Lucius Robe
Fires of Autumn
Evenshade
Sea of Dreams
Purgatory

Other Contemporary Romance:
Lady of Heaven
Darkling, I Listen
In the Dreaming Hour

Multi-author Collections/Anthologies:
With Dreams Only of You (USA Today bestseller)
Sirens of the Northern Seas (Viking romance)
Ever My Love (sequel to With Dreams Only Of You) July 2016

Note: All Kathryn's novels are designed to be read as stand-alones, although many have cross-over characters or cross-over family groups. Novels that are grouped together have related characters or family groups.

Series are clearly marked. All series contain the same characters or family groups except the American Heroes Series, which is an anthology with unrelated characters.

There is NO particular chronological order for any of the novels because they can all be read as stand-alones, even the series.

For more information, find it in **A Reader's Guide to the Medieval World of Le Veque.**

CONTENTS

AUTHOR'S NOTE

The end has come!

The Lords of Thunder Trilogy takes place in the year 1258, which was the year that saw Simon de Montfort come to power in his struggle against Henry III. If you've read the previous two books, then you've had your history lesson already. So let's close this up – on to Tiberius' story.

The year 1258 was probably one of the most eventful in English history for a variety of reasons. One of the main points of contention at this time was the fact that Henry III had allowed many of his wife's French relatives, and other French nobles, into England, and this French contingent was taking over many key castles and English properties, which didn't sit well with the English barons.

There is a small portion of this book that deals with Prince Edward, the future Edward I of "Braveheart" fame, siding with Simon de Montfort. Of course, he had many reasons for this and I've only touched upon one of them. There is so much political intrigue and history going on during this year that to include all of it would have made this book gigantic, so I only touch upon those reasons which are key to the storyline. Also, Prince Edward's siding with de Montfort wasn't official until March 1259, but in my story, the wheels are in motion early on.

And there is knitting! The history of knitting presumes that the actual art of knitting with two needles was invented somewhere around this time, probably in Italy, and there are items in England dated to about 1260 A.D. – a pair of gloves and a seat cushion. In this novel, Lady Douglass is knitting, the newest and latest ladies' activity, although she is probably doing it a few years before it truly became popular.

On to the serious now – in this novel, we come to discover that Tiberius has dyslexia. Of course, back then it wasn't diagnosed. It was simply believed that the person was dense, but in Tiberius' case, that is far from the truth. It's not a major part of this novel, but it is mentioned so if you were wondering what his issue is, now you know.

Overall, I hope this is a fitting ending to the Lords of Thunder Trilogy and I truly hope you enjoy it. Gallus, Maximus, and Tiberius deserve a happy conclusion.

Happy reading!

Hugs,
Kathryn

PART ONE
WINDS OF AWAKENING
AUGUST

And, with the thunder near,
The edge of fear,
The end was clearly in sight.
The time had come,
For all, for one,
With the man known as the Thunder Knight.

~ 13th century chronicles

CHAPTER ONE

1258 A.D.
Isenhall Castle

"HE IS IN Coventry being pursued by de Montfort's agents. We must ride."

The quietly muttered statement came from Tiberius de Shera. Extremely tall, with a crown of soft, dark curls and enormous shoulders, he was the youngest of the de Shera brother trio. He spoke to his brothers, Maximus and Gallus, as they gathered in the small, vaulted-ceilinged solar of Isenhall's enormous block-shaped keep. Tiberius' brothers, however, seemed a bit perplexed at Tiberius' hurried statement.

"*Who* is in Coventry?" Gallus, the eldest of the three, asked. "Whom do you speak of?"

Tiberius appeared quite serious, unusual for the usually jovial knight. He was young, that was true – five years younger than middle brother Maximus, who himself had seen thirty-two years – but Tiberius had always been a mixture of knightly maturity and boyish charm. It was an unusual combination because the knight in him was the best England had to offer. The boy in him was one who could easily find himself on the painful end of a brotherly beating. But the older de Shera brothers had learned long ago to trust Tiberius' knightly instincts, which is why when he spoke of a serious matter, they listened closely.

"De Moray," Tiberius answered. "There is a young man in the bailey who has raced all the way from Coventry. Garran sent a boy with a message – Garran, his father, and a sister were traveling south to their home in Dorset and realized they were being followed by de Montfort men. Now they are barricaded at Coventry and we must save them. They are in trouble."

De Moray is in trouble. That brief explanation clarified the situation quite a bit and the older de Shera brothers began to move. Already, they were heading to the entry of the keep where beyond, in the small and crowded bailey, were located the stables and the armory. There was a sense of urgency as the battle lords, men known as the Lords of Thunder, moved with purpose.

"Were they traveling alone?" Maximus de Shera, the middle brother, demanded. He was a forceful man, curt and to the point at times. "De Moray knows better than to travel without an escort, especially in these times and especially that close to Kenilworth. Did he not think de Montfort men would be about and not recognize him?"

Tiberius was concerned for his close friend, Garran de Moray, son of the great knight Bose de Moray. Up until a few months ago, Garran had been sworn to the House of de Shera and, consequently, Simon de Montfort's cause as the man wrested the power of the nation from Henry III during these dark and turbulent times. But Garran's father, Bose, had been the Captain of the Guard for Henry when the king had been very young. It was a bond that had formed way back then. Henry had even saved Bose's life once.

Therefore, during this conflict, there was no question which side the great de Moray would support and the father had asked the son to ride with him, as he did not want to lift a sword against his own son in battle. Garran, even though he disagreed with Henry's politics, agreed to support his father. It had been a sad parting with the House of de Shera. But Garran was still one of their knights as far as the de Shera brothers were concerned, which meant that they would ride to his aid no matter what.

"I have no idea what Bose de Moray was thinking as he passed through Coventry," Tiberius answered his brother's question. "Mayhap he was coming to Isenhall to visit us or mayhap he was simply heading home. Whatever the reason, we must put our questions aside and extract the man and his family from Coventry before de Montfort's assassins get to them."

They all agreed on that point. Out in the tightly-packed bailey, it was early morning and the sky above was already crisp and blue. The past week had been rather warm and this day promised to be no different. The weather had been quite wonderful and the ground was dry, free from the usual mud that plagued it. As Maximus headed to the knights' quarters to rouse the stable of de Shera knights, Gallus and Tiberius headed to the armory to dress for the occasion.

The air in the armory was stale and warm, so by the time Gallus and Tiberius finished dressing in their usual protection of mail and pieces of plate, they were sweating rivers. Tiberius also smelled rather bad because he tended to sweat quite a bit and he hadn't bathed in a while, so he was sure that noxious odor wafting upon the air was him. He kept sniffing the air and making faces, which eventually prompted his brother to push him out of the armory altogether. Stumbling out of the door, Tiberius turned to his brother, perplexed and insulted.

"Why did you do that?" he demanded.

Gallus shook his head, waving a hand at him. "Because you smell like a rotted corpse," he said. "Why do you not bathe once in a while?"

Tiberius cocked a dark eyebrow. "What for?" he asked. "I do not have a woman in my bed like you and Max do. I do not need to smell sweet for anyone."

Gallus fought off a grin. "Someday you may want to attract a woman," he said as he pulled on his heavy gloves. "All you will manage to do is chase her off with that terrible stench. Besides, you know that certain smells make my wife nauseous in her current state. If you make her vomit because you refuse to bathe, I will take a stick to you."

Tiberius eyed his beloved eldest brother. Gallus de Shera was the Earl of Coventry and the Lord Sheriff of Worcester, a title he had worked hard to achieve. He was a man in his prime, the eldest of the most powerful trio of brothers, and Tiberius adored him. More than that, he believed him when Gallus said he would take a stick to him if he upset his pregnant wife. With a grin, Tiberius moved away from the armory.

"Then I shall stay away from her," he said to Gallus as he walked away, "but I will stick close to you to make sure you smell me until the bitter end."

He could hear Gallus calling after him. "You shall drive the enemy away without even lifting your sword," he shouted. "One smell of you will knock them on their arses!"

Tiberius laughed softly as he headed towards the stables. His middle brother, Maximus, was just emerging. Baron Allesley, otherwise known as Maximus de Shera, was a very big, very powerful man who had recently married. His wife was a lovely woman who seemed to have the ability to tame the savage beast in Maximus because Tiberius had never seen his brother so content or so happy. Or calm, for that matter. The usually curt, rude, and aggressive man he'd known all of these years was now tempered by a slip of a woman. But the fighter in him, that warrior that men feared so much, was still as deadly as ever.

"We are taking a light force with us," Maximus said as he drew near Tiberius. "Both de Wolfe brothers and du Bois are already saddling their horses and I'm having twenty soldiers mount up and ride with us. That should be enough."

Tiberius moved past the man, heading into the stables. "The sooner, the better," he said. "There is no time to waste."

Maximus, who was heading towards the keep, kept walking as he let out a hissing sound. "God's Bones, Ty," he said, putting his fingers to his nose. "There is a cloud of lethal odor following behind you, engulfing everything in its wake. If you do not bathe upon our return, I will put you in the tub myself and scrub you until you can no longer offend anyone."

Tiberius didn't say anything but he made a face at his brother as he entered the stable, his stench mingling with the smell of horses and hay. He was coming to think that, perhaps, he should bathe at some point soon because he knew Maximus would follow through on his threat. But he pushed those thoughts aside as a groom brought forth his big, gray dappled, Belgian charger. In a time when war horses were not commonly used for travel, Tiberius rode one horse and one horse only, even though he personally owned several. But the big Belgian stallion had two attributes that Tiberius liked best – he was oddly calm for a war horse until he was in the heat of battle and he had a pleasing traveling gait that was quite comfortable. Those two factors made him Tiberius' favorite horse. He affectionately greeted the big gray steed with the black mane and tail.

"Storm," he addressed the horse, scratching the animal on the ears because he liked it. "Did you have your morning gruel, old man?"

The groom who had brought the horse nodded to the question. "He likes his cold gruel, my lord," he agreed. "He ate a bucketful of the stuff."

Tiberius grinned and slapped the animal on the neck before mounting the beast. The horse loped from the stables and out into the bailey where men were gathering and Tiberius quieted the soldiers down, explaining what they would soon be doing. Garran de

Moray was in trouble and needed assistance. Tiberius presented the boy who had brought the news and had the young man repeat the message, his youthful voice echoing off the old, circular perimeter walls of Isenhall Castle as he told the hardened de Shera men of the situation.

Tiberius was usually the brother to handle the men while Gallus and Maximus would handle other aspects of their warring life; with Gallus, it was leadership and politics and with Maximus, it was logistics and tactics. Tiberius was the brother who had the ear of the men, the one who allowed himself to become friendly with the soldiers and knights. He had a bit of an unprotected heart which, in his profession, could be a problem at times, but Tiberius never let it interfere with his sense of duty. He was a de Shera to the core and a de Shera always knew his duty.

Maximus soon joined him, coming out of the armory along with Gallus, but Gallus headed into the keep as Maximus went to join the men. They gathered near the gatehouse of Isenhall, a squat, box-like structure that was impenetrable. It had double portcullises and enough murder holes from the second floor above the gatehouse passage to effectively kill anyone trying to enter through the gatehouse. Those old stones had seen decades, even centuries, of death and peace. As the heavily-armed group awaited the earl, Gallus emerged from the keep being trailed by several women and two big dogs.

Taranis, the massive black dog that belonged to Gallus' young daughters, trotted out with his companion, Henry, a very large, leggy mutt that Maximus' wife had adopted during their stay in Oxford a few months prior. The two dogs were good friends and excellent protectors for the women, whom they were very attached to. Henry even had a penchant for sleeping on Maximus' side of the bed, next to his wife, and then growling at Maximus when the man tried to claim his place. There had been a few nights since their marriage back in May when Maximus had been forced to endure the dog sleeping between them.

But it didn't matter, truthfully. Dog or no, Maximus was deeply and endlessly in love with his wife, Lady Courtly. He caught sight of the woman as she emerged from the keep with Gallus' youngest daughter, Lily, on her hip and he immediately headed in her direction to bid her a sweet farewell.

Gallus already had his pregnant wife in one hand and was leading his oldest daughter, Violet, with the other. The children were Gallus' from his first marriage but the girls were young enough that they had taken to Jeniver right away. It was a happy collection of women, girls, and dogs who had come to bid the de Shera men a farewell, but there was one obvious omission – the de Shera brothers' mother, the Lady Honey.

"It seems odd," Tiberius muttered to Sir Stefan du Bois, on a horse next to him, "not to see my mother here, giving us a speech about accomplishing our task because we are de Sheras. She was as much a part of this army as any of us are."

Stefan, son of the great knight Maddoc du Bois, looked away from Gallus and Maximus and their wives and focused on the man who was his distant cousin as well as his friend.

"It will seem strange for a while, I suppose," he said quietly. Young and very brilliant, he had a deep and succinct voice. "It certainly is not the same without her."

Tiberius' gaze drifted over the collection of de Shera men and women. "Honey was only able to meet Jeniver," he said. "I believe she would have loved Courtly very much. It saddens me that she will never see all of this, this empire she helped create and the decent people within it. I have never felt her loss more strongly than I do at this moment."

Stefan nodded in agreement. "She is here," he spoke confidently. "You simply cannot see her. She is here, as she has always been, overseeing the bailey. Watch, now say something foolish and see if a bird does not drop shite on your head in punishment. That is Lady Honey showing you her disapproval."

Tiberius laughed softly, turning to look at his young cousin. "You know exactly how to cheer me up, do you not?" he said. Then he sighed heavily and spurred his charger forward. "No more delays, Stefan. Move the men out of the gatehouse and find de Moray's messenger. He will ride with us. I will go and collect my brothers."

Stefan immediately took up the command, as did the other two knights. Sir Scott de Wolfe and his twin, Sir Troy de Wolfe, took up the cry as well and soon the collection of heavily-armed de Shera men were moving out of the gatehouse, squeezing through the narrowed passage and beneath the twin portcullises, emerging on the other side. Meanwhile, Tiberius was separating his brothers from their wives and children, which proved to be a bigger task than he had anticipated.

"Lovers and ladies," he said in his usual flippant tone, "there are men who will not wait for you and men who mayhap cannot wait for you, so it is with great regret that I encourage you to mount your horses and come with me quickly. De Moray is in need of us."

Gallus kissed his daughters and his wife, in that order, before swiftly mounting his steed. "We should not be gone too long," he told his wife, who was gazing up at him, gingerly rubbing her rounded belly. "I would anticipate we shall be home by sup. Make sure you prepare for guests."

"Ty!" Lily, Gallus' youngest, was calling from Courtly's arms. "Ty, I come with you!"

Lily has just seen her fourth year, a feisty, little girl who was rather attached to her Uncle Tiberius, but Tiberius sadly shook his head.

"Nay, Lee Lee, my dearest love," he said regretfully. "You cannot come. If you do, who will stay with Taranis?"

Lily, or "Lee Lee", as she was known to the family, immediately looked to the dog that was bigger than she was, sitting patiently a few feet away. Thankfully distracted, she slithered out of Courtly's arms and went to the dog, putting her arms around his neck and hugging him. But just as Lily was diverted, Violet spoke up.

"We are strong," she informed her uncle. "I have a pony. I can ride with you!"

Again, Tiberius shook his head as if deeply saddened that he had to deny her. "Not this time, my lovely Vi," he said. "Mayhap another time. You still do not have a sword. You cannot fight without a sword."

Five-year-old Violet knew that it was true. She looked at Jeniver, bewildered, and Jeniver took her hand and smiled.

"Let them go this time," Jeniver said in her sweet, gentle voice. "I would be happy if you would stay here with me. Let us go back inside and draw. Remember that we were drawing flowers yesterday? Let us continue. We will draw a beautiful picture for your Papa by the time he returns home."

That seemed to interest Violet enough and she took off running towards the keep with Lily and the dogs racing after her. The dogs were barking and chasing the girls as the adults watched with some relief. Courtly was the first one to speak.

"Hurry and go," she said, waving her hands at the knights. "Violet is probably going in search of a sword to use, so hurry and leave while you can."

With a grin, Tiberius reined his steed about and headed off towards the gatehouse. Gallus blew a kiss at his wife and followed as Maximus brought his big, black and white warhorse alongside his wife and bent over in the saddle, kissing her sweetly, before following his brothers out of the bailey. When they were finally through the gatehouse, both portcullises began to close, the chains and ropes grinding, and sentries upon the walls shouting that the walls and gatehouse were now secured.

From the noise and chaos of armed men moments earlier, the sudden silence was almost disorienting. Hollow, even, now that the men were gone. Courtly turned to Jeniver.

"Come along, my lady," she said, holding out a hand to her sister-in-law and friend. "Let us get you inside so you may lie down and rest. Your son needs his sleep."

Jeniver smiled as she took Courtly's hand, the sister she never had, her beautiful blond hair wrapped up in a stylish braid encircling her head. Courtly's blond against Jeniver's black was about as different as it could be. From nearly the beginning of their association those months ago in Oxford, different or no, they had been inseparable best friends.

"My son is already as big as an ox," she said, rubbing her swollen belly. "I cannot imagine that I have two more months to go. I already feel as if I am going to burst open."

Courtly smiled, putting her hand on Jeniver's belly as the women headed towards the keep. "Is Bhrodi kicking today?"

Jeniver nodded. "Constantly," she said, weary. "He kicks more when he hears the horses. I do believe he wants to be a knight already."

Courtly nodded as they took the big, wide, stone steps that led up into the keep. "He is not yet born and already a knight," she said. "He is a de Shera. He will be born with spurs on his feet and a sword in his hand."

Jeniver looked at her, horrified. "God's Bones, I hope not," she said. "That would be most painful."

Courtly giggled. "I am afraid it will be painful in any case," she said. Then, she sobered. "But have no fear. I will be by your side. I will not leave you."

Jeniver squeezed her hand as they entered the dark, cool innards of the keep. "I am comforted," she said. "I would be lying if I said that I was not apprehensive, but I do not tell Gallus that. He is more apprehensive than I am."

The darkened interior of Isenhall's keep drew them into the reception room, the first room one came to when entering the keep. It was low-ceilinged but very comfortable, with chairs, benches, a table, and a big, bright fire in the hearth. This is where the wealth of the de Sheras began to come evident. Courtly directed Jeniver into a chair near the hearth as the children and the dogs played several feet away.

"Men are terrified of childbirth," Courtly said. "They fear it more than anything. Gallus wants a healthy son and a healthy wife. I will do my very best to ensure he receives both. We have already spoken to the best midwife in Coventry and the woman will be attending you this birth, so you have little to fear. All will be well."

Jeniver gazed up at Courtly, her brown eyes unnaturally dark against her porcelain-like face. "But if it is not," she murmured, "you will promise me something."

Courtly didn't like it when the conversation about the impending birth turned serious. She was secretly more terrified than any of them because, as the only woman at Isenhall, she was expected to attend to the birth. She felt as if all expectations of the entire de Shera family line were resting on her and the pressure was immense. It was difficult enough for her to keep up her courage without Jeniver growing serious and grim about it, but she allowed the woman her fear. She had every right.

"Of course I will," she whispered. "All you need do is ask."

Jeniver rubbed her belly, thinking on the life inside. "If I do not survive the birth," she said softly, "promise you will take care of my son. Promise you will love him as I would have. Promise me that you will make sure he has the very best in everything."

Courtly was struggling not to tear up. "Of course," she assured her softly. "I already love him. He will not want for anything, I swear it."

Jeniver's gaze was intense. "And Gallus," she said, struggling. "You will make sure… make sure he marries again. Make sure he loves again. I want him to be happy."

Courtly was afraid to speak because of the lump in her throat. Without a word, she sat down beside her friend, taking her hand again and holding it tightly. They sat there, in silence, listening to the children play and thinking of babies born and of men at war. So much potential for death in their happy worlds. So much potential for grief.

It was the silent prayer of both women that neither one of them experience such sorrow anytime soon. Theirs was a wonderful world and they wanted to preserve it as long as they could.

Preserve the happy House of de Shera.

CHAPTER TWO

Coventry

IT WAS LATE morning by the time the de Shera guard rode into Coventry. The day had warmed up considerably and most of the people who had done their shopping or had conducted business early in the morning were now back at home so the streets were relatively empty. That fact made it far easier for the de Shera contingent to hunt for the de Montfort men that were allegedly closing in on de Moray. Heavily-armed men would stand out in an atmosphere such as this because de Montfort wouldn't search out the enemy in secret. He would have his men out in the open as if daring the enemy to come forth.

According to the messenger boy that de Moray had sent to Isenhall, de Moray was barricaded in a tavern called the Castle and Chain, which was one of the more popular taverns in the city. Tiberius had visited it many times for drunken debauchery and knew it well. Therefore, as they entered the city, he sent five groups of two men each to search out any sign of de Montfort men while the bulk of the contingent continued on to the tavern.

The tavern sat at the corner of a big intersection, the apex of two major roads leading into town from the north and the east. It was a two-storied structure with exposed exterior beams and wattle and daub construction, and the entire back portion of the building sagged slightly, as it had sunk into the mud that surrounded it. In spite of the warm temperatures, mud encircled the place because of the dozens of horses that had been tethered to the hitching post from various tavern patrons, enough horses so that their urine and feces created fetid mud all around the place. It smelled like a barnyard.

The de Shera group closed in on the tavern, essentially pushing people out of the way in their attempt to get to it. Dogs scattered, as did a few roaming chickens, creating quite a stir as Tiberius and his brothers invaded the yard behind the tavern. Horses crowded into the yard and two wide-eyed stable boys ran out of the livery, being bellowed at by Maximus for their efforts. He told the boys that if any of the horses ran off or were injured, then he would hold them personally responsible, which caused the boys to grab reins in a panic, trying to collect all of the frothy, excited horses from the heavily-armed men.

About half of the contingent, with Maximus at the head, went around to the front of the tavern while Tiberius, Gallus, and the rest of the men entered through the rear. As soon as Tiberius and the men burst into the common room through the kitchens, the startled patrons let out cries of alarm and made haste towards the front entry, where Maximus was standing. He had them effectively corralled. Tiberius grabbed the nearest tavern wench by the arm.

"You have two knights staying here," he said forcefully. "Where are they?"

The wench, with wildly unkempt, curly, red hair, burst into tears and pointed to the spindly staircase that led to the second floor. Tiberius let go of her and headed for the stairs with Gallus behind him. When they were nearly to the top of the steps, a man with a very big broadsword jumped out at them. Had Tiberius been any slower, the skilled down-parry of the sword would have cut him in half. As it was, he managed to lift his sword just in time. The blow was so forceful, however, that he staggered back into Gallus, who was unable to catch himself on the steps and went tumbling down, all the way to the bottom.

Tiberius couldn't even take his eyes off his opponent to make sure his brother hadn't broken his neck because another extremely heavy blow was forthcoming, one that sent him stumbling down a step, mostly because he was at a tremendous disadvantage being that he was standing steps below his attacker. But he managed to bring his sword up and under his opponent, catching the man on the underside of his arms. It was enough to jar him but not enough to knock the massive broadsword loose. As Tiberius went in for the death blow, he managed to catch a glimpse of his foe's features in the dim light and he stopped himself just in time.

"De Moray!" he gasped. "Cease, man! Do you not recognize me?"

Bose de Moray came to a grinding halt, throwing himself off-balance as he did so. He had to grip the stair rail for support, otherwise he would have pitched over the side. The old knight's black eyes widened in surprise.

"De Shera!" he grunted, shocked. "Dear God... forgive me, please. It is so dark in here that I could not see who it was. I heard you ask for me so I could only assume...."

It was then that Bose spied Gallus at the bottom of the steps, picking himself up with the help of his men. Tiberius, too, turned to see his brother standing up, holding on to his left arm, and both Tiberius and Bose made haste down the steps.

"Gal?" Tiberius reached out to steady his wounded brother. "Did you hurt yourself?"

Gallus was holding on to his elbow. "I do not believe it is too terrible," he said, wincing as he tried to move the arm. He eyed de Moray. "You did not need saving, de Moray. We should have instead saved ourselves from *you*."

Bose cracked a smile, an unnatural gesture on his angular,

scarred face. "I am ashamed that I did not identify you sooner than I did," he said. "You have my deepest apologies, my lord. I hope you are not hurt too terribly."

Gallus shook his head, shaking off the pain in his left arm. "It is my clumsy brother's fault," he said, eying Tiberius irritably. "If there is any blame to be had, it should be directed at him. All that aside, however, we obviously received your missive. Where are these men who have pursued you?"

Bose was rather relieved that the young earl wasn't going to berate him for being too old and too blind to identify him right away. He had asked for the man's help and then he had turned on him when he'd shown up, so he was somewhat embarrassed by his bad manners.

"I am not entirely sure at this point," he said, looking around and noticing more than a dozen de Shera men in the tavern entrance. "Last I saw, they were about four streets over, near the cathedral. Garran has gone out to scout for them, in fact. I...."

He was cut off by the sudden clash of swords outside of the tavern entrance. Startled, Bose, Tiberius, Gallus, and Maximus turned to see a massive fight on the street in front of the tavern. There were bodies clashing and the de Shera soldiers were getting sucked into it. Bose was the first to notice his son, Garran in the middle of it.

"God's Bones," he hissed. "Garran is out there in the fight. I must save my son."

At the mention of Garran's name, all three de Shera brothers prepared to charge outside. Gallus grabbed a soldier near the door as he moved.

"What goes on out there?" he demanded.

The soldier seemed both concerned and perplexed. "Sir Garran had men running after him," he said, pointing to the chaos outside. "He's fighting with them and our men have joined in."

Gallus bolted outside without another word with Maximus close on his heels. Tiberius went to follow his brothers but Bose grabbed him.

"My daughter," he said, pointing up the stairs. "Douglass is in the last room on the left. Guard her with your life, young de Shera. I will help my son but you protect her. She is more important than any of us."

With that, he was gone, a mountain of a man plowing through armed men, swinging his sword with expert precision. It was an impressive sight to see. In fact, Tiberius found himself watching the legendary Bose de Moray as the man fought off men half his age. *The man is truly ageless,* Tiberius thought. But then it began to occur to him that de Shera men were fighting off de Montfort men. Tiberius recognized the tunics of the men who had been chasing Garran. It would seem that Garran found the men who had been following him and his father, and those men had chased him right back to the tavern. There were more de Montfort men than Tiberius would have liked to have seen and that concerned him.

Turning on his heels, Tiberius hadn't taken three steps when someone grabbed him from behind. He turned to see one of de Montfort's men, who glared back at him quite angrily.

"What in the name of all that is Holy are you doing, de Shera?" the man demanded. "Do you have the de Moray party or don't you?"

Tiberius frowned and knocked the man's hand off his arm. The man was a lesser knight, a son of one of de Montfort's favored barons, and Tiberius didn't like him one bit. Sir Lincoln de Beckett was arrogant and dangerous, now in the middle of the fight to capture de Moray.

"You listen to me and listen well, de Beckett," Tiberius snarled. "Take your men and get out of here. De Moray is under de Shera control."

De Beckett, a big man who truly believed himself an equal peer to the Lords of Thunder, didn't back down.

"I have been instructed by de Montfort to bring de Moray to him," he said. "That is exactly what I intend to do."

Tiberius grabbed the man by the neck, towering over him. Tiberius wasn't as bulky as his brothers, but he was seven inches over six feet in height, with a sinewy, muscular body. He was solid and powerful, and by his sheer height he was intimidating. He used all of that intimidation as he hovered over de Beckett.

"De Moray belongs to me," he growled. "Get your men out of here or you will have a real fight on your hands. How will you explain that to de Montfort? You know he will believe Gallus over an arrogant ass like you."

With that, Tiberius kicked out a massive boot and hit de Beckett directly in the chest, sending the man flying backwards. De Beckett hadn't yet hit the ground by the time Tiberius was already halfway up the stairs, running for the last door on the left. He could hear de Beckett yelling behind him and he knew, instinctively, that the man would follow. He had to get to de Moray's daughter before de Beckett did.

The small corridor on the second floor leaned slightly to the left and smelled like a sewer. Tiberius raced to the last door on the left, a rather thin panel, and beat on it.

"Lady Douglass?" he called. "Your father has sent me, my lady. Please open the door!"

There was no response. Frustrated, Tiberius beat on it again, rattling the latch this time, but before he could yell again, de Beckett appeared in the corridor and Tiberius turned to the man, running at him as hard and as fast as he could. De Beckett tried to brace himself but Tiberius hit him like a runaway bull and the knight flipped over the railing and fell to the common room below, crashing onto a table before hitting the hard-packed earth of the floor. The table was enough to break his fall but Tiberius didn't stick around to see if the knight had been seriously injured or not. He had to get to de Moray's daughter.

He raced back to the panel, pounding on it and calling the lady's name. He lifted the latch, positive it would be locked, and was shocked to realize that it wasn't. Giving the door a good shove, he stepped into the room and was greeted by a sharp pain to his head and a burst of stars in his vision.

Something heavy had hit him and Tiberius fell to his knees as another blow cracked him across the back of the head. Pitching face-first onto the floor, he grunted in pain and shock as someone jumped on top of him and began beating him around the head and shoulders.

"You brute!" a female voice seethed. "You'll not take me, do you hear? I will mash you into a pulp!"

Dazed, Tiberius put up his hands, grabbing at the weapon the woman was using. "Lady," he tried to get the words out before she smacked him in the mouth and knocked out his teeth. "I am Tiberius de Shera. Your father sent me, I swear it!"

The beating slowed to a halt but she was still standing on top of him. He could feel a foot against the back of his neck.

"How do I know this is true?" she demanded. "De Montfort's men have been following us since last night. Prove to me that you are not the bastards who have been following us!"

Tiberius grunted. "Look at my tunic, you silly wench," he groaned. "It has the de Shera emblem. How much more proof do you need?"

The woman removed her foot from his neck. "I do not know the de Shera emblem on sight," she said. "Quickly, what is my brother's name?"

Tiberius didn't roll over, afraid she would start whacking him again. "His name is Garran," he replied. "Your mother's name is Summer and your father's name is Bose. You have two younger sisters, as I recall, Lizbeth and Sable."

The woman seemed to stew in confusion. "That is true," she finally said. "But that proves nothing. You could have heard that anywhere."

He sighed drolly. "Then if that is your logic, why did you ask me your brother's name?"

That threw her into deeper confusion and Tiberius took advantage of it. He didn't have any more time to waste. Quick as a flash, he rolled onto his back and used his big legs to knock her off her feet, sweeping her right to the floor. The woman fell heavily and the piece of wood she had been using to assault him flew from her hands and rolled under the bed. Sitting up swiftly, Tiberius reached out and grabbed both of her arms before she could rise, effectively trapping her on the floor. Now he was the one with the advantage, looming over her.

"My name is Tiberius de Shera, Lord Lockhurst," he said, his green eyes drilling into her. "My brother is the Earl of Coventry and your brother, Garran, is one of my very best friends. I am here to save you from de Montfort's assassins and I do not have any more time for your foolery. Behave yourself or I will take you over my knee. Is that clear?"

Lady Douglass Lora de Moray gazed up at Tiberius with a mixture of fear and resentment. She was a striking woman with cascades of golden-red curls, a mass of shockingly beautiful, red hair and her father's black eyes. Her skin was perfect and pale, without the freckles that redheads usually had, and she had a face that was better suited to that of an angel; smooth and porcelain and sweet in every way. But the expression on her face was anything but sweet as she faced off against Tiberius. She was a daughter of de Moray, after all, and she had strength in her. Lifting a booted foot, she kicked Tiberius in the gut. Grunting, he fell off of her.

"You will *not* threaten me," she scolded, frantically searching for her wooden club that had rolled under the bed. "We have been chased since last night by men intent to do us great harm and I have no idea if you are really Tiberius de Shera. I have never met him!"

Tiberius was on his knees, rubbing his belly with a furious expression on his face. "You are meeting him now," he said. Then, a hand shot out and grabbed her again, pulling her face-first onto the floor. "Now, meet the palm of my hand as it blisters your backside!"

He managed to get the first lick in and Douglass howled angrily, trying to move away from him, but as he brought his hand up again, he realized that de Beckett was standing in the doorway, watching everything. In an instant, his focus shifted and he leapt to his feet, slamming the door in de Beckett's face and throwing the bolt. He pressed himself back against the door as de Beckett and his men tried to kick it down.

"You... you *fiend*!" Douglass hurled insults at him. "How dare you strike me!"

Tiberius couldn't believe the situation he found himself in, fighting with a woman he was supposed to be saving. Had he not been so concerned that she might truly be captured by de Montfort's forces, he would have found the entire thing comical. But he didn't have time to laugh. For once in his life, there was no time for laughter. The carefree brother was now the serious knight. They had to flee through the only other portal in the room if they were going to save their skins.

Grabbing the only chair in the room, he jammed it under the iron bolt to give it more support as men on the other side tried to kick the door down. Grabbing Douglass by the wrist, he pulled her over to the window and threw open the shutters. The stable yard was more than a dozen feet below, crowded with de Shera horses.

Still holding on to Douglass with one hand, Tiberius yanked the coverlet from the bed and spun the startled woman around so that she was facing away from him. Then, he looped the coverlet around her torso like a sling. Holding both ends behind her, he shoved her towards the windowsill.

"If you value your life, you will jump," he told her. "I will hold the coverlet so it will ease you to the ground somewhat, but you had better jump, lady. That door will not hold much longer and once de Montfort's men enter, it will be me against a dozen. I cannot promise that I can save you then."

Douglass could hear the urgency in his tone. In truth, he *was* trying to help her, so perhaps he really was who he said he was. She'd heard her brother speak of Tiberius de Shera and tell of the great and sometimes wild adventures they had. Garran had also spoken of Tiberius' arrogance and how the man believed himself to be the greatest knight of all. *The Thunder Knight*, Tiberius would claim. He was part of the Lords of Thunder, after all. He wielded his sword as the storms wield their thunder. With that in mind, she eyed him critically.

"According to my brother, you would consider a fight against a dozen men nearly even odds," she said even as she struggled to climb onto the windowsill. "The odds would be *against* the dozen men, of course."

Tiberius scowled. "God's Bones," he spat. "Garran did not tell me how disagreeable you were. The man has a harpy for a sister."

Douglass' dark eyes narrowed at him. "I am a perfectly sound and agreeable individual around the right sort," she declared. "A man who would take his hand to my backside is *not* the right sort!"

Tiberius shook his head, appalled at the woman's manners. "You are lucky I was interrupted," he said. "I would have beaten you all the way through the floor and you would have ended up lying on the bread oven below. Now, get out of that window, you foolish wench. I am trying to save your life and all you can do is argue with me!"

Douglass opened her mouth but Tiberius put a big boot on her backside, shoving her from the window. As Douglass shrieked with surprise, and a little fear, Tiberius held both ends of the coverlet and lowered her down as far as he could to the livery yard below. Douglass ended up falling the last two feet on her own when he released the coverlet, landing right on her feet. By the time she looked up, Tiberius was climbing from the window, hanging with his long body extended before finally letting go of the sill. He, too, fell the last foot or so, landing awkwardly and stumbling.

"Now what?" Douglass asked as Tiberius picked himself up. "Do we just hang out here with the horses or did you have more of your brilliant plan in mind?"

With a growl, Tiberius grabbed her hand and pulled her through the collection of horses until he came across Storm, his big, gray stallion. He lifted Douglass up onto the saddle, or perhaps he actually threw her, because she nearly pitched off the other side. He wasn't exactly sure how he did it, only that he did. The woman was as fine and beautiful as he had ever seen but her personality had him furious.

Mounting swiftly behind Douglass, he gathered the reins and spurred his charger out of the stable yard and onto the road beyond, heading for Isenhall at breakneck speed but wondering if he should just as well dump the lady onto the side of the road and pretend he didn't see her fall. Nay, de Moray would figure it out sooner or later that it was no accident. Worse yet, the running mouth of Lady Douglass would be sure to tell her father what he'd done. If he hoped to keep peace with de Moray, then he'd better keep the woman safe. But one more negative word out of her mouth and he couldn't guarantee that his hand wouldn't become acquainted with her backside again.

With bunches of wild, red hair blowing annoyingly in his face and blinding him, Tiberius made his way back to Isenhall Castle.

CHAPTER THREE

Isenhall Castle

DOGS BARKED AND scattered as Tiberius and Douglass thundered into the small, crowded bailey of Isenhall.

They'd not spoken a word the entire time during the hour-long ride, fleeing like hunted animals, and by the time they reached Isenhall, it was clear that Douglass was doing all she could to keep her body away from Tiberius'. She'd been holding herself up on the saddle, using the horn to pull forward, since nearly the moment they'd left Coventry. And that hair, all of that red mass of hair, had been in Tiberius' vision the entire way. When he finally brought the steed to a halt and she slid off without benefit of his help, he could see clearly for the first time in over an hour.

Douglass simply stood a few feet away, uncertain and apprehensive, as Tiberius dismounted his charger and sent the horse off to the livery with one of the stable boys. Tiberius was trying very hard not to look at the woman who had assaulted and insulted him, but out of respect for Bose and Garran, he was obliged to be polite. Now that they were at Isenhall, he intended to turn her over to his sisters-in-law and wash his hands of her.

"Please come inside," he said with forced courtesy. "We will wait for your father and brother there."

Douglass eyed the very tall knight. In fact, she'd never seen a taller man. He was muscular, that was true, but not bulky, and he had the widest shoulders she had ever seen. With the soft, dark curls that framed his face and his square-jawed appearance, he was very handsome in a youthful sort of way. She'd realized that the first time she got a good look at his face. If she thought about it, *truly* thought about it, the only reason she came with the man was because he had been extraordinarily attractive and moderately convincing. In hindsight, it had been a stupid decision.

The entire ride from Coventry, she kept thinking how foolish she had been for agreeing to come with him. For all she knew, he had lied to her about who he was and why he had come. Because of her attraction to him, it was possible that she had willingly accompanied one of de Montfort's assassins to this cold and crowded castle where she was about to be thrown in the vault. She was feeling very foolish and very anxious as Tiberius motioned her towards the big, square and squat keep that sat in the middle of the circular fortress.

"I will wait for them here," she said stiffly. "I do not need to go inside."

Tiberius could see that she spoke from fear more than from stubbornness. The combative lady he'd met in Coventry was now uneasy. He suspected she didn't want to go inside and find herself trapped or locked up by a knight she didn't know. Upon reflection, given what she'd been through over the past two days, he didn't blame her sense of caution. Traveling with her father and brother as she was, he was certain she'd latched on to their sense of diligence and, obviously, their sense of fear at being followed by de Montfort. Bose de Moray would make a fine prize if captured. So would his daughter. With that thought, he forced himself to soften.

"My lady," he addressed her steadily, "it is difficult to know precisely when your father and brother will be coming. My brothers' wives are inside the keep and will take great care of you. You do not have to see me at all, I swear it. I will escort you inside and then you shall never see me again."

Douglass eyed the tall knight warily. "Although I thank you for your hospitality, you will forgive me for declining again," she said. "I will wait for my father and brother right here. I am not moving."

"But it is more pleasant inside, out of the sun."

"Nay."

Tiberius wasn't sure what more he could say to convince her. In fact, he was relatively insulted that his softer approach hadn't worked. Resigned, he moved towards her, indicating for her to back up.

"Then stand out of the way," he said. "You are in the path for the gatehouse and I do not want you to be run over. Please stand against the wall if you feel you must wait out here."

Silently, Douglass did as she was told, backing up until her back-side was against the cold, gray stone of Isenhall's circular walls. Tiberius, with nothing more to say, silently excused himself and made haste for the keep. He was just mounting the stairs when the entry door lurched open and women began to appear. Courtly was first, followed by Violet, Lily, and then Jeniver. As the little girls squealed and ran for Tiberius, Courtly addressed Tiberius, curious of the circumstances.

"You were not gone very long," she said. "Where is Lord de Moray?"

Tiberius reached down to pick up the girls as they jumped on him. "I do not know," he said. "I was asked to collect his daughter and I did. I brought her back to Isenhall without delay. The last I saw, de Montfort men and de Shera men were clashing, a rare sight indeed. But the lady is very distrustful. She will not come inside. She insists on waiting by the gatehouse for her father and brother to come."

Perplexed, Courtly and Jeniver strained to catch a glimpse of de Moray's daughter, finally spying her standing against the wall near the gatehouse. Jeniver gathered her skirts and descended the steps with Courtly right behind her.

"What is the matter?" Jeniver wanted to know. "Why is she so distrustful?"

Tiberius, with his nieces in his arms, followed the women as they headed towards the woman near the gatehouse.

"I am not entirely sure," he said, "but I believe it has something to do with de Montfort's men following her father for the past two days. She is not entirely convinced I am a de Shera. I think she believes I am with de Montfort somehow, meaning to imprison her."

Jeniver glanced at him. "Yet she came with you."

Tiberius shook his head. "I did not give her the opportunity to refuse," he said. "Things happened rather quickly and we were forced to flee."

Jeniver and Courtly digested his statement but their eyes were riveted to the woman with the glorious golden-red curls. The woman had a magnificent head of hair, hundreds of spiral curls tumbling all the way to her buttocks. They could see it even from across the bailey. When they drew closer, they could see that she was somewhat tall with porcelain skin and big, dark eyes. She was quite stunning but she was looking at them all rather suspiciously. Jeniver was the first to speak as they drew near.

"My lady," she greeted pleasantly. Jeniver was a truly sweet and friendly woman. "I am Lady de Shera, Countess of Coventry and this lovely woman standing next to me is Lady Courtly de Shera, wife of my husband's brother. We have come to welcome you to Isenhall and to provide you with all of the hospitality we have to offer."

Douglass looked between the women. The countess was a spectacular creature with black hair and brown eyes while her counterpart had beautiful, blond hair in a braid and bright, blue eyes. Truthfully, both women were quite beautiful and Douglass noticed that the countess was pregnant. She also couldn't help but notice Tiberius standing behind the women, playing with two little girls, one in each arm. In fact, it was quite sweet to watch him as he pretended to bite little fingers, making the girls giggle, but she tore her gaze away from him to focus on the women. She dipped into a practiced curtsy.

"I am Lady Douglass de Moray," she said, her manner much more pleasant than it had been in her dealings with Tiberius. "Thank you for receiving me. I pray you are not offended if I wish to wait for my father and brother at the gatehouse."

Jeniver moved towards the woman, who was at least a head taller than she was. "You will be much more comfortable inside," she said, extending a hand to her. "I realize you have had a terrible experience as of late with de Montfort's men, but I assure you that you are safe here. Won't you please come with me? The cook has made some marvelous poached eggs with sauce and we were about to eat. Will you please join us?"

Douglass wanted very much to refuse. She was concerned for her father and brother, and did not want to go inside and enjoy a feast and pretend all was well. All was most certainly not well. But she was coming to feel the least bit comforted with her situation, now realizing that Tiberius de Shera was, in fact, who he said he was. She slanted a look to the man as he played with the little girls, thinking that perhaps she owed him an apology.

"I...," she said, stopped, and started again. "Please do not think me rude, Lady de Shera, but I am very worried for my father and brother. I do not believe I could relax were I to go inside and share a meal with you, pretending everything is normal in my world when it truly isn't. Until my brother and father are safe here, with me, I cannot relax at all."

Jeniver smiled knowingly at the woman. "I understand," she said softly. "I feel the same way whenever my husband rides from these gates. To be truthful, I feel that way now. Since that is the case and there is no shame in admitting that I am concerned for my husband as well, we will wait with you here until everyone returns safely. Would you allow us that privilege?"

Douglass was surprised by the offer. "You do not need to wait with me, truly, Lady de Shera," she said. "Surely you should be inside, resting. I am quite capable of waiting alone."

Jeniver shook her head firmly, turning to Tiberius. "Ty, can you ask the servants to bring food out to us?" she asked. "And mayhap a chair or two. We may be in for a long wait."

Tiberius was distracted from playing with his nieces, knowing that Jeniver was simply being gracious so that Lady Douglass would not have to wait by herself. He also thought it was rather stubborn and selfish of Lady Douglass to make Jeniver and Courtly wait with her simply because she refused to come inside. His thoughts must have been reflected on his features because when he eyed Douglass, the woman was gazing back at him with some indecision and unease.

"If that is your wish," he finally said to Jeniver, although he sounded displeased. "I will...."

"Wait," Douglass cut him off, looking to Jeniver. "My lady, you should not be outside in the elements. I... I will go inside and wait with you, if you will permit me to do so."

Jeniver was glad the frightened woman was being somewhat reasonable because she truly hadn't been looking forward to a long wait in the hot sun.

"Of course," she said, reaching out to take Douglass' hand. "Please come along with Courtly and me. You will tell us all about your traveling adventures while we wait for your father and brother. Where are you coming from?"

She was deliberately changing the subject away from missing fathers and brothers and husbands. Douglass found herself pulled along by Lady de Shera. As small as the woman was, she had the iron will of a thousand men. It was in her manner and everything about her. She was not a woman to be disobeyed or denied.

"I have been fostering at Codnor Castle in Derbyshire, my lady," Douglass said, finding it difficult to speak on something other than her apprehension about her father and brother. "Lord Richard de Grey is a loyalist to the king and a friend of my father's, so I have enjoyed a happy home there for the past six years."

Jeniver and Courtly were listening with interest, although neither one of them commented at the mention of de Grey being the king's loyal baron. Since the de Sheras were on opposite side of that rebellion, it was best not to bring that to the surface, at least not at this early state. But both women silently wondered if Lady Douglass was even aware that the de Sheras fought for de Montfort. Loyalties, and barons choosing sides these days, were complex and sometimes painful issues for the friends and families involved.

"I have never been to Derbyshire," Courtly said, veering the subject away from any discussion of loyalties or rebellion. "Is it quite lovely there?"

Douglass nodded as they crossed the bailey into the shadow of the stalwart keep. "I think so, my lady," she replied. "Codnor is not a very big castle but Lady de Grey and I were close companions. She was very sad to see me go."

Courtly took Lily's little hand as they neared the steps to help the child climb the stairs. "Where are you going?" she asked as Lily took careful steps. "Why did your father collect you from Codnor if you were happy there?"

Douglass was hesitant to answer the question although she wasn't entirely sure why. All she knew was that she could feel Tiberius' big presence walking behind them and she didn't want him to hear the truth. It made absolutely no sense that she didn't want the man to know why she had left Codnor. Perhaps it was the silly woman inside of her who was attracted to him. She didn't want the handsome knight, the one she had insulted and assaulted, to know that she was potentially betrothed because there was something inherent in her that wanted to attract him.

That silly, foolish woman who found him attractive wanted him to think she was unattached and therefore open to his interest, if he were so inclined. But Douglass knew it was an idiotic thought, as the man most certainly would not be interested in a woman who had been rude and aggressive towards him.

"A betrothal, my lady," she said after a moment. "The king has a husband in mind for me and the man is in London. My father is taking me to London to see if an agreement can be reached."

Tiberius heard her. As Courtly and Jeniver pressed her on the wealth and status of her prospective husband, Tiberius trailed behind the women, listening to the chatter, wondering why he felt oddly disappointed at the knowledge that the lady had a husband waiting for her in London. Well, at least a man that could possibly be her husband. Tiberius wasn't surprised, of course. She was well-connected as de Moray's daughter and quite eligible. She would make some man a fine prize.

Tiberius' gaze raked Douglass' backside as she entered the keep in front of him, all the while thinking that she had a rather pleasing backside. Beneath the layers of linen, he could see it. She had a long, slender torso and a heart-shaped bottom when the folds of material would pull tight against it. He wasn't hard-pressed to admit that Garran's sister was quite beautiful, even if she had the disposition of a shrew. Still, all he could feel was displeasure at her statement and he had no idea why. There should be no earthly reason that he should be interested in the woman, but he realized with mounting horror that he was.

He *was* interested.

The dark, cool innards of the keep swallowed them up and he

found himself following the women into the small, vaulted-ceiling solar that was just off the entry. Violet and Lily rushed into the room because the servants had already put bread with cinnamon and raisins on the table and they were begging Jeniver to put butter on the bread so they could eat it. As Jeniver went to do their bidding, Courtly took Douglass in-hand and led her over to a seat at the table, politely making sure she was seated before assuming her own seat. As the servants began to place trenchers of eggs with a custard sauce in front of the women, Tiberius hung back in the doorway, watching, digesting the situation. Mostly, he was watching Douglass.

She was still uncertain and hesitant. It was clear that she was distracted by the whereabouts of her father and brother even as a good deal of delicious food had been placed within her easy reach. The old majordomo, the one who had served three generations of de Sheras, hovered over Lady Douglass to ensure that she, as a guest, had everything she needed. When Violet began calling Tiberius over to the table, demanding he sit and eat with them, Tiberius forced himself out of the observation role and into the situation at hand.

Violet and Lily were quite happy to have their favorite uncle sit between them. The moment Tiberius sat, however, the girls plopped onto his lap and he found it fairly impossible to eat what was put before him. There was no way to move around the little heads that were bobbing and weaving all over the place. But he managed a few bites, keeping his conversation limited to Violet and Lily, mostly because Lady Douglass had made it fairly clear what she thought of him. She had no desire to speak or interact with him at all, so he respected that. Besides, she was sitting on the far side of the table, well away from him. Whether or not he was attracted to her, he would make no attempts to initiate any contact.

"Ty," Courtly addressed him from across the table. "What was happening in Coventry when you left? Was there a fight happening?"

Tiberius nodded his head, swallowing the eggs in his mouth. "From what I could gather, while the lady and Sir Bose remained in their rented room at the Castle and Chain tavern, Garran went out to see if he could find the men who had been trailing them," he said. "When last I saw him, he was racing down the street with about twenty men chasing him. When the lady and I left, there was a rather big scuffle at the front of the tavern."

Jeniver didn't like the sound of that. "Was Gallus fighting?"

Tiberius shrugged, avoiding Lily's hands that were covered in custard sauce. "I think he was trying to ease the situation more than he was actually fighting," he said, daring to glance at Lady Douglass. "But the lady and I had some struggle in order to leave the tavern. We had to jump from the window to escape."

Shocked and dismayed, Jeniver and Courtly turned their attention to Douglass, who had devoured the eggs and sauce and was currently mopping up what was left of it with a piece of bread. She had been hungrier than she originally thought, but when she felt the stares upon her, she looked up from the remains of her meal.

"Indeed, we did," she said, confirming Tiberius' story. "A knight tried to make his way into my room but Sir Tiberius stopped him. We jumped from the window and came here as fast as we could."

She made it all sound as if she and Tiberius had been working together, as a team, when that clearly hadn't been the case. She made it almost sound as if she had been a willing party to everything, which confused Tiberius somewhat. He met her gaze across the table, those same black eyes that her brother had, and he wasn't entirely sure what to say to all of that. Should he mention the fact that she nearly bashed his brains in when he first entered the room? Or should he mention that he had been forced to spank that utterly lovely backside? As he was deciding just how to proceed, Jeniver spoke.

"You were very brave, Ty," she said sincerely. "It sounds as if you did indeed face some opposition."

If you only knew, Tiberius thought wryly. Gazing at Lady Douglass, his eyes riveted to her, he couldn't help the somewhat sarcastic tone in his voice.

"Aye," he replied. "Opposition indeed. Fighting, shoving, yelling… it was quite a struggle to get the lady out of harm's way."

If Jeniver or Courtly read anything into his slightly droll statement, they didn't comment on it. They seemed fixed on the situation itself and on Tiberius' bravery.

"It must have been terrifying," Courtly said with concern. "Lady Douglass was indeed fortunate to have you there to protect her from such ruffians."

Next to Courtly, Douglass cleared her throat softly. "When he says fighting and yelling, I believe he means me," she said, smiling weakly when everyone looked at her with varied degrees of surprise. "I am afraid that I was not very kind when he first came to my aid. I thought he was one of de Montfort's men and, well… I hit him on the head with a piece of wood and tried to beat him unconscious."

Courtly burst out in sharp laughter but quickly slapped a hand over her mouth, looking apologetically to Tiberius. Jeniver was only marginally better in concealing her humor. She was struggling not to smile and losing the battle. Tiberius, his ego somewhat damaged, lifted his hands.

"Go ahead," he said. "Laugh all you want. She tried to fight me all the way to Isenhall. Why do you think she wanted to remain in the bailey? She was convinced I was one of de Montfort's assassins and the moment I took her inside the keep, I would either molest her or lock her in the vault."

By now, both Courtly and Jeniver were grinning broadly. It was clear that Tiberius' pride was damaged by what was apparently a difficult rescue attempt with an unwilling lady to save. As Jeniver shook her head at what she felt was the humor of the situation, Courtly turned to Douglass.

"Tiberius is not an assassin, I assure you, my lady," she said. "He is a true and noble knight. You are in very good hands."

Douglass' pale cheeks mottled a faint red. "I can see that now," she said, although it was difficult for her to admit it. "At the time, however, given that men were trying to kill my brother and father, I had no way of knowing that he was telling the truth."

It was probably as close to an apology as she was going to come, at least at the moment. Tiberius could see that, much like him, she had pride. She also had spirit and was unafraid to protect herself against a man more than twice her size. Taking his wounded pride out of the equation, Lady Douglass de Moray was becoming more intriguing by the moment.

She is betrothed, you idiot, he told himself, but it didn't seem to matter much. Perhaps he could still count her among his many conquests before she went on to her husband. Such things, in his world, had happened before. He'd been known to steal women from the men who had been expecting their purity. But there would be no conquest made unless the situation between them was smoothed over or even warmed. Tiberius was particularly good at warming a woman when the mood struck him and the mood, at the moment, was striking fast.

"No need to feel badly about defending yourself, my lady," he said, rubbing the back of his head. "Men bigger than you have tried to knock my head off. I am sure yours will not be the last attempt."

Jeniver and Courtly giggled as Douglass cracked a smile. She had a lovely smile with straight teeth and slightly prominent canines. In fact, her smile was quite alluring. It had Tiberius' full attention.

"I am very sorry that I knocked you down and tried to beat you," she said. "Did I hurt you much?"

So she apologizes in full, Tiberius thought, relatively impressed that so prideful a woman would admit her mistakes so readily. He continued rubbing the back of his head, feeling a small knot where she had hit him.

"Not much," he replied. "But you used the club well. Did they teach you such things at Codnor?"

Douglass' grin grew and she lowered her gaze, bashfully. "Nay, not really," she said. "Although, there were times when I was forced to fend off an over-zealous knave. Some men do not like to be refused, in any case."

Tiberius was enchanted by the woman's blooming smile but Courtly spoke before he could.

"It seems to me that you have good reason to say that," she said, a twinkle in her blue eyes. "You are quite lovely, something that would not have gone unnoticed by any man. I would like to hear your stories of over-eager men who have met with your wrath."

Douglass laughed softly, flattered. "It would be a tale for women only," she said. "I would not want to offend Sir Tiberius by laughing at his sex's foolishness."

As the women giggled, Tiberius shook his head. "I have seen enough foolish men to know that there are plenty in this world," he said. "You could not offend me with such talk, my lady. I could probably tell you much the same stories from my perspective."

That drew more laughter from the women. The situation in general had settled down a tremendous amount since Tiberius and Douglass arrived at Isenhall, and Tiberius was thankful. He was trying to think of something witty to say when the dogs that roamed the entry began to bark and charge towards the door. Excited servants began to move about, including the majordomo. The little man with the white hair and bony body stuck his head into the solar.

"More men have returned, Lady de Shera," he told Jeniver.

"There are soldiers entering the bailey."

Jeniver leapt up as quickly as her swollen body would allow, followed swiftly by Courtly. There was excitement, and some anxiety, in the air. The hope from the women was that Gallus and Maximus had returned and as Jeniver rushed out, she took a quick moment to speak to Tiberius.

"Please take Lady Douglass in-hand," she asked. "Will you keep her entertained until we know who has returned?"

Tiberius nodded but Douglass rose to her feet. "My lady," she said, almost pleadingly. "I should like to see if my father and brother have returned. May I come with you?"

Jeniver waved her off. "Please remain here," she said. "The bailey can become very chaotic and I do not want you injured in the swirl of men and animals. I will send someone to tell you as soon as your father and brother have been located."

With that, she was gone, leaving Douglass and Tiberius alone in the solar. Violet and Lily had remained behind because they were enjoying licking the custard sauce meant for the eggs off of their fingers, but they were off in their own little world at the moment as Tiberius stood up, his gaze fixed on Douglass. Her focus was on the entry where Jeniver and Courtly had so recently disappeared, her expression wrought with apprehension. But she caught movement out of the corner her eye and noticed Tiberius standing there, watching her. For a split second, she looked rather surprised to realize they were alone, but that surprise quickly dissolved into a timid smile.

"So you really are a de Shera," she said. "Forgive me for doubting your word. And forgive me for trying to mash you into a pulp before we were properly introduced. I did not know, after all. I am not entirely trusting by nature, especially in a situation such as that."

Tiberius grinned. "Aye, I really am a de Shera," he said. "I am the youngest and most handsome de Shera. Surely you have heard legend of my beauty."

Douglass laughed softly at his jest. "I have heard legend of you from my brother," she admitted. "But not of your beauty because I am sure he would not have said such things. However, he tells many stories about the two of you. He says you are quite brave."

"I am."

"And quite reckless at times."

Tiberius frowned. "He lies."

Douglass laughed again. "I will tell him you said so."

Tiberius nodded, still frowning, although it was clear that he was not entirely serious. "You will tell me what he has told you about me," he said, moving around the table so he wasn't shouting across the room at her. Moreover, he found he simply wanted to move closer to her now that she wasn't threatening him bodily harm. "Come, now, be truthful. What lies and half-truths has he told you?"

Douglass shook her head firmly even though she couldn't help but notice he had come closer to her. He was standing just a few feet away and it began to occur to her that the very handsome knight smelled slightly rotten. She had noticed the smell a couple of times at the tavern but not at all when they had fled for Isenhall, probably because she was seated in front of him. She wasn't entirely sure it was appropriate to bring up the man's horrific smell but it was so strong that she actually took a step away from him.

"I will not give my brother away," she said firmly. "Honestly, I've not seen the man that much over the past several years so the stories he has told me about you have been very few. He did, however, tell me about a trip to Leicester when you were involved in a brawl at church. He said that the priests took to chasing you with one of those long iron sconces that hold the fat, white tapers. He said you had to fend them off with your broadsword."

Tiberius' frown deepened. "He told you about *that*?"

She giggled. "He said you that you were on horseback when you followed a woman inside a church."

Tiberius shut his eyes tightly and shook his head, lowering it in shame. He was going to have very strong words with Garran for telling his sister such a thing. "I was not *on* horseback," he said, weakly defending himself. "I was leading my horse behind me. And the woman stole something from me. I had to get it back."

Douglass was enjoying his discomfort. "Garran said she stole your purse."

Tiberius' eyes opened and he looked at her, mortified. "Did he tell you more than that?"

Douglass shook her head. "He did not," she said, seeing that there must be quite a tale behind the stolen purse simply by the expression on Tiberius' face. "How did she come so close to stealing your purse? Most men carry their purses very close to their bodies. How on earth did she get so close to you to have the opportunity to take it?"

Tiberius was quickly slipping into utter embarrassment and horror. There was no way he was going to tell Lady Douglass that the woman who stole his purse had been a prostitute and that she had stolen the purse when he had been sleeping after several hours of exhausting sex. He shook his head, firmly.

"It would not interest you," he said, desperate to be off of the subject. "But know that I will mash your brother to a pulp when next I see him for telling you such tales. You must have a terrible opinion of me already and we have only just met."

Douglass didn't push the purse story. She had only just met the man, after all, and this was the first civil conversation they had shared. Already, he was agitated with the subject and she didn't want to push the man into annoyance. Still, she could see that Tiberius de Shera was very charming and witty, and his boyish mannerisms and expressive face made him very endearing, but she had the impression that he knew very well that he was charismatic and handsome. He was certainly very comfortable speaking to a woman. All things considered, she was coming to feel very bad for her actions towards him when they first met and the silly woman who had initially found him so attractive now found him even more attractive. It would be quite easy to be infatuated with him.

"The only opinion I have of you is of a man who tried to help me and I was reluctant to let him do so," she said after a moment, watching the corners of his eyes crinkle when he smiled. "Mayhap… mayhap we can begin again. Start over, as it were. Let us pretend we are meeting for the very first time under much more pleasant circumstances. That being the case, I will introduce myself. I am Lady Douglass Lora de Moray and I am honored to meet you, Sir Tiberius."

She curtsied with a practiced flare, her glorious, red hair splaying across her shoulders and arms when she bent over. Tiberius, his eyes glittering with great interest, reached out to take her hand. In a complete breach of protocol, because it was quite improper for him to touch the woman in any fashion given that they were not courting or married, he brought her hand to his lips and kissed her tender flesh quite sweetly.

"The pleasure is all mine, Lady Douglass," he said softly, his voice tinged with a suggestive tone. "I hope we are able to know one another better before you continue on your journey to London."

There was magic in the air, but it was a sweet and heart-pounding moment abruptly interrupted by a herd of people entering the keep. Bose de Moray and Gallus chose that moment to shove through the entry door, followed by Jeniver, Courtly, Maximus, a pack of de Shera knights, and finally Garran de Moray.

Tiberius heard the entry door slam back and the commotion of men, but he was too slow in releasing the lady's hand. He released it so swiftly that it ended up looking as if he had been caught doing something he shouldn't have, as if he were guilty for having touched the woman when he had no right to. The truth was that he should not have touched her, even her hand, and he was well aware of the fact. Tiberius knew by the expression on de Moray's face that he would have some explaining to do.

All he could do was smile, tell the truth, and hope the man didn't try to kill him for laying a hand on his daughter.

CHAPTER FOUR

T HE GREAT HALL of Isenhall Castle was in full swing this night, with food and wine flowing freely, a massive fire in the pit in the center of the hall, and three minstrels in the corner of the room trying desperately to be heard over the noise of the diners. Tonight, the great Bose de Moray was an honored guest and the House of de Shera would show him all due respect.

Tiberius sat at the feasting table with his brothers, their wives, Scott and Troy de Wolfe, Garran and Bose, and finally Douglass. There had been a good deal of eating, drinking, and storytelling going on and, fortunately for Tiberius, Bose hadn't brought up anything about Douglass and Tiberius' flight from Coventry nor had he mentioned the kiss to his daughter's hand from a man she was not betrothed to. Bose was a man of great wisdom with a calm, even manner, but he also had a legendary temper that was common knowledge. It took a great deal to push him into anger but when he reached that state, the results were often deadly.

Therefore, Tiberius' focus had been on his brothers and the knights. He ignored Douglass completely, who was sitting next to her father. He didn't want to look at her and see Bose by default. He was still afraid of incurring the man's wrath so he spent his time speaking happily with his brothers.

Course by course of food passed before them, expertly prepared by the de Shera cook who had been helped in her skills by Maximus' wife, Courtly, who had learned the art of cooking from her patroness, Lady d'Umfraville of Prudhoe Castle. There was pork in a thick sauce of coriander and caraway, stewed pigeons, cabbage and turnip pottage, and a variety of breads. There was even a sweet gingerbread with raisins and nuts for Violet and Lily, who sat with their father and step-mother, happily gorging themselves. There was also a variety of red and pale wines, and even an apple cider that had quite a bite to it.

Tiberius had started in on the cider almost as soon as it appeared. He was nervous with de Moray in the room and upset that he couldn't give his full attention to Douglass, as he had wanted to. Therefore, he hit the cider fairly hard and ate very little, mostly distracted with talk of the last major battle the de Sheras had been a part of at Warborough back in May. Since then, there had been a few smaller skirmishes but nothing of note. Since Bose and Garran were at the table, men who were sworn to Henry, politics and loyalties never came up. No one would discuss them out of respect for the friendship they had that superseded loyalties to kings and rebels. It was a fine balancing act, however.

As the evening wore on and the conversation grew louder, Tiberius was fairly drunk. He ended up sitting on the table itself while he told a rather exciting story about a battle when he had been newly knighted, one of the few times he had actually fought alongside his father. The battle had been some skirmish along the Welsh border, but Tiberius had a great twist for every part in the story, mostly making himself out to be a demi-god in battle. As his brothers shook their heads in amused doubt and the knights laughed uproariously at Tiberius' antics, Bose spoke from across the table.

"And it is this same Thunder Knight who rescued my daughter from de Montfort's men today," he said, his unmistakable bass-toned voice filling the table. "Douglass said you threw her out of a window, Tiberius. Is this true?"

Drunk, without his usual control, Tiberius looked to de Moray in a mixture of fear and defiance. "I had to in order to get her out of the chamber," he said frankly. "There were at least six men at the door, including Lincoln de Beckett, and I had to remove her from the room any way I could. I eased her down in a coverlet sling although I should have tossed her out on her head. Do you know she attacked me when I first entered the chamber? She nearly knocked me senseless. Then, what would have become of her? She would have become fodder for de Beckett and his men. She is lucky I saved her at all!"

The table had quieted down dramatically by that point, listening to Tiberius all but scold de Moray and his daughter. It was clear how drunk and emotional he was. Gallus, quickly seeing that the situation could turn very bad indeed, cleared his throat softly.

"I am sure it was not that bad, Ty," he said, reaching out to grasp his brother's arm. "I believe Lord de Moray is thanking you for rushing to her aid."

Tiberius yanked his arm out of his brother's grip, disgusted. "She knocked me right across the back of the head," he said, shifting on the table and sending Scott de Wolfe's trencher into the man's lap. "I told her who I was but she would not believe me. I was wearing a de Shera tunic, for Christ's sake. Who did she think I was? Who else but a de Shera would have risked his neck to save such an ungrateful wench?"

Gallus cast a sidelong glance at Maximus, who took the hint and immediately stood up. "Come along, Ty," Maximus said to his brother, reaching out to grasp the man by both arms and pulling him off the table. "You have had a trying day. I think you need to retire."

Tiberius struggled against his brother but Scott stood up and helped Maximus pull the man off the tabletop.

"I will not be chased away like a naughty child," Tiberius said, unhappy. Then, he turned back to Bose and the wide-eyed Douglass with drunken flare and pointed at the lady. "*Look* at her. Look at that beautiful woman. She is simply beautiful. Beautiful, beautiful. And already you have a husband selected for her? Why not give someone else the opportunity to offer for the woman? I saved her! She should be offered to *me* as a reward for risking my life to save her!"

Maximus threw his big arm around his brother and began pulling him away from the table. "Shut up," he hissed. "You are making an ass of yourself."

Tiberius frowned at his brother. "But she belongs to me," he said, slurring his words as he thumped his own chest. "I saved her. She belongs to *me*. I want her, do you hear? Tell de Moray to give her to me."

Stoically, Maximus didn't reply as he pulled his very drunk brother away from the table, leaving those left behind appearing rather awkward, especially in light of Tiberius' last few words. As Maximus and Scott escorted Tiberius from the hall, Gallus turned to de Moray.

"I do apologize, my lord," he said. "Tiberius is a passionate man and drink sometimes brings out more passion in him than he can control."

De Moray took a drink of the fine, red wine. "He is young and brilliant and brave," he replied. "I am most fortunate that he was the one to rescue my daughter."

Seated next to her father, Douglass was both mortified and thrilled by Tiberius' words. Was it possible that he actually meant them? Or was it the drink talking? She couldn't dare to hope that it was the truth.

"I *did* strike him, Papa," she said, putting her hand on Bose's arm. "I thought he was one of de Montfort's men."

Bose looked down his shoulder at his lovely daughter, his heart, his love. "He is," he replied quietly. "Did you not know that the House of de Shera serves de Montfort? Tiberius fought off one of his own men to take you to safety. He is a man loyal to friendship and family over all. Is that not correct, Lord Gallus?"

Gallus nodded faintly, thinking the situation, overall, was much more complex than that. "Aye," he replied simply. "It is. The House of de Moray and the House of de Shera may have different loyalties at this time, but ultimately, our loyalties are to each other over all."

Bose eyed Gallus. "Is that how you are going to explain this situation to de Montfort?"

Gallus cocked a thoughtful eyebrow. "The man is the godfather of Davyss de Winter," he muttered. "Davyss serves the king. If de Montfort was given a choice between Henry or Davyss, he would choose Davyss every time. The man, therefore, understands the complexities of loyalty. Blood and bond are often stronger than king and crown."

Douglass was listening carefully to what the men were speaking of, loyalties and crown and the blurred lines of fealty. It was all quite confusing. "I do not understand," she whispered to her father. "If they are loyal to de Montfort, why did you ask them for help?"

Bose patted her soft hand. "Because they would give it," he said simply. "Do not trouble yourself over the loyalties of the House of de Shera. As we have said, friendship and blood sometimes supersede fealty to the king or de Montfort."

Douglass digested the statement, still baffled but trusting her father's judgment. Moreover, the de Shera brothers had already proven that they were loyal to the House of de Moray by their actions of the day. Was it possible, then, that her father might consider a betrothal between her and Tiberius even if the de Shera brothers were siding with de Montfort? But only if Tiberius truly meant what he said, of course. People often said things they did not mean when they'd had too much to drink. It was a perplexing situation, indeed, but one that she felt some excitement with. Having the tall, handsome Tiberius de Shera as a husband did not distress her in the least. But she said nothing; at least, not at the moment. Later in private, she would broach the subject with her father.

As Douglass mulled over a future in the House of de Shera, Gallus has been lost in a world of reflection of his own. Thoughts of Tiberius and Maximus and how much the three of them had been through over the course of the year, converged in his brain. A great deal had happened, enough to rattle the most stalwart heart. As Bose poured himself more wine from the pitcher at the table, Gallus spoke again, softly this time.

"You must also know, my lord, that the death of our mother has hit Tiberius very badly," he said to Bose. "Tiberius is the youngest child and my mother treated him like her baby up until he was a young man. When Tiberius was sent away to foster at ten years of age, it was to Kenilworth Castle, which is very close to Isenhall. It was so my mother could visit him monthly, which she did until he became a squire and asked her not to come so often because the other squires were shaming him. Do you know my mother went to find those boys who had been teasing my brother and she belted every one of them? They never teased Tiberius again. The point, however, is that my mother and Tiberius were quite close. He still sheds tears for her and he thinks that we do not know. His behavior tonight… he does not normally do this. I believe it is his grief more than anything that caused him to behave so."

Bose was listening with some sympathy but it was Garran who spoke first. The black-eyed knight was Tiberius' closest friend and when he opted to serve with his father and, therefore the king, a few months ago, it had been very difficult for Tiberius to accept. Garran had served the House of de Shera for many years. But Tiberius understood that the man's loyalty was to his father and not to the king. Still, it had been a difficult decision for all of them, including

Garran, to accept. Aye, there were perhaps more reasons than one behind Tiberius' outburst.

"Let me go and sit with him until he comes to his senses, my lord," Garran begged softly. "I have not seen him in months. Mayhap... mayhap he needs an old friend to talk to."

Gallus looked to Garran, a man he still trusted with his life. "Max will see that he is tended," he said. "You needn't sit with him now. He is probably already asleep."

Garran smiled weakly. "If I know Ty, and I believe I do, he is currently trying to strong-arm Maximus into letting him back into the hall," he said. "I would go to relieve Maximus of this burden, my lord. Please."

Gallus grinned faintly. "Although I have great faith in your abilities, are you sure you are strong enough to fight Ty off if he attempts to return to the hall?"

Garran nodded. "I have done it before."

"Then go."

With a nod of gratitude, Garran rose from the table and quit the hall, moving out into the dark bailey beyond. He had been in this bailey thousands of times, both during peaceful times and warring times. He had spent the past four years serving the House of de Shera and knew the layout of Isenhall Castle intimately. As soldiers walked the walls, guarding the occupants against threats in the dark and with only the distant stars as company, Garran headed into the keep.

The big, square keep smelled the same to him as it always had; like smoke and dogs and Lady Honey's incense of sage and rosemary, which she liked to burn throughout the keep to mask the musky odors of the old stone. Even though Lady Honey had died back in May, Jeniver and Courtly kept with that tradition because it was of comfort to the sons.

The main staircase of Isenhall was off to the right of the entry, an unusual staircase in that it was straight from floor to floor rather than being spiral. It was also wide, and easy to travel, and Garran made his way up to the third floor where Tiberius' bedchamber was. By the time he hit the landing on the third floor, he could already hear Tiberius' agitated voice and Maximus' deep, calm tone. Carefully, he opened the old oak door into Tiberius' chamber.

It smelled of unwashed bodies and urine because Tiberius often let the dogs into his chamber and they would pee in the corners. Tiberius was standing over by the lancet window that overlooked the eastern portion of the bailey, slumped against the wall, as Maximus stood several feet away with his arms folded across his chest. It was clear that the brothers had been in some manner of discussion and, from the expressions on their faces, it had been a serious subject. Maximus caught sight of Garran first.

"De Moray," he greeted. "I hope your father is not too offended by Ty's behavior. Did you come up here to berate him? He will not listen, you know."

Garran shook his head as he came into the room. "My father is rather forgiving," he said. "He has not even mentioned it. I have come to relieve you of the duty of sitting with your brother so that you may return to your wife. I have not seen Ty in a few months. We have much to catch up on."

Maximus looked to Tiberius, who was focused on Garran. He had his hands on his face, wiping the drunken tears from his cheeks.

"You were not here for my mother's funeral," Tiberius said to Garran, sorrow in his tone. "In fact, I missed it, too. We all did. By the time we received word of her passing, she had already been buried in Isenhall's chapel next to my father. I was not able to tell my mother farewell."

His eyes were filling with a pond of tears and Garran glanced at Maximus, who simply shook his head with some regret.

"You did, Ty," Maximus said softly. "You told her farewell before we left to go to Oxford those months back. Remember? Now, why don't you lie down and try to sleep? You have had far too much to drink, more than I have ever seen from you. You need to rest."

Tiberius wiped the tears that seemed to keep falling. He looked away from his brother and his friend, his gaze finding the bright carpet of stars in the night sky.

"She was ashamed of me," he whispered, his lower lip trembling. "Gallus was her shining star and Maximus was her strength. What was I? A misfit. A *comic*. I was her youngest son that had not accomplished anything to make her proud of me. Gallus married Catheryn and had two children, and then he married Jeniver and she will bear him a son. And now Maximus has married Courtly and they are very happy. What have I done to perpetuate the de Shera name? Nothing of note. I have done... nothing."

Maximus didn't want to hear any more of his brother's drunken self-pity. As far as he and Gallus were concerned, Tiberius, the baby, had always been Honey's favorite son. Maximus moved towards the man and pulled him away from the window, towards his bed.

"Go to sleep," he said. "Garran will sit with you so you do not drown in your own vomit. Come along, Ty, lay down. You will feel better when you have had a chance to sleep."

Oddly enough, Tiberius didn't fight him. He let his brother push him down on his messy, smelly bed. All of that terrible cider had finally caught up with him and he could hardly keep his eyes open.

"Garran, your sister," Tiberius rambled on, grabbing hold of Garran's arm when the man helped Maximus pull up the coverlet. "She tried to beat me when I first found her in that room, you know. She is a brave and strong woman. She is also quite beautiful. Did you know that?"

Garran cocked a patient eyebrow at the man. "Men do not usually think their sisters to be beautiful."

Tiberius was very serious. "But she is," he insisted. "Why did you not tell me you had such a beautiful sister?"

Garran shrugged, trying to peel Tiberius' hand off of his arm. "I told you," he said. "Men do not go around telling others that their sister is beautiful. That would be strange."

Tiberius' cider-muddled mind tried to make sense out of that statement. "I saved her from de Montfort's assassins," he said. "Therefore, she belongs to me. You will tell your father, will you not? Lady Douglass is mine. I intend to keep her."

Garran knew there was no arguing with a drunken man. "As you say, Ty," he said. "She belongs to you."

Satisfied, Tiberius let go of Garran and drowsiness quickly came upon him. "She will be the mother of my sons," he muttered, his eyes fluttering closed. "She is a fine woman. My mother would… would be proud of me to marry such a fine woman."

He continued muttering, trailing off and falling dead asleep in a matter of seconds. Maximus and Garran stood over him as he began to snort loudly.

"I will stay here for a time," Garran said, looking at Maximus. "You may return to the hall if you wish. I will make sure he comes to no harm."

Maximus nodded as he headed for the door. "He will not remember any of this come the morning," he said. "I hope your father does not think he is truly interested in your sister. Although your sister is a beautiful woman, Tiberius is not a man to wed, at least not at this point in his life. I am not entirely sure he is capable of being true to one woman."

Garran snorted. "Well I know it," he said. "I would approve of Lucifer as a husband for my sister sooner than I would approve of Ty. I have seen what that man is capable of with the opposite sex."

Maximus had to wriggle his eyebrows in agreement. Tiberius was quite legendary with women and there was rumor of at least one de Shera bastard in London. But they didn't discuss that particular aspect of Tiberius' character as Maximus left the chamber and shut the door softly behind him. Garran pulled up a chair near the hearth and sat, taking a deep, cleansing breath as he thought on the day's adventures. It had been quite a full day, for all of them.

As Tiberius snored away, Garran couldn't help but wonder if the man, once sober, would continue to show interest in Douglass. Although Garran loved Tiberius like a brother, as he had told Maximus, he had seen what the man was capable of with women. He was handsome, charming, and always got his way in everything. Many a maiden had been ruined by Tiberius de Shera's sweet talk and wooing ways, and Garran intended to make sure that his sister did not fall prey to the likes of his friend. He wondered, darkly, if he would find himself fending off Tiberius at some point. He hoped not because he would unquestionably defend Douglass to the death.

Perhaps even Tiberius'.

PART TWO
WINDS OF BETRAYAL

CHAPTER FIVE

H E WASN'T SURE if there was actually pounding on the door or if it was simply the pounding in his head. Tiberius was trying to sleep, trying to ignore the massive headache that was throbbing against his forehead, but the pounding on the door assured him that he could no longer sleep. Someone was not only pounding on the door but they were calling his name. Frustrated, and ill, he struggled to lift his head.

"Enough!" he roared to whomever was doing the pounding. "I am awake."

The voice on the other side of the door was muffled. "Lord Gallus requests your presence in the armory," someone said. "He requests it now."

Tiberius braced a hand against the wall next to the bed as he pushed himself into a sitting position. His head hurt so badly that he was sure it was about to explode and send brains and blood all over the floor. Surprisingly, it didn't burst, although he fervently wished it would. Perhaps it would relieve the pressure. He was in more pain than he'd been in for quite some time. He wasn't one to overindulge, at least not as much as he had last night, so he was rather angry at himself for having imbibed too much. Now, he was paying the price.

He was also angry at himself for another reason. Oddly enough, he could remember certain things he said the previous night. He remembered telling de Moray that Lady Douglass belonged to him since he had saved her from de Montfort's assassins. Bits and pieces of memories came back to him, like weeping for his mother, but the rest of it was mostly a blur. He didn't like the blur, fearful of what else he had said in his inebriated state. Drunken men usually said embarrassing and odd things, and he had a feeling that he had utterly humiliated himself in front of Lady Douglass. With a grunt of absolute pain, he stood up unsteadily from the bed.

More pounding on the door startled him, shooting bolts of pain through his head and he nearly fell over with it all. The soldier sent to deliver Gallus' message called to him again and Tiberius angrily chased the man away, assuring him that if he caught him on the other side of the door when he opened it, then he would promise the man pain of his own. The soldier ran off as Tiberius yanked open his door.

Hand on his head, Tiberius staggered from the chamber. His usual custom in the morning was to sing at the top of his lungs. He did it almost every morning to the point where Maximus would become enraged and try to shut him up. Prior to marrying Courtly, Maximus had been known to throw punches in order to quiet him down, but since marrying his lovely bride, the man would simply sit and stew and throw punches when his wife wasn't looking. It was fairly amazing how marriage had changed the man.

But Tiberius wasn't thinking about marriage at the moment and he certainly wasn't about to sing. He was thinking on Lady Douglass and how he needed to apologize to her for his drunken antics. In fact, it was nearly the only thing on his mind. As he took the stairs down to the first floor, he could hear Violet and Lily and the barking of their dogs. He could also hear Courtly and Jeniver as they went about their chores for the day, instructing the servants to wash bed linens on this day and clean the floors.

As Tiberius reached the landing, he could see his nieces playing with the dogs, the very big, black Taranis and the equally leggy

Henry the hound. When the girls saw him, they squealed and ran to him happily, but he refrained from picking them up because it hurt his head too much to bend over. But Violet wouldn't be put off so he ended up picking her up, groaning in pain as he did so. The sounds of pain he was emitting had the attention of Courtly and Jeniver.

Courtly emerged from what used to be Lady Honey's chamber. Now, it belonged to Courtly and Maximus. When Courtly saw her brother-in-law, she grinned.

"I am surprised to see that you are up and moving," she said. "I thought for sure you would spend the day in bed."

Tiberius couldn't even shake his head to refute her statement. The action hurt too much. He rubbed his bloodshot eyes. "Gallus has summoned me, 'else I would surely still be sleeping," he muttered, setting Violet on her feet because holding the girl hurt his head. "I would assume your husband has been summoned as well?"

Courtly nodded, thinking it quite humorous that Tiberius looked so terrible. He also smelled horrible. "He has already gone to Gallus," she said. Then, she eyed the man carefully. "I am afraid to ask how you are feeling."

Tiberius grunted. "How do you think?" he said grumpily. "I feel as if my head is about to pound right off of my shoulders."

Courtly laughed softly. "Then let it be a lesson to you to never again drink so much of that devil cider," she said. "That stuff has fallen many a man here at Isenhall."

Tiberius rubbed his eyes again. "I will never touch it again," he swore softly. Then, he looked at her, blinking his red eyes. "I am afraid to ask just how much I embarrassed myself."

Courtly sobered a bit. "Maximus removed you before you did too much damage."

"But I *did* embarrass myself."

She shrugged. "It was the drink. Everyone knows that."

He grunted, unhappy. "I *knew* it," he said. "I made an arse out of myself in front of Lady Douglass and her father, didn't I? Something about Lady Douglass belonging to me because I saved her?"

Courtly was trying not to laugh. "You were quite adamant about it."

Tiberius was feeling increasingly miserable. "Has de Moray left yet?"

Courtly shook her head. "Nay," she said. "He is breaking his fast with Lady Douglass and Garran in the great hall. Jeniver and I were going to join them shortly. Will you come?"

Tiberius looked at her, thoughts of Lady Douglass rolling through his pain-hazed mind. Strangely enough, even though he knew he said that she belonged to him, he didn't regret it. At the time, he truly meant it, and now... well, he meant it still but he knew it was an unreasonable assumption. However, he *was* sorry that he had spouted off so and he wanted to tell Lady Douglass that without her father or brother hanging about. He would apologize to them as well, but for the lady... he wanted to apologize privately.

"Not at the moment," he said. "I want you to do something for me."

Courtly nodded. "Anything. What is it?"

Tiberius hesitated. "Will you bring Lady Douglass to the solar?" he finally asked. "I fear... I fear that I must make apologies to her for my behavior last night and I wish to do it in private. I am sure her father will not let her meet with me, alone, so I would ask that you bring her to me. De Moray will let her go with you as an escort."

Courtly's blue eyes twinkled. "You want to see her alone?"

"Aye."

Courtly regarded him a moment. "Tiberius de Shera, if you want to see her alone to do something unseemly, then I will have no part of it."

He waved her off. "Nay, I swear it," he said. "Nothing unseemly. I simply wish to apologize to her. Will you please help me?"

Courtly's gaze held steady on him. Her brother-in-law was a bit of a rake and quite randy with the women. He flirted and he conquered, and under normal circumstances she would not have trusted the man alone with a lady. But there was something in his manner that told her this situation was different. She didn't know why, but there was something about him that was unusual for Tiberius. Could it possibly be the very real trappings of humility? For once, did he truly wish to apologize to a woman for his actions? She wondered.

"Very well," she agreed. "But under one condition."

"Name it."

She put her fingers to her nose. "That you bathe yourself," she said. "You smell like a barn animal. Go and bathe yourself this very minute or I will not summon the lady. I would be ashamed to."

Tiberius sniffed himself, realizing that he did smell rather bad, although he'd known that for days. He hadn't cared until this moment. If it would get him what he wanted, he would do what he was told.

There was a room off to the side of the kitchen that was used for bathing with a massive copper tub that was half-buried in the floor. Once, the tub had been used to strip carcasses but over the years, the men of Isenhall realized it was big enough to bathe their rather enormous bodies in and that was where they did their bathing these days, close to the kitchen and close to an endless source of hot water.

Tiberius made his way down to this room, ducking through the doorway to enter the low-ceilinged chamber. He'd passed through the kitchen on his way and told the cook what his intentions were, so there were already servants bringing forth hot water from a supply that was usually kept simmering off to the side of the enormous kitchen hearth. The cook's husband, a big man with a round belly and no teeth, began filling up the big, copper tub with buckets of hot water, splashing some of it on the floor as Tiberius began to undress.

As the hot water went in, the clothes came off. Truthfully, Tiberius couldn't remember when he had last bathed or even changed his clothes, so he asked the cook's husband to remove his soiled clothing to be boiled and told the man to bring him some fresh clothing. All the while, his head throbbed and he knew that Gallus would be angry that he was ignoring the man's summons by taking the time to bathe, but he didn't much care. He had priorities in his life and sometimes those differed from Gallus'. For now, his priorities were of more importance to him. He needed to speak with Lady Douglass before her father took her away, perhaps forever. Gallus would have to wait.

Tiberius plunged into the tub that was half-full with hot water. He hooted and gasped, as the hot water made his head throb even more, but it didn't matter. In a way, it actually felt good, and after splashing water all over himself, he grabbed a horsehair brush and a bar of white, lumpy soap that smelled of rosemary and went to work. Lathering up the brush with the white, milky froth from the soap, he scrubbed himself from his feet all the way up to his hair.

The cook's husband came back into the room bearing clean clothing and Tiberius had the man hunt down a razor so he could shave. Carefully, with a very sharp razor and a bronze mirror, Tiberius shaved his face clean. In the reflection of the mirror, he could see that his hair was rather long, hanging in his eyes, so he had the cook's husband cut several inches from his hair with the same razor he'd used to shave his face. His hair, now much shorter, kinked up in dark curls all around his face, but at least it was out of his eyes. Rinsing himself off one last time, he climbed out of the tub and dried off with a big piece of linen that was used for just that purpose.

Still damp, he pulled on leather breeches and a big, linen tunic. His feet, now clean, went back into his heavy, leather boots. As he made his way from the small, bathing room and back through the kitchens, he stuck his fingers in his wet ears, trying to dry them out, and ran his hands through his hair several times as he attempted to dry it somewhat. He was just moving towards the stairs that led to the upper levels to tell Courtly that he was prepared to meet Lady Douglass when a soft voice from the solar caught his attention.

He was somewhat surprised to see Lady Douglass standing in the solar archway, smiling rather timidly at him. In the early morning light that was filling the chamber, he could see how glorious she was. Clad in a deep purple surcoat of very soft wool, the garment had a square neck and tight bodice that emphasized the woman's curvaceous figure. And her hair… all of that marvelous, curly, golden-red hair, framed her like a dance of light. The sun glistened off it, creating bursts of stars. Tiberius saw all of this and more as he approached the woman. He met her smile, nearly as timid as hers.

"My lady," he greeted politely. "You are looking quite lovely this morning."

Douglass' smile turned modest. "Thank you, my lord," she said, lowering her gaze coyly. "Lady Courtly said you wished to speak to me."

Tiberius' smile faded. Forgetting his throbbing head, all he could focus on was the woman in front of him, more glorious than he had remembered her. At that moment, he knew that he could not let her go to London to meet her prospective husband. He wasn't sure how he was going to intervene, but he knew that he had to. He'd never felt like this for a woman, not ever. Aye, he was interested in her, but this went beyond mere conquest or lust. There was something more to it, although he wasn't sure what that could be. All he knew was that he felt it, whatever it was, and it consumed him.

"Please," he said softly, indicating the big table a few feet away. "Will you sit?"

Silently, Douglass complied and perched herself on a bench at the corner of the table as Tiberius towered over her, staring down at her. Realizing that he was, in fact, towering over the woman, Tiberius quickly sat at the end of the table, next to her. His gaze never left her face.

"Did… did you sleep well, my lady?" he asked politely.

Douglass nodded. "I did, indeed," she replied. "There is something very strong and peaceful about Isenhall but I awoke to a very noisy bird perched on my window. He awoke me before dawn."

Tiberius grinned. "Show this bird to me and I will punish him," he said with feigned gallantry. "How dare the bird disrupt your slumber."

Douglass laughed softly and Tiberius was again enchanted by her bright smile. "I chased him off, I assure you."

Tiberius laughed because she was. She could have been laughing at anything and, still, he would have laughed. Her smile was infectious.

"I do not doubt it," he said. "As I saw yesterday, you are a very brave woman and unafraid to wield a weapon. It is an admirable quality."

Douglass sobered, gazing into Tiberius' freshly-washed face. He was clean and shaven, his hair even cut, and she thought that perhaps he was the most handsome man on the face of the earth. Truly, she had never seen finer.

"I suppose I should thank you for your kind words," she said, "but I am not sure wielding a weapon in the face of someone who is trying to do you a good deed is an admirable quality. You are kind to say so, however."

He shook his head. "I was not trying to illicit another apology from you for whacking me on the head," he assured her. "I was simply making an observation. You are a remarkable and beautiful woman."

Douglass' cheeks flushed and she lowered her gaze. "Thank you, my lord."

Tiberius watched her as she averted her gaze, studying every hair on her head, the angle of her cheeks, and the soft pout of her lips. He was becoming more infatuated by the moment. He would have been content to stare at her all day except he knew their time was limited. He had to say what needed to be said before de Moray dragged her off to London. *London!* God's Bones, he didn't want to see her go.

"Well," he said finally, thinking on what he needed to say. "In truth, I did not wish to see you alone to pay homage to your beauty or, at least, that is not the only reason. I wanted to apologize for my behavior last night. It has come to my attention that I may or may not have embarrassed myself in front of you with my excessive drinking. If I offended you, then I must apologize. I am deeply sorry if I made you uncomfortable."

Douglass' head came back up and she looked at him, smiling. "You did not offend me," she assured him, "although I appreciate your apology. Rest assured, however, that you did not insult me in the least."

"You are certain?"

"I am."

Tiberius breathed a sigh of relief. "Then I am at ease," he said, running his fingers through his damp hair again. "I thought for certain that I had left you with a terrible lasting impression of me."

Douglass shook her head. "You did not," she said. "In fact, you were quite humorous at times. You told my father that I belonged to you because you had saved me from de Montfort's assassins."

Tiberius watched her giggle, thinking that perhaps he should play into that subject a bit. Perhaps if it was done in jest, he could determine if the woman had any interest in him. He was willing to take the chance.

"You do," he insisted, although it was clear he was teasing. "I saved you and therefore you belong to me. When shall we wed?"

Douglass' laughter grew. "I think you should speak to my father first."

Tiberius scowled. "I would rather marry you first and ask forgiveness later. Your father cannot become overly angry with me once I marry you. Surely he would not kill the father of his grandchildren?"

Douglass snorted. "So we have children already, do we?"

Tiberius shrugged as if it were the most logical thing in the world. "Of course," he said. "I would say six to ten sons would be sufficient, and mayhap a daughter or two so you will not feel entirely lonely in a house full of men."

She smirked wryly. "Thank you, kind sir."

He grinned broadly. "You are welcome, my future wife," he said. Then, he was back to scowling, only this time, he was rather serious about it. "Tell me of this man your father intends to betroth you to. Who must I fight for your hand?"

Douglass wondered just how serious he was. Much like he was doing, she decided to play the game to see, in fact, if his interest was serious. If he wasn't serious, then she could claim she was teasing. But in her heart of hearts, she prayed that the man was sincere. It might break her heart if he wasn't.

"He comes from a very fine Cornwall family," she said. "His name is Tallis d'Vant and he hails from St. Austell Castle. I know that he is twenty-seven years of age and that he has been in the service of the king since he was very young. His father is Dennis d'Vant of the Cornwall d'Vants. His mother is a cousin to the king."

That is tremendous competition, Tiberius thought. But no matter. "It sounds as if he is a fine match," he said. "But I have decided this man shall not have you."

Douglass lifted her auburn eyebrows. "Is that so?" she said.

"What do you intend to do about it?"

Tiberius snorted arrogantly. "I told you. I will fight him for you, of course," he said. "Then your father will have to give you to me."

Douglass laughed quietly. "I hear that Tallis d'Vant is a very fine knight," she said. "His father is a very fine knight. He may put up a good fight."

Tiberius looked at her. "I am The Thunder Knight," he said. "There is no finer fighter or tactician in all of England. As good as d'Vant is, he will fall to me, mark my words."

"Then you know of him?"

"I have heard of him."

Douglass studied Tiberius a moment. He was jesting mostly, that was true, but there was a seed of truth in his behavior. Perhaps his declaration that she belonged to him was, indeed, the truth. Like a game of strategy, a great game of chess that would decide her future, Douglass made the next tactical move in the conversation. The stakes were growing very high, indeed.

"Then you shall not have to face him," she said. "We shall be married today. I will run off with you this very moment and defy my father. Will you take us to the nearest priest?"

Tiberius looked at her with surprise. "Now?"

"Now."

He blinked, considering her proposal. "Would you truly marry me?"

"Would you truly marry *me*?"

"I would."

She lifted her eyebrows again. "Then know this," she said. "If I marry you, there will be no more women for you. I do not share and any infidelity from you would be unhappily and mayhap even violently met. I would haunt you until the end of your days, which would be sooner than you think should you betray me. Now, do you still wish to marry me?"

Tiberius was looking at her with a slight grin on his face. "The moment I met you, all other women in the world ceased to exist for me," he said softly, all of the jesting gone from his tone. "Would you truly have such a sinner as me for your husband? If you would, then I can promise you that you would never regret it. You, and only you, would always be my forever."

The light, teasing tone that they had so recently enjoyed had vanished, replaced by something sweet and warm and thrilling. Douglass' breath caught in her throat. For a moment, as she gazed into his eyes, she forgot to draw in air. It was as if time itself had stopped, just for that moment. In that instance, she knew he felt the same way for her that she did for him. There was interest. There was hope.

It was the truth.

"And you would be mine," she whispered.

Tiberius grinned a bright, dazzling smile that lit up his entire face. But the moment he moved to take her hand, Courtly suddenly appeared in the doorway. She headed directly for Douglass, reaching down to snatch the woman away.

"Come along, my lady," she said rather urgently. "I saw your father out in the bailey from my window. He will be looking for you and more than likely should not find you alone with Tiberius."

Douglass leapt up, following Courtly even though her gaze was on Tiberius. "Will... will you come to the hall, Sir Tiberius?" she asked, not wanting to let the man out of her sight, not even for a moment. "Have you broken your fast yet?"

Tiberius stood up from his seat, feeling the throbbing in his head begin again. But, much like Douglass, he didn't want to be separated from her. However, Gallus was expecting him and he was already late. Torn, he suspected he needed to find Gallus before he joined the guests in the hall. If he didn't, Gallus would come looking for him and the results could be quite unhappy.

"I have not yet," he told her. "I will come as soon as I can. Please do not leave before I have had a chance to bid my farewells."

Douglass was scooting along with Courtly as the woman threw open the entry door. "I will not leave," she told him. "I promise, we will not leave before you come."

That was good enough for Tiberius. Smiling gently, he waved to Douglass as Courtly led the woman out of the keep. He followed her trail to the doorway, standing there and watching as Courtly and Douglass met Bose in the middle of the bailey. After a brief discussion, the three of them headed back into the hall. Tiberius watched Douglass' red head until it disappeared from view.

You will always be my forever. He had meant every word. God's Bones, he never realized how much he meant them until this very moment.

He had finally found his forever.

IN THE BRIGHT, beautiful, early morning hours, Maximus found Gallus sitting in the armory of Isenhall with an unrolled piece of parchment in his hands. Gallus had received the missive at dawn and, after reading it, sent for both of his brothers to join him. Even though the knights were up and going about their duties, and Bose de Moray and his family were in the great hall breaking their fast before continuing on their journey, Gallus had only requested the company of his brothers. There were serious dealings afoot, according to the missive he'd received from de Montfort, and he wanted his brothers to be the first to know.

"Good morn," Maximus greeted his brother as he entered the dim, cool armory that smelled strongly of leather and dirt. "You summoned me?"

Gallus nodded, his features drawn and tense. "Where is Ty?"

Maximus shook his head. "I have not yet seen him," he replied. "He is probably still drunk from all of the cider he consumed last night. Shall I go and rouse him?"

"Nay," Gallus said, looking at the parchment in his hand. "I sent a soldier for him. He will be here."

Maximus couldn't help but notice that Gallus was focused on the rolled parchment in his hand. He could see the broken seal on it and flashes of carefully-scripted writing when Gallus unrolled it again to look at it.

"What is that?" Maximus finally asked. "Who sent the missive?"

Gallus was reading it again. He'd already read it no less than ten times that morning but he was reading it still again. He sighed heavily, his focus still on the yellowed, brittle parchment.

"It is from de Montfort," he said. "It was sent from Kenilworth this morning."

Maximus lifted his eyebrows. Kenilworth was a little more than an hour's ride from Isenhall to the west. "De Montfort is at Kenilworth?" he asked. "Last I heard, he was traveling the south of England to drum up support."

Gallus nodded. "I know," he said quietly. "Evidently, he has drummed up quite a bit of support, mayhap more support than he bargained for."

Maximus leaned back against the stone wall, folding his big arms across his chest. "What do you mean?"

Gallus held out the missive to Maximus, who took it and unrolled it, reading it carefully and slowly as Gallus spoke.

"Henry's son and heir, Prince Edward, is apparently siding with de Montfort now," he said. Then, he shook his head, baffled. "I cannot believe I just said that. It is preposterous at the very least, but Simon assures me that it is true. That is Simon's signature on the missive. Therefore, it must be true."

Maximus looked at his brother, shocked, before returning his focus to the parchment. "Simon wants us to come to Kenilworth immediately," he said, lifting his eyes to his brother again. "Edward must be there. He wants us to meet with the prince."

Gallus shook his head, unhappy and unnerved by the entire happenstance. "Edward is the next king of England," he said flatly. "Does de Montfort not realize this? Edward is a brutal warrior and a man of great vision. He will rule England with an iron fist and facilitate absolute rule, whereupon de Montfort's efforts for change will be destroyed. Everything we are working towards now will be destroyed. I do not want to go to Kenilworth and listen to Edward's lies."

"What about Edward?"

Tiberius's voice was heard as the man entered the armory, smelling like rosemary soap and clean-shaven. In fact, he looked quite different, causing both Gallus and Maximus to take notice. Gallus reached out and tugged on the sleeve of the tunic Tiberius was wearing.

"Isn't that mine?" he asked, suspicious. "My wife made that for me. What are you doing in my clothing?"

Tiberius pursed his lips wryly. "I had nothing else that was clean to wear, my dearest love," he said. "What would you have me do? Walk about nude until my clothing has been cleaned and dried? I am sure that would impress the women of Isenhall deeply. It would cause them to realize how inadequate you two are as husbands and they will lament the fact that they should have married me instead."

Gallus grinned in spite of the insult as Maximus rolled his eyes. "I've not yet had the need to measure my manhood but I would wager it is better than yours."

Tiberius scoffed arrogantly. "It is *not* better than mine," he said. "Mine satisfies a woman as food satisfies the hungry. We are speaking of a massive side of beef as compared to your tiny, pork sausage."

Maximus burst out laughing as Gallus cut his brother an intolerant expression. "Mine is better than yours for one good reason," Gallus said. "It will produce the next Earl of Coventry. You and your inadequate manhood cannot make the same claim."

Tiberius shrugged, conceding the argument at that point. He pointed to the missive in Maximus' hands.

"What is that?" he asked, changing the subject. "And what about Edward? I heard his name mentioned as I came in."

They went back to the subject at hand. Gallus took the parchment away from Maximus and looked at it again. He made no move to give it to Tiberius because the man was a terrible reader. He mixed words up or misplaced them entirely, so he was never given anything to read. Something happened between Tiberius' eyes and his mind that twisted everything around when he was reading or figuring mathematics.

One would have thought Tiberius was dumb but for the fact he retained knowledge that was verbally relayed to him as tightly as a vault. He could visualize numbers in a way that wasn't normal, but he could still figure the most complex mathematics in his mind and come out correct. And, much like Maximus, Tiberius could recall conversations, events, or facts from years prior or two minutes ago – his total recall was infallible. Unlike Maximus, however, Tiberius didn't see only two sides to a coin or to a situation. Maximus' world was black and white, with nothing in between. Tiberius, however, could see all colors of a situation with great clarity. In that capacity, he was invaluable. The man was clearly not dumb. He was the most brilliant of all three of them.

"This missive is from de Montfort," Gallus told him. "Apparently, Prince Edward, the king's heir, has joined de Montfort's cause and de Montfort has summoned us to Kenilworth immediately to discuss it."

Tiberius' eyes widened with surprise. "Edward?" he repeated. "The man has withdrawn support of his own father?"

Against the wall, Maximus grunted. "It is as Gallus said," he said quietly. "If Edward inherits the throne from his father at this moment, he will have to deal with the Savoyard and Poitevin element that Henry has allowed into this country, greedy Frenchmen who are soaking up English properties for themselves. Edward wants them out of England as badly as we do, I would suspect. Siding with de Montfort will gain him what he wants."

Tiberius knew all of that but the reality was still shocking. He shook his head, hissing. "I do not like this," he muttered. "Edward has properties in Gascony he is having trouble with. Mayhap he wants de Montfort's help with those, which means we could quite possibly be sent to France to fight Edward's wars. Throwing his support behind de Montfort will indebt de Montfort to him. He could easily ask for the man's help."

Gallus couldn't argue the fact. "If that is the case, then I do not want to fight for a greedy prince," he said. "I will threaten de Montfort with changing loyalties if he intends to send us to France. England needs us right now and I'll not spend my time or resources in France fighting for a futile cause."

Maximus nodded in agreement. "Nor I," he said firmly. "Let de Montfort send someone else to France if he will pledge support for Edward there. I will fight in England for Henry before I will fight in France for Edward."

The armory fell silent a moment as each man pondered the course of the immediate future. With Prince Edward siding with de Montfort, things were uncertain indeed. But the thought of Edward inevitably brought on thoughts of Henry and, along with him, thoughts of de Moray, who was a great supporter of the king. Tiberius looked to Gallus.

"I wonder if de Moray knows any of this," he ventured quietly.

Gallus shrugged. "My guess is that he does not," he said. "For his own sake, I should tell him. The man needs to know who his allies and enemies are and if Edward's loyalties have indeed shifted, then de Moray must know."

Maximus sighed with resignation. "When do we leave for Kenilworth?"

Gallus glanced at the parchment in his hand. "He has summoned us immediately so I imagine he wants us at Kenilworth today, tomorrow at the latest," he said, moving to the armory doorway and gazing out across Isenhall's bailey. This was his empire, what he was fighting and living for. He thought of Jeniver and the son she carried. He thought of a world with no conflicts, only peace. It seemed like a dream to him. He wondered if it was something he would ever truly see. "Be ready to leave by dawn tomorrow. I am not overly anxious to leave my wife today."

Thoughts of a wife brought about thoughts of Douglass to Tiberius. He fervently wished that he had a wife to leave behind, that he had *her* to leave behind. As Gallus moved to leave the armory with the intention of speaking to de Moray, Tiberius stopped him.

"Wait, Gallus, please," he said hesitantly, eyeing both brothers as they looked at him curiously. Suddenly, he felt rather embarrassed and uncertain but he charged on anyway. "I… I wanted to apologize for embarrassing you last night. I am afraid the cider loosened my tongue far more than I would have liked."

Both Gallus and Maximus grinned at the change of subject. "Apologize to Max if you must," Gallus said, pointing to the middle brother. "He was the one who suffered when he took you back to your chamber."

Maximus was waving him off even as Tiberius turned to him. "It is not even worth mentioning," Maximus said. "I seem to remember you taking care of me once or twice when wine had gotten the better of me."

Tiberius smiled weakly at the memories of a drunk and combative Maximus, a fearsome beast indeed. Maximus was the meanest drunkard he had ever seen. "It was no trouble," Tiberius said. "You are my brother. It is my duty to take care of you."

Maximus nodded his head firmly. "And I, you," he said. "You were no trouble at all, really. Well, except when you were telling de Moray that you wanted his daughter. You were quite adamant about it."

Tiberius' smile faded. "I know," he said. "I remember that part."

Maximus was mildly astonished. "You do?" he asked. "That is surprising considering the amount of cider you had consumed. I think de Moray has forgotten about it, however, so you are safe."

Tiberius emitted a heavy sigh. "Nay, I am not."

"Why?"

Tiberius was having difficulty looking his brothers in the eye. "Because it was not the cider forcing my words last eve," he said quietly. "I... I am not even sure how to speak on this subject. I rescued a woman who beat me, fought me, argued with me, yet for all of that, she is on my mind like no other woman has ever been and I cannot seem to shake her. At first, I thought I was simply interested in another conquest but now... now I am not so sure. All I know is that I do not want her going to London where a potential husband is waiting for her. I do not want her out of my sight."

That softly uttered confession brought Gallus back into the armory. Both Gallus and Maximus closed in on Tiberius, their expressions laced with both disbelief and humor.

"Is this true, Ty?" Gallus asked as if he hadn't heard his rakish brother correctly. "You have feelings for Garran's sister?"

Tiberius was feeling embarrassed and confused and joyful, all at the same time. "It is possible," he said. "I do not want her leaving for

London. Can we keep her here somehow?"

Gallus looked at Maximus, both men shrugging at a seemingly impossible endeavor. "I do not know much about de Moray's contract with her potential husband," Gallus said. "I suppose I could ask him if you are truly serious about her. *Are* you serious, Ty? Are you certain she is not meant to be another one of your conquests? To do that would sorely damage the relationship between the House of de Moray and the House of de Shera. Surely you know that."

Tiberius nodded. "I know," he said quickly. "I assure you that is not my intent, at least not now. Mayhap it was yesterday but… but that is not my intent today. Something about the woman moves me in a way I've never known before. Is that what it is like to love someone?"

Maximus let out a hiss. "Love, is it?" he said. Then, he shook his head as if Tiberius were a fool. "You are speaking of something quite serious, Ty. You do not love someone so quickly. It takes time."

Tiberius was looking at him. "How long did it take for you to know you loved Courtly?"

Maximus backed down a bit. "Well," he said slowly, having difficulty looking Tiberius in the eye. "More than a day, in any case."

Gallus was looking at Maximus rather drolly. "It took you exactly one day to declare your intentions for the woman," he said. "Do not forget, I was there. We were *all* there. We know what you went through for Courtly. It is perfectly plausible that Ty is indeed feeling the first seeds of love, but be that as it may, the fact remains that Lady Douglass already has a suitor waiting for her in London. I would imagine that de Moray has already given the man his word and that will be a difficult bond to break."

Tiberius knew that and struggled not to feel discouraged. "The suitor was picked by Henry himself," he told them. "According to Lady Douglass, the knight Henry has selected for her is Tallis d'Vant."

That drew a reaction from both Gallus and Maximus. "D'Vant?" Gallus repeated. "Of the Cornwall d'Vants?"

Tiberius nodded. "We all know who he is," he said, sounding defeated. "He is a great knight in the arsenal of Henry's armies. The man is well-connected and has a fine reputation."

Maximus simply looked at Gallus. He would let his older brother handle this situation because it involved politics and that was Gallus' strength. Maximus simply put a hand on Tiberius' shoulder in a comforting gesture before turning away to ponder the situation. He didn't want to tell his youngest brother that the situation was hopeless, but it sure sounded that way. As he wandered away, Gallus spoke.

"The House of d'Vant holds most of Cornwall," he said. "As I recall, Tallis is the eldest son of the house, which means he will inherit it. That would be a position of prestige for Lady Douglass."

Tiberius was starting to feel quite inadequate against Tallis d'Vant. "I have my own lordship," he insisted. "I inherited Lord Lockhurst from grandfather and my lands produce an excellent income, plus Keresley Castle belongs to me. I am not a pauper."

Gallus patted him on the shoulder to quiet him. "I know," he said. "But you must admit that d'Vant and his Cornwall estates are rather attractive."

Tiberius frowned. "Will you speak to de Moray on my behalf or not?"

Gallus was trying not to smile at his brother, who was being quite forceful about it. He honestly couldn't tell if the man was being serious about his feelings or if it was just an infatuation he was dealing with. Knowing Tiberius, he tended to think it was the latter. Sighing heavily, he looked to Maximus.

"Well?" he asked him, rather shortly. "What do you think?"

Maximus was leaning against the cold wall of the armory, digesting everything that had been said. "I think we should not discourage him," he said. "I know what it is like to fall in love with a woman on sight, so I cannot discount him completely. However, knowing our dear brother as I do, I am not entirely convinced that he has genuine feelings for the lady and the only way he is going to know is if he spends time with her."

Gallus shook his head. "He cannot spend time with her if they are leaving for London today."

"He can if he rides escort," Maximus said, cocking an eyebrow to emphasize his suggestion. "I will ride on to Kenilworth to see what de Montfort has to say about Edward while you and Ty escort Lady Douglass and de Moray into London. It is foolish for de Moray to be traveling alone, anyway. He got into trouble with it so we shall ride with him to London to ensure he doesn't get into any more trouble. It will be a perfect opportunity for Tiberius to speak with Lady Douglass further and determine if, in fact, it is not simply infatuation he is feeling."

It was a reasonable plan. Gallus glanced at Tiberius' hopeful face before returning his focus to Maximus. "And if it is *not* infatuation?" he asked. "What then?"

Maximus sobered. "Then you must speak to de Moray about Tiberius' desire to court his daughter," he said. "You are the only one who can do it, Gal. As the earl, you can offer much that d'Vant cannot."

"Like what?"

Maximus scratched his neck in thought. "Ty already holds the Lockhurst lordship," he said. "Tell de Moray that you will grant him the title of Viscount Sherborne to sweeten the deal against d'Vant."

Gallus frowned. "Viscount Sherborne is a title for my son."

Maximus cocked his head. "*If* you have a son," he said. "It is quite possible that Jeniver will have another girl. You asked my opinion, Gal. I am simply telling you what I think. Do nothing and let Tiberius stand on his own, then. He is a de Shera, after all. That would be enough for most men."

With that, both brothers looked to Tiberius, who was coming to see that his battle for lovely Lady Douglass' hand was to be uphill all the way. He pondered the situation seriously before speaking.

"I am willing to offer myself on my merits alone," he said. "I am a de Shera and there is no need to sweeten the deal with more titles or promises of wealth. Let us send word to de Montfort that we shall join him in a few days at Kenilworth and then we will escort de Moray to London under the guise of protection. All three of us must ride together. We have never been separated and I do not wish for this to be the first time. Moreover, Maximus would be facing de Montfort's wrath that all of us did not answer the summons and that is not fair to him. Therefore, either all of us go to London or none of us go. If that is the case that none of us goes, then I will have to figure another way to deal with the situation."

Gallus' gaze lingered on his youngest brother a moment before turning to Maximus. "Then we all go to London," he said. "Agreed?"

Maximus nodded. "Agreed."

Gallus returned his attention to Tiberius. "Then we all ride to London so that you may try to win over Lady Douglass," he said. Then, he grew serious. "But I will say one thing, Ty. If you are simply out to toy with this woman, I will hold you down while de Moray beats you and then I will take a turn at you myself. Is that clear?"

Tiberius didn't flinch. "Perfectly."

"I am putting myself and my reputation on the line for you."

"Understood. You will not be sorry."

Gallus simply nodded, giving his brother a lingering look as he headed out of the armory. Maximus followed, giving Tiberius more of a sympathetic expression as he, too, stepped out into the mounting dawn.

Tiberius followed his brothers somewhat, pausing in the armory doorway and watching as the men headed for the great hall. So many things rolled through his mind at that moment; how fortunate he was to have such loyal brothers and how he truly didn't want to let them down. Gallus was noble, Maximus was strong, and Tiberius very much wanted to be worthy of their loyalty and brotherly love.

Tiberius had spent the last several years of his life being rather careless and wild, but that wasn't the kind of life he wanted to lead forever. There was a beautiful, red-haired woman in the hall that had managed to capture his spirit and he truly wanted to come to know her better, but not because he wanted to discover if she was worthy of him. He wanted to discover if *he* was worthy of *her*.

It was time for Tiberius de Shera to grow up.

CHAPTER SIX

VIOLET AND LILY were running in circles out in the bailey with the dogs chasing after them, barking happily. It was some sort of game that had Violet chasing Lily, tapping her, and then Lily would turn around and chase Violet until she was able to tap her in return. On and on it went as Taranis and Henry chased the girls. Taranis wasn't a jumper but Henry was and, when extended on his hind legs, he was as tall as the women, so when Henry got too excited and jumped on Lily, pushing her over, Courtly wrangled the mutt and made him sit with her over on the big steps that led into the keep.

Courtly and Jeniver were sitting on the steps, watching the girls play in the sunshine while Jeniver worked on some kind of clothing for the baby. It was a lovely day, two days after Gallus, Maximus, and Tiberius left to escort Bose and Garran and Douglass from Isenhall to London, and the ladies were passing the time until their husbands returned. It was a pleasant sort of passage.

But there had been an ulterior motive behind the de Moray escort. Both Gallus and Maximus had mentioned to their respective wives that the escort was mainly a ruse so that Tiberius could spend more time with Lady Douglass with the hopes of wooing her. In that respect, neither Jeniver nor Courtly had issue with the men being gone for a few days. However, what neither Gallus nor Maximus had mentioned was that after London, they would be headed to Kenilworth before returning home.

Gallus knew that his wife would not have been happy with those plans, as she wasn't particularly a de Montfort enthusiast, so he kept the business end of their trip to himself. Not strangely, however, Jeniver knew that the brothers were going to Kenilworth, anyway, when a soldier happened to mention their plans to the majordomo who, in turn, told Jeniver. She was therefore planning to have strong words with her husband when he returned for not telling her the truth.

But in the grand scope of things, it really didn't matter. One way or another, Gallus and Maximus and Tiberius would be returning home and all would be right in the world again. As Jeniver sewed the little sleeve on the baby's clothing, Courtly sat beside her, petting the pouting dog as he watched his playmates cavort.

"Have you ever been to London, Jeni?" Courtly asked as she stroked Henry's head.

Jeniver nodded. "Earlier this year," she said. "When my father took me to Paris for my birthday, we passed by way of London."

Courtly sighed. "I have never been there," she said. "Maximus said he would take me some day, very soon. He told me of a Street of the Merchants with all manner of exotic things to purchase. It all sounds quite wonderful."

Jeniver smiled as she stitched. "My father bought me scented oil on the Street of the Merchants," she said. "The city is a vast, dirty place. I was not particularly impressed with it."

Courtly shrugged longingly, petting the dog as he whined, but both women looked up when the sentries on the wall began to take up the call.

Evidently, riders were approaching and the de Shera sentries had a protocol for such things. The exterior portcullis would be raised to admit the riders but the interior portcullis, the second one, would remain closed. Then, the exterior portcullis would close, effectively trapping the visitor until they declared their business. Depending on their business, they were either chased back outside of the gatehouse by men wielding spears, or they were ushered into the bailey. The de Shera guards were very efficient so neither Jeniver nor Courtly gave the event of incoming riders much thought. They returned their focus back to the children playing before them.

It took some time for the riders to finally enter the gatehouse, trapped between the portcullises, but the women weren't paying attention by this time because Lily had fallen and scraped her knee. Courtly picked the child up, cradling her, as Jeniver tended the scrape. Meanwhile, Violet was off and running with the dogs, not particularly concerned with her sister's weeping.

But the tears were short-lived. After Jeniver wiped off the barely-bloodied knee and cleaned it with a witch hazel solution that the majordomo brought her, Lily was back on her feet running and screaming in delight as the dogs chased her. Jeniver and Courtly were about to resume their seats on the steps when they noticed Scott de Wolfe heading their way.

Scott had been left in charge of the castle, along with Stefan, while Troy rode with the de Shera brothers to London. Scott had the day watch and Stefan had the night watch. In the event of an attack or other military situation, Scott was the senior commander. He was only twenty-five years of age, as was his twin, but he had the maturity and wisdom of a man who had seen much in life. As the son of the legendary Wolfe of the Border, William de Wolfe, Scott was a greatly respected knight not only for his family ties but for his own skill. Scott and Gallus were particularly close. Jeniver glanced over when she caught sight of the big, blond knight.

"Greetings, Scott," she said, addressing him informally. "'Tis a fine day, is it not?"

Scott was a very handsome man with pale green eyes and fair skin. He smiled weakly. "It is indeed, Lady de Shera," he said. "I was wondering if I may have a word with you."

Jeniver nodded, moving in Scott's direction as Courtly took a seat upon the stone steps of Isenhall's keep to maintain a vigilant eye over the children. Scott politely took Jeniver's elbow and led her over towards the gatehouse where they would have some privacy. When they had moved far enough away from prying ears, he let go of her elbow and faced her.

"I wanted to make sure we were away from Lady Courtly," he said, lowering his voice. His expression seemed to morph between confusion and concern. "It would seem we have a situation on our hands involving her husband."

Jeniver grew instantly concerned. "What is it?" she gasped. "Has Maximus been injured? Is he ill?"

Scott could see the panic in her expression and he hastened to reassure her. "Nay, my lady," he said quickly. "Nothing of the sort. Maximus is perfectly fine as far as I know. The situation I am speaking of is rather... unique. I do not know how to bring it up to Lady Courtly so I will rely on you for your counsel."

Jeniver was growing increasingly perplexed. "Of course, Scott," she said. "What is it?"

Scott scratched his head, struggling to figure out where to begin. "I have known Gallus and Maximus for many years," he finally said. "We fostered together at Kenilworth. All of us squired together for knights who were close friends, which meant we spent nearly all of our time together. My lady... did Maximus ever mention to you that there was a girl he was quite fond of when he was around seventeen years of age? Or has Gallus ever told you anything about that?"

Jeniver thought seriously on his question. "Courtly has mentioned it to me," she said. "Neither Gallus nor Maximus have ever told me anything directly, but in conversation once, Courtly mentioned that he had been in love with a girl when he was a lad. Antoninus de Shera sent the girl away to end the budding romance and I think Courtly said that Maximus was told later that she had died of a fever. Why do you ask?"

Scott puffed out his cheeks, clearly struggling. "What Lady Courtly told you is true," he said. "I was there when Maximus fell in love with young Rose. She was the daughter of a smithy at Kenilworth. Maximus wanted very much to marry her but Antoninus caught wind of the budding romance and had de Montfort send the girl and her father away. Maximus was devastated. I truly believe he loved the girl, but they were both so young and marriage simply wasn't possible. I was also there when Maximus received word that Rose had died of a fever. He was shattered after that for quite some time."

Jeniver was still confused about the entire conversation. "I see," she said, pretending she understood when she really didn't. "Why are you telling me all of this? What has happened?"

Scott hissed softly. "There is no easy way to tell you this so I will be frank," he said. "There is a man at the gatehouse I recognize. He is the smithy that de Montfort had sent away those years ago along with his daughter."

Jeniver still wasn't understanding the man's sense of apprehension but she knew, instinctively, that there must be a reason behind it. "God's Bones," she exclaimed softly. "After all of these years? What is he doing here?"

Scott lifted his eyebrows, resigned to what he must say. "The man has returned with a lad who is nearly sixteen years of age and who is the exact image of Maximus," he said, watching Jeniver's eyes widen as she came to realize what he meant. "My lady, the smithy told me that his daughter did not die of a fever. She died in childbirth, and now the smithy has brought Maximus' son to Isenhall because he feels the boy should have all of the privileges of a de Shera. He has come to claim the boy's birthright as Maximus de Shera's son and he is demanding to see Maximus."

Jeniver's mouth popped open in shock as the news sank in. In all her wildest dreams, she could not have imagined this would have been the reason behind Scott's edgy demeanor or the reason behind the visitors at the gatehouse. Shocking wasn't quite the word she had in mind; staggering was more like it. It was too staggering to believe and she quickly clapped a hand over her gaping mouth.

"Maximus has a *son*?" she gasped. "Scott, is this true?"

Scott nodded firmly, his expression suggesting he was as shocked as she was. "It is," he said softly. "I swear to you, my lady, that this boy is Maximus' son. He looks exactly like him. I believe the smithy without question."

Jeniver's hands moved to her head, astonished beyond measure. But just as quickly, she thought of her friend, Courtly, and how the woman would handle the news of her husband's bastard. She could hardly catch her breath, knowing that Courtly's entire world was about to be shaken to the core. But she quickly composed herself, knowing that this was not her battle to fight. It was not her right to feel anything other than sympathy for her friend and for Maximus, who would undoubtedly be stunned by the news. Therefore, she took a deep breath and faced Scott. Decisions had to be made and made quickly.

"I will take Courtly inside the keep and distract her," she said. "You will bring the smithy and the boy into the castle and settle them in the knights' quarters. Once you have settled them, you will help me explain the situation to Courtly. But before you do anything, you must send a messenger riding as hard as he can for Gallus. My husband must know what has happened so that he can tell Maximus. Max will take the news better if it comes from Gallus. Is that clear?"

Scott nodded. "It is, my lady," he said. "I agree completely."

Jeniver nodded shortly. "Good," she said. "Go now. Send the

messenger, settle the visitors, and then come to me in the keep. We must tell Lady Courtly that her husband's bastard son has arrived."

She said it with some sadness and Scott could understand why. It was a shocking and saddening situation for all involved. As Jeniver headed back across the bailey towards Courtly, who was now sitting on the steps with Lily on her lap and the dogs milling about her, Scott headed off towards the gatehouse where the big, sickly, wheezing smithy was waiting with a very big lad who was the image of Maximus de Shera in his youth. The entire situation was astonishing but Scott focused on what he needed to do. With the de Shera brothers gone, this was his keep now and he was in charge. He would make the correct and necessary decisions, with the guidance of Lady Jeniver, for all concerned.

A trusted soldier was soon racing for London bearing a shocking missive for Gallus de Shera.

BECAUSE IT WAS nearing the nooning meal, Jeniver and Courtly herded the little girls into the small solar off the entry where they usually had intimate family meals as opposed to eating in the vastness of the great hall. As Taranis and Henry milled around the table, mostly over by Violet and Lily who they knew would feed them scraps, Courtly oversaw the dishes the servants were bringing in. Jeniver sat down and poured herself some boiled juice made from apple juice, pear juice, a tiny amount of wine, and mashed rose petals. The little girls received the same drink and Lily tried to pick the rose petals out.

As those at the table helped themselves to drink, Courtly stood at the door of the chamber and inspected the dishes as they were brought in.

"This is the apple pie I was telling you about," Courtly said to

Jeniver as a servant set a large, baked pie onto the table. "It is made from mashed apples, figs, raisins, honey, and a small amount of spice and saffron. Ty tried to describe this to me as a dish he favored as a child so I have tried to recreate it. I hope it turns out well."

Jeniver smiled weakly as a servant presented her with a slab of the pie. "Anything you do turns out wonderfully," she said, taking a big pewter spoon and scooping up a small bit. Putting it in her mouth, she chewed. "It is delicious. Ty will be thrilled."

Courtly smiled, relieved and happy that her pie was a success. As the servants brought in bread, butter, fruit compote, and warmed-over pork and gravy from the night before, she sat down next to Jeniver and took a piece of pie for herself. Spooning a bite into her mouth, she crowed with delight.

"It *is* good," she said. "I can already tell that Ty will confiscate the entire thing for himself, which means I will have to make several pies so everyone can have some. Why are men such little boys some-times?"

Speaking of little boys.... Jeniver thought as she eyed her friend. She took another bite of the delicious pie before using her spoon to cut up the small piece of pie on Lily's little wooden trencher. She then returned to her own food, accepting a piece of bread when a servant passed her a trencher filled with it.

"I spent my entire life with only my father and a few cousins and servants as company," she said. "Most of them were old men or young women, so I have not spent a good deal of time around men in general. I can only imagine that Lady Honey had her hands full with her sons but it seems that she ruled the nest, not the other way around."

Courtly was almost finished with her pie. "I am very sorry that I was not able to know the woman," she said. "When we first returned to Isenhall after her death, I know that Maximus was truly devastated that she had been buried shortly after her death and he had missed her funeral. For weeks, he would get up in the middle of the night and go to the family vault where he would simply sit beside her crypt for hours. Do you remember how Ty actually slept next to his mother's crypt for the first week following her death? It was truly sad to watch."

Jeniver remembered all of that. She had caught Gallus, several times, talking to his mother's crypt. Three months later, he still did it. But Jeniver knew it gave him comfort. "What about you?" she asked Courtly. "Your father was buried in Kennington shortly after you and Max were married. Do you miss your father as your husband misses his mother?"

Courtly sighed faintly. "I do, at times," she admitted. "But my father grew very odd towards the end. His protectiveness over me and over my sister grew to unhealthy proportions. I have not yet forgiven him for trying to kill Max on the field of battle. I am not sure if I ever will."

Jeniver nodded. She knew of Courtly's resentment towards her father following her marriage to Maximus. Kellen de Lara had tried to kill Maximus under the guise of battle and might have succeeded had Bose de Moray not saved Maximus' life by killing Kellen. It had been a shocking and deadly turn for Kellen de Lara's anger towards Maximus.

"Sir Bose apologized for killing your father when he came to pay his respects to Lady Honey after the battle at Warborough," Jeniver said softly. "Did he make any mention of it again with his most recent visit?"

Courtly shook her head. "There is no need to," she said. "I told him that there was nothing to forgive, as my father had gone mad. I thanked the man for saving Max's life. I am indebted to de Moray, just as Max is. We owe him our happiness."

Jeniver let the subject drop, mostly because the situation at the time of Honey and Kellen's deaths had been turbulent, indeed. They were not particularly happy times other than Courtly and Maximus' marriage. Jeniver finished off the last bite of her pie.

"And your sister?" she asked, changing the focus somewhat. "Will she be coming to Isenhall to stay with you? You speak of her so often I feel as if I already know her."

Courtly smiled at the thought of her younger sister, Isadora, who had been at her family's castle of Trelystan over the summer months, having been sent there by Kellen back in May before the chaos surrounding Courtly and Maximus' marriage. The younger de Lara sister had been removed from most of her father's madness during that time, fortunately.

"I have written her three missives over the summer," Courtly said. "Isadora has written back to tell me that she is very happy at Trelystan because she is the Lady of the Castle now with my father and me gone. Kirk St. Héver has remained there as well to help her oversee things since my father's death. Technically, the castle now belongs to Maximus through his marriage to me but my husband has no desire to live there or even see it right now. He is content to let St. Héver command the castle for now. As for my sister, she seems happy there and Aunt Ellice has even gone to Trelystan to live with her. Isadora is in very good hands and I am content."

Jeniver recalled the spinster aunt who had been so instrumental in ensuring Courtly and Maximus' relationship. "Aunt Ellice is quite a woman," she said, recalling the woman's bravery in the face of Kellen de Lara's resistance to his daughter's romance. "Isadora is very lucky to have Ellice as her guardian."

Courtly, too, was thinking on her aunt, a woman she had not particularly cared for until the incident with Maximus. Then, Ellice had proven herself an exceptional and courageous ally. "It is a comfort to know and understand the woman after so many years of disliking her," she said softly, "but my father was terrible to her and she reacted in kind. Now, with my father gone, Ellice is truly one of the family and I believe she will be a good influence on Isadora. I hope they will visit Isenhall someday but, until then, I know they are happy at Trelystan."

Jeniver was about to reply when the keep entry opened and Scott stepped through. From where Jeniver was sitting, she could see the knight right away and his gaze found her almost immediately. Jeniver's humor faded as she braced herself for the conversation that was to come. Scott had arrived and it was time to inform Lady Courtly de Shera of her husband's youthful indiscretion. Although Courtly was a level-headed and pragmatic woman, it was hard to know how she was going to react. Still, they could not delay. She had to be told.

"Greetings, Scott," Courtly said as the knight entered the solar. "We have plenty to eat. Are you hungry?"

Scott nodded as he sat down at the long, scrubbed table. The dogs shifted their attention from the girls to their latest visitor and Scott patted Taranis on his big, black head before moving to help himself to the food at the table.

"Ah," he said, taking hold of the apple pie and helping himself to a massive slab. "More of Lady Courtly's culinary experiments. I am happy to eat it all before Max gets to it."

Courtly and Jeniver laughed at him. "That was for Ty," Courtly pointed out. "It is a pie he described to me, something Lady Honey would make for him when he was young. I tried to recreate it."

"And you did a magnificent job," Scott said, his mouth full. "It is delicious."

Pleased, Courtly watched the knight wolf down a big portion of the pie. "You had better eat your fill now," she said. "You know what will happen when Maximus and his brothers return."

Scott swallowed an enormous bite. "I know exactly what will happen," he declared. "I will get nothing but crumbs. I am glad they are away for the next few days so that I can eat my fill before the hungry hounds return."

Courtly giggled. "Hurry and eat what you can, then," she said, noticing that Violet and Lily had finished their food and were now under the table with the dogs. She turned to Jeniver. "Jeni, mayhap the girls need to be taken away for their naps. When they crawl under the table, you know it is prelude to them laying down and sleeping there."

Jeniver nodded, peering under the table at Lily and Violet. "Indeed it is," she said, lifting her head and calling to the nearest servant. "Please send for the nurse. Lady Lily and Lady Violet must be returned to their chamber."

As the servant headed off, the room fell into comfortable silence. Scott was eating everything in sight and Courtly was finishing off the last of her pie. The nurse soon appeared and pulled Lily and Violet out from underneath the table, escorting the children out of the solar.

When they were gone and there was no one left in the low-ceilinged room but the three adults, Jeniver cleared her throat softly. The time was upon them to delve into the disturbing dealings at hand and she would waste no more time. It wasn't as if they could avoid the subject. The longer they delayed, the worse it would be. It was time to speak.

"Courtly," she began casually. "Did you notice the visitors we had today at the gatehouse?"

Courtly sipped at her fruit juice. "I did," she said. "Who was it?"

With that simple question, the opportunity had presented itself to tell her everything and Jeniver chose her words carefully. Courtly would be upset enough with the subject matter so Jeniver tried to present a calm, even front. She could only pray that her calm attitude helped Courtly somehow. God only knew how Jeniver would react if she had been presented with Gallus' bastard. She couldn't even imagine. Therefore, she fell back on how Scott had presented the situation to her in the hopes that it would help Courtly understand the freakish turn of events. She could only pray.

"Love is a strange thing, isn't it?" she ventured softly. "Love is the greatest motivator in the world. It can be the greatest gift or the heaviest burden. Sometimes people fall in love and have no idea that when that love is gone, there are still lasting effects they might not even be aware of."

Courtly was looking at her, a curious smile on her face. "I suppose so," she said. "What does that have to do with the visitors we had earlier?"

Jeniver glanced at Scott, who had stopped eating. He was looking at Courtly, gauging her reaction. But he caught Jeniver's look and took the hint. It was time for him to help explain the situation from his perspective.

"Lady Courtly, I have known Maximus since we were children," he said. "I am a few years younger than he is, but we squired together and my brother and I would tail around after him and Gallus and Tiberius. I have, therefore, seen all three brothers go through a great deal. In particular, I was there when Maximus fell in love with the young peasant girl, Rose. He has told you about Rose, has he not?"

Courtly nodded, not at all concerned with the path the conversation was taking. "Aye," she said. "He was seventeen and she was fourteen, as I recall. She was the daughter of a smithy and Max's father sent the girl and her father away to stop the romance. Max has spoken of that event with some sadness. As a young man, I think it deeply marked him."

Scott nodded in agreement. "I remember," he said. "He was heartbroken about it, as any young man in love would have been. I'm sure you can understand that."

"Of course," Courtly agreed. "But what does that have to do with the visitors today?"

Scott continued as gently as he could. "I was with Max about a year later when a soldier passing through Kenilworth told him that Rose had perished of a fever," he said. "At that point, she was nothing more than a fond memory although news of her death did sadden him for a time. To the best of my knowledge, that is the last time he received any news about Rose. He never heard about her again… until today."

Courtly's eyebrows lifted. "Did the visitors bring more news of Rose?" she wanted to know. "*Who* are the visitors?"

Scott didn't dare look at Jeniver for fear that Courtly would see their apprehensive expressions and it would send her into a state. Therefore, he kept his eyes on Courtly, strong and reassuring, as he delivered what would perhaps be the most shocking news of her life.

"Rose's father came today," he said. "He has come seeking Maximus."

Courtly frowned. "Why on earth should he do that?"

Scott was very good at maintaining a somewhat passive expression, masking the pity he felt for the woman. Before he could speak, Jeniver grasped Courtly's hand gently and continued.

"Maximus was told that Rose died of a fever, but that was evidently not true," she said gently. "Rose's father came today to inform Maximus that Rose, in fact, died in childbirth with Maximus' child. He has brought the boy here to Isenhall because he feels the boy is due his birthright, as a de Shera. He has come to seek it for the boy."

Courtly stared at Jeniver. It was clear that she was processing what she had been told. She stared at Jeniver an excessive amount of time, her eyes glittering and her features flexing slightly as she digested the information. She wanted to speak but she couldn't. Thoughts were rolling through her head but she couldn't grasp just one. Should she shout? Cry? Become angry? Her husband had bedded another woman and had produced a child. *What should I feel? I don't know!* Finally, when the wait became nearly unbearable, her quiet voice filled the air.

"Max has a *son*?" she repeated. "He and Rose had a son?"

Jeniver nodded. "Aye."

"How do you know this for sure?"

Scott spoke quietly. "Because the boy looks exactly like him," he said. "I knew Max at that age. His son is the mirror image of him. There is no denying he is Maximus de Shera's son, my lady."

Courtly was looking at him as he spoke, further processing his words. When reality finally struck, she stood up swiftly, pulling her hand from Jeniver's grasp and making her way over to the lancet windows that overlooked a portion of the bailey. She wrapped her slender arms around her torso, hugging herself, smelling Maximus on her skin because she had not washed off his scent since he had left her two days before. She slept with one of his tunics because it smelled of him. Her whole world revolved around him. She didn't even know how to feel at this moment. All she could feel was bitter, nauseating shock. Gazing up at the blue sky above, she could see her husband's face, somewhere in the clouds. Nebulous and handsome, he smiled back at her.

"Max could not have known about the boy," she muttered.

Scott was up, following her towards the windows. He didn't even know why. Perhaps he was afraid she was going to go mad and try to jump through one even though it was only a few feet to the ground below. Moreover, the windows were big enough to climb through. Still, he felt the need to move close to her in case insanity swept her. Although Courtly had proven herself stout and reasonable, women were odd creatures sometimes, especially when it came to those they loved.

"Nay," he said firmly. "I strongly believe he had no knowledge of the boy. You know Max. Had he known, he would have brought the boy to live here at Isenhall or, at the very least, arranged for his schooling. He would not have ignored him."

"Scott is right," Jeniver said, rising from her chair. "Max would not have neglected his own flesh and blood and, had he known, he would have most certainly told you. Do not think he was keeping a secret from you, Courtly. I am positive Max knows nothing of this."

Scott nodded. "As am I," he said. "But he must be told. I have already sent a soldier with a message for Gallus. Gallus must tell him."

Courtly looked at Scott. She was pale with shock but not unreasonably so. In fact, she had handled the entire situation quite calmly until this point. More calmly than either Jeniver or Scott had given her credit for. But it was clear she was struggling with the news as her features tensed and twisted, powerful emotions flooding her heart. After a moment of contemplating Scott and Jeniver's opinions on what Maximus did, or did not, know, she simply nodded her head and looked away.

"Aye," she said softly. "He should be told."

Jeniver was moving towards her, her heart aching for the woman. She could hear simply by her tone that perhaps all was not as well with her as she was laboring to pretend.

"Tell me what you are feeling, Courtly," she murmured, putting her hands on the woman's shoulders. "I know this must be terribly shocking to you. Please tell me what you are feeling."

What am I feeling? Courtly rolled the question around in her mind. In truth, she didn't know. She was still too stunned to feel anything at all. She needed to go off by herself to think. As much as she loved Jeniver, she didn't want to talk about her feelings, at least not at the moment, and certainly not in front of Scott. Her first conversation about her feelings should be with Maximus. She would give her husband that courtesy.

"I... I am not sure what I am feeling," she said. She looked up at Jeniver, seeing pity in the woman's eyes, and it angered her. There was pity there because, in her eyes, perhaps Maximus has shamed her. But Courtly didn't feel shame, not in the least. She looked at Scott. "You said you have sent word to him already?"

Scott nodded. "Aye, Lady de Shera."

All Courtly could think about was the return of her husband. She wanted him back at Isenhall. She had to see him, to ask him what this bastard son meant for the future of their own children. Was it possible that this boy, this son of a peasant, would usurp her own children? Now, she was starting to feel some angst. It was starting to come. She could feel it building up in her chest, unreasonable feelings of anguish and sorrow. *He loved Rose, after all, before he loved me. Will he love this boy more than he loves our own children?* So much of her mind was in turmoil. She could feel it building.

"Please," she begged softly, pulling away from Jeniver and heading for the chamber door. "I... I need to be alone. I must think. Please... please let me be alone."

She fled before Jeniver could stop her. Her footfalls were rapid on the stairs that led to the first floor and they heard her chamber door slam, hard. It reverberated against the old, stone walls that had seen much pain and sorrow in the de Shera family. They would soon see more. Wide-eyed at Courtly's quick flight, Jeniver looked at Scott.

"He had better come quickly," she hissed. "Dear God, Max had better come quickly and sort this mess out. Meanwhile, you keep that smithy and the boy in the knights' quarters. They are not permitted anywhere else in the castle, including the hall and the keep. Is that clear?"

Scott nodded. "Aye, Lady de Shera."

"They are not allowed anywhere outside of the knights' quarters unless I say so."

"Aye, my lady."

Frustrated, and rubbing her swollen belly, Jeniver left the chamber as well, heading up the stairs to be close to Courtly if she needed her.

Scott remained in the solar long after the women had left, thinking over the day's events and hoping, praying, that Maximus would be able to deal with it all. For certain, something like this could tear families apart and to a new marriage, an event such as this could ruin it for life.

Scott hoped that Maximus and Courtly were stronger than that. For all concerned, this was a nightmare.

CHAPTER SEVEN

London

A FTER FOUR DAYS of travel, Tiberius' hopes of getting to know Douglass better hadn't exactly come to fruition.

It all started when they left Isenhall. Bose de Moray must have sensed something was up with him, as if those onyx-black eyes could look into Tiberius' soul and know he had plans for his daughter. The entire trip to London, Bose had never left Douglass' side and the few attempts Tiberius had made to speak with her had been summarily thwarted by the man. That went on for two days until Gallus and Maximus began to casually gain de Moray's attention while Tiberius would make his move to speak with Douglass. However, while Bose was occupied, Garran would step in and make sure he was between his sister and Tiberius at all times. At no point during the travel was Tiberius allowed to speak with Douglass alone and the night before they reached London, Tiberius knew he was almost out of chances. If something didn't happen tonight, tomorrow would see the end of it.

On the outskirts of the city, they had secured several rooms at the Pig and Fiddle Tavern in the dirty, crowded berg of Wycombe. Even after the sun went down, men were out on the streets, drinking and being generally loud, and the three big taverns on the main avenue through town were beyond capacity. People spilled out into the street, singing and laughing for all to hear, including Tiberius. He could hear them quite clearly. As he stood at the window of the second floor minstrel's balcony that he and his brothers had managed to snare, they had a bit of privacy and could watch the activity in the room below.

"I am surprised de Moray agreed to stay here," Tiberius finally said. "There are men peeing all over the place, pulling out their manhoods for all to see. He has his daughter with him, after all. I would not want her to see this."

Maximus, who was seated at the poorly-constructed table, had a cup of very bad ale in his hand. He pointed to the room below.

"And they are fornicating, too," he said, indicating the loud couple in a shadowed corner of the common room as they engaged in sexual intercourse. "It is making me miss my wife very much."

Gallus, seated next to Maximus, was stuffing his mouth with food. He was starving after a very long day of travel. When he saw Troy de Wolfe collect a leg of chicken from the platter full of cooked chicken pieces that the tavern keeper had brought them, he yanked the leg right out of Troy's hand and took a big bite. The young knight, unwilling to fight his liege over a chicken leg, made a dejected swipe at another piece of chicken.

"Watching that man poke himself into a prostitute makes you miss your wife?" Gallus asked Maximus, incredulous, with his mouth full. "I am sure Courtly would be thrilled to hear that particular sentiment."

Maximus grinned and took another drink of the ale in his hand. "She will never know unless you open your big mouth and tell her," he said. "But it makes me inclined to believe that we should return to Isenhall first before continuing on to Kenilworth. There is no knowing how long we will be kept there and I would like to see my wife at some point in the next few months. If we do not stop on our way to Kenilworth, we run the risk of not seeing the women for quite some time. You may even miss the birth of your son."

Tiberius turned away from the window and the party in the

street. "We will not speak of returning to Isenhall," he said, interrupting his brothers. "I have not had one opportunity to speak with Lady Douglass alone and it has been four days. Tomorrow, she will disappear into London and I will never see her again unless you help me. What am I to do?"

Gallus took a big swallow of the cheap, fermented ale. "De Moray has made sure to be with her at all times," he responded. "Garran, too. He must have told his son not to allow you near the girl when he was not in a position to fend you off himself."

Tiberius plopped his big, mail-clad body down on the chair beside his brother. He was starting to smell badly again, as he always did when he had not bathed in a few days. His hands were dirty and there was a shadow of beard on his chin and, in general, he looked rather slovenly. But the glitter in those brilliant eyes sparkled with fire for the subject at hand.

"De Moray knows," he said, disillusioned. "The man knows I am interested in Douglass and it is clear that he is trying to discourage me. I must have a few moments alone with the woman this night or all will be lost, forever. There is no more time to waste. Will you please help me?"

Gallus swallowed the bite in his mouth. "Well," he said slowly, "it seems to me that we must play our hand. Ty, if you are serious about courting the woman, then I should probably tell de Moray. That might make him more lenient, or at the very least, more understanding. He will not be concerned that you are merely trying to make a conquest."

Tiberius shook his head. "It might make him more defensive, too," he said. Then, he eyed Gallus. "Did you tell him of Prince Edward's support of de Montfort yet?"

Gallus shook his head. "There has been no opportunity," he said. "But I suppose I should create an opportunity or, much like your Lady Douglass, de Moray will be gone tomorrow and I will not have another chance."

"Then we pull de Moray and Garran into a private meeting and tell them," Maximus said. "While we are telling de Moray of the prince's loyalties, Tiberius can speak with Lady Douglass."

Gallus wriggled his eyebrows in thought. "It seems logical enough," he said. Then, he looked at Tiberius. "I am not entirely sure how long we can corral de Moray so if you have something important to say to the lady, say it quickly. Where is she?"

Tiberius pointed across the balcony to the area on the other side of the building where a flight of old, wooden steps led to a corridor with a series of doors in it. "The last I saw, Garran put her in one of those rooms," he said. "We have been sitting here ever since and I've not see her come out, so I can only assume she is still there."

Gallus and Maximus gazed across the smoky room to the other side. The malfunctioning hearth was spitting more smoke into the room than it was through the chimney and it was all gathering up near the ceiling, creating a choking, blue haze that burned the eyes.

"Where is de Moray?" Gallus asked.

Tiberius stood up from the chair and went to peer from the window overlooking the street outside. Across the avenue, through the torch-lit street, he could see a livery on the other side, crowded with de Shera horses. He could also see a pair of knights milling about and he pointed.

"There," he said. "They are across the street at the livery. Garran's horse is coming up lame and they are tending it."

"Then Lady Douglass is alone."

Tiberius snapped around, looking at his brothers as if a great thought had just occurred to him. *She is alone!* He realized he'd been very stupid, not realizing she was alone before now. As he bolted across the balcony, heading for the lady's chamber on the far side of the tavern, Gallus and Maximus rose to their feet.

"Let's go," Gallus said, pulling Maximus along with him. "Let us see how long we can distract de Moray before he figures out that we are deliberately stalling him."

Maximus grunted in agreement, hoping they could delay the old and wise knight long enough for Tiberius to say what he needed to say.

"Ty," he called after his youngest brother. "You will hurry, whatever you do!"

Tiberius heard his brother call after him, waving the man off as he moved swiftly across the catwalk that connected the balcony with the second floor chambers on the other side. He turned to look over his shoulder, once, to see that Gallus and Maximus had descended the stairs and were heading for the front door of the tavern. Suspecting he would have minutes, not hours, to do what needed to be done, Tiberius made haste to the side of the tavern that had the series of sleeping chambers.

He'd last seen Lady Douglass enter the last door on the right so he planted himself in front of the door and knocked softly. Immediately, there was a quiet voice on the other side.

"Who comes?" Douglass asked, her voice muffled.

Tiberius could feel his heart race at the sound of her voice. "It is Tiberius, my lady," he said. "May… may I speak with you?"

The door flew open so fast that Tiberius took a step back, startled. Douglass was standing in the doorway, clad in a dark blue surcoat that revealed a good deal of her pale and luscious décolletage. Her dark-eyed gaze was wide with surprise.

"What are you doing here?" she asked. "Do my father and brother know you are here?"

Tiberius shook his head, unsure how to answer. "Nay," he said. Then, he pointed weakly over his shoulder. "They are at the livery with my brothers and I thought…."

Douglass cut him off, reaching out to grab his hand and yanking him inside her chamber. She slammed the door and bolted it.

"Praise God," she muttered. "I have had enough of their shadowing every time you come near me. They are mad, do you hear? Mad!"

Tiberius fought off a smirk. "Then you have noticed it, too?"

She threw up her hands, frustrated. "Of course!" she said. "I swear that they believe you are attempting to ravage me every time you come near me! I have had enough of them, do you hear? Enough!"

Tiberius started to chuckled. "They are only trying to protect you, my lady."

She put her hands on her hips, angrily. "From what?" she demanded. "You? I took you down once and if you try anything inappropriate, I shall not hesitate to do it again."

Tiberius' eyebrows shot up as if he was fearful of her threat. "God's Blood," he muttered. "I shall stand right here and not make a move, then. I am not fond of being knocked on the head."

Douglass' angry stance took a hit and she started to giggle. "I would not really do it," she said. "Well, I suppose if I had to, I would. But you will not give me a reason to, will you?"

Tiberius shook his head firmly. "I will not, I vow," he said. His gaze glimmered warmly at her. "I simply wanted to speak with you. Tomorrow, you go on to London and we return home. If I do not say what I wish to say now, then I suspect I will never again have the opportunity. Will you listen?"

Douglass grew serious. "Of course," she said, indicating for him to sit on a small stool while she moved to the only chair in the room. "Please speak. I have not had the chance to truly speak with you since this journey began. Are you well, Tiberius?"

He smiled faintly as he took the stool, folding his very tall body on top of it. "Of course," he said. "May I say that for these past four days, you have been looking exceptionally well yourself."

Douglass grinned. "Is that what you wished to speak to me about?"

The time was upon him. Tiberius felt a tremendous sense of urgency, fearful that de Moray and Garran would be pounding on the door at any moment. He began to grope for words, knowing that this could possibly be the most important conversation of his life and he didn't want to sound like a fool.

"Nay," he said after a moment. "I wished to speak to you about me. That is to say, the conversation we had back at Isenhall is all I have been able to think on. My lady, I do not pretend to be a perfect man. I am not, you know. I have my flaws. But the one area where I demand perfection is with my honor. I am an honorable man to the death. My word, once given, is my bond, and I have never broken my word. I may not be as prestigious as Tallis d'Vant but I have a lordship that provides me with an excellent income. I carry the de Shera name, which is far more impressive than the d'Vant name. And I am loyal to the death. My devotion, once given, can never be broken or distorted. Do you understand what I am trying to say?"

Douglass had an idea and her heart was full to bursting with joy. Four days of not being able to speak with Tiberius, to have him chased off every time he came close to her, had driven her to the brink of rage and frustration. Although she knew her father and brother were only doing what they felt best, for once, she didn't want their protection. She wanted them to go away and let Tiberius come forth. She wanted to go back to that moment at Isenhall when such lovely, sweet things had been said between them. She wanted to continue that conversation. Therefore, in that respect, she suspected what Tiberius was trying to say but she wanted to hear him say it. She did not want to guess.

"I think so," she replied. "But be plain, tell me your thoughts, Tiberius, and do not hold back. You may never have another chance."

So she realizes that, too, he thought. It began to occur to him that she was thinking the same thoughts he was. At least, he hoped so. His heart was pounding so that he was sure it would burst from his chest as he looked her in the eye, savoring her beauty, praying that she felt the same way he did. If she didn't, he would be crushed forever. For all of those hearts he had broken, for all of those women he had made cry when he had left them wanting for him, his broken heart would be just payment for their anguish. He would finally know what it would feel like to long for someone you could never have. He could only pray it would not happen to him.

"What I am trying to say is that I will speak to your father about courting you if you are agreeable," he said softly. "But I will not do it if you are set on marrying d'Vant. I only wish to see you happy."

So he said it. Everything Douglass had wanted to hear was out in the open, words of joy and happiness floating in the air between them like sparks floating upon a fair breeze. She wanted to reach up and grab these words, holding them to her heart.

"I am agreeable," she said quietly, the light of joy in her dark eyes. "But you must speak to my father right away. He is planning on meeting with d'Vant very soon."

Tiberius was grinning so broadly that his face threatened to split in two. "I will," he said. "You… you have made me the happiest man in all of England. I swear to you that you, and only you, will have my loyalty and my heart for the rest of my life. You will be my wife and worthy of such respect. You will always be my forever, Lady Douglass. You have my vow."

Douglass smiled, touched by his words, sweet words she'd heard back at Isenhall and sweet words that were coming to represent Tiberius in her heart and mind. "And you will be mine," she said softly. "Mayhap… mayhap you should write up a contract for my father and present it to him. If you do that, he will believe you to be very serious indeed. It will prove to him that you mean what you say."

Tiberius' smile faded somewhat. "Would that I could," he said. "I will have to have my brother draw up a contract. You may as well know that I do not write. That is, I was educated on the mechanics of it, but it is very difficult for me to do."

Douglass cocked her head seriously. "What do you mean?"

He shrugged, realizing he was about to admit something fairly embarrassing to a woman he very much wanted to impress. "You may as well know now," he said. "It is very difficult for me to read or write. I mix words and numbers up terribly. That is why I take to memorizing everything, so I will not have to read or write."

Douglass looked at him with concern. "Is this true?"

"It is."

Her concern turned thoughtful. "I knew a knight like that, once," she said. "A friend of my father's. He was a very smart man but he would mix sentences up all of the time when he was reading."

Tiberius nodded, somewhat ashamed. "As do I," he replied. "It is not something I generally tell people. Only my brothers really know of my problem. I pray it does not diminish your opinion of me."

Douglass immediately shook her head. "Of course not," she said. "I can read and write. The lady of Codnor Castle, my patroness, taught me how and she permitted me to teach the pages and young squires of Codnor. I truly enjoy educating people. Mayhap... mayhap you will allow me to help you read?"

Tiberius was touched by her offer, deeply touched. "Then you are not ashamed?"

She shook her head firmly. "Nay."

He smiled timidly. "I would be honored to read with you, then," he said. "But I warn you, it will not be an easy task for you. I can be rather stubborn about things. You may run away screaming."

Douglass laughed softly. "I would never run," she insisted. "I can be rather stubborn myself at times. You will learn or I will beat it into you."

Tiberius chuckled. "It would not be the first time someone has tried."

Douglass merely smiled, so very thrilled that they had been given the opportunity to speak their minds and declare their intentions. Now, there was nothing assumed or unspoken between. He knew her mind and she knew his. Silence settled, although it was not uncomfortable, and she indicated a pitcher on the nearby table.

"Can I offer you some ale?" she asked. "Have you eaten?"

Tiberius looked over at the table bearing the remnants of her meal; bread, cheese, fruit, and something in a bowl that he couldn't quite see. He nodded his head.

"I have eaten," he replied. "But that is the worst ale I have ever tasted, so you will understand if I refuse. I will make sure you have better food tomorrow."

Douglass was already feeling protected by the man, nurtured and cared for. It was flattering and sweet. "We will be in London tomorrow," she said. "My father usually stays in a small manor near the city's center that belongs to my mother's side of the family."

Tiberius cocked his head thoughtfully. "Garran has spoken of it before," he said. "Leadenhall House, I believe. Your mother's family is from Chaldon Castle, are they not? In Dorset?"

Douglass nodded. "Have you been to Dorset?"

"I have been everywhere."

Douglass laughed. "I would believe that," she said. "Do you have a favorite place to visit?"

Tiberius pondered the question. "I like Paris a great deal," he said. "It has beautiful... buildings. Aye, beautiful buildings."

Douglass' laughter grew. "You were *not* going to say buildings."

"I wasn't?"

"Nay," she shook her head. "It is okay for you to tell me that there are beautiful women in Paris. I have heard that also."

He puffed out his cheeks, relieved. "As beautiful as they are, they cannot compare with you," he said sincerely, watching her flush prettily. His gaze was soft upon her. "Truly, I shall murder your brother for not telling me of you sooner. I could have offered for your hand years ago. As it is, I find myself scrambling to prevent a catastrophe."

Douglass grinned. "It is not as bad as all that."

Tiberius snorted. "That remains to be seen," he said, rather ominously. But he didn't want their precious time together spent with negative thoughts, of him perhaps doing battle against d'Vant to win her hand, so he shifted the subject. "Let us instead spend a few moments and speak of nothing else but you. I want to know all about you. What do you like to do to fill your time, Lady Douglass?"

Douglass laughed softly as she reached over into a small satchel on the bed and pulled forth what looked like two big, iron pins. She also pulled forth a neat roll of silk thread, although it was thicker than the thread used to sew. It was a beautiful, red color and Tiberius could see that, on the other end of the thread, some kind of weaving was taking place. He watched with interest as Douglass used the two big pins to continue weaving the silk thread into some manner of finely woven material.

"The lady of Codnor Castle, Lady Peverel, discovered this wonderful way of weaving when she and her husband traveled to Italy last year," she said, holding up the woven square she was constructing. "One knits the thread into this fabric. I have made a pair of gloves already. This will be a pillow cover for Papa's bed. I have been passing the time doing this since we have been on our journey but, of course, you would not know that since you have not seen much of me."

Tiberius' eyes glimmered with humor. "I would like to see much more of you from now on."

He let his eyes trail down her body when he said it and Douglass opened her mouth with some outrage. "That is a bold and lascivious statement, my lord," she pointed out. "You are seeing as much of me as I will allow."

She was indicating her state of dress, awkwardly trying to cover up her bosom with her arms, and Tiberius burst out laughing.

"I did not mean see *that* part of you," he said. "I simply meant in general. I hope to see more of you in general, my lady. I meant nothing lascivious in the least."

Douglass fought off a grin as she resumed her knitting. "Then I apologize," she said. "I thought you were being most improper."

"For once in my life, I am not."

Douglass was prevented from replying when something heavy and powerful hit the chamber door. Tiberius leapt up, putting himself in front of Douglass, as the door suddenly exploded and Garran stood there, his massive broadsword in hand. Tiberius could see, by the look on the man's face, that this was not a social call.

Garran had come to kill.

"Leaving Tiberius to spend time alone with Lady Douglass is not the best or brightest thing we have ever done," Maximus said as he and Gallus opened the entry door to the tavern, spying the livery across the street. "You know how he is with women. I cannot believe we are trusting him not to do something unsavory to de Moray's daughter."

Gallus stepped out into the avenue, kicking aside a drunkard who wandered too close to him, begging for coins for more drink.

"Our baby brother has promised he does not want another conquest," Gallus said. "He swears that his intentions are honorable."

Maximus was torn. He knew what Tiberius was capable of when it came to women yet he wanted to believe that his younger brother truly wanted to mend his wicked ways. He truly wanted to believe that Tiberius had met the woman that would tame him. He grunted unhappily.

"I know what he said," he replied. "I heard him. I want to believe him. But is it truly wise to do so? With Garran's sister, no less?"

Gallus didn't reply. He was thinking the same thing. He did not want to doubt Tiberius but the man's reputation spoke volumes. "Quiet, now," he told Maximus. "De Moray is up ahead. Careful he does not hear us."

Maximus didn't say another word as they slugged through the mucky livery yard, full of animal dung, approaching Bose from behind. The older knight was bent over Garran's big, brown steed with Garran holding the animal's head. Garran was the first to see the de Shera brothers approach.

"My lords," he greeted.

Gallus forced a pleasant smile as Bose stood up and faced him. The elder de Moray wiped a bit of sweat off his brow with the back of his hand.

"Lord Gallus," Bose greeted. "What are you doing out here? It is much more pleasant, I am sure, inside with drink and food."

Gallus shrugged. "It is very loud and very smelly in there," he said. "In truth, Maximus and I have come to speak with you on a matter of great importance and I fear if we do not do it now, we will not have another opportunity before tomorrow morning. You are continuing on to London tomorrow, are you not?"

Bose nodded. "Indeed we are," he said. "Henry is expecting us."

"Business with the king?"

Bose regarded the man for a moment. "Are you asking for de Montfort or simply making conversation?"

Gallus' pleasant expression faded, mildly insulted that de Moray would not have more faith in him than that. "If I were asking on de Montfort's behalf, I would certainly not ask you to your face," he said. "Moreover, I have a horde of spies in my employ who would tell me when you met with Henry, what you spoke of, and what you drank. And you would know absolutely nothing about it."

Bose could see that he had offended the man. "My apologies," he said. "It was a foolish question. Forgive me, please."

Gallus waved him off. "Suspicions are what keep us alive during this troubling time," he said. Then, he cast de Moray a long glance. "As we have said before, sometimes blood or friendship is stronger than loyalties to a king or to a rebel. This is one of those cases, as I am about to tell you something that no one outside of de Montfort's inner circle knows. You must not tell anyone, not even Henry."

Bose grew serious. "Why not tell the king?"

Gallus lifted an eyebrow. "Because he would want to know where you heard it and you could not tell him the truth," he said. "To do so would be to jeopardize your position with the crown. What I tell you must be kept in confidence but it is information I must tell you for your own good."

Both Bose and Garran, who was listening closely, looked around to make sure there was no one within earshot. Gallus did as well, going so far as to send Maximus to prowl around and chase any servants or nosy soldiers away. With Maximus off stalking in the warm summer night, Bose spoke quietly.

"I am listening," he said to Gallus. "What is it?"

Gallus' voice was soft. "I have received word from de Montfort that Prince Edward has joined his cause," he whispered. "I am not sure if Henry knows this yet so it would be prudent not to tell him. It might throw you into a world of suspicion with the king because he will want to know how you knew. It is better to keep it to yourself for now, but in case you have future dealings with Edward, know that he has joined de Montfort against his father. Protect yourself."

Bose's black eyes glittered in the moonlight as his mind mulled over all of the possibilities that bit of information entailed. "I will say that I am not shocked by the news," he finally said. "Edward has been rumored to have been unhappy with his father for quite some time. I do not believe Henry wants to believe it, but if what you say is true, he will have to."

Gallus folded his arms across his broad chest as he considered the situation. "De Montfort might be happy to have Edward but I am not," he said. "There is something strange going on here, something I cannot quite put my finger on to say it is the definitive cause. Edward is siding with de Montfort because he wants the French out of England as we all do, but there is something more to it. I can feel it."

Bose knew that. "Whatever it is, take your own advice," he said. "Protect yourself. Do not trust Edward, at least until you know and understand his motives."

Gallus thought of the missive he had received, asking him to come to Kenilworth. "De Montfort is expecting me at Kenilworth very soon," he said. "I am assuming Edward is there with him but I do not know that for certain. When the morrow comes, we will be heading there."

Bose sighed heavily, leaning against the hitching post. He didn't like the direction this conversation was taking, none of them did. It was convoluting an already complex situation because the stakes were changing. If Prince Edward sided against his father, then that would give de Montfort a tactical edge. With Edward came power.

"So the son sides against the father," Bose murmured. "That move alone will weaken Henry's ranks because now the dynamics will change within his power structure. Henry has many close Savoyard relatives that advise him. Edward was the only buffer between the French and his father. Now, with Edward gone… it will be interesting to see what happens."

Interesting, but not in a good way, Gallus thought as he watched Bose lean against the post, fatigue and concern evident on his face. "What will you do now?" Gallus asked.

Bose shrugged his shoulders. "I am not entirely sure there is anything to be done," he said. "I will simply continue along my same path."

Gallus hesitated a moment before speaking. "De Moray, you are English," he said. "Don't *you* hate to see hordes of greedy French taking over prosperous and strategic English properties?"

Bose was nodding before Gallus even finished speaking. "Of course I do," he said. "But it is the king's privilege to do as he wishes with crown properties."

"It is wrong."

"He is our king and beyond our reproach."

The last two sentences were spoken over one another, choppy and with passion. It was clear that Gallus and Bose saw the situation two different ways. Bose was a staunch supporter of the monarchy because he owed a life-debt to Henry for having saved his life once. Had he not owed such a debt, things might have been different. The fact remained, however, that the situation was irreversible for him, no matter how foolish or corrupt or careless Henry seemed to be. Bose would support Henry until the death. De Moray finally took a deep, long breath, struggling to clear his head.

"For now, my loyalties lie with Henry," he said simply. "There is nothing more I can do about it, although I greatly appreciate your confidence in telling me. I will not repeat it, I swear."

Gallus knew that. Men like Bose de Moray did not give their word lightly. "I know," he said softly. "I just wanted you to be aware in case you have dealings with Edward. He is not allied with his father."

The mood surrounding them was now somber, almost edgy. The

situation was changing rapidly and that made all of them uneasy. The future, for now, was murky as loyalties shifted from one to the other, back and forth. Soon, they would not know enemy from ally. But one thing was certain. The strength between the House of de Shera and the House of de Moray would never change. Bose was grateful.

"You have been a true friend and ally, my lord," Bose said sincerely. "We shall never forget what you have done for us. We owe you a great deal."

Gallus smiled weakly. "You saved Max's life on the battlefield," he said. "It is we who are indebted to you."

Bose's lips twitched with a smile, remembering that moment in time Gallus spoke of. As he thought on it, he looked over his shoulder to his son, knowing how hard all of this was on him. Garran hated Henry and he hated Edward even more. The only reason he was allied with his father was because the man had asked it of him. Bose wanted to say a few things to Gallus without his son hanging about so he thought swiftly for an excuse to send Garran away.

"Garran," he said, turning to the horse that was sporting a big wrapping on its right foreleg. "Go and make sure your sister is settled in for the night and then go to the kitchen and have the cook make another mustard plaster. If we cannot settle the swelling in this animal's leg by morning, we will have to leave this very expensive horse behind."

Tiberius is with Douglass, Gallus thought, feeling some panic at Bose's directive to Garran. He wanted very much to tell the knight not to go but to do so might look seriously odd, enough to put Bose and Garran on their guard. They would question why Gallus did not want Garran to go and check on his sister. And then they would look around and realize that Tiberius was missing.

A ruse. They would then know it was a ruse to allow Tiberius to get close to Lady Douglass with her father and brother occupied. Therefore, Gallus had to keep his mouth shut and pray that Tiberius had been truthful when he said he had no plans for Lady Douglass to become another conquest. He had to have faith in his brother in that nothing unseemly was happening between him and the lady, because if it was and Garran discovered it, the situation might turn very bad indeed. Still, he had to act as if nothing was amiss. He had to pretend all was well!

"Garran," Gallus said casually. "If you happen to see Tiberius in your travels, please send him to me."

Garran was already moving away. "If I know Tiberius, he is curled up with some wench on his lap," he said, grinning. "I will check the common room. If I see him, I will send him to you."

He is probably curled up with some wench on his lap. Gallus cringed as Garran said it, hoping that wench wasn't Douglass. And if it was, he hoped Garran didn't see it.

Please, Ty... for once in your life, do not be improper with a lady!

CHAPTER EIGHT

"**N**AY, GARRAN!" DOUGLASS leapt up, putting herself in between Garran and Tiberius as her brother burst through her shattered chamber door. "Garran, what on earth is the matter with you? Why did you do that?"

Garran's black eyes were glittering dangerously at Tiberius. He had come to check on his sister for the night but when he heard soft strains of Tiberius' voice inside the room, he'd panicked. He had busted down a fairly substantial door and now stood in the ruins, his broadsword in his hand and rage on his features. He never took his eyes off Tiberius, not even for a second, and the tension in the room soared to a splitting capacity as Garran and Tiberius, the best of friends, now faced off against one another.

"What in the hell are you doing here, alone with my sister?" Garran growled.

Tiberius remained calm. "Truly, Garran?" he asked wryly, indicating the sword. "Are you truly here to kill me? Then I do not know why I should answer your question if you think you already know the answer."

Garran was struggling not to shove his blade into Tiberius' gut. "I *know* you," he fired back. "I know how you operate with women. I cannot believe you would make my sister your next victim!"

Douglass was aghast. "Victim?" she repeated. "Garran de Moray, you are wicked and terrible! Whatever do you mean by that?"

Garran was enraged, a rare state for the usually calm knight. Tiberius had seen the man in the heat of battle, calm and collected, so this state of fury was unusual for him, indeed.

"*What* is he doing here?" Garran asked his sister angrily. "Why did you let him in? You know you should not have done that. I warned you against it."

Douglass put her hands on her hips, incensed and furious at her brother's behavior. "I was alone in my chamber and I have been for hours," she said. "Tiberius came to talk. We were simply talking. Do you really think it was something more than that, something... *unseemly*? Do you really think I would allow such a thing?"

Garran's fury was now tinged with uncertainty. "I know you would not," he said, eyeing Tiberius. "But I have known Tiberius for many years. You have no idea what he is capable of, Douglass."

As Douglass hissed angrily, Tiberius spoke up. "You are correct, Garran," he said calmly. "I am capable of quite a bit, but not with your sister. I thought you trusted me more than that."

Garran gave him an expression of disbelief. "I trust you with my life," he said. "I trust you on the battlefield. I trust you not to let any harm befall me or my family if you can help it. But I do *not* trust you with my sister's honor."

Douglass shrieked angrily. "Tiberius has been a perfect gentleman, the same of which cannot be said about you," she said, pointing an imperious finger at the door. "Get *out*. Get out and go find me a chamber with a door on it. You can sleep in this one for all I care."

Garran refused to be made the villain in this situation. He lowered his sword, shaking his head at his sister as if she were the most ridiculous creature in the world.

"I do not care what he has told you," he said. "Tiberius de Shera is only interested in another conquest. He's very good at that sort of thing. He'll lavish attention and gifts on a woman for a day or two and then when she believes herself in love with him, he claims her maidenhood and then runs off to the next woman. He's done it a dozen times before and I refuse to allow you to become his next conquest."

Furious, Douglass reached out and slapped her brother across the face. "In order for him to conquer me, I would have to be willing," she snarled. "I am not willing to be a man's conquest but I am willing to be a man's wife. *That* is what we were talking about, Garran. You have a dirty, nasty mind to think differently."

Garran's jaw popped open in shock. He could hardly believe his ears. "Wife?" he gasped, looking at Tiberius. "You… you proposed marriage to my sister?"

This wasn't exactly the way Tiberius had wanted to inform everyone that he had offered for Douglass' hand but Garran could not un-hear what he had just heard. Therefore, Tiberius had no choice but to confess everything and pray Garran didn't try to use his broadsword on him.

"I did," he said, softening in the hopes that his sincerity would soften Garran. "Garran, I know that you and I have had many adventures together. I know there have been… women. I have done things that I am not entirely proud of. But all men must grow up, even me. Your sister was special to me from nearly the moment I met her and I swear that I would make her a fine husband. I would be faithful to her until I die."

Garran stared at him in disbelief. "Nay, Ty," he muttered, begging. "Not my sister. Choose another."

"Why?"

Garran was starting to appear ill, ill and bewildered. Although he loved Tiberius as a brother, he didn't want to trust the man with his precious sister. He knew too much about him, too many unsavory things. The entire situation, as he was coming to realize it, was overwhelming him. Tiberius wanted Douglass and Douglass wanted Tiberius. It was a nightmare any way he looked at it.

"Because," he said simply, shaking his head, shocked and perplexed. "You are not a man who can be tied to one woman. Haven't you told me that before?"

Tiberius nodded patiently. "I did," he said. "Many times. But that was before I met Douglass. I… I cannot tell you what changes a man's mind, only that minds do change. Men change. Will you not at least allow me that opportunity?"

Garran looked at his sister, seeing her expression of hope and disappointment and resentment. There was quite a mixture in her features, which confused Garran all the more.

"He is not a man I would pick for you," he said earnestly. "You must have a man who… who…."

Douglass cut him off. "How many times have you told me how much you love Tiberius?" she demanded, although there was no force behind it. "How many times have you told me that he is a loyal, perfect knight? And now he is not good enough for me?"

Garran was losing the fight. He could sense it. He grunted unhappily. "He treats women as if they are disposable commodities," he said. "I have seen it time and time again. I do not want him to treat you like rubbish, too."

"And I won't," Tiberius said firmly. "Garran, I am not entirely sure how much clearer I can be about this. Your sister… she has changed something in me. You must believe me. I would have her and no other. Either you believe me or you don't. Have I ever lied to you?"

Garran shook his head without hesitation. "Never."

"Then you will believe what I am telling you. It is the truth."

Garran stared at him, pain in his eyes as he felt his defeat. He was surrendering, unable to fight against Tiberius and his word of honor.

No man in England had a more powerful bond. If Tiberius said that Douglass was the woman he wanted to marry and that he would honor and respect the woman as his wife, then Garran had no choice but to believe him. If he didn't, then his relationship with Tiberius would be damaged forever. He found himself faced with a horrible, life-changing choice… to believe or not to believe.

To have faith in a man's honor or spit upon it. God, he was so torn….

"Drop the sword, Garran."

Maximus' voice suddenly filled the chamber. Garran immediately dropped his sword, feeling the sharp tip of Maximus' weapon in the small of his back. Douglass gasped, frightened, as Tiberius put up his hands to ward off Maximus' threat.

"He was not going to use it, Max," Tiberius said steadily. "Everything is well."

Maximus didn't drop the sword. He kept it against Garran's back as he looked at the smashed door.

"I can see that," he said drolly. "This door looks well, indeed."

Tiberius went to his brother and put his hand on his sword, removing it from Garran's back. "Ease down, brother," he said, a smile on his lips. "All is well, truly."

Garran wandered into this sister's chamber and sat heavily on the small bed, despondent, as Maximus looked between Tiberius and Douglass. They both had smiles on their faces so he surmised that perhaps all was not as it seemed. He was growing confused.

"Why is the door shattered?" he wanted to know, "and why was Garran armed? Why do I come up to Lady Douglass' chamber and find things in shambles?"

Douglass blurted before Tiberius could answer. "The lock on my door was stuck," she said, lifting her shoulders as she spoke as if that would convince Maximus she was telling the truth. "Garran had to break it down."

Maximus didn't believe her for a moment but he didn't say so. He merely turned to Tiberius. "What really happened?"

Tiberius chuckled softly. "Do you not take a lady's word for it?"

Maximus emitted something that sounded between a grunt and a groan. It was meant to express his impatience and disbelief.

"Then you will tell me later," he said. "Meanwhile, I believe Gallus and de Moray are finished speaking so you had better come with me. It is time to leave the lady to her sleep."

Tiberius looked at Douglass, who was smiling timidly at him. He didn't want to leave her but he knew he had to go. Reaching out, he took her hand gently as Garran, seeing the gesture, buried his face in his hands.

"I will speak to your father immediately," he assured her softly. "Come the morning, we shall see if you, in fact, go to London. You may just as easily come back with me to Isenhall."

Douglass squeezed his big fingers. "I can only hope so."

Tiberius squeezed her hand in return and let it go. He thought kissing it might be too much for Garran to take. He looked at the man, sitting despondently upon the bed.

"Well?" he said. "Are you coming, Garran?"

Garran simply shook his head and Tiberius didn't push. He wanted very much to speak with his friend, to clear things between them, but he thought that perhaps now was not the time. Moreover, he had more important things to do, like discussing his offer of marriage with Bose. In the long run, Garran would not make that decision – Bose would – so it was more important that he speak with Bose.

"Come along," Maximus encouraged, cutting into his thoughts. "We must leave."

Tiberius didn't say another word. He followed Maximus from the chamber, kicking aside the broken pieces of the old, oak door, and casting Douglass a wink just before he left completely. She smiled in return, giving him a brief wave. It was a wave of hope and of longing. Already, he could see that she missed him. He missed her, too.

Thoughts of Douglass were heavy on his mind as he headed away from her room, down the darkened corridor. But those thoughts were interrupted when he suddenly smacked into the back of Maximus, who had come to a sudden halt. When Tiberius looked to see why Maximus had stopped, he realized that Bose was standing directly in front of him.

But de Moray wasn't looking at Maximus or Tiberius. He was looking at the shattered door that belonged to his daughter's chamber. Then, the black eyes went directly to Tiberius.

"*Why* is my daughter's door smashed?" he wanted to know.

Tiberius could see that the man was holding his composure together by a mere thread. Thoughts of a ravaged daughter were clearly rolling through his head and, by the way he was looking at Tiberius, it was quite possible that Bose thought he was to blame. To that end, Tiberius did the only thing he could do. He told the truth.

"Garran did it!"

HAVING LEFT DE Moray several minutes earlier, Gallus was back in the minstrel's gallery overlooking the common room of the tavern. He had a clear view of the catwalk, the stairs, and the area across the building that had the sleeping quarters on the second floor. He saw, clearly, when de Moray intercepted Maximus and Tiberius as they were coming out of Lady Douglass' chamber and he noted there was a brief exchange before Maximus and Tiberius continued onward. Bose continued to his daughter's destroyed chamber door and Gallus could see the man kicking pieces of broken wood aside.

Gallus couldn't begin to guess how Lady Douglass' door had

been destroyed but he was positive it had something to do with Tiberius. In fact, both brothers were heading in his direction, across the catwalk and through the smoky haze. Gallus poured himself a measure of the terrible ale as Maximus and Tiberius resumed their seats at the table. The first thing Tiberius did was drain an entire cup of that awful alcohol.

"Well?" Gallus asked. "What happened? Did you talk to her?"

Tiberius nodded and poured himself another full cup. He slurped it down as Gallus looked at Maximus with concern. In fact, both brothers were rather concerned at Tiberius' manner but Tiberius finished the second cup, wiped his mouth with the back of his hand, and took a deep breath.

"She is agreeable," he said, thrill evident in his voice. "She feels for me as I feel for her. She is agreeable to a marriage contract."

Gallus smiled broadly. "Congratulations," he said. "But why is her door smashed?"

Tiberius' smile faded. "Garran did that," he said. "He heard us talking through the door and, fearing the worst, smashed it down."

"So that is why the door was broken," Maximus muttered into his cup. "I thought you did that to get to her."

Tiberius shook his head. "Not at all," he said. "She is a warm and wonderful woman. She is different from the empty-headed chits I have chased from one end of England to the other. She is intelligent and kind. I am wholly unworthy of her but I intend to do my best to make her an excellent husband."

Maximus glanced at Gallus, who simply lifted his eyebrows in understanding. Both brothers still had their doubt that their free-loving youngest brother could indeed settle down with one woman, but Tiberius seemed convinced that he could and since the lady was agreeable, there wasn't much they could say about it. The truth was that neither one of them had ever seen Tiberius so excited about anything, and especially a woman. It was touching.

"And so you shall," Gallus finally said. "What is your next move?"

Tiberius pondered his response over his third cup of disgusting ale. He was so wrapped up in thoughts of Douglass that he couldn't even stop to think about the fact that he was drinking swill.

"I want to marry her immediately," he said, overlooking any sense of propriety. "I will speak to her father tonight and then marry her."

It was a simple and rather selfish plan. Gallus lifted his eyebrows as if not entirely believing what he was hearing.

"De Moray will not allow you to marry her tonight, Ty," he said, trying to force his brother to see some reason when, in fact, men in love were seldom reasonable. "You must ask her father for permission to court the woman. Once he gives his consent, you may start planning the wedding, but this will not be a quick process. Did you really think it would be?"

Tiberius frowned. Drinking three straight cups of the nasty ale and its high alcohol content already had his head buzzing. "Maximus married Courtly within two days of knowing her," he said. "You helped him marry her as quickly as he could. Why am I any different?"

Maximus sighed heavily and looked at Gallus for an answer, but Gallus merely scratched his head. "It was different and you know it," he said. "We were dealing with a father who was being unreasonable and mad at times. De Moray is not unreasonable and he is not mad, and he will most certainly be more formidable than Courtly's father was. Do you truly wish to anger the man?"

Tiberius backed off somewhat. "Of course not."

"Then you and I will go to him tonight and ask permission to enter into negotiations for the woman," Gallus said, explaining the situation as plainly as he could. "This is a different situation altogether, Ty. We must observe proprieties or you will have a very angry Bose de Moray on your hands and that would not be a healthy thing for any of us."

Tiberius didn't say anything, knowing his brother was right. He hung his head, looking to the empty cup in his hand, before inevitably turning his attention in the direction of Lady Douglass' chamber. He could see, across the mezzanine level they were on, that Bose was assisting his daughter from the room and moving her to a chamber with a door on it that had not been kicked in by an over-zealous brother.

Gallus and Maximus noticed where Tiberius' attention was. They, too, could see the woman with the mane of golden-red hair as she moved from one room to another. Gallus sat back in his chair, watching Tiberius, wondering when the man was going to demand they go running over to de Moray to plead for the woman's hand. It didn't take long.

"Mayhap we should go now," Tiberius said. "He is settling Douglass in another chamber. It will be the perfect time to speak with him."

Gallus frowned. "How did you determine that?"

Tiberius shrugged. "Because I...."

He was interrupted when one of Gallus' soldiers suddenly appeared on the catwalk, capturing Gallus' and Maximus' attention. But Maximus frowned when he saw the man's face. Illuminated by the dim light of the tavern, they could see the man quite clearly as he drew near. A sense of apprehension immediately filled the air.

"That is Chambers," Maximus said, his tone edgy. "We left him behind at Isenhall."

Gallus knew that. Already, he was on his feet as the man approached. "What has happened?" he demanded of the soldier. "Why are you here?"

The soldier bearing the de Shera colors was exhausted. He was dirty, sweaty, and had mud all over the lower half of his legs, as if he had ridden very hard and very fast through anything and everything in his path. He came to a weary halt, wiping at his eyes.

"I saw some of our men in the street below, my lord," he said, addressing Gallus. "They told me where you were."

Gallus couldn't help but notice the soldier hadn't answered his question. "And so I am," he said, eyeing the man with great concern. "Is my wife well?"

The soldier nodded. "She is very well, my lord," he said, looking to Maximus also. "Lady Courtly is also well. Be at ease, my lords, the women are fine."

Gallus was vastly relieved but he was also increasingly perplexed. "Then why are you here?"

The soldier looked directly at Gallus, apparently having difficulty answering. He seemed to be groping for words. "Sir Scott has sent me, my lord," he said, strained. "I have a message for you and you alone. Sir Scott has asked me to deliver it to you in private."

Gallus' brow furrowed. He was weary and unhappy that he was away from his pregnant wife, so cryptic messages were not pleasing him at the moment. "What on earth about?" he demanded.

The soldier shook his head faintly. "Please, my lord," he begged quietly. "It will only take a moment."

Gallus rolled his eyes, looking to Maximus and Tiberius, who simply waved him on. They didn't care about the contents of a private message because they knew that Gallus would tell them both eventually. They delved back into the food on the table, or what was left of it, as Gallus pulled the soldier with him along the smoke-hazed catwalk leading to the staircase on the other side. When they were about halfway across the walk, Gallus came to a halt and turned to the man.

"No more foolery," he said, his voice low. "You have come a very long way to deliver an urgent message to me. What did Scott want you to tell me?"

The soldier cleared his throat softly. He had been with the House of de Shera for many years, as had his father. He was a legacy soldier, the second generation fighting for the Lords of Thunder, and he was a senior soldier in the ranks. That meant he had the trust of the de Shera brothers and it was something he did not take lightly. Scott had known it, too, which is why he had sent the man. He knew that Gallus trusted him and would believe him. He was about to put that trust to the test.

"Two days after you left Isenhall, a man and a boy appeared and demanded to speak to Sir Maximus," the soldier said quietly. "Since Sir Maximus was gone, the man spoke to Sir Scott. My lord, Sir Scott wishes for me to tell you this: the girl that Sir Maximus loved in his youth at Kenilworth Castle, the one that your father sent away, did not die of a fever as he was told. She died in childbirth with Sir Maximus' son. Now, the girl's father has come to Isenhall with Sir Maximus' son and seeks all birthrights for the boy. Sir Scott asked me to tell you this information in private so that you could relay it to your brother. He says that Sir Maximus should return to Isenhall with all due haste."

Gallus listened to the message with mounting astonishment. By the time the soldier was finished delivering the message, Gallus was staring at him with genuine shock. He opened his mouth to say something but found that he couldn't. He had no idea what to say. He finally put a hand over his mouth to cover up his gaping lips.

"I cannot believe it," he finally hissed. "Is it possible that it is true?"

The soldier nodded. "I saw the boy myself, my lord," he said. "He is the exact image of Maximus. You will see for yourself and know that the lad is a de Shera."

"You are certain of this?"

"I am, my lord."

Gallus was overwhelmed with the news but he knew it was nothing compared to what Maximus would feel. In fact, his gaze moved to his middle brother, sitting over on the minstrel's balcony, tearing apart a big piece of bread. Aye, he knew that Maximus would be rocked to the bone by the news.

Already, he ached for his brother. The man had found such happiness with Courtly after years of being a rather cynical, unhappy man. And now this. Sickened, Gallus returned his focus to the soldier.

"The man who brought the boy," he muttered, "said that he was the boy's grandsire?"

The soldier nodded. "Aye, my lord."

Gallus exhaled slowly, thoughtfully. "Maximus would no doubt recognize the man."

Again, the soldier nodded. "I would presume so, my lord."

Gallus pondered that particular reunion, knowing it would not be a good one. "Were they still at Isenhall when you left?"

"Indeed, my lord," the soldier replied. "Sir Scott told them to remain while he sent for Sir Maximus."

Gallus' gaze lingered on the man for a moment. "And Lady Courtly?" he asked. He was almost afraid to know. "Does she know who this boy is?"

The soldier nodded. "Sir Scott told her," he said softly. "He had no choice."

The reply hit him like a blow to the gut. *God's Bones*, Gallus thought. He closed his eyes a moment, tightly, to ward off the utter shock and sorrow Courtly must have experienced to be confronted with Maximus' bastard. And a demanding bastard, evidently. With that in mind, Gallus knew he could not delay in telling Maximus. He swiftly moved past the soldier, heading back to where his brothers were sitting.

"Come with me," he ordered. "I may need you to answer any

further questions Max may have about all of this."

Obliging, the soldier followed. They made their way back across the catwalk to the minstrel's balcony where Maximus had finished his food and now had his big feet upon the table, yawning. Tiberius was still focused on Lady Douglass so his attention was over where the sleeping rooms were. When Gallus returned, Tiberius tore his gaze away long enough to speak to him.

"I have not seen de Moray emerge from Douglass' chamber," he said. "He is still in there, now with Garran present. Should we go over there now?"

Gallus shook his head. "Now is not the best time, Ty," he said, eyeing Maximus. "It would seem that Maximus has received some news he must deal with. Max, a message has come to you regarding an unexpected situation back at Isenhall."

Maximus looked at his brother, not particularly concerned. His wife was well and that was all he really cared about. He yawned again, folding his big arms behind his head and leaning back.

"What is it?" he asked.

Gallus sat down and fixed on his brother. After a moment, he shook his head. "I am sorry if this is blunt," he said. "I am not entirely sure how to say this, so bear with me. This has to do with Rose."

Maximus didn't seem to understand what his brother meant. Clearly, a romance from sixteen years ago wasn't at the forefront of his thoughts. "Rose?" he repeated. "Rose who?"

Gallus could see that the news was going to hit Maximus from out of nowhere, for the man had no idea what he meant. "*Rose*," Gallus said again, softly. "Rose from Kenilworth."

That drew a reaction. Maximus' brow furrowed. "Rose?" he said yet again, now obviously upset by the statement. "What in the...? What is the meaning of this?"

Gallus reached out and put a hand on his brother's arm. "Quietly, Max," he admonished softly. "Be quiet and listen. Will you do this?"

Maximus' feet came off the table, slamming onto the floor with enough force to rattle the balcony. His dark green eyes were blazing at his brother and his jaw worked angrily, off-balance and off-guard by the subject matter. He was confused and agitated, a dangerous combination where Maximus was concerned.

"Listen to *what*?" he nearly shouted.

Gallus remained calm. "I have no idea why you are so angry," he said. "Calm yourself or this will not get any easier if you do not."

Maximus was struggling with his composure but he took a deep breath, laboring to relax. "Speak, then," he said through clenched teeth. "I am listening."

"Quietly?"

Maximus simply rolled his head around in a marginally affirmative action. It looked more like an act of desperation. "I will try," he mumbled. "Speak, Gallus. What is this all about?"

Gallus could see that the situation was edgy already. Rose was an emotional subject for Maximus, even after all of these years. Tiberius, concerned, moved closer to Maximus because, if the man veered out of control for some reason, by his sheer size alone, Tiberius was the only one who could control him. He hovered over Maximus as Gallus spoke.

"Listen to me," Gallus said, grasping Maximus' hand. "I must ask you a question. Do you recall that after Father sent Rose and her father away from Kenilworth, you were told that the woman had later died of a fever?"

Maximus' jaw was tensed and he nodded shortly. "From one of de Montfort's men," he said. "Rose and her father had been sent to one of de Montfort's outposts and the soldier told me she had perished from a fever. He knew this because he had just come from the outpost."

"But he told you nothing more?"

"Nothing," Maximus replied. "I never knew how or why, or even where she was buried. Gallus, why are you asking me these questions? What has happened?"

The flash of rage that Maximus had experienced had quickly faded and he was more in control of himself. Gallus was so very sorry to tell him what was transpiring, now, sixteen years after Rose and Maximus had shared their brief affair. He squeezed his brother's hand in a silent show of support, of strength, of solidarity in that nothing could break the bond between them. Not even news such as this.

"Evidently, two days after we left Isenhall, Rose's father showed up at the castle and demanded to see you," he said carefully. "He was not alone, Max. He brought his grandson with him. He told Scott that Rose did not die of a fever. She died in childbirth with your son. Rose's father has brought the boy to Isenhall to claim his birthright as a de Shera. As the son of Maximus de Shera."

Maximus stared at him for a moment before his eyes narrowed and his features twisted. The shock, the denial, in his eyes was paramount as Maximus sat back in his chair, heavily, and stared at his brother.

"A son?" he repeated, his voice oddly hoarse. "I… I cannot believe it. I will *not* believe it."

Gallus turned to the soldier, who had been watching the entire scene with some trepidation. An enraged Maximus de Shera was a happenstance that all men feared. But when he saw Gallus' expression, encouraging him to speak, he didn't hesitate.

"I saw the boy, my lord," he told Maximus. "He is the exact image of you. He is quite large and well-formed."

"It could be a ruse! A lie!"

"I do not think so, my lord. He looks exactly like you."

Maximus blinked at the soldier, as if the words from the man's mouth had somehow slapped him in the face, startling him. After several long moments, he emitted a long, hissing sigh and hung his head, wiping his hands over his face in a weary, disbelieving gesture.

"A son," he muttered. "God's Bones, is it true? Could it actually be true?"

Gallus watched him carefully, glancing at Tiberius to see that the man looked deeply concerned and deeply shocked, just like the rest of them. Gallus put a hand on Maximus' slumped shoulders.

"You bedded the woman, did you not?" he whispered. "It *is* possible, isn't it?"

Maximus nodded slowly. "I loved her," he breathed. "I wanted to marry her. She loved me in return. Aye, I bedded her, so this is entirely possible. I should be shouting my denial to the heavens but I find… I find that I cannot. Dear God, it wasn't the fever that killed her… it was me. *I* killed her."

Gallus shook his head. "You did not kill her," he said firmly before Maximus went on a tangent of self-pity. "You conceived a son with the woman but that does not mean you killed her. You cannot blame yourself."

Maximus was still hanging his head, overcome with all he had been told. "A son," he murmured again. "Does this son have a name?"

Gallus didn't know. He looked at the soldier, silently prompting the man to speak. "Cassius, my lord," the soldier said. "He gave his name as Cassius de Shera."

Maximus put his hands over his face. "Oh… God," he hissed. "She knew… Rose knew that all de Shera males had Roman names. We discussed it a few times, jesting about what we would name our son. She gave him a Roman name as a final show of respect for me. Dear God, I can hardly believe any of this."

Gallus let Maximus wallow in sorrow and shock for a few moments. In truth, he wasn't sure he could say anything to ease the man's agony. Maximus would have to come to grips with what had happened and the sudden turn his future had taken. But there was something else Maximus needed to know and, after a several moments of allowing the man to grieve, he spoke quietly.

"There is something else, Max," Gallus confided. "Courtly knows about the boy. Scott had to tell her, so you should make all haste to return to Isenhall. There is much waiting for you there to sort through."

Maximus' head shot up, the dark green eyes fixed on Gallus with horror. "God help me," he rasped. "He *told* her? Scott told my wife who the boy was?"

Gallus nodded. "I am not certain of the circumstances," he said, "but you know that Scott would not have told her unless he had no choice. Regardless of the circumstances, the fact remains that she knows and you must return home immediately."

Maximus was already nodding, his thoughts centered on his wife and how she must have taken the news. His heart was shattering for the humiliation and shock she must have suffered. He abruptly stood, knocking over his chair.

"I must go now," he said. "I will have my horse saddled immediately. I must go home now."

Gallus stood up alongside him and motioned the soldier forward. "Have your horse prepared," he said. "Take Chambers with you. Mayhap he can answer any more questions you might have."

Maximus merely nodded. He didn't know if he had any more questions at the moment because his mind was a chaotic mist of shock, anguish, and not surprisingly, some happiness. *He had a son!*

God, was it really true? He intended to find out for himself.

Gallus and Tiberius watched Maximus storm out of the tavern with the soldier on his heels. Mostly, he staggered, so very stunned by everything. When Maximus burst through the tavern entry, out into the street beyond as he headed towards the livery, Gallus turned to Tiberius.

"I suspect that one of us must return with him," he said quietly. "I should go on to Kenilworth and confer with de Montfort so mayhap you should go with Maximus."

Tiberius frowned, trying not to appear selfish. "I cannot help Max with this and neither can you," he said. "He is a grown man and will have to face this himself. We cannot and should not make any decisions for him."

Gallus sighed heavily. "You are more than likely correct," he admitted. "I was thinking that mayhap he needed our support. But I do not suppose there is anything we can do."

"I do not think so," Tiberius agreed. "Moreover, I have my own issues to deal with. I must speak to de Moray about marrying his daughter and I most definitely require your help. Will you go with me to do this? I fear... I fear that the man may not take me seriously."

Gallus looked at his youngest brother, thinking that there was too much trauma and turmoil going on in the House of de Shera. Maximus and an unexpected son, and Tiberius who decided he wanted to become a husband. He wondered how things had gotten so out of control. He could handle warfare and politics quite easily. It was human emotion he sometimes had trouble with.

"Very well," he said, resigned. "Has he come out of her chamber yet?"

Tiberius shook his head. "Nay," he replied, somewhat anxiously. "Mayhap we should go to her chamber and ask de Moray for a few moments of private conversation. I realize this seems rushed but I fear that if I do not do it now, it will be too late by tomorrow."

Gallus nodded wearily, distracted for a moment as he heard Maximus outside, bellowing over at the livery across the street. The man had a voice that could carry for a mile.

"Then let us get this over with," he said, eyeing Tiberius a moment. "You *are* certain about this, aren't you? You will not marry the woman and abandon her in a month?"

Tiberius' expression was steady. "I am certain," he said softly. "I will never leave her side as long as I live."

Gallus didn't respond other than to lift his eyebrows in acknowledgement. Then, he turned for the catwalk that led to the sleeping rooms on the other side of the building. It was time to procure Tiberius a wife.

And try not to make an enemy in the process.

CHAPTER NINE

"**M**Y SON HAS told me about your… exploits," de Moray said, his black eyes as hard as cold steel. "You will forgive me for not readily accepting your proposal. Although I love and respect the House of de Shera, you will understand when I say that I am reluctant to pledge my daughter to the brother who possibly has one or more bastards running about England, and who furthermore has a reputation for deflowering maidens or stealing them from their husbands."

The conversation was ugly from the start. Gallus, Tiberius, and Bose were in Bose's chamber, next door to Douglass' new chamber. Garran was over in her old sleeping chamber trying to piece together the door he had destroyed. The initial conversation between Gallus and Bose had been brief and to the point, and now they were coming to the meat of the situation. As Tiberius had feared, the look in de Moray's eyes was not promising.

"The same could be said for many men," Gallus pointed out quietly, seated on a small chair that was barely able to hold his considerable bulk. "That does not necessarily make them unworthy or unfit."

Bose nodded. He was looking particularly weary this night, exhausted from travel, from drama perpetuated by his son and daughter. The marriage proposal from Tiberius de Shera was not surprising at all. In fact, he had been expecting it from the way

Tiberius and Douglass had been looking at each other. Bose was no fool. But he was also not inclined to hand his daughter off to a knight with a reputation for women.

"I realize that," Bose said. "I know many fine men who have a bastard or two, men who have, in fact, married good women and have good marriages. But they were older and wiser when they married. I certainly mean no offense to your brother, but he is young still. Women at his age are a fascination and, much like a feast, must be sampled in abundance. I am not convinced that Tiberius is ready to settle on one woman."

"Then what would it take to convince you?" Tiberius asked earnestly. "Name it, my lord, and I will produce or provide it. But let me say this, I realize that I am young and that I have managed to earn myself a reputation that some might consider unsavory. Never have I been ashamed of that reputation until now. It is difficult to say what changes a young man into a wise man, or a man who understands what he wants out of life. All I can tell you is that the moment I met your daughter, something inside of me changed. Douglass changed it. I swear to you upon my honor that I would be a good and true husband to her. I would never knowingly hurt or disappoint her."

Bose was listening to Tiberius with reservation but he could see how genuine the knight was being. He was telling the truth, or at least the truth as he believed it. Infatuated young men often meant what they said and truly believed they were capable of such things, but the reality was that the lure of being young and happy and lusty could override such promises. Bose grunted softly, his indecision evident.

"I will confess something," he said. "I spoke with my daughter at length about you earlier. When I saw the broken door to her chamber, I originally thought you had broken it trying to get to her. Even though you told me that Garran did it, I did not believe you until both of my children confirmed that to me. But Garran told me he did it because you were alone with my daughter in her chamber and he broke the door down with the intention of saving her honor. You were alone with her in her chamber, were you not, Tiberius?"

Tiberius nodded his head. "I was," he said honestly. "But nothing unseemly happened, my lord. We were simply talking."

Bose eyed him. "I know," he said. "Douglass told me. And I know my daughter well enough to know that she would not have permitted anything unseemly to happen. Still, the fact remains that you were bold enough to overlook propriety to get to her."

Tiberius didn't know what to say to that for a moment. To his credit, he maintained eye contact with Bose even though he knew the man was right. It was like being caught stealing or committing another petty crime. He knew he was guilty of what he had been accused of.

"It was without ill-intent, I assure you, my lord," he said quietly. "I simply wanted to speak with her and that is all we did."

Bose's dark gaze lingered on him. "I was a young man myself, once," he said. "I know what lies in the heart of youth and talking isn't among it. However, to your credit, I will say that my daughter told me the same thing. I commend you for your restraint. I do not, however, commend you for your boldness. I do not appreciate my daughter being put in such a position that her honor could be questioned."

Tiberius understood that. "She is beyond reproach," he replied. "She is perfect and mannerly in every way. My lord, I realize that you are hampered by rumors and by what you perceive as a less than desirable reputation, but I will again say that my intentions toward your daughter are completely honorable. I will make a fine and noble husband for her and I beg you consider my suit."

Bose could tell that Tiberius was sincere simply by the look on his face. Bose remembered what it was like to be young and infatuated, as if nothing else but the sweet face and dulcet tones of the object of your fascination existed. But as much as he sympathized with Tiberius, he had to think of his daughter's welfare. He had to think of her future.

"You are already aware that another match has been selected for her, are you not?" he asked.

Tiberius was stoic. "She told me, my lord," he said. "She told me that Henry has selected Tallis d'Vant. A good knight from a good family."

Bose sighed softly. "And this is another matter altogether," he pointed out. "You and I do not support the same cause. How would it look if I were to pledge my daughter to a man who not only serves de Montfort, but he is a de Shera as well? We will be on opposite sides of the battle, Tiberius. Would you lift a sword against your wife's father in battle?"

Tiberius could see where this was going. Not only was his reputation at question but so were his loyalties. Everything that could possibly be against him, in fact, was. Being a calculating man, he was willing to sacrifice in order to gain his wants and, at this moment, he wanted Douglass more than he had ever wanted anything in his life.

There were things in life he was willing to accept and things he wasn't. He was not willing to accept that Douglass de Moray would never be his. He could see that bargaining was not going to work with de Moray. The man needed more than words. He needed proof. As Tiberius pondered the situation, he knew that he was going to have to make a sacrifice bigger than himself in order to achieve it. He was going to have to make a choice he did not want to make. If he truly wanted Douglass, it was time to act.

He was going to have to change his destiny.

"I have already faced off against you in battle but my sword was never wielded in your direction," he said softly. "It never will be. I can do nothing about my reputation. It is set and I cannot erase it.

All I can do is change the future and it is my intention that Douglass be a very big part of that future. I can see, however, that you will need convincing. I will need to prove to you that I am a far better man that Tallis d'Vant and that will be no easy feat. I cannot do it if I am sworn to de Montfort but I can do it if I am sworn to you. Will you accept my fealty, my lord?"

Gallus nearly fell off the chair he was sitting on. He had remained quiet throughout the exchange, hoping Tiberius could convince de Moray of his intentions without Gallus' help. Tiberius' proposal of fealty to de Moray had been completely unexpected and Gallus was shocked to the core. Stumbling to his feet, his eyes were wide with astonishment on his youngest brother.

"Ty," he hissed. "Have you gone mad? You cannot do such a thing."

Tiberius looked at him. "Why not?" he asked calmly. "Gallus, you are my brother and I love you dearly. You are the blood that flows through my veins. But there comes a time in every man's life when he must choose his own path and to achieve my wants, mayhap my path is not with you. Mayhap I must go my own way to learn and grow and prove that I am the knight I am born to be. To prove I am the *man* I was born to be."

Gallus was speechless. "But…," he said after a moment, "but this is not the way, Ty. You cannot swear fealty to whoever suits your purposes at the moment. You *know* that. Fealty is based on convictions and beliefs and bloodlines, among other things. Do I really need to explain this to you?"

"My fealty can be given at my discretion. That is every knight's privilege."

"But it belongs to me. I will not release you."

Tiberius didn't waver. "If you were in this situation and it was Jeniver we were speaking of, what would *you* do?"

That stopped Gallus in his tracks. At that moment, he knew he was going to lose Tiberius. He could see it in the man's face and, more importantly, he couldn't deny his question. They both knew, very well, what he would do if Jeniver were involved. He knew what it was to want a woman so badly that he would do anything to have her. Aye, he knew very well and the realization sickened him. It was then that Gallus realized that the Lords of Thunder, as England knew them, might no longer exist. He was devastated.

"Then you will be lifting a sword against me," he said, a lump in his throat. "You will be fighting against Maximus. Is that what you want? Is Douglass more important than your brothers?"

Tiberius could see the glimmer of emotion in his brother's eyes and it nearly did him in. In fact, his eyes started to water. There was such pain in his heart that he could hardly stand it.

"Nay," he said hoarsely. "But there is a time in every man's life when he must follow his heart. This is the time when I must follow mine. Please do not hate me for it, Gallus. I must do this."

Gallus couldn't help it. His eyes filled with tears. "Because of her?"

Tiberius lost his composure. His eyes watered and spilled over, shattered by what was taking place.

"Because of *me*," he whispered. "Don't you see? I must become a better *me*. I must prove to myself, most of all, that I am no longer this young and foolish knight who only cares for himself. I care for someone else now and I must prove to me, and only to me, that my feelings are right and true. If you cannot understand that, then I am not sure what more I can say. I love you, Gallus. You are my oldest brother, the man I have always looked up to and hoped to be. Now, you must let me become a great man by following my own path. Let me soar out from under your protective wing to see how high I can rise."

Gallus closed his eyes, the tears spilling over. He was so very distraught. But he also understood what Tiberius was telling him. Perhaps it was time for the youngest brother, the young knight who had lived in the shadow of two very powerful, older brothers, to finally find his own way. As much as it pained Gallus, he understood completely. God help him, he did.

"Are you sure?" he whispered.

Tiberius nodded. "I am."

There was nothing more Gallus could say. Reaching out, he pulled his brother's forehead against his lips and kissed him.

"Do what you must, then," he said comfortingly. Then, he looked to de Moray as he wiped away the tears. "Take good care of him, my lord. Please."

With that, he walked from the chamber and Tiberius stood there a moment, struggling not to sob. He wiped quickly at his eyes, composing himself, before turning to de Moray. At that moment, as their gazes locked, something changed between them.

Bose had an expression of abject sorrow on his face but, in some small way, he saw Tiberius through new eyes. A man could speak persuasive words as he tried to convince those around him that he was sincere, but a man who gave up something that was most precious to him in order to prove his sincerity was something altogether different. Perhaps young Tiberius meant what he said. Any man who would break from his beloved brothers was a man to be considered.

"Are you certain you want to do this, Tiberius?" Bose asked softly. "This is all rather sudden. I understand if you wish to think it over."

Tiberius took a deep breath, pulling himself together. "I do not need to think it over, my lord," he said. "I will swear fealty to you and fight by your side. Much as Garran does, however, it is you I support and not Henry. I still do not believe in the man or his ideals.

Therefore, it is you I fight for and not the king. But if we end up in battle siding with Henry, so be it. I want to prove to you that I am the right man for your daughter and if this is the way to do it, then so be it. You have my complete loyalty."

"What if I do not want it?"

"Then I will follow you wherever you go, so you may as well accept it. I am yours whether or not you want me."

Bose didn't dare deny him, not after what he had just seen. He wondered how Henry was going to react knowing that Tiberius de Shera was now fighting for his cause. In fact, he wondered how all of England was going to react knowing that the Lords of Thunder were now two instead of three because Tiberius had defected to the enemy. It would make Bose a fairly hated man by de Montfort, of that he was sure. He also wondered how he was going to explain to Henry how the marital contract between his daughter and d'Vant would need to be delayed because Tiberius de Shera was now competing for her hand. In truth, the addition of Tiberius de Shera could be a great upheaval in more ways than one.

Only time would tell.

PART THREE
WINDS OF DESTINY

CHAPTER TEN

London

THE TREES ABOVE were heavy and moist with the humidity from the Thames and Douglass, as she rode her small, gray palfrey, was sticky with it, too. She felt like one of those trees, wilting and drooping, and that certainly wasn't what she wanted to feel like. There was something in her midst now, something of great and utter importance, and the last thing she wanted was to look like a drooping tree. She wanted to look her very best.

Tiberius was riding off to her left, slightly behind her. He had been since they had left the tavern early that morning. Her father had explained to her the night before that Tiberius would be traveling with them for "some time", although he hadn't clarified what that meant and he really hadn't told her any more than that. All she knew was that Tiberius was now in their midst, astride his big, gray beast that seemed to foam at the mouth constantly. The horse worried the bit to death and he kept shaking his head, throwing foam onto those near him so Tiberius was riding well to the rear of their four-person party. Douglass suspected his frothing horse was the reason he had not ridden beside her.

Or, it was one of the reasons. She was sure there were others. For instance, Garran seemed particularly distant from Tiberius. After the debacle last night when Garran had broken down her chamber door, she was certain that Garran and her father were going to do all they could to keep Tiberius away from her so it was strange that he was traveling with them this morning. His brothers, the earl and Sir Maximus, had turned back for Isenhall. Now, the de Shera brothers were split and Douglass wasn't sure of the reason behind it but she knew there *was*, in fact, a reason. Everything seemed oddly tense all around.

But she kept her attention ahead and not on Tiberius, which was very difficult for her to do. She wanted to turn back and look at him but she couldn't do it and not be obvious about it, so she kept her attention forward, on the dark, dirt road with the heavy ruts in it from the wagons that passed along it constantly. Sunlight streamed between tree branches and birds frolicked in the leaves above. As the de Moray party passed quietly along the path, the outskirts of London proper began to come into view.

Poorly constructed residences bunched up here, many of them lining the road. There were people about, going about their business, children and dogs playing in the road, and women beating their wash down by the dirty river. There was a breeze coming off of the gently flowing waters of the Thames, providing some relief from the stickiness in the air. Even though Douglass had braided her curly mane tightly to keep it off her neck, she still found herself lifting the hair off the back of her neck, allowing the soft wind to cool her. Once, as she lifted her hair, she managed to sneak a glimpse back at Tiberius only to discover he was looking right at her. She smiled faintly and he smiled back.

Giddy, she faced forward, fanning her face with her hand and thinking on their destination for the night. She assumed it was Leadenhall House, but her father hadn't said much to her that morning so she truthfully wasn't sure. As she delicately wiped the sweat off her brow, she spoke to her father who was riding point several feet in front of her.

"Papa?" she called. "How long until we reach Leadenhall?"

Bose didn't turn around. With his helm on, he couldn't turn his head anyway, so he simply spoke loudly so she could hear him.

"We are not going to Leadenhall right away," he said. "My army is with the de Winter army at Wintercroft so we will be going there first so I can claim my men."

Douglass understood. She lifted her hair again as a particularly strong breeze came off of the water. "I do not understand why you did not bring them with you when you came to collect me at Codnor Castle," she said. "It seems very odd that just you and Garran would have come for me. Why did you not bring your men?"

Bose grunted. "Because I would have been compelled to feed and house eight hundred men for at least a month on the road," he said. "It was much easier, and much less expensive, simply to leave them mingled with de Winter men. Besides, armies in transit often attract unwanted attention and I would be traveling close to Kenilworth. I did not want to attract de Montfort's attention by moving enemy troops through his lands."

Douglass eyed her father. "You attracted de Montfort, anyway," she said. "That is why the de Shera brothers had to come and save us."

Bose grinned, without humor. "A fateful day that was."

"What do you mean?"

Bose shook his head, thinking that it was the day Tiberius had been introduced to Douglass but saying nothing about it. "Nothing," he said. "I simply meant it was an eventful day. That is the last time I travel anywhere near Kenilworth. De Montfort has eyes and ears everywhere."

"You remember Davyss de Winter, don't you?" Garran, riding a few feet off to her right, turned to ask his sister. "I think you met Davyss about six or seven years ago when he came to Ravendark Castle with his father. I think they were traveling from one point to another and stopped for the night. Father, do you recall?"

Bose nodded his big head, recalling that day years ago when Davyss and his father stopped at the de Moray fortress to rest in their travels. Ravendark Castle, near Salisbury, had been Bose's home for many years, ever since the king had granted him the property. It was yet one more thing he owed Henry.

"They were coming from Dunstan Castle, I believe," Bose said. "Grayson de Winter, Davyss' father, had some business there and they were heading home. That family owns most of Norfolk and all of Surrey, you know. The de Winters have more land in England than anyone save the royal family, including Wintercroft. It's their London base."

Douglass thought back to the vague memories of a muscular, young knight with shaggy, dark hair. "I think he pinched me," she said thoughtfully. "When Papa wasn't looking, Davyss de Winter pinched me on the arse."

Garran burst out into snorts while Bose actually tried to turn around and look at her, his dark eyes narrowed.

"Did he truly do this?" he wanted to know.

Douglass nodded. "I was only twelve or thirteen," she said. "He pinched me and it hurt. He laughed!"

Garran continued to snort as Bose shook his head. "Then I shall have a word with Davyss and make sure he does not pinch you again," he grumbled. "He will not like my reaction if he tries."

"Nor mine," Tiberius said from several feet back. "In fact, I can promise you he will not like it in the least."

Garran stopped snorting and turned to look at Tiberius. "Would you challenge him?" he asked, almost incredulous. "That would be like fighting one of your brothers, Ty."

Tiberius looked at him. "It would be like fighting you and that almost happened, too."

Garran pursed his lips with some frustration, turning away because he didn't want to engage in any kind of verbal argument in front of his sister. Already, the situation was extremely strange and he wasn't sure he liked it. He was still trying to decide how he felt about all of this.

His father told him that Tiberius had sworn fealty to him because he wanted to prove himself to de Moray, to prove that he would be a good enough man for Douglass' hand. It was clear that Tiberius was quite serious about his sister and Garran was having difficulty adjusting to that. Was it possible that Tiberius was actually serious about one woman? It was all still quite shocking to Garran even though he was glad to be with Tiberius once again. He had missed him terribly. But the circumstances were still unnerving to him. It was going to take time for him to get used to it all.

No one said anything more as they plodded along the road, passing through stretches of housing and then stretches of thick trees and fields all around. The river was constant, to their right as they moved, and soon enough the more crowded area of London came into view.

Smoke trailed from leaning and malfunctioning chimneys, hanging in a gray haze above the rooftops. In the distance, they could see the spire of Westminster with the sun hanging behind it in a sort of hazy backdrop. Gulls, that had followed the river in from the sea, swarmed in the sky above, dropping into streets and onto rooftops looking for food.

And it smelled horribly in the August heat. With the moisture from the river, the stench of man was cloying, like breathable grease, and Douglass resisted the urge to pinch her nose as they turned northeast to skirt the edge of the city. She wrinkled it against the smell, sneezing as they moved onward, past children dressed in rags and toothless men, fat, who were on the side of the avenue trying to fix a broken wheel. All of these people stopped what they were doing to watch three big knights and a small lady move through the town, looking upon them with suspicion and curiosity.

As they moved further into the city, a few children began to follow them. Tiberius was bringing up the rear and his head was on a swivel, watching all angles for any signs of threat, including a gang of children that was following behind them at a distance. When one of the children threw a stone that hit his horse in the buttocks and caused it to jump, Tiberius whirled the animal around and roared at the gaggle of children, causing them to scream and scatter. That brought a smile to Douglass' lips as she watched Tiberius growl and bellow and the children shriek. It was quite hilarious to watch.

It also made her fond of the man just a little bit more. He wasn't afraid to show his humor, unusual when knights were usually so controlled and austere. He wasn't afraid to smile, or wink, or speak his mind, even if it was on a subject that he was emotional about. She appreciated a man who wasn't afraid to be himself, unhindered by the severe trappings that knighthood sometimes brought about. He was different, very different from any knight she had known, her father included. Tiberius was a man who was unafraid to show his passion, in any aspect of his life.

They moved on, sans the flock of children that Tiberius had scattered to the wind. They were now entering a part of the city where the smells of food were mingled with the smells of human habitation. It was past the nooning hour and Douglass was hungry, sniffing the air to see where the smells were coming from. As Bose turned down an avenue that seemed to take them away from the marvelous smells, Douglass stopped him.

"Papa?" she called. "I am hungry. Can we please get something to eat and rest for a few moments? I am exhausted."

Bose pulled his big steed to a halt, looking at their surroundings. They had been on the road several hours and Douglass had held out admirably considering she had never been the greatest traveler. She had been terrible to take anywhere as a child. He pointed to a street that led off to the south.

"That is the Street of the Bakers," he said. "We can find you something to eat there."

Happily, Douglass followed her father into the narrow street that smelled heavily of baking bread and other cooking smells. They moved the horses over near the end of the avenue and dismounted. Garran moved to hand his reins over to Tiberius so he could follow his sister and father, but Tiberius turned the tables on him and handed him his reins instead. Disgruntled, Garran remained behind with the horses and possessions while Bose, Douglass, and Tiberius went to find something to eat.

The street wasn't particularly busy since most people had done their shopping and eating earlier in the day. Bose found a Scottish vendor who sold a variety of goods; lamb pies, puffy little cakes made from oats, butter, honey, raisins, and eggs that Douglass fell in love with, and great loaves of bread with cheese and herbs baked into them. In all, Bose purchased a feast for the four of them and they carried their booty back to where Garran was waiting with the horses.

Starving, Garran and Douglass plowed into the food while Bose pulled a loaf of bread apart and enjoyed it. Tiberius devoured his lamb pie but failed to get any of the sweet little cakes because Douglass had eaten those first. He simply grinned at her while Garran fussed.

"You could not have shared those with me?" Garran demanded of his sister. "I wanted some, too."

Douglass brushed her brother off. "There were only a few," she said. Then, her manner turned taunting. "They were delicious."

Garran made a face at her. "I will permit Davyss to pinch you now," he said. "That will be your punishment for being such a glutton."

Douglass giggled as Tiberius shook his head. "Davyss will lose a hand if he touches her," he muttered. "He may consider the risk too high."

Garran turned to him, distress on his face. "This is too strange, Ty," he said, agitated. "You speaking of my sister this way. I cannot adequately deal with it so do not make your comments around me. It makes my head want to explode."

Tiberius was amused. "Why?"

Garran wasn't sure how to explain it. "It is not natural," he said. "You are as a brother to me and when you speak of my sister in a romantic fashion, it reeks of something dark and dirty. It is too strange."

Tiberius laughed softly and pointed to Bose. "Then go stand over there by your father," he said. "You are not wanted in this conversation. Go over there like a good lad."

Garran grunted in frustration and moved away, going to complain to Bose that Douglass had eaten all of the sweet oat cakes. Tiberius thought it was rather funny to watch Garran when he was around his father and sister. The usually composed, serious knight seemed to revert back to childhood and become a petulant brother again. As Garran expressed his disappointment to his father, Tiberius turned to Douglass.

"I am glad you ate all of the cakes," he said, a twinkle in his eye. "It is quite humorous to watch Garran have a fit over it."

Douglass grinned. "I did save one," she admitted. "But it is for you. He cannot have it."

Tiberius smiled. "You are gracious my lady," he said. "I am honored."

Douglass laughed softly as she unwrapped the remnants of her meal, producing the last oat cake. Offering it to Tiberius, he took it, his eyes riveted to her as he bit into it. Douglass looked into his eyes as he chewed, her heart doing strange things against her rib cage, feeling overwhelmed and giddy as she'd never felt in her life. This man she was so enamored with, a gentle knight who had thus far shown none of the lascivious behavior she had been warned about. He had been kind, sweet, and attentive, and she was falling further and further under the man's spell. Interest and attraction had turned to something else.

"How long will you be with us?" she asked softly, watching him chew. "Why did you not return to Isenhall with your brothers?"

Tiberius could see in that instant that Bose hadn't told her anything of what had transpired. He pondered why the man would have withheld such information but Tiberius saw no reason to. He wanted Douglass to know that he was here because of her, because he was trying to prove to her father that he was an honorable man who would be an excellent match for his daughter. He wanted her to know the lengths he would go to for her, to prove himself to her. Swallowing the bite in his mouth, he spoke quietly.

"I will be with you indefinitely," he said. "It would seem that your father is uncertain if I am worthy of you so I have sworn fealty to him in order that I may prove my merit. I could not let him take you to London and on to a potential marriage contract, Douglass. I cannot and will not lose any hope of ever having you for my wife."

Douglass' eyes widened dramatically. "So you swore fealty to my father?" she repeated, astounded. "I... I cannot believe it. What about your brothers? Surely they did not want you to do this!"

"They did not, but they must learn to get on without me for now."

Douglass was clearly astonished. She could hardly believe the man would give up everything he had worked for simply to follow her. Romantic tales often told of men pursuing women to the ends of the earth, but she never truly believed it would happen to her. Men often spoke of romance and passion but to see a demonstration of it as he had done amazed her. The actions of the man spoke far louder than any words ever could.

"You would *do* this for me?" she asked in disbelief.

He nodded, wishing he could take her hand. He very much wanted to. "I would," he murmured. "When I told you I wanted you for my wife, I was serious. I will do whatever is necessary to see that come to fruition. I will therefore be at your father's side from now until the day I marry you, and mayhap even after that. I will never let you out of my sight, Douglass, not ever."

Douglass smiled at him in a gesture of utter elation. Her entire face was glowing. She, too, wanted to reach out and take his big hand but she dare not touch him with her father and brother watching, and especially Garran. The situation had only just calmed between her brother and Tiberius. She didn't want to stir things up again.

"No matter what my father says," she hissed at him, "I will not marry d'Vant. I will not permit it."

Tiberius' grin was a grateful one but he was interrupted from replying when Garran broke away from Bose and came near. He tugged on his sister's sleeve.

"We must go if we are to make Wintercroft by this evening," he said, eyeing Tiberius because he thought the man might be standing too close to Douglass. "Let me help you onto your horse."

Douglass balked. "Can't Tiberius help me?"

Garran nearly snarled. "Nay," he said flatly, tugging on her arm again. "I will help you up."

Douglass shrugged him off. "I can get on the horse myself," she said, pushing him away when he tried to help her again. "Leave me alone, Garran. Go mount your own horse and leave me be."

Garran made a face at her but he didn't move away. He remained with her until she deftly jumped onto her small horse herself. She tried to push him away with her foot, then, and he had no choice but to move away. Mounting his charger, he fell in beside his sister as she followed their father back through the avenue and onto the main road that headed off to the northeast. Tiberius brought up the rear, watching the woman with the spectacular golden-red hair when he should have been watching the area for threats. Douglass had his full attention.

As he watched her curly hair blow softly in the moist breeze that was sweeping in off the river, he couldn't help but think on their destination. Wintercroft. He'd been there before, many times in his youth, as Grayson de Winter had been Antoninus de Shera's best friend. They'd spent many a summer there as young children, visiting Davyss and his brother, Hugh, and Grayson and Katherine de Winter. Lady de Winter was the sister of the Earl of Surrey, a slender woman who always wore a severe wimple that made her look rather frightening. As a child, Tiberius had been afraid of the woman and she would give him treats to try and warm him to her, but to no avail. In this day and age, he wasn't afraid of her any longer but he had a healthy respect for her. She ruled the House of de Winter far more than Grayson did.

Tiberius also wondered what Davyss was going to say when it was made public knowledge that Tiberius de Shera now fought for Bose de Moray and, subsequently, the king. Tiberius was prepared for questions and perhaps even condemnation, but he was determined to stand his ground. He suspected the condemnation might come from Grayson more than Davyss. Grayson's opinion of loyalty was that it could only be given once. Given that the de Winter and de Shera families were so close, Tiberius felt much as if he were about to face his father with what he'd done. He had to admit that he wasn't looking forward to it.

But it was worth it. As his gaze lingered on Douglass' head, he knew without a doubt that his actions had been worth it. He would get what he wanted in the end and that was all that mattered.

He would have Douglass.

CHAPTER ELEVEN

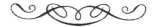

Wintercroft Manor

IT WAS JUST before sunset when Tiberius, Douglass, Bose, and Garran reached Wintercroft Manor. The manor was set north of the river, back in a massive forest of trees that stretched as far as the eye could see. The four of them traveled for some time down the forested road as the sun lowered in the sky, creating phantoms and shadows in the canopy overhead, until the heavily foliaged trees parted and a gray stoned wall came into view. The wall was inordinately high and there was a massive wood and iron gate cut into the middle of it. As they drew near, Bose called to the sentries and announced himself and the gate began to crank open, allowing them to enter.

As they made their way into the bailey, the structure of Wintercroft loomed before them. Although it was a fortified manor, it looked more like a small castle. It was pale-stoned, bulky and gloomy. The yard was littered with small outbuildings and a fairly large stable block off to the south. The house itself was odd. There was a heavy, iron door on the first floor but no windows anywhere on the floor. All of the windows were on the second floor but there was also a strange addition that projected off the north side of the house, creating a third and fourth floor. It was like an enormous tower had been added to half of the house. All of this oddness made it very peculiar in appearance and as the four of them drew close to the manor, the door opened and a big knight with shaggy, brown hair appeared.

"De Moray!" the man called, followed shortly by an older man emerging from the door behind him. The young knight that was dressed in mail and sloppy, leather breeches lifted a hand to Garran. "You're an ugly ape of a man, Garran, but I am happy to see you."

Garran waved off Davyss de Winter, who stood there laughing at Garran as the man balled a fist at him. But that laughter faded when Davyss saw Douglass tucked in behind her brother's charger. Gallantly, he bowed.

"Ah," he said. "Lady Douglass de Moray. I would recognize that beautiful hair anywhere. Welcome back to Wintercroft, my lady."

Davyss was a flatterer of women and, much like Tiberius, had something of a scandalous reputation that followed him around. Douglass could tell just by the man's manner that the rumors were true. He had a bright smile, was very handsome, and he knew it. She fought off a grin, trying to appear stern.

"I was hoping you would not be here, Davyss," she said as she reined her palfrey to a halt and he came out to help her from her horse. "I told my father that the last time I saw you, you pinched me."

Davyss appeared shocked. "I did no such thing."

"You did."

He pretended to be very contrite. "It was an accident, I am sure, my lady," he assured her. "I would never have knowingly done such a thing."

"And you had better not do it again or you will have to answer to me."

The threat came from Tiberius, the last rider in their party, as he came up behind Douglass' palfrey. Davyss had been so fixed on the glorious Douglass that he hadn't noticed Tiberius riding in with Bose and Garran. Tiberius was not wearing his de Shera tunic and, quite frankly, Tiberius was the last person Davyss would have expected to see with de Moray. He stared at Tiberius as if he were seeing a ghost.

"Ty?" he finally gasped. "What in God's name are you doing here?"

Tiberius smiled faintly at one of his oldest and dearest friends. "An explanation for another time," he said, indicating quite clearly that he didn't wish to discuss his presence in the open for all to hear. "Suffice it to say that I am here and I am not a prisoner of de Moray. I am here of my own free will. Greetings, Uncle Grayson."

He was speaking to the older man who was standing behind Davyss. Grayson de Winter had graying temples and a muscular, compact body that suggested he'd spent many years being active as a knight. He simply had that look about him. Grayson gazed steadily up at Tiberius with his dark hazel eyes.

"What are you doing here?" Grayson asked.

Tiberius glanced at Douglass, then at Bose, as the man was climbing of his steed. "I told you," he said, lowering his voice. "I am here of my own free will."

"That is not what I asked."

"That is the only answer I will give you at the moment."

That wasn't good enough for Grayson, not in the least. After instructing Davyss to escort Bose, Garran, and Douglass into the house, he returned his focus to Tiberius.

"Get off the horse," he told him in a tone that suggested he dare not be disobeyed. "Come with me."

Much as Tiberius had feared, he was about to face some manner of fatherly interrogation with Grayson. It was inevitable that Grayson involve himself in his business. Obediently, he dismounted his animal, muzzling the beast before handing it off to a hovering stable boy. Like a guilty child, he followed Grayson to the north side of Wintercroft where there was a heavy door that led inside.

It was dark and musty in the structure, with low ceilings and close walls. Tiberius, with his extreme height, had to duck his head as they moved down a corridor so that he would not smack his forehead. He was positive that the de Winter family built this place for midgets. Grayson led him into a small room that faced the north side of the bailey and the heavy copse of trees on the other side of the wall.

"Now," Grayson came to a halt in the small but comfortable solar and faced Tiberius. "What are you doing with Bose de Moray? Where are your brothers?"

Tiberius drew in a thoughtful breath, collecting his thoughts before he explained. "I want to marry Douglass de Moray," he said simply. "Her father is not entirely certain I am a desirable husband for his daughter so I have sworn fealty to him in order that I may prove myself."

Grayson was not pleased by that explanation. It was clear by his expression. "You cannot simply swear fealty to a man because you want his daughter," he said, verging on anger. "You are a Lord of Thunder. Your heart is with de Montfort and everybody knows it."

"My heart is with Douglass."

That seemed to bring on more anger. "Just because you are thinking with your manhood and not your brain, that does not mean you can switch allegiances so easily," he snapped. "Your father would have your head for this. What in the hell are you thinking, Tiberius? This is a foolish and dishonorable move."

Tiberius struggled not to feel guilty. "I told you," he said evenly. "I want to marry Douglass and the only way to prove to Bose that I am worthy is to serve him. Actions speak louder than words, Uncle Grayson."

Grayson scowled. "That is ridiculous," he said. "I want you to go back to Isenhall where you belong. God help us if Henry gets wind of this. If he knows de Moray has you, he will demand you be brought to him and do you know what will happen then? You will be lucky if throwing you in the vault is all he has in mind. He knows that you are privy to the inner workings of de Montfort's rebellion. He may try to torture every last detail out of you!"

Tiberius' jaw ticked faintly. "I am not going back to Isenhall."

Grayson nodded his head firmly, quickly. "Aye, you are," he said. "You are putting everyone who knows you in danger, Tiberius de Shera. Do you think I would stand by and watch Henry take you to sport? Of course I would not. You would ruin everything I work for just so you can fuck another man's daughter? I am ashamed of you."

Tiberius felt as if he'd been struck. He suddenly felt very foolish and very weary. He sighed heavily, searching for the nearest chair to plant his body on. Plopping onto the nearest bench, he tried not to feel too confused or devastated.

"I do not want to bed her," he muttered. "I want to marry her."

Grayson could see that he had successfully beat Tiberius down and there was a natural guilt with that, being stern to someone he loved. He softened slightly, but not too much. He had a point to make and he could not do it if he crumbled because Tiberius' feelings were hurt.

"Ty," he said, putting his hand on the man's shoulder. "I am not trying to be cruel, but you have put yourself in great danger by doing this. Trust me when I tell you that we cannot always have the women we want. That does not mean there is not another fine woman waiting for you, somewhere."

Tiberius looked up at him. It had only recently become common knowledge that Grayson had been very fond of Honey de Shera. That had been established during Honey's very lengthy illness when Grayson had come to Isenhall to pay a visit. That had been back in April. As Honey lay dying, Grayson had said a few things to her that he probably shouldn't have, intimating that Honey was the woman he had always loved. Strangely enough, it hadn't mattered much to

Honey's sons, as they had always looked to Grayson as an uncle and as part of their family. Even now, as Tiberius looked at Grayson, he could see the sorrow of a lost love in his eyes.

"You are speaking of my mother," he murmured quietly. "Don't you regret not marrying her?"

Grayson hesitated a moment before shaking his head. "I have a fine wife and fine sons," he said. "I have no regrets and neither will you. Go home, Tiberius. Forget about Douglass de Moray. There will be other women for you."

Tiberius shook his head. "I do not want another woman," he said. "I want Douglass. I intend to have her and I am sorry if that causes you to be ashamed of me. I would think that you of all people would understand my heart."

Grayson could feel his ire rise again. "I understand completely," he said. "But I also understand that you have had many women in your young life and you probably believed yourself in love with half of them. Douglass, too, shall pass."

Tiberius stood up, facing the considerably shorter Grayson. "This is different," he said. "And I am not leaving. You cannot force me to go home."

Grayson was unhappy that Tiberius was not doing as he was told. "Then there is this to consider," he said, trying another angle. "Henry has chosen a husband for her already. That was why de Moray went to Derbyshire to collect his daughter and bring her to London. I do not know how you became involved in this or how you met her, but Bose has brought her to London to meet her betrothed. Did you know that?"

Tiberius looked at him suspiciously. "I did," he said. "How did *you* know that?"

Grayson didn't falter. "Because it was arranged that de Moray should bring her to Wintercroft to meet her intended," he said. "Do you think it was by pure coincidence that he brought her here? Of course not. He left his army here and he intended to return here. It was logical, then, for her intended to meet her here when de Moray returned. In fact, her intended has been here for about a week, waiting for her to arrive."

A bolt of shock coursed through Tiberius as the realization hit. "D'Vant?" he asked, stunned. "Tallis d'Vant is here?"

Grayson nodded. "He is indeed."

Tiberius ran from the room before Grayson could stop him.

DOUGLASS HAD NO idea where Tiberius was going, following Sir Grayson around the side of the keep, but having him out of her sight made her edgy and anxious. As her brother practically shoved her into the gaping entry door of Wintercroft, she lost sight of the bailey, which distressed her. Onward Garran gently pushed her into a small and dark entry, with an enormous, stone, spiral staircase to the right and a large, windowless hall to the left.

As she entered the enormous hall, she could see that there were slits at the top of the room for ventilation. In all, Wintercroft was a very oddly designed building but the hall itself was more comfortable than most. There was a colossal table in the center of the room with smaller tables around it. There were cushions on the benches and beautiful tapestries on the walls, indicative of the de Winter fortune. There were even fine works of art against the wall, paintings on thin, wood panels, and the panels drew Douglass' attention.

Propped against the wall in regular intervals, the scenes were quite detailed – they depicted scenes from the Bible and Douglass called her father over to take a look at them. Bose grunted when he saw what she was looking at.

"I have seen these," he said. "There is the scene from the Garden of Eden as Adam and Eve are banished, and there is the scene of Daniel in the lion's den. There are eight of them in total. Lady de Winter had them brought all the way from Italy on the backs of donkeys."

Douglass was impressed. "They are beautiful," she said. "Is Lady de Winter here at Wintercroft?"

Bose shook his head. "Lady Katherine de Winter prefers her own castle of Thetford," he replied. "She lives there and if Grayson is a very good lad, he is permitted to visit her once in a while."

Douglass glanced at her father, grinning. "Is she so strict with him?"

Bose laughed softly. "If your mother was as strict with me, then you children should have never been born," he said, turning his attention to the entry of the hall when he heard a noise. Abruptly, his features grew serious. "Oh… God's Bones…."

Douglass heard the softly-uttered words. It sounded as if her father was hissing out a curse. She turned to see a tall, blond, very broad and very handsome man standing in the entry. Garran was already speaking with the man and Douglass looked at him curiously.

"Who is that?" she asked her father.

Bose didn't sound entirely pleased. "That," he said, "is Tallis d'Vant. I did not know he was already here."

Startled, Douglass grasped her father by the elbow, almost fearfully, as she eyed the knight who was speaking to her brother.

"What will we do?" she whispered. "Tiberius is here, also. Mayhap that is why Sir Grayson took him away, so that he would not see Sir Tallis."

Bose shook his head. "Grayson does not know why Tiberius is with us," he muttered. "He would have no reason to separate him from Tallis."

Bose didn't say what he was truly thinking at the moment. At some point, Tiberius would join them in the hall. Tiberius would know who Tallis was but Tallis would have no idea who Tiberius was or what he wanted, and Bose had no doubt that Tiberius would make his wishes known. Bose didn't want the two young knights in the same room because, like two dogs circling around the same bone, the situation could get quite violent quite quickly. He hadn't expected d'Vant to be here already. He thought he'd have some time.

"My lord," Tallis called from across the room when he noticed Bose standing there. "'Tis good to see you again."

Jolted from his thoughts, Bose lifted a hand to him as he muttered to his daughter. "We may as well introduce you," he said. "It is not as if I can hide you now because he has seen you. Come along, daughter."

Douglass didn't want to move. But Bose pulled her with him, practically dragging her across the floor as they headed for the young knight. As Douglass drew close, she could see Tallis more clearly. He had a neatly trimmed blond beard, neatly trimmed blond hair, and pale blue eyes. When he smiled, he had big, white teeth and prominent canines. He was, in truth, a very handsome man and when Bose came close, he looked the man straight in the eye.

"Greetings, young d'Vant," Bose said steadily. "We were not expecting you so soon."

Tallis smiled politely. "The king sent me to greet you, my lord," he said. "He also sent me with information for both you and Sir Grayson, which we shall discuss in private."

Bose nodded. Since there wasn't much more to say to that, he turned to indicate Douglass. She was, in fact, the entire purpose of Tallis being at Wintercroft so it was best to make introductions and get on with it.

"You have not yet met my daughter," Bose said. "Sir Tallis d'Vant, this is my daughter, Lady Douglass de Moray. Douglass, Sir Tallis is one of the king's premier knights, an impressive accomplishment at such a young age."

Tallis' blue eyes glimmered at Douglass as he bowed politely. "It is an honor to meet you, my lady," he said. "I trust your journey from Codnor Castle was pleasant?"

Douglass thought about the adventure they'd had since leaving Codnor. "It has been exciting to say the least, my lord," she said, sounding not entirely pleased to meet him. "But we have made it to Wintercroft safely."

Tallis appeared properly concerned. "I hope that you did not meet with any misfortune," he said, looking between her and Bose. "Is there anything I can do to assist?"

Bose shook his head. "Nothing, although I thank you for your offer," he said. "We had a bit of a run-in with de Montfort's men in Coventry, but it was minimal."

Tallis was obviously concerned now. He looked at Douglass with great sympathy. "I am very sorry to know that, my lady," he said. Then, he indicated the big, scrubbed feasting table. "Will you sit, then? I will order refreshments immediately."

He had a very genteel way about him, polite to a fault. Douglass looked at her father, absolutely not wanting to sit with the young knight. She didn't want anything to do with him. But Bose simply took her by the elbow and escorted her over to the table with Tallis following, seating her on a cushioned bench. Douglass refused to let her father go, however, afraid the man would walk off and leave her alone with Tallis. But the young knight could see how she was clinging to her father and he hastened to reassure her.

"Everything is fine, my lady," he said sincerely. "You need not fear. You are safe now."

Douglass was having a difficult time even looking at him. "I am not afraid, my lord," she said. "Why would you think so?"

She was denying her apprehension even as she clung to her father. Tallis, fearing he had insulted her somehow, politely backed off the subject. "I do apologize, my lady," he said. "I thought… mayhap you are simply weary from your journey."

Douglass looked at him, irritated by a man who would be so polite to her when she didn't even want to speak with him. He seemed to be going out of his way to be kind when she was only being brittle and snappish. Mayhap… mayhap if she was brittle and snappish enough, he would not agree to the betrothal. An idea occurred to her and, abruptly, she could see her way through the situation. *Be a terrible shrew and he will not want to marry you!* she thought. *Let him see the devil inside!*

"What makes you think I am weary?" she demanded. "Do I *look* weary?"

Tallis was deeply apologetic. "Nay, my lady," he said sincerely. "You are fresh and lovely. 'Tis only that you have traveled a very long way today and that would be taxing on anyone."

Douglass turned her back on him. "You will not assume anything about me, sir."

Tallis was mortified, terrified that she had misconstrued his words. He looked at Bose with great remorse in his eyes but Bose was looking at his daughter. It wasn't like Douglass to be so disagreeable. In fact, it was very out of character for her. If he didn't know better, he would think she was pretending to be angry. Her rudeness was forced simply because it wasn't in her nature. He eyed her suspiciously, curious of her behavior.

"He was not assuming anything, Douglass," he said patiently. "I believe he was simply being kind. If you are not feeling well, then mayhap you should retire until the evening meal. You will be in a better humor then."

Douglass kept her back to Tallis. "I do *not* want to retire," she said petulantly, praying her father didn't become too angry with her. "I want to remain here."

"Mayhap it would be better if you did not."

"I said I am *staying*. You cannot force me to go!"

Bose wasn't sure where this bad behavior was coming from but he knew he didn't like it. She was making a bad impression on Tallis but, as he thought about it, perhaps that was her plan. If she discouraged Tallis, then the path would be clear for Tiberius. Aye, he could see through her scheme quite clearly. Frustrated, he resisted the urge to swat her on her arse. Grabbing her arm to get her attention, he leaned down into her ear.

"You will cease this behavior or you will not like my reaction," he whispered. "You are embarrassing me. Be kind or not only will Tallis not want you, but I can assure you Tiberius will never have you, either. Is that clear?"

Douglass knew he meant it and she had never been very good at taking a stand against her father. So much for her clever plan for discouraging Tallis. With a heavy sigh, she begrudgingly turned to Tallis.

"My apologies for being snappish, my lord," she said. "I… I suppose the trip was more exhausting than I thought. Will you please sit? I understand your family is from Cornwall. Tell me of it."

She said it simply to make her father happy but the relief on Tallis' face was obvious. The man literally breathed a sigh of relief as he took a seat across the table from her, not too close but enough so that he could look her in the eye. Everything Tallis had done so far had been polite, thoughtful, and considerate. He had been well-schooled with his manners.

"Thank you, my lady," he said sincerely. "I was born at St. Austell Castle in Cornwall. It has been my family's home for several generations. The castle guards the bay of St. Austell and when I was a very young lad, my father used to take me with him to inspect the ships that docked in the bay. As a result, I have a great love for the sea but, unfortunately, I do not have the opportunity to see it much. Have you ever been to sea, my lady?"

He was animated as he spoke, describing the bay with big, sweeping motions of his hands. Douglass shook her head at his question.

"I have not," she admitted. "My father's castle of Ravendark is far from the sea but my mother's family's castle, Chaldon, is very close to the sea. I have walked along the rocky shore, many times."

Tallis smiled. "Then we shall have to remedy that," he said. "I have my own cog. I have sailed to France and Spain many times. I would like to invite you and your father to sail with me sometime."

Douglass smiled weakly, looking to Bose, who was shaking his head. "I do *not* sail for pleasure," he said frankly. "The rocking of ships makes me ill. I only travel on boats out of necessity."

Tallis laughed softly, prevented from answering when heavy and swift bootfalls sounded in the entry. He turned, unconcerned, as did Bose and Douglass, to see Tiberius entering the hall. It was clear by his expression that he did not look pleased and Bose, who was closer to him, realized that Grayson must have told him about Tallis' appearance. It was clear as if Tiberius had shouted it. As Tiberius stormed towards the table, Bose had to do some very fast thinking or the situation was about to turn bloody very quickly. He stood up to intercept him.

"My lord," Bose said, putting his hand on Tiberius' chest to stop him from charging d'Vant. "Have you met Sir Tallis d'Vant yet? He is one of Henry's great ones. Surely he has heard of you, as... well, as young King Alexander's personal guard. Sir Tallis, this is Sir Eric du Bonne, a man appointed by Henry to protect the young Scots king. Will you greet him?"

Tiberius looked at Bose as if the man had lost his mind but the ruse momentarily worked. Tiberius was so off-guard by Bose's words that he paused in confusion long enough for Tallis to rise from his seat and approach him. Now, Tallis was on the offensive as Tiberius stood in bewilderment.

"Sir Eric," Tallis greeted politely. "It is an honor, my lord. I apologize that I have not heard of you but I am sure you are very accomplished. Where did you foster?"

Tiberius was still looking at Bose, greatly perplexed. He couldn't quite figure out why de Moray had said such a thing and his first reaction was to call the man out as a liar. But just as quickly, he realized he could not do that. De Moray's reputation was beyond question and to declare the man a fabricator would only make Tiberius look foolish and mad. Whatever de Moray was up to, it had been a clever move on his part. Tiberius had no choice but to confirm whatever the man said, especially if he wanted to marry de Moray's daughter. He was trying to impress the man and calling him a liar would not be the best way to go about doing that.

"I...," Tiberius stammered, struggling to concoct a story. "I fostered at Nottingham. And you?"

Tallis smiled politely. "Alnwick," he replied. "I have heard the du Bonne name. Where is your family from?"

"Du Bonne is my wife's family name," Bose said, averting that subject. "Come, let us sit and become better acquainted."

Tallis went to resume his seat but Bose had to shove Tiberius to get him moving. Tiberius was looking at Bose as if the man had lost his mind but Bose shot him an expression that suggested he'd better go along with whatever was said. As the three of them moved to the table where Douglass was now standing, looking anxiously at Tiberius, Grayson came rushing in through the entry door.

"Ty!" he sounded, rounding the corner into the hall. "Tiber...!"

Grayson shut his mouth when Bose whirled around and gave him a cleaving motion with his hand to shut him down. As Tiberius went to take a seat next to Douglass, Bose made his way back to

Grayson and muttered a few short words to the man. Grayson's eyes flickered in understanding but he didn't react other than that. The mood, however, was set. Something covert was afoot. Bose returned to the table as Grayson called for refreshments.

"How do you like Scotland, Sir Eric?" Tallis asked courteously. "I have personally never been. I hear it is quite cold with big mountains and wild Scots."

Tiberius had never been to Scotland, either. He eyed Bose as the man took his seat as if to say *damn you, man!* Clearing his throat softly, he answered.

"All Scots are wild," he said, joking his way out of it without directly answering the question. "But let's not speak of me, let us speak of you. You must spend a great deal of time in London with the king. What brings you to Wintercroft?"

Everyone in the room knew why he was at Wintercroft but it was a clever way of turning the conversation around and off of him. Tallis smiled genuinely. "I am here on the king's business," he said simply, a proper answer for a knight who was not supposed to go around running his mouth, not even with trusted colleagues. "I have never been here before, actually. I must say that it is a rather strangely-built place. Whoever designed Wintercroft, Lord Grayson?"

Now it was Tallis' turn to be clever, putting the focus on their host, Grayson. So far, both Tiberius and Tallis had been shrewd enough to take the focus off of themselves and turn it on to others in the room. Grayson, seeing he was now the subject of focus, gave everyone a forced smile.

"My parents," he replied. "My mother wanted a manor but my father wanted a working fortress. Wintercroft's odd shape is the result. Odd or not, it is quite impenetrable and quite comfortable. Sir Bose, of course, has quite a mighty fortress in his home of Ravendark. Lady Douglass, were you born there?"

The focus was bouncing all over the place. Douglass, who had been looking at Tiberius, was suddenly very self-conscious with all eyes now on her.

"I was," she said, not wanting to be the center of this very strange and tense gathering. "Sir Tallis, tell us more about your cog – the one you were speaking of earlier. How far have you sailed it?"

Now it was back on Tallis, who was quite happy to speak with Douglass, so much so that he was oblivious to Tiberius' dark expression. Grayson noticed it, however, and he kicked Tiberius under the table, right in the man's shin. Tiberius grunted in pain, covering the noise with a cough and then appearing apologetic when both Douglass and Tallis looked at him curiously. He pointed to his throat.

"Dry," he said, a lame excuse. "Long ride."

It was a good enough excuse and Tallis returned his attention back to Douglass just as a pair of servants entered the hall with pitchers and cups.

"I have sailed as far as Corsica," Tallis said as the pitchers and cups were set on the table and wine began to flow. "I would like to sail to the north of Africa someday or mayhap even to The Levant. Do you like to travel, then, my lady? Even if it is not by boat?"

Douglass opened her mouth to reply when both of Grayson's sons entered the hall. Davyss was followed by his younger brother, Hugh de Winter, a compact and muscular knight just like his father. Unfortunately, neither man knew of the ruse to disguise Tiberius' identity from Henry's knight and before Grayson could get to either of them, Hugh spoke up.

"Davyss said you were here," he said to Tiberius. "It has been a long time since we have seen a de Shera within these old walls. Well? What do you have to say for yourself, Tiberius? Why have you not come to visit us before now?"

Hugh was already upon Tiberius, clapping the man on the shoulders and giving him a manly hug. It was evident that he was quite happy to see him and as Bose and Grayson rolled their eyes, realizing their deception was over, Tallis simply appeared confused.

"De Shera?" he repeated. "There is a de Shera here? At Wintercroft?"

Bose was closest to Hugh. He grabbed the man by the arm and yanked him away from Tiberius.

"Sit down," he rumbled. "Shut your mouth."

Hugh, dragged down by the massive de Moray, looked very confused as Davyss, standing over by his father, had no idea what had just happened. He thought it rather odd for de Moray to grab Hugh as he did but he couldn't help but notice that everyone at the table appeared rather odd, sickened and perhaps even afraid. Grayson stood up, pushing Davyss away from the table.

"Come with me," he said to his eldest. "We have some business to attend to."

Davyss was now vastly confused as to why his father was pushing him away from food and drink. "What is it?" he demanded quietly. "Can it not wait? I have not seen Tiberius in months. I want to speak with him for a few minutes."

By this time, Tallis was starting to put the pieces of the very strange puzzle together. He eyed de Moray and de Winter before turning suspicious eyes to Tiberius. Tiberius could tell from the look on the man's face that he was starting to realize that the Eric du Bonne introduction had been a cover. Rather than try to continue the deception and insult d'Vant's intelligence, Tiberius made the decision to tell the truth. It might cause a terrible scene, but that was already where they were heading. Better to get it all out in the open.

"I will apologize on behalf of de Moray and de Winter," Tiberius said to Tallis. "They were trying to protect me. I am Tiberius de Shera and I am here because it is my intention to marry Lady

Douglass. De Moray and de Winter did not want this to be a blood bath between us so they sought to not tell you who I was or what my presence at Wintercroft meant. Their deception was not meant to insult you but rather to protect me and, quite possibly, you. It was my intention to do you great bodily harm."

To his credit, Tallis didn't change his expression. He didn't rage. He simply sat there, looking at Tiberius, digesting the fact that there was a real and true de Shera sitting before him. *A Lord of Thunder in the flesh.* The fact that Tiberius had essentially threatened him had no meaning to him at all.

"I have heard a great deal about you," he finally said, his tone rather neutral. "Everyone knows of the Lords of Thunder and their support of de Montfort."

"That is true."

Tallis inspected Tiberius, his gaze moving down the man's arms, looking for weapons or any hint that Tiberius was about to move against him. Tiberius was indeed armed but his hands remained in the open. He appeared relaxed and not ready to do battle. That, in turn, kept Tallis calm.

"You have come to pledge for Lady Douglass?" Tallis asked.

"Aye."

"Does the king know of your interest?"

Tiberius shook his head. "He does not," he replied. "There is no way he could."

Tallis appreciated the straight answers but he was nonetheless a bit insulted that the older knights had tried to deceive him. He looked at de Moray.

"Rather than tell me the truth, you would lie to me about de Shera's interest in your daughter?" he asked.

Bose sighed faintly. "As Tiberius explained, I was protecting him more than I was attempting to insult you," he said evenly. "I was not attempting to insult you at all. I was trying to keep the peace since a de Shera in the walls of Wintercroft could be considered treason against Henry. I did not want your opinion of de Winter to be tainted and I take full responsibility for the deception. It was my idea."

Douglass, knowing that her father's honor was now in question, stood up and put her hands out as if to stop all conversation. She looked pointedly at Tallis.

"Wait," she said. "Sir Tallis, this is my fault. My father is in this situation because of me. Sir Tiberius and I wish to be wed but my father, being an honorable man, had already given his word to you about negotiating a marital contract. He is here to see that through but I have allowed Sir Tiberius to come with us and create this terrible situation. If there should be any dishonor had, it should be mine. I do not mean to offend you in the least, Sir Tallis, because you seem like a kind and noble man, but I wish to marry Sir Tiberius. I am sorry that you have been caught up in this situation."

Tallis listened to her seriously. "Well," he said, scratching his head, "at least this is starting to make some sense. I was genuinely questioning what du Bonne, or de Shera, was doing here in the first place. At least I am no longer confused."

Douglass nodded, somewhat regretful. "I *am* sorry," she said sincerely. "I hope you do not think too poorly of the de Moray family. We are usually quite honorable people but when there are feelings and strong wills involved, sometimes things become a bit... complicated."

Tallis was studying Douglass quite closely, seeing a strong and beautiful woman there. He had been imaging what she would look like for a few months and now that he knew, and now that he had met her, he wasn't so quick to walk away. At least, he wanted to know more about the situation before he did. Women like Douglass were very rare. He didn't want to give her up if he didn't have to.

"I do understand that," Tallis said, his gaze moving between Douglass and Tiberius. "Tell me something, my lady. Are you in love with him?"

Douglass was embarrassed by the question. It was such a personal thing to answer in front of all these men. She glanced at Tiberius.

"I… I am quite fond of him," she said quietly. "I wish to marry him."

"But do you love him?"

"I am not entirely sure that is any of your business, Sir Tallis. That is between me and Tiberius."

Tallis shrugged. "If you expect me to relinquish my suit, then it *is* my business."

Douglass shook her head. "Then I will respectfully decline to answer," she said. "But I ask that you relinquish your suit anyway. You certainly do not want a bride who is fond of another man."

Tallis simply looked at her as if pondering her reply. Then, he nodded his head and stood up.

"You will forgive me, my lady," he said, "but I will not relinquish my suit. I can see that there is doubt in your mind and as long as there is doubt, there is hope. Your father and I will still discuss the contract as planned and hopefully come to an agreement. Now, if you will excuse me, I have other business to attend to."

With that, he moved away from the table and headed from the hall. Tiberius, however, rose to his feet with the full intention of following the man but Bose and Garran stopped him, each man holding him back to a certain extent. Even Douglass put her hands on his chest.

"Nay, Tiberius," she begged softly. "Let him go. You will not confront him now. Let my father speak with him first."

Tiberius' jaw was ticking angrily. "You heard what he said," he pointed out hotly. "He intends to go through with the contract. I cannot allow this."

Bose removed his hands from Tiberius' shoulders and moved away from the table, following Tallis' path.

"I will speak with him," he said. "I must make sure he understands the situation for what it is. I must also make sure he does not run back to Henry to tell him that the House of de Moray and the House of de Winter are harboring an enemy de Shera. That would prove difficult for all of us."

Tiberius watched de Moray as the man headed to the hall entry. "I will not be left out of negotiations for Douglass," he said. "If you are hearing Tallis' terms then you will hear mine also. I can offer more than d'Vant can."

De Moray paused in the entryway, his black eyes intense on Tiberius. "That remains to be seen," he said. "For now, you will behave yourself and keep a low profile at Wintercroft. Too many of Henry's loyalists abound and that could be trouble for you as well as for us. I will not tell you again."

He quit the hall, leaving behind confused and tense occupants. As everyone tried to gather their thoughts and return to the food and wine on the table, Hugh, still seated where de Moray had planted him, looked around at the worried faces and threw up his hands and looked at his father.

"What just happened here?" he demanded. "What is Tiberius talking about? And who is Eric du Bonne?"

Grayson couldn't even answer. All he could do was drink.

CHAPTER TWELVE

Isenhall Castle

THERE WAS JUST too much happening.

As the great circular fortress of Isenhall came into view, Maximus could only think on what lay in store for him inside those great, old walls. He'd spent the past four days rolling the situation over in his mind, thinking of Rose and the son she had given him. In truth, he still wasn't over the shock of learning that not only had the reason behind her death been a lie, but a child – *his* child – had caused that death. Now, he had a fifteen year old son, nearly a man grown, and his astonishment was still fresh. As the walls of his home appeared on the horizon as he and Gallus rode in from the southeast, apprehension swept him.

This has all happened so fast....

And then there was Courtly. How was his wife taking the news? She was such an even-tempered, wise woman that he was certain she had handled it admirably, but he was still anxious to see her and speak with her, even more than he wanted to see his son. Courtly was his world, his everything, and he could only pray that something like this had not damaged her opinion of him. He couldn't even stomach the thought. Maximus, the consummately controlled knight, was in perhaps the greatest turmoil of his life.

As Maximus, Gallus, Troy, and about twenty de Shera men approached Isenhall, they could hear the sentries on the walls take up the cry that the Lords of Thunder had returned home. Men were shouting and shifting around and, soon, both portcullises began to crank open. Chains creaked and ropes strained, and the smell of burning fiber wafted upon the late-morning air. Soldiers emerged from the bailey to greet them at the first portcullis as Maximus and Gallus passed through the gatehouse tunnel and emerged into the small bailey on the other side.

Those in the keep had already heard the cries from the sentries so Jeniver, Violet, and Lily were already on the stairs of the keep, ready to greet Gallus. Courtly was slower to emerge from the keep but eventually she, too, stood upon the stairs as the collection of men and animals gathered in the ward. As the stable grooms came out to collect the horses and the knights disbanded the weary soldiers, Maximus and Gallus separated from the group and headed towards the keep.

Violet and Lily squealed with excitement when they saw their father, rushing down the stairs to greet him. Smiling wearily, Gallus swooped down to pick up his daughters, kissing soft, little cheeks as Jeniver went to him and kissed him sweetly on the lips. As Gallus was reunited with his loved ones, Maximus mounted the steps towards Courtly.

His stomach was in knots as he gazed into her beautiful face, so very terrified that she was about to spit in his eye or, even worse, simply turn away from him. To his surprise, she did none of those things. She smiled warmly at him and wrapped her arms around his neck, squeezing him tightly.

"You are home," she whispered. "Praise God for your safe return."

Maximus was holding her so tightly that he was nearly squeezing her to death. His eyes, tightly shut, stung with tears. "Courtly, my love," he whispered. "I received word about... about...."

Courtly cut him off, releasing his from her embrace and taking him by the hand. "Come inside," she said, pretending there wasn't a thing wrong in the world. "You must be weary. I pray your journey was without incident. Did de Moray make it to London safely?"

Maximus followed her inside, simply following like a dumb animal. As she pulled him into the cool, dark innards, he inhaled deeply drawing in the scent of Isenhall's keep. It was a comforting smell, a smell that renewed his strength. Courtly was pulling him towards the small solar but he came to a halt, yanking on his wife and snapping her right back into his arms. The force of his emotion, his passion, was driving his actions.

"Gallus told me what happened," he said, looking into her startled expression from having been yanked upon. "Is it true? Did a lad claiming to be my son arrive?"

Courtly gazed up at her husband. The truth was that she was much calmer now than she had been in days. There had been a time when her emotions had the better of her but now, seeing Maximus, she took strength in his presence and in their love. At the moment, all she could feel for him was her love.

"I have sent for Scott," she said calmly. "He can tell you better than I can. I've not yet met the boy."

Maximus' brow furrowed. "But...," he said, cocking his head curiously. "But he has been here for over a week, hasn't he?"

Courtly nodded. Then, she pulled herself from his embrace, took his hand again, and led him into the small solar. "Sit, Max," she said. "Let us discuss this calmly. I am sure it was a great and terrible shock to you."

Maximus let her push him into a chair but the moment she moved away from him, he grabbed her hand, clinging to it.

"Courtly, please," he begged softly. "I... I am so confused. You have not yet met the boy and he has been at Isenhall over a week? Please tell me what is happening."

Courtly ended up sitting upon his knee, her hands clutched in his two big ones, holding them against his chest. She could see how terribly distressed he was and her heart ached for the man.

"I did not want to meet him before you did," she said softly. "It is your privilege to meet him first, Max. It is not my place. It is true that I was deeply shocked and perhaps even jealous when I first learned of him. I wondered what it would mean to our relationship and even to our children. If we have a son, will this boy supersede him in your heart and mind? I had many terrible thoughts and questions but I realized that this is not my battle to fight – this is yours. Something very drastic has happened and it is not my right to become upset about it. My duty is to support and comfort you, and that is what I intend to do, so you needn't worry about me. The bigger issue is how *you* feel about all of this. Will you tell me?"

Maximus was truly astonished by her reaction. He had expected... in truth, he wasn't quite sure what he had expected. All he knew was that he had feared terrible things and his relief upon realizing Courtly wasn't hateful or resentful about the news gave him relief such as he had never known. He was utterly, deeply astonished by her response.

"God's Bones," he hissed, closing his eyes briefly to give thanks. "I thought... I had no idea how you were going to react. I was fearful that I would return to Isenhall and you might not even be here, having fled in anger and shame. If this situation is really true and the lad is my son, then I will say this – he was not conceived out of lust. I did love his mother but not nearly as much as I love you. If this situation has brought you shame, then please know how deeply sorry I am. I would never knowingly shame you. I hope you know that."

Courtly touched his lowered, dark head. "Of course I do," she admitted. "Max, you are a true and honorable man. You were honest about Rose. You told me about her. It is not as if you kept anything from me and I know you were unaware of any child. If you had known, I know you would have taken care of him."

Maximus nodded. "It would have been my duty," he said. Then, he smiled weakly. "Thank you for not hating me and for not feeling ashamed. Your support means more to me than you can ever know. This situation has me quite unbalanced, as you can imagine."

"I would believe that."

"But this boy will never take precedence over the children you and I have together. They will be my heirs. I want you to understand that."

"I do."

"And it is you who have been the greatest love of my life, not Rose."

Courtly smiled with gratitude. "And you are mine."

Maximus kissed her hands gratefully, feeling the warmth and joy of the moment. But he couldn't let himself get too upswept in it. His thoughts were still lingering on the boy. "I supposed I should meet the lad," he said, both reluctantly and curiously. "Do you know where he is?"

Courtly nodded but refrained from speaking as Scott abruptly entered the keep, heading straight into the solar when he caught sight of Maximus. Maximus stood up as Scott marched into the room.

"My lord," Scott greeted him. "I was just speaking with Lord Gallus. He says that you received the message I sent about the boy."

Maximus nodded, his expression wrought with apprehension and even some confusion. "My wife tells me that the lad is still at Isenhall," he said. "What can you tell me about this situation, Scott? Have you spoken with the lad or the man who brought him at length? Is any of this really true?"

As Scott suspected, Maximus had many questions. Scott had been sitting on top of a fairly volatile situation for days, waiting for Maximus to return. It had been hours of apprehension, of conversations with the old smithy, and of observing the young man who looked very much like Maximus. He had a few answers for Maximus but not many.

"I have spoken with the smithy at length, my lord," he said. "He is indeed the smithy we remember from Kenilworth. There is no mistake. Would you have me go over everything he has told me or would you prefer to hear it from him?"

Maximus didn't really know. He simply wanted answers to his questions so he lifted his big shoulders. "You will tell me," he said. "At least I may have an inkling of what I am to face before I see the smithy. Does he still speak with a stutter?"

Scott nodded. "He does," he said. Then, he indicated the seats around the small feasting table. "Will you sit and be comfortable? I will tell you what I can."

Courtly pulled Maximus down to sit again and the two of them sat together, holding hands tightly, as Scott sat down opposite Maximus so he could better see the man. He took a moment to collect his thoughts. He could see how unnerved Maximus was.

"The smithy's name is Albert, my lord, in case you have forgotten," Scott finally said. "As Albert explains it, his daughter perished in childbirth with your son about seven months after leaving Kenilworth. To give you some background, when the smithy realized she was pregnant, he wanted to send word to you but his daughter would not allow it. In her mind, since the two of you could not be together, there was no reason to tell you. Therefore, she spent the next several months concealing her pregnancy so no one knew of it. When she finally gave birth, it was in secret. When she died, Albert paid the midwife well not to tell anyone what had happened and that is how the rumor of Mistress Rose dying of a fever was started. Albert did not want his daughter's legacy to be that of dying to bear a de Shera bastard."

Maximus was struggling not to relive those feelings of desolation and sorrow he'd known when Rose had been taken from him but, more than that, he was feeling some rage.

"He is not too proud to try and capitalize on a de Shera bastard's bloodlines now," he growled. "He shows up fifteen years later and demands money for the boy."

Scott shrugged. "He wants what is the boy's due, as your son," he said. "But I have not yet spoken to the lad, to be truthful. I have only seen him. Albert keeps him well hidden from us. He says he will not let anyone but you speak with him."

Maximus shook his head. "That seems quite odd," he said. "Why keep the boy out of sight? He comes to Isenhall and demands that the boy be recognized as a de Shera, so why keep him hidden?"

Scott could only shake his head. "You are here now, my lord," he said. "Mayhap you can find out."

Find out, indeed. Maximus looked at Courtly, who squeezed his hand encouragingly. "Do you want me to come with you?" she asked softly. "I will accompany you if you wish it."

Maximus thought on that. Then, he reached out to touch her cheek. "Would you mind if I went alone?" he asked softly. "This is something… I suppose I must reconcile it myself at first. I think I should go it alone for our first meeting."

Courtly kissed him on the cheek. "Go, then," she said. "I will be here. Send for me if you need me."

Grateful, Maximus kissed her hands, her forehead, before rising and following Scott from the keep. Out in the bailey of Isenhall, the sky above was bright blue and the warmth milder than it had been in weeks. It was a generally pleasant day and as Maximus and Scott descended the steps leading from the keep, Maximus could see Violet and Lily as they ran about and chased each other. Gallus and Jeniver were watching them but when Gallus looked over and caught Maximus' attention, Maximus waved the man over.

"I am going to see the lad now," Maximus said as Gallus came near. "Courtly is going to wait for me in the keep, but you… I think I should like you to go with me. Will you come?"

Gallus nodded. "Of course," he said. "Where is the lad?"

Scott spoke. "In the knights' quarters," he replied. "I will wait here with Lady de Shera unless you wish for me to accompany you."

Maximus shook his head. "Gallus will attend me," he said. "But I thank you for your skill and wisdom in this situation, Scott. It could not have been an easy one."

Scott smiled knowingly. "You are welcome, my lord," he said. "I wish you luck in your conference with the boy."

With that, Maximus and Gallus continued on to the knights' quarters which was really just a series of connecting rooms built against the eastern wall of Isenhall, to the east of the keep and great hall. Much like everything else at Isenhall, they were crammed together because of the lack of space within the walls, but the rooms were still fairly comfortable. There was a larger common room and then six smaller sleeping chambers.

Maximus opened the door to the common room, a heavy, oak door that was latticed with iron strips. The panel creaked open, revealing a dimly lit room beyond that smelled heavily of smoke and dirty men. As his eyes grew accustomed to the dim light, he could see the remnants of a meal on the table and a fire burning low in the hearth. He remained at the door until his eyes began to grow more in tune with the darkness of the room, as knights were taught not to enter a situation they could not clearly see. That training kicked in with both him and Gallus, but as they lingered by the door, they heard a quiet voice come from the corner over to the left.

"Sir Maximus?"

Maximus turned sharply in the direction of the voice, seeing a big, round, human shape and little more. "Identify yourself," he commanded.

The figure stood up with a grunt, laboriously shuffling towards

Maximus and into the light. Maximus' gaze fell on the face and he immediately recognized Rose's father, the smithy. A definitive shock ran through his veins because he realized, now, that there could be very little chance of a mistake as far as the reasons behind the man's visit. He recognized the smithy and the smithy, most definitely, recognized him.

"It is A-Albert, m'lord," the smithy said, stammering. "I was at K-K-Kenilworth when you knew my daughter. D-Do you remember me?"

Maximus nodded slowly, with confirmation. "I do," he said, unbalanced and apprehensive. "I have been told why you have come. Where is the lad?"

Albert wasn't finished studying Maximus yet. His old, dark eyes were riveted to the middle de Shera brother, reacquainting himself with the man his daughter had been so deeply in love with. The reason why his daughter died. When Maximus lifted his eyebrows at the man, expecting an answer, Albert smiled weakly, embarrassed that he had been caught in reflection.

"F-Forgive me, m'lord," he said. "Seeing you reminds me of my Rosie. The last t-time I saw you was nearly the last time I saw her."

Maximus' composure took a hit but he hid it well. Memories of Rose began to fill him as well. "The same thing could be said for you," he replied quietly. He regarded the man a moment, re-familiarizing himself with the old and lumpy features. "If this lad you have brought is truly my son, why haven't I known about him before now?"

The smile on Albert's face faded. He looked much older than Maximus remembered him, lines of sorrow and hopelessness on his face. He averted his gaze, grasping for the nearest chair and sitting his big, jelly-like body down. When he spoke, his gaze was distant, as if remembering things he'd rather not have recalled. There was grief in his memories, long past.

"I-I was respecting Rose's wishes, m'lord," he said quietly. "She did not want you to k-know of the boy. She did not want you to f-feel obligated, I suppose. She said that the c-child belonged to her, as it would b-be the only thing she ever had of you. But C-Cassius is older now and I-I cannot provide for him as I would like to. I-I am old and it is hard to work my trade, as m-my hands are painful and swollen. When C-Cassius started to go hungry because there was no b-bread, I knew I had to seek you out. It is not fair to C-Cassius not to have benefit of the de Shera name."

That explained quite a bit and Maximus was starting to feel sad and sorrowful for many reasons. A dead love, a starving son... aye, he was coming to feel quite emotional about the situation. He glanced at Gallus, who had much the same expression on his face.

"So you have brought the boy to me now," Maximus said softly. "How old he?"

"He has seen f-fifteen years, m'lord," Albert replied. "He was b-born on the first of December of the year we left Kenilworth."

Maximus thought quickly back to the last time he had bedded Rose and realized that an early December birth would have fit quite nicely into that time frame. Much like Tiberius, Maximus could remember the slightest detail from two minutes ago to twenty years ago. His memory was perfect in every aspect so he clearly remembered the last time he and Rose had been together and the timeline for the birth was feasible, indeed. He braced himself for what was to come next, the inevitable introduction. He was both anxious and excited about it.

"Then let me see him," he said. "Let me see if he is, indeed, my son."

Albert nodded, resigned, and called over his left shoulder. "Cass?" he lifted his voice. "C-Cass, come out here, if you would."

They could hear a door opening down the short corridor where three sleeping rooms were located. Albert laboriously stood up and moved to the corridor entry just as a young man appeared.

The lad was very big for his age, dressed in a ragged tunic and hose, with broad shoulders and shaggy, brown hair. In fact, it was the first thing Maximus noticed. The lad had his hair. Already, the boy looked like him. But when the lad lifted his face, it was Gallus who gasped.

"God's Bones," Gallus muttered. "He looks just like you."

Maximus drank in the first sight of a boy who was, in fact, an indisputable de Shera. There was absolutely no question in his mind as his gaze moved over the strong features, the square jaw, and the dark green eyes beneath dark brows. He had the handsome lines and the intelligent features. He was a de Shera to the bone.

"He looks like Father," Maximus murmured, stunned.

Gallus shook his head. "He looks like *you*."

Maximus forced himself past his shock and lifted a hand, motioning the lad forward. "Come into the light," he said. "Let me see you more clearly."

The boy did as he was told with Albert by his side. The old smithy had his arm around the boy's big shoulders but it was clear that the lad was very nervous. Although he met Maximus' eye, there was apprehension in his face. As the boy came to a halt in front of Maximus, for a moment, no one spoke. They simply looked at each other. It was a moment filled with a million words, yet not one verbal sound came forth. It was a moment when expressions spoke far louder than words ever could as father and son faced each other for the first time.

Maximus took a good look at what he truly believed to be his son, feeling emotions wash over him, feelings he never knew he had. It was prideful and paternal. The boy was almost as tall as he was but he was still growing. Maximus could only imagine how big the boy was going to get. To think of this young man without food, without hope, and raised by a grandfather who lived in poverty nearly brought Maximus to his knees. *My blood,* Maximus thought. *He is my blood!*

"Tell me your name, lad," Maximus said, his throat tight with emotion.

The young man swallowed nervously, looking to his grandfather, who nodded his head. The lad then returned his attention to Maximus and swallowed hard once more before speaking.

"C-Cassius, m'lord," he replied softly.

He has the smithy's stutter, Maximus immediately thought. No wonder the smithy hadn't let anyone close to him! To hear the boy's stutter would have brought shame at the very least, an imperfect young man bearing the de Shera bloodlines. But the lad had a beautiful, deep voice, very much reminiscent of Maximus' tone, and in those short few words, Maximus knew without a doubt that he was looking at his very own son. His heart soared and it was all he could do to keep the smile off his face, and he could feel his eyes stinging with tears of joy. Something he had felt such apprehension over, the appearance of his bastard, now seemed silly in reflection. Blinking away the tears, he focused on the nervous young man.

"Do you know who I am?" he asked hoarsely.

Cassius glanced at his grandfather before shaking his head. "N-Nay, m'lord."

Maximus smiled faintly. "I am your father," he said. "My name is Maximus de Shera. I loved your mother very much, once. I am very sorry you have been kept from me, lad, but I understand why your grandfather did it. Now that you are here, however, I should like to come to know you. Are you agreeable to that?"

Cassius' nervousness seemed to morph into something else. He stood a little taller now, his gaze peering seriously at Maximus. He was curious and interested, but he still held a glimmer of doubt. He looked at his grandfather again, for reassurance, before speaking.

"I-I didn't know about y-y-you until a f-few months ago, m'lord," Cassius said. "E-Even when I-I knew, I-I did not w-want to come to see you. I-I did not want anything f-from you but m-my grandfather insisted."

Maximus' brow furrowed. "But you are my son," he said. "You are due all rights and privileges that the de Shera name can bring you."

Cassius seemed to grow frustrated. "M-My grandfather and I do w-well enough," he insisted. "He h-has taught me his t-trade and I am a good smithy."

"He is one of the very b-best, m'lord," Albert put in. "The l-lad has skill and s-strength beyond compare."

Maximus' smile grew. "I am proud to know that," he said. "But he is a de Shera and should be a knight. That is his heritage."

Cassius shook his head, almost violently, and moved away from the men. It was clear that he was agitated. "I-I cannot be a knight," he said, pointing to his grandfather. "I-I told you I d-did not want this. I want to g-go home!"

Maximus looked at Albert with some confusion and concern as Gallus, who had been observing everything quite closely, moved around Maximus and took a few steps towards Cassius.

"Cassius," he said evenly. "I am the Earl of Coventry and you are my nephew. Your father is my brother. Lad, you are the finest example of a de Shera I have ever seen. You are big, strong, and intelligent. I assure you that you can and will be a knight. I will ensure that you are trained by the best."

Cassius looked at Gallus, stricken. "I c-cannot, m'lord."

"Why not?"

Cassius was overwhelmed with what seemed to be embarrassment. He didn't want to answer Gallus but he knew that, out of respect, he had to. He had to give the man an answer. "C-Can they teach me to s-speak without s-sounding like a f-fool, m'lord?" he finally said, pain in his voice. "I-I cannot be a k-knight and shout o-orders like this. Nay, it is b-better to be a s-smithy."

"Why?"

"B-Because I will shame the de S-Shera name, stuttering c-commands as men laugh."

Gallus was heartbroken at the lad's attitude. What a horrible opinion the young man had of himself because of his stuttering speech. But he suspected the lad had suffered a lifetime of ridicule because of it and he knew nothing else. It was heartbreaking, indeed.

"No one will laugh at a de Shera, I assure you," Gallus said. "But I will hire the finest teachers to help you with your speech and I will hire the finest knights to teach you how to become what you were born to be. Cassius, it is a much better life that you will have this way and so will your grandfather. We will take care of him as well. Don't you understand what this means? You and your grandfather will never go hungry again. You will be part of the House of de Shera and you will be given all honors to that regard. Your father is the greatest warrior England has ever seen and I have no doubt that you will be a fine warrior as well. Already, you honor us. Let us show you how much."

Cassius stared at Gallus, overcome by the man's impassioned speech. After a moment, his features twisted somewhat into an expression of pain. "B-But...," he stammered. "B-But t-this was not my wish. It was my grandfather's."

"I understand," Gallus said. "But you must give us time to at least show you what it means to be a de Shera. I am pleased that you did not come here expecting anything. That shows true humility. But you are a part of the House of de Shera whether or not you want to be. It is your birthright and a right that many men would love to have. Spend some time with Maximus. At least understand what it is you will be turning down before you refuse it completely."

Cassius pondered the words a moment before nodding his head reluctantly. "I... I- I will do that, m'lord," he said, his gaze moving to Maximus. "I-I will come to know my father, as t-that is what my g-grandfather wishes."

Maximus smiled at the young man. He was coming to see that Cassius was very confused, and very humble, and the idea that he was part of a greater family clearly overwhelmed him. It had only been him and Albert for so long and now he was being introduced to a father who was a great warrior and an uncle who was an earl. For the young man of simple upbringing, it was too much for him. Maximus was coming to see that Albert hadn't been hiding the boy as much as the boy was probably hiding himself. The stutter in his speech and being very large in size had a hand in his wish to remain hidden from the world. Therefore, Maximus proceeded carefully.

"I have a few duties to attend around the castle," Maximus said to Cassius. "You may accompany me if you wish or you may remain here. It is your choice."

Cassius appeared rather dubious, looking to his grandfather as if the old man could tell him what to do. Albert, however, simply lifted his shoulders. He had brought Cassius this far and it was time for Cassius to make some decisions on his own. Brow furrowed, Cassius turned back to Maximus.

"I w-will remain with my grandfather, m'lord," he said. "I-I do not want to l-leave him alone."

Maximus didn't argue with him. He simply nodded his head. "Very well," he said, looking between Cassius and Albert. "I do hope you will both join us in the hall this evening for supper. I should like you both to meet my wife and the rest of the de Shera family."

Cassius merely nodded, watching as Gallus and Maximus turned for the door. Gallus went through first, out into the daylight beyond, and as Maximus was moving through the door after his brother, Cassius suddenly spoke up.

"M'lord," he said, watching Maximus turn around to face him. "I-If you w-want me to come, I... I-I suppose I will. I-If you still w-want for me to, that is."

Maximus was very glad that Cassius was at least showing some interest. A few moments ago, he was feeling deeply disappointed that Cassius didn't seem to want anything to do with him. Now, there was a bit of hope. Even though Cassius still seemed indecisive, nervous still, at least he was showing some interest. At the moment, that was enough.

"I will always want you to come with me, Cassius," Maximus said.

Cassius eyed Albert, who gave the boy a shove forward in Maximus' direction. Cassius made his way to Maximus, looking the man timidly in the eye, giving him a quick and humorless smile, before heading out into the sunlight. Maximus lingered in the doorway a moment, watching the boy as Gallus began speaking to him. Then, he turned to Albert. His gaze was moist as he looked at the old man.

"Rose would have been very proud," Maximus whispered. "He is a fine boy."

With that, he proceeded out to where Cassius and Gallus were speaking, or mostly Gallus was speaking, and together the three of them continued on across the bailey, heading towards the armory on the other side. From the doorway of the knights' quarters, Albert watched with tears in his eyes.

Aye, Sir Maximus, he thought to himself. *Rose would have been very proud, indeed.*

CHAPTER THIRTEEN

Wintercroft

"**P**SSSST!"

Douglass heard the very odd sound, like someone hissing. At sunset, she was seated in a small solar that Grayson had graciously allowed for her private use while she was a guest at Wintercroft. She had been knitting most of the afternoon, ever since her father went off with Tallis. Grayson, Garran, Davyss, and Hugh took Tiberius away, leaving Douglass to be settled by servants into the small solar. It was a lovely room and very comfortable, but Douglass was very edgy knowing that Tiberius and Tallis were wandering about somewhere, perhaps to go head to head at any moment.

"*Pssssst!*"

There was that sound again and Douglass set down her knitting, peering curiously around the room. There were two long and slender holes for ventilation at the top of the room, holes that could also be used as arrow slits in case of attack. The sound seemed to be coming from there. Setting her knitting down, she dragged a chair over to the wall and stood on it to peer out of the ventilation holes.

"Greetings, sweet!"

Half of Tiberius' face appeared in the hole and Douglass shrieked softly in surprise. She nearly fell off the chair, grasping at the windowsill to keep from tumbling over.

"Tiberius!" she gasped, precariously holding her balance. "What on earth are you doing out there?"

Tiberius' eyes and nose were visible through the slit. "I am hiding from Grayson and Davyss, who seem quite anxious to keep company with me," he said. "They follow me around like lost puppies, never leaving my side, and of course it is to keep me away from Tallis. But I told them I wanted to check on my horse and they let me go alone, but I came looking for you instead."

Douglass grinned, flattered and happy to see him. "How did you find me?"

"I paid a servant to locate you for me."

Douglass laughed softly. "Clever, my lad," she said. Then, she sobered. "Have you seen Tallis at all? I have been consigned to this foolish room and have not seen anyone. I have not even seen my father."

Tiberius reached a big hand through the small window and she grasped it, holding it tightly. "I have not seen him lately," Tiberius said, caressing her soft fingers. "The last I saw of him, he was with d'Vant and, as you know, I've had to lose my shadows of Grayson and Davyss. They are probably out searching the grounds for me right now, so I will have to make this visit short."

Douglass' face fell. "Must you?" she asked, disappointed. "Must you leave so quickly?"

Tiberius squeezed her hand again. "I am afraid so," he said. "But I must speak to you, no matter how short our time together. I have been afforded a good deal of time to think on things, Douglass. I have done nothing but think all day. It is clear that the winds of favor are blowing in Tallis' direction. The king has selected him for this marriage and it is my sense that your father wants him as well. After all, Tallis was planned for you long before I came along. It is my feeling that your father wants to stick to the bargain in spite of what you want."

Douglass' brow furrowed unhappily. "I will not marry him," she said firmly. "It is you I will marry."

Tiberius toyed with her fingers, his eyes glimmering at her. "And it is you I will marry, too," he murmured. "But I fear unless we take matters into our own hands that it will not happen."

"What do you mean?"

"I mean to take you out of Wintercroft and marry you immediately."

Douglass' eyes opened wide with shock. "But...," she gasped. "But how can we do that? My father... God's Bones, Ty, if my father catches you, he will do terrible things to you and you know it. It will also damage relations between the House of de Shera and the House of de Moray. Are you willing to risk that?"

"Are *you*?"

It was a blunt question and Douglass was taken back a bit, pondering the question. Was she willing to risk a rift, possibly a life-long one? Gazing at Tiberius, she knew that she could not go on without the man. She could not marry Tallis d'Vant when she loved Tiberius. Aye, she loved him. She couldn't remember when she hadn't. Everything revolved around that enormously tall knight and his dashing smile. He was reckless, skilled, brilliant, and a rake, but he was hers. He had all of her. She clasped his rough hand with both of hers, squeezing firmly.

"I am," she said. "Absolutely, I am. When shall we go?"

Tiberius was thrilled with her response. He honestly hadn't been sure what her reaction would be and to hear that she was agreeable meant everything to him. With Douglass by his side, he could move mountains and to hell with those who tried to separate them. He would fight to the death for her. He already knew that. But he hoped it didn't come to that.

"You will always be my forever, Douglass," he whispered. "I will make a good and true husband, Douglass, I swear it. You will never regret it."

She smiled, holding his hand against her cheek. *You will always be my forever.* Those sweet words rang so true. "I know I will not, my love," she agreed. "Every moment I am away from you is absolute torture. When shall we go?"

Tiberius thought on that particular question. He'd been pondering stealing her away most of the day but he hadn't a particular plan in mind because he wasn't sure she would agree. Now that she had, he was forced to think quickly.

"Whatever we do it must be stealthy," he said. "It must be done under the cover of darkness and it must be well planned. Let me ponder what will be done and we will discuss it tonight at some point. There will be an evening meal that both of us will be attending, so I will see you there. I will find a way to speak to you, I promise."

Douglass was giddy with fear and excitement, but she was also apprehensive about her father and how he would react to marrying Tiberius without permission. Bose de Moray was extremely formidable and she didn't want her father killing the man she loved in a fatherly rage.

"Will you do something for me, Ty?" she asked softly.

"Anything."

"Will you please speak to my father one last time about marrying me the proper way before we take matters into our own hands?" she asked. "As much as I want to be your wife, the thought of being at odds with my father for the rest of my life is sorrowful. He and I are very close. I would hate to lose that bond between us."

Tiberius was able to pull her hand out of the ventilation slit enough so that he could kiss two of her fingers. "Of course I will speak to him one last time before we take this matter upon us," he said. "I would rather have your father as an ally than an enemy. That does not please me. But seeing you married to d'Vant would please me even less."

Douglass smiled gratefully. "Thank you," she whispered. "But know whatever comes that I am with you. You, and only you, will always be my forever."

Tiberius started to say something but voices caught his attention. He could hear men approaching the north side of the structure where he was and he was almost certain that it was Davyss and Grayson, so he quickly let Douglass go and moved well away from the building. The last Douglass saw of him, he was walking casually away from her, pretending not to even notice the structure behind him. He was looking up at the sky overhead, seemingly without a care in the world.

Douglass climbed off the chair and moved it away from the window, back to its original position by the small hearth. Her knitting was still there, crumpled upon a stool, and she reclaimed her seat and collected her knitting, all the while keeping her ear cocked to the faint male voices in the bailey outside. She could pick Tiberius' voice out as he spoke to whoever was out there with him. She thought she heard her father but she could not be sure. Still, to hear Tiberius' voice made her heart swell. *We must take matters into our own hands,* he had said. She was ready. It was a terrifying and thrilling prospect, but she was ready.

A knock on the door jolted her from her thoughts and she glanced at the door, seeing it was unlocked. She called out to the caller.

"You may enter," she said.

The door opened and instead of seeing Bose or Garran, or even one of the de Winters, Tallis was standing there instead. Shocked at the unwelcome sight, Douglass lowered her knitting into her lap.

"My lord," she greeted. "How may I help you?"

Tallis smiled confidently. The man seemed to have an abundance of confidence, as she'd seen from the start, and this moment was no different. He remained by the door and made no attempt to enter.

"Your father has given me permission to speak with you, my lady," he said. "May I come in?"

Douglass' brow furrowed. She didn't like the idea of being alone in the room with the man. "Nay," she said. "You will remain where you are. It is not proper for you to be alone in this room with me without a chaperone."

Tallis wasn't discouraged. "I was going to leave the door open, of course," he said. "But if you are more comfortable with me in the doorway, then I will happily remain here. I was hoping we might come to know one another and your father agrees it that it is a good idea. I have had a long talk with him, my lady. I like your father a great deal."

Douglass knew she couldn't dissuade him completely so she didn't try, but she wasn't going to let him come past the door. If he tried, she had two iron knitting needles that could be turned against him and she would not hesitate. She returned her focus to her knitting in a gesture that suggested she had little interest in coming to know d'Vant. The message was clear.

"My father is a great man," she said simply. "What is it you wish to know about me?"

Tallis could see, in that moment, that this would not be an easy task. Not that he expected it to be. The woman seemed fairly determined to marry de Shera and Bose had explained that Douglass could be stubborn. But in order to give Tallis a fighting chance to win the lady's affection, Bose suggested that Tallis open some manner of dialogue with her. He was giving the young knight that opportunity. As Bose had gone off to find the youngest de Shera knight and keep him distracted, Tallis had made his way to the small solar where the lady was occupying her time.

"Let me see," he said, pretending to be thoughtful when he already knew a great deal about her thanks to her father. "Tell me what your favorite food is."

Douglass was rather surprised by the question. She glanced at him as she continued knitting. "Apples with honey and cream," she said, not particularly friendly. "What else?"

Tallis fought off a grin, amused by her stiff demeanor. He decided to try another approach. "When I was a young boy, my father took me down to St. Austell Bay because a great, pirate ship had docked," he said, watching her knit furiously. "It was called the Gemini and the pirate was a friend of my father's, for some odd reason. As it proceeded, I was taken aboard this ship and I found it an incredibly fascinating and incredibly terrifying experience. The men shipboard were unlike anything I'd ever seen before; sunburned, dirty, smelly rats. I was horrified. As I was walking towards the bow or, as was really the case, cringing in fear with every step I took, the rail of the ship suddenly came alive and this terrifying vision with no teeth came up over the side, hurling threats at me as he fell to the deck. In truth, it was a shipmate who was simply doing his work, but to my eyes, it was a monster out of the sea. Well, I was so terrified that I ran blindly until I hit the rail on the other side and flipped over the railing, plunging to the sea below. Fortunately, I could swim, but I heard my father and the pirate laughing on the rail overhead until they choked. That is one of my fondest childhood memories."

By this time, Douglass had stopped knitting and she was listening to him. He was an engaging storyteller. When he finished with a rather comical conclusion, she fought off a grin.

"Fond?" she repeated dubiously. "It sounds terrible."

Tallis laughed softly. "At the time, it was," he said. "At least, to me it was. But in hindsight, I suppose it *was* rather humorous to watch a terrified child flip his way over the side of a boat."

He continued to snort and Douglass' grin broke through. But when she realized she was smiling, she quickly straightened her lips and turned back to her knitting. She didn't want him to think she actually found his story charming.

"I have no such humorous memories," she said, somewhat stiffly. "My childhood was all quite normal and my father is *not* friends with a pirate."

Tallis could see that she was being stubborn, which he didn't mind in the least. He rather liked a challenge. It would make the victory all the sweeter.

"Surely you have a humorous story somewhere in your history," he said, encouragingly. "Something with your sisters, mayhap? Or your brother?"

Try as she might, Douglass couldn't stop thinking about one incident in particular when she, Garran, and their younger sisters were caught doing something they shouldn't be doing. Even thinking of it made her smile and, inevitably, she couldn't help but tell the tale. Perhaps if she did, Tallis would be satisfied and go away.

"Well," she said reluctantly. "When I was small, our sow gave birth to a litter of piglets. I was around six years of age, I believe, and Garran was nine or ten. It was just before he was sent to foster. My younger sisters were quite small. Lizbeth was four and Sable was no more than two. Garran wanted very much to see the piglets and play with them but my mother had warned us against going near them because the sow was very mean. Still, Garran insisted, so one day we snuck down to the stables and to the pen where the sow and her piglets were. Of course, we had to take the piglets out of the pen and play with them, but they made such a racket that our mother, who had been inside the kitchens, heard us. We heard her voice and panicked, and put the piglets back as quickly as we could. Garran, however, was inside the pen and the sow began to chase him. As my mother came outside to see what all of the fuss was about, Garran was running circles in this pigpen, trying to keep away from a sow that was easily four times his size. My mother screamed, my father came running, and he managed to pluck Garran out of the pen before the sow got to him. My father was quite calm about it but my mother took hold of Garran and spanked him soundly. He couldn't sit down for a week."

She was trying very hard not to laugh as she finished with her story and Tallis, too, was biting back a snort. When she saw that he was ready to burst into laughter, she broke down into gales of it. Tallis followed, laughing deeply at the thought of Garran de Moray being chased by a sow. As he'd hoped, however, now the mood between them was lightened. Tallis was very clever that way.

"And you?" he asked. "Did you permit your brother to take all of the punishment?"

She shrugged lazily. "Of course," she said. "I would not tarnish my image as a perfect angel."

Tallis liked that but he sighed in mock disapproval. "I see," he said, pretending to be critical. "Then I am sure you have more stories like that where you have permitted your brother to take the blame for other things you were a part of."

"Of course I do. But I will never speak a word of it."

"Tell me."

"I will not!"

It was a playful exchange but when Douglass realized it, she quickly turned back to her knitting. Tallis d'Vant was quite charming and she realized, with some horror, that if she had not met Tiberius first, she would have been most agreeable to a marriage contract with d'Vant. He was kind and humorous. But the fact remained that she had met Tiberius first and he had her heart. She didn't want to give Tallis hope where none existed. Rather than be coy or cold about it, she thought it would be best to be honest with the man again and try to persuade him to end his suit.

"Sir Tallis," she said after a moment, dropping her knitting into her lap again. "May I be truthful?"

Tallis leaned against the doorjamb. "I would expect nothing less."

Douglass sighed softly. "Then may I say that I am very flattered with your interest in a marital contract, but I still must stress that I wish to marry Tiberius de Shera," she said, looking at the man. "You asked me earlier today if I love him and the truth is that I do. I want to be his wife. You deserve a woman who wants to be your wife and that woman is not me."

The warm expression on Tallis' features faded. "I see," he said, but his manner was still pleasant. "May I ask how long you have known Tiberius?"

"A few days."

"So you have only just met him."

"Aye."

Tallis didn't reply for a moment, but he was most certainly thinking. The lady thought herself in love with a man she'd only known a few days. That bespoke of infatuation, not true love. That being the case, he wasn't ready to concede yet. He was going to have to play harder and dirtier than de Shera was. If the lady was only infatuated with de Shera, surely he could turn her head and change her mind. He was determined to try.

"I hope you have enjoyed our conversation as much as I have, my lady," Tallis finally said, pushing himself up off the doorjamb. "I will leave you to your tasks, then, and see you tonight at sup. May I have the privilege of escorting you?"

Douglass sighed, frustrated. "You will understand when I say I would rather not."

Tallis nodded his head graciously, not at all deterred. "I will abide by your wish, then," he said. "I look forward to seeing you later when we can speak further on piglets and raging sows."

Douglass didn't reply as he left the room, quietly closing the door behind him. But even after he left, his presence lingered, so much so that Douglass eventually had to put her knitting down.

Tallis d'Vant was a very nice man and a perfect knight. There was nothing unsuitable about him in the least and, in that respect, she felt badly that she had no interest in him. Running off with Tiberius would surely upset d'Vant and it would definitely cause him to see the de Morays as a dishonorable family. Was that really what she wanted her father's legacy to be? A rebellious daughter who defied him and shamed him? Certainly, she didn't want that. She loved her family too much. But she also loved Tiberius and she did not want to be married to Tallis d'Vant. Much like letting Garran take the blame for the sow incident, she hadn't taken responsibility for her part in it. Maybe, for once in her life, it was time to act responsibly. Perhaps that meant not running off with Tiberius and doing what her father wished for a change.

Confused, sickened, she set her knitting down completely and wandered to the slit window, the last place she had seen Tiberius. God, she wanted to be with him so badly, but was it right to be so selfish?

All she knew was that once she chose her path, there was no turning back. There would be no reversing the harm she had done.

Would it be a matter of sacrificing her happiness for the sake of her family's honor?

She wondered.

CHAPTER FOURTEEN

T HE EVENING MEAL was an hour or so away. Tiberius could tell because the servants were busily working in the hall, sweeping away old and rotted food, stoking the hearth, and chasing the dogs away who would simply regroup and return to the room. Pitchers of wine were being placed on the table, heavy pewter pitchers that were indicative of the de Winter wealth. Moreover, there were pewter chalices as well and not wooden cups. The de Winter wealth was much like the de Shera wealth in that they made sure to display it at important events to important people. With wealth came strength and these were two of the strongest houses in England.

But Tiberius wasn't thinking much about strength or pewter chalices. He was thinking about Douglass. He'd been thinking about her all afternoon and more seriously since she gave him her pledge that she would indeed run away with him to be married provided he speak with Bose one last time to try and obtain the man's consent.

Even though Tiberius had spent a good amount of time with de Moray earlier that afternoon, it had been with Grayson and Davyss in their company also and he didn't want to have that particular conversation with an audience. When he spoke to Bose about marriage, one last time, it would be man to man and knight to knight. He had to convince de Moray that he was a suitable candidate because d'Vant, unfortunately, was a very fine candidate indeed. It was Tiberius' worst nightmare.

As Tiberius strolled across the bailey, just having come from the stables to ensure his charger was fed and didn't bite someone's hand off in the process, he looked around the darkening bailey of Wintercroft, up to the walls where the sentries were. There was a walk platform that extended from the gatehouse but it didn't go all the way around the walls. It only went part way. The complex had four towers, not including the gatehouse, and the towers functioned as their own fortified battlements. Men patrolled out from these towers, meeting in the middle somewhere along the walls, before patrolling back the other way. It was excellent coverage for walls that weren't built with the ability to mount them all the way around.

There was, however, a postern gate, built into the thick of the wall back by the kitchen yard. Tiberius had walked by it earlier in the afternoon to see how easy it would be to escape through it. It was heavily fortified, and guarded, but it would be a simple thing for Douglass to walk from it as long as the guards either let her pass or, better still, were distracted and she was allowed to slip through. He would have to think of a way to distract them so Douglass could escape while he himself passed through the gatehouse under the guise of returning home. He would then pick up Douglass and make haste for London and for a priest to marry them. Much like Douglass, he was reluctant to ruin the relationship between the House of de Shera and the House of de Moray, but he was resigned by this time. He had to do what was best for him and for Douglass. He was determined to have no regrets.

But the fact remained that he had promised Douglass he would approach de Moray one more time about a marriage contract so on this evening, as the torches were being lit on the walls against the darkness, he made his way from the stable yard to the house, hoping to find de Moray alone so he could speak with the man. As he entered the house, he asked the nearest servant where de Moray was and the servant pointed up the stairs.

It was a big, wide, spiral staircase that led to the upper floor. A long corridor ran nearly the length of the building and there were three doorways off of it that he could see in the darkness, all three of them arched in the Norman design fashion with heavy, oak doors. Not entirely sure which room he would find de Moray in, Tiberius went to the first door and lifted his hand to rap softly but before he could lay his knuckles against the wood, he heard voices coming from inside.

It was Davyss and the man sounded quite serious. Tiberius wasn't sure who he was talking to but he didn't want to interrupt. Laying his head against the wood, he could hear voices but not words. He could make out at least three voices, possibly four. They seemed to be speaking quite agitatedly at one another. Perhaps they were even speaking of him and his desire to marry Douglass, since it was a subject they all seemed to be quite willing to give their opinions on. If they were speaking of him and Douglass, then he wanted to know what was being said.

Concerned, Tiberius noted that the door next to this one, down the hall, was slightly ajar. Curiosity drove him down to that door where he could hear much better because, evidently, that room was connected to the one Davyss was in. Voices were much clearer. Carefully, he leaned into the door to see if he could hear what was being said. Davyss had stopped speaking but another voice he suspected to be d'Vant was now spilling his worth, speaking passionately on a subject he believed in.

"… and that is why Henry sent me," d'Vant was saying. "Henry understands that the House of de Winter and the House of de Montfort are close. He told me to tell you that, Sir Grayson. He told me to tell you that he is very sorry that he must give this command, but it is essential to his strategy. Henry has made the decision not to honor the provisions given to him by de Montfort and his followers back in May. He is the king and his rule is absolutely without the interference of de Montfort and men like the de Shera brothers or Hugh Bigod or Richard de Clare. He is therefore amassing a massive army to march northward and confiscate Erith Castle, one of de Montfort's most prized holdings. Once Erith is secure, he will move northward and continue securing the north, but Erith Castle is essential for that plan. It is well situated and well supplied. The king has asked that the House of de Winter and the House of de Moray summon their allies and move north, converging in the village of Ingleton, whereupon Henry will join his armies and march on Erith."

Davyss looked at his father, exasperation on his face. "I have no problem meeting de Montfort on the battlefield, but taking one of his properties is another matter," he said. "How would we feel if de Montfort came to Wintercroft and laid siege?"

Grayson had listened to d'Vant's message from Henry with growing distress. When young d'Vant said he had come bearing information from the king, he suspected it might be something like this. Tensions had been growing all summer since the Oxford council meeting back in May when men selected by de Montfort and men selected by Henry had met. De Montfort's council had made demands of Henry and had levied provisions against him, provisions Henry had sworn to follow. Now, the king was no longer willing to fulfill what he considered an affront to his absolute rule. Grayson knew it was bound to happen sooner or later. He sighed heavily.

"Henry is well aware that Simon de Montfort is my closest and oldest friend," he muttered, looking to Tallis. "He knows that Simon is Davyss' godfather. Regardless of that fact, Henry is asking me to march on the man's castle. I want to be clear about this."

Tallis nodded. "He is asking for your support, my lord," he said. "The king has chosen to take the offensive with ten thousand French mercenaries and yeomen behind him. They are coming to England's shores as we speak."

Davyss rolled his eyes and hung his head. "French mercenaries," he grumbled. "The King of England must rely on his Poitevin and Savoyard supporters to bring French mercenaries to England so he can fight against his own English barons. Am I the only one that sees anything wrong with this?"

Bose, standing over near the door, cleared his throat softly. "He is the king," he said quietly. "He can do as he wishes, for this is his country and it is his right to rule it as he sees fit. Even if you do not respect the man, young Davyss, respect his position in life. It is a great burden that I am sure no one in this room should like to bear in his stead."

Next to his father, Garran, who they all knew to be a de Montfort supporter, was shaking his head with great remorse.

"But he is allowing the French to take over," Garran said. He could keep silent no longer. "Father, you know I support you, as my presence here proves, but do not spout off divine rule as being Henry's right. He is obligated to protect England from the French that want it, and by bringing in French mercenaries... God's Bones, do you know what they'll do? They'll descend upon the countryside like locusts, raping and burning and pillaging... and we are supposed to *let* them because we support Henry's right to divine rule? That is madness."

Bose looked at his son. "We are English," he said frankly. "We will not allow them to ravage our country. We will watch them and we will police them if necessary. Did you truly think I would stand by and watch Frenchman tear up my country? A country meant for my children and grandchildren?"

Garran simply shook his head and turned away. He was sickened by this news and he was truly starting to question his decision to support his father. Although he would not go back on his word, he was clearly unhappy with what was happening.

"I am not going to argue with you," Garran said to Bose. "But this is wrong and you know it. And now we have been ordered to confiscate Erith Castle from de Montfort. This is full-blown civil war, Father, for once we attack Erith, de Montfort and his stronger barons will retaliate."

"De Shera?" Grayson asked softly.

Garran turned to the elder de Winter knight. "Aye, de Shera," he said. "And Bigod and de Clare. They will retaliate and it will become very, very ugly, especially given the fact that French mercenaries are now being brought in to fight Henry's war. This is utter and complete madness, all of it."

"There is something else," Bose said quietly to the men in the room. "Something I swore not to reveal but I find that I must. It is very important to the king's cause. I have been told by a very reliable source that Prince Edward is siding with de Montfort now. If that is the case, then this war will be more violent and deadly than you know."

The men in the room looked at him in shock. "Who told you this, Bose?" Grayson asked, aghast.

Bose shook his head. "Someone I would trust with my life, many times over," he said. "I will not reveal his name but I know he tells the truth. He would not lie about something as serious as this."

It was a horrible thought, for all of them, and one that caught them all off-guard. Davyss put his hands on his head and turned away, overwhelmed with the thought, while Garran stood there, shocked, knowing that Gallus or Maximus must have told his father about Edward. It was the only explanation. He also knew that Bose would never betray them, but that piece of information was very crucial. He looked at d'Vant.

"Do you believe Henry knows this?" Garran asked the knight. "That his son is siding with de Montfort?"

D'Vant appeared genuinely stunned by the information. "Nay," he said. "I am sure he would have said something. He must not know at all."

Bose grunted, pushing himself off the wall he had been leaning on. "Then you must ride to London and tell him," he said. "I will mobilize my men and I am certain Grayson will, too, and we will ride for Ingleton to await Henry's arrival. But the king must be made aware that Edward sides with de Montfort."

Tallis nodded firmly. "Without question, my lord," he said. "I will ride at dawn. If you do not mind, I should like to feast tonight here at Wintercroft with your daughter before leaving. I hope that is acceptable."

Bose nodded. "It is," he said. "A few hours will not make a difference."

Garran, having heard enough, excused himself from the room. He was tired of hearing about French mercenaries and a king who would go back on his word to his barons. He went to the chamber door and exited into the corridor outside, shutting the door before realizing there was someone standing at the other door a few feet away down the corridor. When he looked up, he found himself looking into Tiberius' familiar eyes.

"Ty?" he said, cocking his head curiously. "What are you doing here?"

Tiberius opened his mouth but d'Vant started talking and his voice floated out of the slightly open door that Tiberius was standing beside. Tallis was continuing the conversation about Henry and the French mercenaries and, at that moment, Garran knew exactly what Tiberius had been doing. His eyes widened.

"You *heard* all of that?" he asked.

Tiberius, his expression serious, nodded. "I did," he said. "But in my defense, I was looking for your father. I happened across the conversation quite by accident."

"But you heard everything?"

"I did."

Garran gave him an expression suggesting that the situation was quite serious, indeed. Tiberius had heard private information that d'Vant had delivered to Bose and Grayson in what the man assumed was confidence. Now, one of the most important knights in de Montfort's arsenal was privy to the future battle plans of the king. It was a dire situation, indeed.

"What are you going to do?" Garran hissed.

Tiberius appeared surprised by the question. He moved away from the door, making his way towards Garran. "What are *you* going to do?" he turned it around on Garran. "At the very least, you should be telling your father what I have heard."

Garran was greatly torn. Scratching his head, he slumped back against the wall, seemingly despondent. "I... I do not think I can," he said. "Did you hear d'Vant speak of ten thousand French mercenaries?"

"I did."

Garran's expression was wrought with urgency. "Then you must go to Isenhall, now, and tell your brothers," he whispered. "They must know what Henry is doing!"

Tiberius knew that. God help him, he knew that. But there was the small matter of Douglass. "I know," he muttered. "But Douglass... I cannot just leave her."

"If you do not, then Gallus and Maximus will be riding into a slaughter and you know it."

It was a shot straight through Tiberius' heart. He very much wanted to marry Douglass, to take her away and claim her for his own, but he couldn't let his brothers ride to their deaths. Perhaps there were some things more important than him and his love for the lovely Lady Douglass and if she truly cared for him, she would understand. She would wait for him. For now, Garran was correct. He had to tell his brothers what he had heard, regardless of the fact that he had sworn fealty to de Moray. His faith, his true honor, was with his brothers. They had to know.

"You are correct, of course," Tiberius said, inhaling deeply in resolve. "I must go to Isenhall but I must tell Douglass why. I will leave tonight, Garran. Will you help me?"

Before Garran could reply, a voice came from the open door that Tiberius had just been standing beside.

"You are not going anywhere, Tiberius."

Tiberius and Garran turned to see Grayson and Davyss standing there as Bose and Tallis emerged from the first door. Tiberius thought many things at that moment. How he could fight his way out of this or charm his way out of it. Either way, he knew he was in a world of trouble.

"Unfortunately, I am," he told Grayson steadily. "I must return to Isenhall."

Grayson didn't seem angry or threatening, simply weary. He shook his head in a gesture that suggested frustration.

"I would assume you heard most, if not all, of what we were speaking of?" he asked.

Tiberius shrugged. "I heard enough," he said. "I cannot let my brothers ride into a slaughter. You know this."

Grayson shook his head again, suggesting he was weary of the entire situation. "I know," he said. "But I cannot let you tell them what you know. Everything I stand for screams against it. Do you understand that, lad?"

Tiberius didn't pull any punches. He could see where this was going. He turned straight to de Moray. "We saved your life and the lives of your children in Coventry when de Montfort's assassins were looking for you," he said. "You may now pay that debt. Let me go back to Isenhall."

The focus swung to Bose, who met Tiberius' demand with a steady eye. "I do indeed owe you and your brothers," he said, knowing that the situation was far more complex than that. "Let me speak with de Winter and see if we can come to an agreement."

"No agreement," d'Vant said. The congenial knight was now hard and deadly as he gazed at Tiberius. "The man overheard privileged information. He is, therefore, a spy. Spies will be executed."

Both Garran and Davyss put themselves between Tiberius and Tallis in a protective gesture. "Try it, d'Vant," Garran snarled. "You'll get more than you bargained for and I can promise you that you will not leave Wintercroft alive."

The men were armed, all of them, so before blades could be drawn, Bose put himself in the middle of it, holding out his hands to cool young, heated heads.

"You will not fight," he commanded as only Bose de Moray could. "Garran, you and Davyss take Tiberius with you. Do not let him out of your sight. D'Vant and Grayson and I will remain here and discuss this situation. Go now, get out."

Garran didn't hesitate. He took Tiberius by the arm while Davyss got in behind him and, together, the two knights forcibly escorted Tiberius from the corridor. With the men shuffling down the hall and moving down the big, spiral staircase, Bose turned to d'Vant.

"If you ever threaten a de Shera again, I will kill you where you stand," he said quite calmly. "Is that in any way unclear?"

D'Vant didn't flinch. "Aye, my lord."

Bose's jaw ticked as he studied the young knight, so strong and loyal to Henry's cause. His absolute stance would make for a difficult situation. In these complex times, older knights like Bose and Grayson knew that one had to be flexible and that old friends and family loyalties exceeded those of kings and barons. Tallis had not yet learned that. But perhaps it was time he did.

"Get back into the chamber," Bose commanded d'Vant again, pointing to the room they had been meeting in. "Stay there for now. If you come out, I will punish you personally. Do you comprehend?"

"I do, my lord."

"Stay there until I come for you."

Tallis didn't respond other than to go into the chamber and shut the door. When the young knight was gone, Bose turned to Grayson. It was clear they were facing a very difficult decision. Hearts and souls and minds and bloodlines were about to be prioritized, and it was Grayson who spoke first.

"What do you want to do?" he asked Bose softly. "Tell me and we shall do it. But d'Vant might prove to be a problem."

Bose sighed, his clever mind working on a solution to this seemingly terrible problem. "Not if I distract him with something more important," he muttered.

"What?"

"My daughter."

Grayson didn't like the sound of that. "What do you intend to do?"

Bose was sick at the mere thought. "Mayhap a marital contract might distract him from Tiberius," he said, saddened. "Mayhap that is what I must do in order to allow Tiberius to flee back to Isenhall without d'Vant trying to kill him as a spy. If d'Vant thinks he is going to be married to my daughter, then he will be mostly focused on that and Tiberius will fall by the wayside. At least, that is what I am hoping."

Grayson shook his head, sorrowful. "Tiberius will not go if he finds out you intend to pledge Douglass to d'Vant."

Bose knew that. He rubbed his brow and then his eyes, wearily. "Then he will not know."

"How can you do that?"

Bose looked at Grayson, the greatest turmoil on his face that he had ever allowed to show through. He couldn't believe what he was about to say, but in order to save Tiberius from d'Vant, in order to make it so the man would be able to return home, he had to make a choice. He had to compromise his honor. It was killing him because he knew it would kill Douglass, too.

"Lie."

It was a dirty word that hung in the air between them but Grayson knew it was a necessary one. It was something that had to be done in order that Tiberius should be allowed to return to the Isenhall in a complete act of treason. Aye, it was treason. Both Bose and Grayson knew it, but family lines and loyalties were crisscrossed these days like a spider's web. Bose knew that he had to save Tiberius. He was obligated to. And Grayson would not betray the man who was like another son to him. They were both in this so deeply that they couldn't get out.

The lies had to be done.

In silence, Bose entered the room he had so recently banished Tallis to. When he entered, followed closely by de Winter, he found Tallis standing over by the lancet windows that overlooked Wintercroft's crowded bailey. The young knight turned expectantly to the older knights, without a hint of anger or distress on his face. He trusted Bose and he trusted Grayson. It was written all over him. That being the case, Bose thought very carefully about what he was going to say next.

"Now," Bose began. "Obviously, there is a good deal going on at Wintercroft but you should only be focused on returning to Henry with news of Edward's betrayal. Is that clear?"

Tallis nodded, but there was doubt in his expression. "What about Tiberius?"

Bose cocked an eyebrow. "You will let me worry about Tiberius," he said. "I suspect he will find himself in the vault before this day is over, which will more than likely be his permanent home for the weeks and months ahead. As for the accusations of being a spy, he is no more a spy than I am. He is not the sneaky and dishonorable type and I will not have you spreading rumors to that effect. Is that clear?"

"It is, my lord."

"If I hear tale of Tiberius de Shera being a spy, I will come for you personally and you will not like what I have to say."

"Aye, my lord."

Bose critically eyed the young knight a moment before averting his gaze and moving to a chair that was lodged back against the wall. The chair was cushioned with silk pillows and very comfortable. There was also a footstool next to it. Bose lowered his big body onto the chair and pulled forth the stool, plopping his massive boots on it. He was feeling his age this night, stress brought on by passionate young men and their passionate ideas. With a grunt of satisfaction, he sighed.

"Let us move on to another subject, d'Vant," he said. "I permitted you some time alone with my daughter. You will tell me how that went."

Tallis was still lingering on Tiberius de Shera and his need for punishment but he forced himself away, focusing on Douglass instead. It was a much more pleasant subject, anyway. He thought back to their brief conversation earlier in the day.

"It went well enough, my lord," he said. "We were able to converse fairly easily."

"About what?"

Tallis shrugged. "I relayed a story from my childhood," he said. "She told me something of hers. It was pleasant."

"Did she relax somewhat?" Bose asked. "Or was she still unsociable?"

Tallis shook his head. "Mayhap she was at first," he said, trying to be tactful. "But I was able to educe a smile from her, in any case.

She is quite charming when she's not trying to ignore me."

Bose cocked an eyebrow. "Charming enough to marry?"

Tallis nodded. "Without question," he said. Then, he relaxed somewhat, looking at de Moray with a resigned expression. "I am not a fool. I know she is infatuated with de Shera, but I also know she has only known the man a few days. I believe I can quite adequately erase him from her mind given the chance. I would like to be given that chance, my lord. I would make her a fine husband."

Bose pondered the request or, at least, he pretended to. Having Tallis' interest in Douglass was all part of his plan. *A part of his lies.* He pretended to be thoughtful.

"If I say yes, then there is much more to it than simply my permission to marry my daughter," he said. "She will inherit a great deal from her mother. Her uncles are all powerful warlords in their own right. When you marry into the House of de Moray, the House of du Bonne comes with it because her mother is a du Bonne. They are the guardians of Dorset. Are you aware of this?"

Tallis nodded. "As my family *is* Cornwall," he said confidently. "Our marriage will merge two great shires."

Bose signed heavily, mulling the situation over. *Say what you must to keep his mind off Tiberius!* he thought to himself. *Try not to promise anything if you can help it!* He wasn't used to lying but he was used to games of skill. He considered this an utter test of his skills of persuasion.

"Her mother will want to meet you before we enter into any manner of contract," he finally said. "When this business of Erith Castle is finished, you will come to Ravendark Castle and meet her mother. Most men believe I am a fool in that I take my wife's opinion into consideration in matters such as these, but the truth is that you must have Lady de Moray's permission before anything is finalized. Are you willing to come to Ravendark and meet with my wife?"

Tallis nodded his head. "Aye, my lord."

"I will give her final say over the matter."

"I understand, but do I at least have your support?"

"You do."

Lies! That was the biggest lie of all because Tallis did not have his support. Bose realized with horror that Tiberius did. *Tiberius, I am doing this for you. Do not disappoint me, lad!*

"Very well," Bose said, standing up. "Then you will leave Wintercroft after the evening's meal and ride for Henry and you will leave Tiberius de Shera to me. You and I will discuss a time for meeting Lady de Moray when the matter with Erith is finished."

"Do I have your word, my lord?"

"You have my word that we will meet, aye."

Tallis seemed satisfied and Bose was satisfied, too, that he hadn't given the man any more than a promise that they would meet again. It was not a promise of marriage. Bose looked to Grayson before quitting the room.

"Did you have anything more to say to this, Lord de Winter?" he asked.

Grayson shook his head. "I do not," he replied. "You and I can discuss what to do with Tiberius in private."

Bose wriggled his eyebrows. "Something terrible, I am sure."

"A thrashing at the very least."

Bose nodded in agreement although it was all for show. He had no intention of doing anything to Tiberius other than spirit him out of Wintercroft because Tiberius had been correct. Bose owed him. Much as Bose was repaying a life-debt to the king by supporting him during this troubling time, he owed the House of de Shera the same life-debt. It was Gallus, Maximus, and Tiberius who had saved him and his two children from de Montfort's assassins, and Bose was in the habit of repaying his debts. By sending d'Vant along his way and then giving Tiberius a chance to escape for Isenhall, he was doing just that. There was no question that it needed to be done, now settled in his mind. The idea that he was betraying Henry by letting Tiberius leave for Isenhall never entered his thoughts because he was doing what he had to do, for himself and for his family. For his honor.

As the three of them took the wide, spiral staircase down to the ground level of the manse where the great hall was, they began to hear voices. Garran, Tiberius… and then there was Douglass. They most definitely heard Douglass. Tallis picked up his pace because he, too, heard her voice, but by the time they reached the bottom of the steps, it was not the situation they had expected to see. They found Garran and Davyss standing side by side while Douglass stood with Tiberius. In fact, he seemed to be holding on to her.

The next thing anyone realized, Tallis had his mighty broadsword unsheathed and he was bolting in Tiberius' direction.

ONCE THEY LEFT the upstairs corridor, Tiberius, Garran, and Davyss ended up in the great hall of Wintercroft. Once they came down off the stairs, Garran and Davyss herded Tiberius right into the room. Tiberius wandered into the room, frustrated and edgy, as Garran and Davyss stood by the door, watching the man. It was clear that they were all edgy and unsure what to say to one another. As Davyss and Garran watched, Tiberius abruptly unsheathed his sword and turned to them.

"I can see I am going to have to fight my way out of here," he said, his focus riveted to the two knights. "I never thought I would hear myself say those words but I fear it is true."

Neither Garran nor Davyss flinched because they knew if they did, Tiberius would rush them and as tall as he was, and with his incredibly long arm span, he would be most formidable. Garran was an excellent knight and Davyss had already made a name for himself as he fought with the sword of his forefathers, *Lespada*, but neither man wanted to face a Lord of Thunder in combat and they certainly didn't want to fight Tiberius. Davyss sighed heavily.

"Are you truly going to kill me, Ty?" he asked, holding up his hands to show that he had no intention of unsheathing his sword. "I will not lift my blade against you."

"Nor I," Garran said. "Put the sword away. Let my father negotiate your right to leave Wintercroft."

Tiberius shook his head. "That is not going to happen and you know it," he said. "Bose and Grayson must imprison me, don't you see? D'Vant will run back to Henry and tell the king that two of his premier barons have been unfaithful and that will badly mar the trust between the king and those two great men. Grayson was right. My presence here will ruin all he has worked for. Even so, I do not regret coming and I will still marry Douglass. But our marriage will have to wait. My brothers' lives are at stake and I must return to Isenhall."

Garran was deeply sickened by the entire circumstance. "There is a great part of me that hopes d'Vant goes back to the king and tells him that my father is a traitor," he said. "Then my father will have no choice but to fight for de Montfort. But on the other hand, my father is a legendary knight with a great reputation and I do not want to see that damaged. He is a man of honor. I do not want to see him dishonored."

Tiberius didn't lower his sword but it was clear he, too, was affected. "Nor do I," he replied quietly. "Your father is a great man and Uncle Grayson has been my father-figure since the death of my own father. Clearly, this is an emotional situation so I beg you both, please let me go. Tell them that I overwhelmed you and fled. Let me at least give Gallus and Maximus a fighting chance."

"Garran?"

A soft, female voice came from the darkened corridor near the stairwell, directly across from the hall. Garran, Davyss, and Tiberius turned to see Douglass emerging from the corridor. Her lovely face was full of curiosity and concern, and even fear, when she noted that Tiberius was holding a sword. She pointed at the man.

"Why is Tiberius armed?" she asked her brother. "What is happening here?"

Garran frowned. "Where did you come from?"

Douglass pointed back into the darkened corridor. "I was consigned to a solar back there," she said. "But I have grown restless and hungry. What is going on?"

Tiberius spoke before Garran could reply. "Come here, sweetheart," he said, holding out his hand to her. "Please come to me."

Garran grabbed on to his sister. "Don't go to him," he told her. "Not... now. Go back where you came from."

Douglass yanked her arm from her brother. "I will not," she said flatly. "What is wrong? You are frightening me."

Garran tried to grab her again but she managed to stay out of arm's length. "Douglass, *stop*," he commanded. "Do not go to him."

Douglass was already halfway across the hall, looking at her brother as if he had completely lost his mind. "What is the matter with you?" she demanded. Then, she looked to Tiberius, who was a mere few feet away. "Why is your sword drawn? What is happening here?"

Tiberius kept his hand extended to her and she took it. Rather than pull her against him in a possessive gesture, he simply stood there and held her hand, gently.

"It would seem that there are political dealings afoot, my lady," he told her calmly. "I have come into some information that my brothers must be made aware of and your brother and Davyss do not want to let me go. For their cause, it would be stupid to let me walk out of here but for my cause, de Montfort's cause, it could mean the matter of life or death. Life if I am allowed to leave and death if I am not."

Douglass held on to his hand with both of hers, gazing up at him seriously. "Are you planning to fight your way out, then?"

He smiled weakly, looking at his sword just as she was. "I was thinking on it," he admitted. Then, he looked at her. "Come with me, Douglass. Come with me back to Isenhall and we shall be married, just as I told you we would. Will you come?"

Douglass didn't hesitate. "Of course I will," she said. "But you must put your sword away. I will not go with you if you intend to fight my brother or father. There will be no bloodshed. Is that clear?"

Tiberius immediately sheathed his blade. "It is, my lady," he said. "But you must understand that it will be difficult for you and me to simply walk out of here if I do not present a weapon."

Douglass turned to her brother. "Is this true?" she asked him. "Are you preventing Tiberius from leaving to return to his brothers so that he must fight his way free?"

Garran nodded. "He overheard information that must not make it to de Montfort," he said. "Father has asked Davyss and I to hold him here until he decides what is to be done."

Douglass frowned. "What does that mean?" she wanted to know. "Why must you decide what is to be done with Tiberius?"

Garran was losing his patience with his sister, who had now put herself in a precarious situation with a man who could quite easily take her hostage. Garran didn't truly believe Tiberius would do that, but he also knew that Tiberius would do anything to get to his brothers. The situation was growing more tense by the moment.

"Come here, Douglass," Garran said, trying to manipulate her into leaving Tiberius. "I must tell you something in confidence. Will you please come to me?"

Douglass shook her head. "I will not," she said, looking between her brother and Davyss. "There is something terrible happening here and I will not leave. You will not hurt Tiberius if I remain next to him."

Garran sighed faintly. "We do not wish to hurt Tiberius in any case," he told her. "How could you think that?"

Douglass didn't answer. She was still glaring at her brother. After a moment, she turned to look at Tiberius.

"What has happened that you must flee to Isenhall to warn your brothers?" she wanted to know. "Will you tell me what you know?"

Tiberius smiled at her, a gesture that had the ability to completely disarm her. How could anything be wrong in the world with a smile like that?

"The details would not concern you," he said softly. "Suffice it to say that I must go or my brothers will die. As much as I adore you, nay... as much as I love you, I must return to Isenhall. I must fight with my brothers, Douglass. I should never have left them but my heart was with you... I had to make a difficult choice. Now I must make another one. I must return to Isenhall any way I can. Even unto the death."

Douglass reached out, grasping his hand and holding it fast. "I love you, also," she whispered, tears in her eyes. "Oh, Tiberius, of course I do. I told you that you would always be my forever and I meant it. Where you go, I go, and we are going to Isenhall."

He lifted her hand to his lips, kissing it sweetly. For a moment, it was just the two of them in that room; no Garran, no Davyss, no Henry, and no de Montfort. Just them and the love they had declared for one another. Tiberius wanted very badly to take her in his arms but he didn't want their first true embrace and their first kiss to be public. For once, he didn't want to make a spectacle of something as intimate as a kiss. He wanted it to be something just the two of them would witness, something meaningful and special. He wanted to show their newly-found love the respect it deserved.

"Then get behind me," he commanded after a moment. "I am going to try and walk out of here without a fight. Stay close."

Nodding fearfully, Douglass tucked in behind him, her hands on his waist. He was so tall that her head only came to mid-back on him, and she laid her head against him for a moment, feeling his warmth and strength. It was a thrilling moment for her, but it also served to fuel her fear. She was terrified that Tiberius was going to get hurt if he tried to leave without being able to brandish a weapon, as he had promised her he wouldn't do. She didn't want to see her father and brother injured but she didn't want to see Tiberius injured, either. Slowly, Tiberius began to walk towards Davyss and Garran.

"Will you let me pass, Davyss?" Tiberius asked. "I am asking that you let me pass without resistance. As a personal favor to me and to Gallus and Maximus, I ask you. Will you honor me?"

Davyss was preparing to hold his ground, as miserable as he had ever been. "I cannot," he muttered hoarsely. "You know I cannot, Ty. Please do not ask me."

Tiberius didn't slow down. He kept a slow, steady pace, drawing ever-closer to Davyss as Garran drew close to Davyss as well, shoulder to shoulder, in a show of solidarity.

"Don't, Ty," Garran begged softly. "Please don't push this matter. We cannot let you go."

"Is it because of your sister?" Tiberius asked softly. "Is it because she has joined herself to me?"

Garran shook his head. "It is not that, not any longer," he said. "You have convinced me that your feelings for her are true. I know you too well. I know what it is when you are infatuated, but with my sister... it is different. I know it is different and I am no longer resistant. Just do not prove me wrong, ever, or I will kill you. You know that."

Tiberius paused. He was only a few feet away, looking at Garran and knowing the man spoke the truth. All he could do was nod. But more than that, he could see that he was going to have to lay hands upon both of the knights to move them out of the way. His heart was aching in so many ways that it was difficult to isolate just one. All he knew was that this situation, the one they had always feared would separate them from their closest friends, was about to do just that. He was about to hurt his friends and he almost couldn't stand the pain. But he couldn't stand the loss of his brothers even more.

"Please," Tiberius begged, one last time. "Please move aside so that I may save Gallus and Maximus. For my brothers' sakes, will you please move aside?"

There was such sorrow in the room, such grief between them. Garran was stricken with it, as was Davyss. But before they could reply, denying Tiberius yet again and undoubtedly entering into some manner of physical altercation with him, they all heard the sing of metal as a sword was unsheathed. Tiberius turned in the direction of the sound only to see Tallis flying off the staircase and hurling himself in his direction, weapon drawn.

Quite quickly, the situation turned deadly.

PART FOUR
WINDS OF LOYALTY

CHAPTER FIFTEEN

T IBERIUS WAS ABLE to remove his sword in time to ward off
d'Vant's blow, but the pure power behind it sent him reeling.

Douglass screamed in fright, throwing herself out of the way as
Tallis nearly bowled over Tiberius. But the de Shera brother was as
skilled as he was powerful. As he stumbled away from Tallis, he
brought his sword up from the floor in an upwards sweeping
motion, immediately catching d'Vant, who was bearing down on top
of him, in the midsection. Clad in mail with a heavily padded linen
tunic beneath, it wasn't enough to prevent Tiberius' sword from
gashing him quite significantly from the top of his right thigh to the
middle of his chest. As quickly as that, the first blood was spilled.

To his credit, Tallis did nothing more but quickly reverse his
momentum, preventing Tiberius from cutting him up to the neck.
As it was, his mail coat was damaged and blood was already seeping
from the snags in the mail. It had happened so quickly that it was
over and bleeding before he even felt the sting of the wound. But it
didn't stop him. Tallis put up his sword as Tiberius, much taller than
he was, came down on top of him, all sword and elbows and feet.
Tallis found himself kicked in the gut and thrown to the floor.

As Bose, Grayson, Garran, and Davyss watched with horror and
great concern, Tiberius went on the offensive. Tallis was already
down, and already bleeding, but Tiberius didn't hold back. He
kicked the man when he was down, picking up a chair and smashing

it on his head as he tried to rise. Tallis, realizing he was already at a terrible disadvantage, ducked under the feasting table to stop the onslaught. Tiberius' feet were there in big, leather boots so he lashed out his sword, catching Tiberius in the shin and cutting through the leather. Tiberius grunted with pain but the agony fueled him. He upended the feasting table to get at Tallis.

It was an incredible show of strength as the enormous table rocked onto its side. Tallis, however, was already at the other end of the table, leaping to his feet. Tiberius charged after him, his sword glinting wickedly in the weak firelight, and clashing against Tallis' raised weapon. Now, the sword fight began in earnest as the two powerful knights went at each other, thrusting and parrying, each trying to outfight the other. The sounds had awoken the entire manse and even Hugh de Winter, who had been on duty out in the bailey, came rushing in to see what all of the noise was about. He could only stand in the entryway alongside his father and brother, mouth agape at the fight he was witnessing. It was truly something to behold.

Douglass, on the other end of the room, standing on a heavy table that was meant to hold big sides of beef or a side of pork, shrieked and gasped as Tiberius and Tallis battled to the death. It was clear that Tiberius was the more skilled of the two but Tallis was not to be discounted in the least. He was clever and, very quickly, learned to use Tiberius' height against him. Tiberius had a long arm range but he was rather blind down around his knees, so at one point, Tallis lashed out a big boot and caught Tiberius in the kneecap. As the big knight went down to one knee, Tallis tried to decapitate him.

But Tiberius was too fast and too skilled for that maneuver. He ducked low, rolled onto the ground, and came up with a slice that would have cut Tallis in two had the man been any slower at defending himself. On and on the fight went, over tables, breaking chairs, as Bose tried to get Douglass off the table and over with him. She refused, going so far as to throw something at her father when he tried to move towards her. Bose received a small, wooden cup on the forehead for his trouble. He glowered at his daughter.

It wasn't that Douglass was trying to be difficult. It was the fact that if her father got a hold of her, she was afraid he would carry her away and she would never see Tiberius again. She would never see the end of this horrible and bloody fight. She was terrified that Tiberius was going to be killed but, on the other hand, it was quite a sight to watch the man fight. He was skilled, powerful, and clever, and it all seemed to look quite effortless to him. But the fact remained that Tallis was an excellent fighter as well, so the battle going on was truly a nasty one.

It grew worse when Tallis made a thrust at Tiberius and lost his balance. Tiberius grabbed the man by the throat and, with the hilt of his sword, smashed him across the face. Blood spurted but Tallis didn't go down. He managed to get a knee into Tiberius' gut. It turned into a fist fight from that point on even though they were still holding swords. Now, it was turning deeply bloody and brutal as Tiberius and Tallis tried to beat each other into a pulp.

The slugs and kicks grew very heavy. The men shuffled in Douglass' direction as she saw Tallis land a particularly heavy blow on Tiberius' jaw. Tiberius stumbled, brought up an elbow, and planted it in Tallis' neck. Tallis fell back, into the table Douglass was standing on, and she shrieked in fright. But she also saw an opportunity. Hanging on the wall near her right hand was a heavy, iron bar, one used to manipulate large sides of beef. Collecting the bar, she smashed it over the top of Tallis' head. The man fell like a stone, unconscious.

Breathing heavily and splattered with blood, Tiberius kicked Tallis before he realized the man was out cold. When d'Vant didn't fight back or try to rise, Tiberius bent over him, noting that, indeed, the man had been knocked unconscious. Looking rather baffled, he peered up at Douglass.

"You knocked him silly," he said, pointing. "Why did you do that?"

Douglass still had the iron rod in her hand. Tiberius' question had her nearly screaming in frustration. "Are you mad?" she bellowed. "I did it to save your life!"

Tiberius grinned at her, his lips swollen and bleeding and an eye already showing signs of a bruise. "Although I thank you for your gallantry, I did not need saving," he said. "I was preparing to deal the man a death blow."

Douglass rolled her eyes and climbed off the table but she didn't drop the iron rod. She held it with both hands as she faced off against her father and Grayson, who were starting to come into the room to see if d'Vant was even still alive. Douglass made sure to stay well away from the men.

"Papa," she said as Bose bent over d'Vant. "Tiberius must go home to Isenhall and I am going with him. He has already had to fight d'Vant this day but I swear I will fight each and every one of you if I have to. You will not prevent us from leaving. Is that clear?"

Bose straight up and faced his daughter. He could see how edgy and frightened she was, while Tiberius appeared very calm. Still, there was a great deal of tension in the air because of Tiberius' uncertain future within the walls of Wintercroft. The man still knew something he shouldn't, something important to Henry's cause. The fight with d'Vant didn't erase that fact.

"I am willing to let Tiberius flee," Bose said quietly. "I always have been willing. But you are another matter."

Both Tiberius and Douglass looked at Bose in various stages of shock. "Is this true?" Douglass gasped, eyes wide. Her gaze moved back and forth between Tiberius and Bose. "You... you are willing to release him from his oath to you and let him go home?"

Bose moved away from d'Vant as Grayson and Davyss looked the man over to make sure there was not something more seriously wrong with him. As the de Winter men rolled d'Vant onto his back, Bose focused on his daughter.

"His oath was never really mine," he said quietly. "I knew that from the start. He only came with me to be close to you and I knew if I did not permit him to do so, that he would follow me and create more of a problem. It was better to have him with me than to constantly be looking over my shoulder, waiting for him to steal you away."

Tiberius was no longer grinning. "You have my oath, my lord," he said seriously. "That has not changed. But I must go and tell my brothers what I know."

Bose looked at him. "And then what?" he asked. "Will you return to fight with me against your brothers? I think not. Go home, Tiberius. Go home where you belong. Tell Gallus and Maximus what you have heard this day so that they are prepared for it. Your brother told me about Edward's turn against his father so this is the least I can do."

Douglass would not be left out. "But what about me?" she asked. "Papa, I love him. There, I've said it. I love the man and I want to be his wife. I want to go with him to Isenhall. Will you please let me go?"

Bose looked at his daughter, *really* looked at her. There was a great deal rolling through his mind, not the least of which was the unconscious knight on the floor and the potential marriage he had discussed with the man. But that was all for naught. He knew it. He always had.

"I think I lost you the moment you met Tiberius in Coventry," he said pensively. "From that moment on, your focus has been on him. I knew it from the start but I thought it would pass. I thought if you knew all of the terrible things about him that you would push the man aside. But I can see that I was wrong because he is truly not a bad man. Tiberius may have his faults, but we all do. He is a fine, noble knight. I do not suppose I could keep you from him even if I wanted to. See how my attempt to give you a choice of suitors has failed?"

Douglass felt sorry for him. "You did not fail, Papa," she insisted softly. "It was because of you that I met Tiberius. To me, that is a great victory. May I go with him... *please*?"

Bose smiled ironically. *As if I have a choice.* He then looked at Tiberius, who was looking quite beaten at the moment. He looked the man up and down, studying him. "Are you well enough to ride tonight?" he asked.

Tiberius nodded. "I am."

Bose lifted his eyebrows at the finality of that statement. If Tiberius thought he was to be permitted to ride back to Isenhall, he would have done it with two broken legs. He would have crawled if he had to.

"I believe you," Bose said with a twinge of humor at the knight's determination. Then, he hesitated. "If I try to keep Douglass here, she will be miserable. But if I let her go with you, I will be miserable. What shall I do?"

Tiberius took the question seriously. "I swear to you that I will show her only chivalry and kindness on our journey to Isenhall," he said. "When we reach home, I will turn her over to my brothers' wives for safekeeping. I swear to you upon my oath that I shall not molest her in any way until we are properly wed. This I will do because it is not as Grayson said. I did not swear fealty to you because I wanted to bed your daughter. I swore fealty to you because I love her. Let me have her and I swear that you shall not be sorry."

Bose could hear the sincerity in his voice. "I have always known you and the Lords of Thunder to be honorable men," he said quietly. "I do not expect this should be any different. Take her, then, and go swiftly. I suppose she really does belong to you, de Shera. On that first night at Isenhall when you became drunk and said that I should give her to you because you saved her, I suppose you were right all along. There was a magic to the moment you took her from Coventry, something that bonded the two of you. Now, I will give her to you. You have proven to me that you deserve her."

Tiberius looked at Douglass, who was looking at him with tears in her eyes. There was so much joy and relief in his heart that he could hardly think straight. All he knew was that he had been given permission to marry her. He had been given her. Sword still in his hand, he made his way over to her and pulled her into a crushing embrace with only one arm. It was the best, most satisfying thing he could think to do. Finally, the youngest de Shera brother, the rake with a reputation, had earned something only a true man earned – the love of a good woman. He'd never felt more like a man than at this very moment. He had his love now and he would never let her go.

"Go," Bose hissed at them. "Before d'Vant wakes up."

Douglass wiped the tears from her eyes as she turned to her father. Releasing Tiberius, she went to Bose and collapsed in his powerful embrace.

"Thank you, Papa," she whispered. "For everything, thank you."

Bose hugged his eldest daughter tightly, fighting back tears. He knew she would be happy with Tiberius but it was very difficult to let her go. "Your mother and I will come to Isenhall when time permits," he assured her. Then, he pulled back, cupping her lovely face between his two big hands. "Be happy, my sweet. That is the greatest gift you can give me."

The tears were back as Douglass nodded, biting back a sob as she hugged Bose one last time and kissed his cheek. She then moved to

Garran, standing next to their father, and hugged him, too. Embarrassed at the display of affection, Garran hugged his sister tightly before pushing her away.

"Hurry up," he said gruffly, covering for his emotions. "Get out of here. Hurry before d'Vant wakes up and runs after you."

Douglass wiped the tears from her cheeks. "But what will you tell him?"

"That Tiberius escaped and took you with him," Bose said. When Douglass and Tiberius looked at him with some surprise, he simply shrugged. "What would you have me tell him? That a woman knocked him unconscious and I rewarded her with Tiberius because she won the battle? He would never live that down."

Tiberius grinned. "I could live with that."

Bose waved him off, fighting off a grin as he looked at d'Vant. The man was starting to stir. "Hurry now," he waved his hand at Douglass and Tiberius again. "Get out of here."

Douglass flew at her father one last time, kissing him on the cheek and handing him the iron rod that was still in her grasp. As Tiberius and Douglass said their farewells to Grayson and Davyss before fleeing the hall, d'Vant began to lift his head. Bose took the iron rod that Douglass had given him and smacked the man on the head again, sending him out cold. When Grayson and Davyss looked at him in surprise, he simply lifted his big shoulders.

"They need time to get away," he said. "Meanwhile, let us eat and drink. D'Vant will come around shortly and he can join us."

Grayson looked at the young knight sprawled across the floor. "I have a feeling joining us will be the last thing on his mind."

Bose knew that. God's Bones, he knew that. But he tried not to think about it. Letting Douglass go with Tiberius complicated the issue greatly, not the least of which was the fact that his daughter would marry a de Shera. For those who saw the black and white of Henry against Simon, that would be a problem.

Dark times were to come, indeed.

TRAVELING AT NIGHT was never the best option but, in Tiberius and Douglass' case, they had little choice.

Before collecting Storm from the stables at Wintercroft, Tiberius had allowed his future bride a few stolen moments to collect what she could of her possessions, things that would be easy to carry for the rough ride ahead. Douglass collected two gowns, a shift, toiletries and combs, and tossed a heavy cloak over her shoulders. With her possessions wrapped up in a green woolen surcoat, she and Tiberius had fled for the stables.

The big, gray warhorse was happy to see Tiberius, as he was usually quite restless when housed in unfamiliar stables. Tiberius pulled the giddy, nipping horse from his stall and had the groom quickly saddle him, and soon they were riding from Wintercroft's gates. Quickly, very quickly, they moved down the road that took them into thickets of forests where moonbeams pierced the darkness, streaming to the ground like fingers of silver.

The horse had an easy traveling gait, one that was quite comfortable, so Douglass tucked in behind Tiberius and held on tightly as they cantered down the road. Even though there was a bright half-moon in the sky, the landscape surrounding them was still very dark, full of phantoms. Douglass didn't like the darkness so she squeezed her eyes shut, laying her cheek against Tiberius' broad back as they thundered down the road.

The traveling became monotonous very quickly. Once the fear of d'Vant following them died away, the apprehension for their undertaking took hold followed shortly by the tedium of the trip. There were a great many emotions Douglass was feeling as the big, gray horse charged down the road. She wasn't entirely sure what

Tiberius was feeling, but she was most definitely feeling a slurry of emotions. Surprise, fear, realization, and above all, the hope that they make it safely to Isenhall. It was still a few days away and a great deal could happen in a few days.

But Douglass kept her mouth shut, holding tightly to Tiberius as the man directed his horse south. At some point, Douglass must have fallen asleep with the rhythmic rocking of the horse because when next she realized it, she was inhaling the stench of smoke and human habitation. She wrinkled up her nose, lifting it from Tiberius' back as she became aware that she had smelled that stench before when they had traveled on the outskirts of London. They were back in the mix of one of the greatest cities in the world and she looked around, seeing dark and vacant streets.

"Will we stop for the night or do you intend to ride all night?" she asked Tiberius as he slowed the horse to an easy trot.

Tiberius shook his head. He was riding in full armor, a state that was both an invitation and a deterrent to those would see a knight, alone in his travels. Some men would try their hand at defeating a fully armed knight while some would turn tail and run.

"We will stop," he said. "We will go to the Carmelite Monastery in White Friars for the night. They will marry us and give us shelter. After that, I hope you can stand riding hard for Isenhall because that is what I intend to do."

Douglass was rather surprised by his intentions. "We will be married *tonight*?"

He directed the horse off to the right when they came upon a fork in the road. "Indeed," he said. "Did you truly think I would wait any longer than necessary?"

A smile crossed Douglass' lips. "I had not thought on it, to be honest," she said. "I assumed we would at some point very soon, after you have had a chance to deal with the crisis."

"What crisis?"

"The crisis you are going to tell your brothers about, of course."

He shrugged. "That is secondary to our marriage," he said. "But I will say that I am impressed that you have not pressed me to tell you what it is."

She didn't seem distressed about it. "I assume if you want me to know, you will tell me."

He smiled faintly. "That is wise," he said softly. "You are wise, my lady, so very wise. And I am so very fortunate. That is why I must find a priest at this very moment to marry us, so that I may once and for all claim all of that wisdom and beauty for my very own… so that I may claim *you* for my very own."

Douglass thought on the implication of marriage and all of those things it would make her part of and privilege to. Certainly, she would support Tiberius, as his wife, and keep their home if they ever had one of their own. He had a small castle but she had no idea if he'd ever lived there.

"I am pleased that you are being sensible," she said after a moment. "Pleased that I do not have to go through the next several days trying to discourage you from molesting me before marriage, as you promised my father you would not."

Tiberius snorted. "Why do you think we are finding a priest tonight?" he said. "My willpower will only hold out so long. It is best not to tempt fate."

Douglass giggled. "So it *is* all about molesting me," she said. "And I thought you were a chivalrous man."

"I am," he insisted. "Chivalrous enough that I will keep my promise to your father. But in order to do it, I must marry you quickly."

Douglass simply grinned. "He was a young man, once," she said. "I am sure he remembers those days of unbridled passion. He is still very affectionate with my mother, although he tries to keep his actions discreet. The truth is that he cannot. It is obvious in everything about them that they adore one another."

Tiberius smiled when he thought of Bose de Moray being frisky with his wife. "I will confess," he said, "that I intend to follow your father's lead. I intend to be quite affectionate with my lovely wife, forever."

Douglass' cheeks grew warm, even under the moonlight. The thought of Tiberius touching her as only a husband should made her heart race with apprehension and excitement. She could hardly believe that after all of the struggles and denials that they were finally about to be married. It seemed surreal. But thoughts of the marriage also brought about thoughts of children, as she would now bear Tiberius', producing a proud de Shera son who would have a mix of de Moray and de Shera bloodlines. What a mighty son he would be, indeed.

"Tell me," she said softly. "Now that I am to marry you, I must ask, for my own sake. Is it true what my brother said about you?"

"What do you mean?"

"That your behavior towards women has been less than… chivalrous."

Tiberius thought on the question a moment. It was one of those questions that he suspected had no easy answer. "Would it change your mind about me if it were true?"

"Nay," Douglass said without hesitation. "The Tiberius de Shera I have known has always been very kind and polite. Never have you displayed anything lascivious towards me. But I have come to understand that restraint with a woman is not common behavior with you."

Tiberius pondered his answer. He wanted to marry the woman so badly that he could taste it and he didn't want to chase her away with terrible tales of his past exploits. It would crush him. The only time he had ever regretted his lustful ways was when he had met Douglass. Now, he was coming to regret his behavior a great deal. She deserved far better.

"Garran was not wrong," he finally said. "I have paid more attention to women than I should have, but I am young and unattached... or, at least I was. But everything changed the moment I met you, Douglass. You make me want to be a better man."

Douglass smiled with appreciation, at both his sweet words and honest answer. "Do you really have a bastard?"

"I do not honestly know," he said. "I have heard rumor of one but I have never seen proof."

"Then some day we may see a de Shera offspring showing up at our doorstep?"

"It is possible," he replied, cringing inside. "I will apologize in advance for the shame you will suffer. Please know I would never intentionally do anything to embarrass you."

Douglass knew that he was quite regretful. She could hear it in his voice. "It does not affect me because it happened before I met you," she said. "Whatever you did before I met you is your affair, Ty, but what you do after our marriage is my affair, indeed. But I will say this, you will not have to worry about my father and brother if you shame me after our marriage. You will have to worry about me, and I am far more formidable than they could ever hope to be. Do I make myself clear?"

Tiberius started to laugh but he fought it, mostly because he remembered the woman who had nearly brained him with a piece of wood when he was trying to save her from de Montfort's assassins. He knew she was brave and fearless, a woman to be most proud of. He believed her implicitly.

"You do, my lady," he said sincerely. "I seem to remember you swearing upon me great bodily harm once before in the solar at Isenhall should infidelity tarnish our marriage. I believed your threats then as I believe them now, but not as threats. As a promise. I can only swear that I shall not fail you."

"See that you do not," she said firmly, although she was grinning. He couldn't see because she was behind him, yet she could feel his body heaving as he laughed at her. "You would be a very unhappy man."

"I have no doubt."

Douglass' grip on him tightened, a silent gesture indicating that she believed him. She felt more settled now that the mention of Tiberius' past had been brought into the light. Now, there was truth between them. As the darkened surroundings passed by them, she spoke again.

"Speaking of sons, bastard or otherwise," she said, "you and your brothers have great Roman names. Are we expected to name our son after a dead Roman, too?"

Tiberius laughed, happy that the subject of his lustful past has been pushed aside. He was eager to speak on other things. "Absolutely," he said. "Do you not know the story behind the de Shera name?"

"Nay."

"Then I shall tell you," he said, spurring his horse into an easy canter to make better time. "My family descends from a lost Roman legion that was stationed at Chester. Family legend states that we descend from the House of Shericus, an ancient and noble Roman family. When my ancestor came with his legion many centuries ago, the name was shortened to Shera. My father remembers his grandfather speaking of the days before the conquest when our family was still known as Shera. It was the Normans who changed it to de Shera, or 'of Shera', in order to make it more fitting with their own customs and surnames. Having an ancestor who sought to work with the Normans rather than oppose them, he agreed to the change and the House of de Shera was born."

Douglass was listening with interest. "Then it is true," she said, feigning resignation. "All of our sons really *must* be named after dead Romans."

"I am afraid so."

She sighed, pretending to be disappointed about it, but the truth was that she thought it was all rather prestigious. "Do you already have these dead Roman names we must use?"

Tiberius shrugged. "I've not thought much about it, truthfully," he said. "But legend says that the original de Shera was named Magnus Flavius Shericus and I often thought I would like to name a son Magnus unless my brothers have sons before I do."

"Lady de Shera is with child," Douglass pointed out. "Mayhap the earl will name his son Magnus."

Tiberius shook his head. "His son's name is already Bhrodi, after Jeniver's grandfather," he said. "Jeniver is the hereditary princess of Anglesey, you know. She has almost a greater family lineage than we do. She wants her son to bear a Welsh name and Gallus agreed."

"That is gracious of him."

Tiberius tried to turn around and look at her but his helm made that difficult. "I will tell you a secret."

"What?"

"If you wanted to name our son something else, I would agree, too. I would not want you to be unhappy."

Touched, Douglass grinned and laid her head on his back in a sweet gesture. "I like Magnus," she said. "May I name all of our children, then?"

Tiberius was relishing the feel of her against his back, her warmth against his. "That depends," he said. "If they are foolish names, you may not."

"It is all a matter of taste."

"Let us hope we have the same taste."

Douglass laughed softly but fell silent after that, watching the bulk of the city pass to the south of her. The walls of London were tall this night, illuminated by the half-moon in the dark sky above, and they were on a slightly raised angle so that they could see the moon glimmering on the waters of the Thames in the distance. It was a very clear night with few clouds in the sky, as the day had been warm and breezy. Now, the night was cool and gentle. As they crested a hill on the road and the river came into full view, Douglass could see ships along the shore of the river, moored deep. Thoughts of ships brought back thoughts of Tallis and his cog.

"Have you ever sailed anywhere, Ty?" she asked softly.

Tiberius shook his head. "Not really," he said. "I have been to France, of course, and took a ship across the sea to reach her, but I've not been on a long voyage. I did not like being caged up on a ship with miles of sea all around me."

Douglass imagined what a trip on a boat might be like. "I should like to go to Rome someday," she said. "The city has always fascinated me. When I saw Lady de Winter's artwork at Wintercroft, it reminded me of Rome and of the wonderful sights I have heard of."

Tiberius' eyes narrowed. He could see their destination in the distance, nestled along the old, city wall. He could just see the tops of the roofline and he directed the horse down a smaller road, heading for the distant cluster of buildings.

"If it is your wish to visit, then we shall go," he told her, encouraging the horse to go faster. "But we must wait until this madness with Henry has at least settled down. It would do no good to leave and then be summoned home weeks later."

Douglass was forced to agree. She didn't want to be traveling with her husband only to turn back because the wars in England were surging again. She did not have to remind herself that she was marrying one of the greatest warlords of all, someone whom Simon de Montfort depended upon. She knew very well that a knight was married to his vocation more than his wife, although her father had been an exception to that rule. He would have chosen his wife, Lady Summer, many times over any conflicts that had to do with the king. Douglass wondered if she and Tiberius would ever reach that point, where he would easily choose her over any conflict. She wondered if, from a Lord of Thunder, such a thing was even possible.

Lost to her thoughts, the remaining travel until they reached the monastery in the White Friars area of London passed quickly. The next thing she realized, Tiberius was drawing his steed to a halt in front of a square, block-like building that was rather oddly shaped. It had more than four walls, it seemed, and a thatched roof. Tiberius pulled the horse to the side door and secured the animal, knowing that the beast had a bad enough temper that no one would be able to get close to it to steal his belongings. He dismounted and reached up to pull Douglass off as well, setting her carefully to her feet. Holding Douglass with one hand, he pounded on the door.

It took several more knocks before a small window in the door slid open and a pair of eyes appeared.

"Who comes?" a thin voice demanded.

Tiberius didn't hesitate. "I am Tiberius de Shera, Lord Lockhurst," he said. "My brother is the Earl of Coventry. My lady and I wish to be married and I shall pay handsomely for the service. Will you admit us?"

The eyes in the door peered at Douglass, who frowned because the man seemed to be studying her longer than he should have. She didn't like the way he was looking at her. He was making her vastly uncomfortable.

"Stop staring at me as if you have never seen a woman before," she said, disturbed. "Open the door and summon your superior. We wish to be married."

The eyes in the door blinked rapidly and the little door panel slid shut. Tiberius looked at Douglass and shrugged. "I have no idea if they will open the door," he muttered, looking at their surroundings, formulating a back-up plan. "If they do not, then we shall move on until we find a church that will marry us this night."

Douglass held his hand tightly, looking around because he was. "It seems very foreboding here," she said. "Where are we, exactly?"

Tiberius looked east, to the massive wall that encompassed most of the city. "We are on the west side of London," he said. "Westminster is south of us, along the river. That big wall to the east is the ancient wall, one meant to protect the entire city from invaders. Some say the Romans built it. Mayhap my ancestors even built it."

Douglass was looking at the big, dark wall with interest. "I would not be surprised," she said. "The men of the House of de Shera seem to be quite accomplished."

Tiberius was looking at her, digesting her delicate profile as she studied the city wall. "Have I told you recently how fortunate I am?" he asked softly.

Douglass looked up at him, a smile on her face. "You have, but you may tell me again."

"I feel like the most fortunate man in all of England right now," he confessed. "Never did I imagine that you would be with me this night. I thought... I truly thought that I would have to bide my time in order to take you away with me."

Douglass' smile faded and she reached up, gently touching his swollen lip, injured in his fight with d'Vant. "But you wanted to run away tonight," she reminded him. "Did you think we would not be able to?"

He shook his head, an uncertain gesture. "I do not know," he said honestly. "I was making plans, of course, but I had to go through five very fine knights in order to see my plan through. I truly thought I was going to have to fight your father or, at the very least, Garran."

Douglass was watching his expression, sensing his distress.

"Would you have really fought them?"

He sighed faintly. "I would have," he said. "You are worth that and more to me. But I do not believe injuring your father or brother in my attempt to abduct you would have started our relationship off very well. We would always have that shadow over us."

Sensing his depression and perhaps confusion, Douglass leaned against him, wrapping her arms around his tight torso. Tiberius put his arms around her, holding her close and savoring her warmth, when the door next to them suddenly jerked open. Standing in the darkened doorway was a priest in brown robes. The man was smoothing at his thin, brown hair.

"What 'tis thee wish?" he asked.

He had a very strange accent. Tiberius peered at the little man. "We wish to be married," he said. "I will pay for the service."

The little man frowned. "Who are you?"

Tiberius had enough of questions. He wanted to marry Douglass so that even if d'Vant was pursuing them, he couldn't legally take Douglass away. Tiberius didn't want to leave anything to chance but the more time this was taking, the more frustrated he was becoming. Reaching out a big, long arm, he shoved the door back and pushed his way into the church.

"My name is Tiberius de Shera and my brother is the Earl of Coventry," he repeated. "I am a premier knight for Simon de Montfort and unless you want de Montfort, Bigod, and the de Shera brothers down around your ears, I suggest you do as I ask. Bring a priest now to marry the lady and me."

The church was so dark inside that Douglass literally had a hand out in front of her to prevent her from banging into any walls. It smelled very strongly of burnt fat and smoke, odd smells from the Carmelite order of priests who burned such things. She had a good hold on Tiberius, who was following the priest, so she essentially clung to him in the darkness as they made their way to a large, circular-shaped sanctuary.

There was a small bank of pasty-white, tallow candles burning, dripping fat onto the floor, and this room was better lit. Douglass could see much more; the uneven dirt floor, the pillars that held up the ceiling, and the rather ornate ceiling itself. The altar, conversely, was without adornment other than a red, silk covering over the wooden altar itself, and there were acolytes, young boys, scurrying around. As Douglass watched, the priest who had brought them into the room issued commands to the boys and they fled. Once the acolytes vanished, the priest turned to them.

"Now," he said, looking mostly at Douglass. "Who gives permission for this woman to be wed? I do not see her father present."

"My father is dead," Douglass said quickly, realizing they would have a very big problem if her living father did not personally give his consent. "My parents are both dead. I was fostering at Codnor Castle and have pledged my troth to Lord Lockhurst. Will you marry us, please?"

The priest's gaze lingered on her a moment before fixing on Tiberius. "Your intentions are honorable, my lord?"

"Of course they are."

He sounded snappish and Douglass gently squeezed his hand, easing the man's manner. Tiberius realized, very quickly, that a soft touch from Douglass doused any fire of rage or frustration he might be feeling. It was quite surprising, actually. He never realized a woman could have such power over him.

"My intentions are quite honorable," he said, more calmly. "We are traveling to my home and rather than travel in sin, as two unmarried people, we will do the honorable thing and be married. Will you do this for us?"

The priest didn't appear convinced. "So you want to marry the woman only so you will not be traveling in sin?"

"I want to marry the woman because I love her."

That gave the priest pause. "Can this not wait until morning for a proper mass?"

"It must be done now. I am expected home on an urgent matter."

The priest eyed them both, trying to determine if there was any duress going on with the lady. Was she being forced? He didn't get that sense. In fact, they both seemed quite comfortable with one another. The Carmelites, a contemplative order, emphasized prayer and service over all else. There was no vow of poverty as there was with some orders. His focus returned to Tiberius.

"Show me your coin," he said. "You will make a sizable donation for this service in the dead of night, which is most irregular."

Tiberius produced several gold coins and gave them to the priest, who seemed satisfied. The acolytes he had sent away a few moments earlier now returned with a white prayer mantle for the priest, a cup full of wine, and a few other items including sacramental oil. All of these things were very carefully laid upon the altar except for the mantle, which went over the priest's shoulders. After kissing the mantle, the priest pointed to the floor.

"Kneel," he commanded.

Tiberius and Douglass went to their knees, listening earnestly as the priest began to intone the wedding mass. It was done rather quickly, and almost routinely, as if there were no true feelings to it, but they nonetheless paid strict attention to what the priest was saying. *Is this really happening?* Tiberius thought to himself. *Am I truly marrying her?* It seemed unbelievable to him, finally marrying this woman that he'd fought so hard for. True, he'd only known her a short time but it felt as if he'd known her for years. Years of fighting for something he very much wanted. *Can you see me, Honey?* He offered up prayers to his beloved mother, having been dead these past few months. *I wish with all my heart you were here. Douglass is much like you and I know you would love her. I will make you proud, I swear it.*

Thoughts of Honey de Shera faded as the priest offered him the cup of wine to drink from. He took a heavy drink of the tart, cheap wine and passed it to Douglass, who also took a deep drink. She smiled at him after she swallowed it and he handed the cup back to the priest. The man took the cup, made the sign of the cross over them, and intoned the final prayers, sealing the marriage.

It was done. Tiberius could hardly believe it. He helped Douglass to stand and held her hand tightly as the priest signed the book that documented births, deaths, and marriages. Tiberius knew he was expected to sign also and he felt some trepidation at that, given that his name was nearly the only thing he could sign. Anything else ended up just a jumble of words in whatever order his brain told him to put them. The priest eventually handed him the quill and he was able to write his name in the correct order, to his relief.

Now, she truly belonged to him. Tiberius turned to Douglass, smiling at her with all of the joy in his heart. He couldn't help but wrap his arms around her and squeeze her tightly, feeling her heated response against him, listening to her giggles of happiness.

"Let me be the first to address you as Lady Tiberius de Shera," he murmured. Pulling back, he kissed her sweetly, feeling his blood instantly flame. The woman had that effect on him. "Now, we should find a place to rest for a few hours before continuing on. I would assume you are weary."

Douglass put her hands on his face, gazing into his eyes. "I am hungry more than anything," she said, her thumbs stroking his cheeks. "Mayhap we can find a place to eat?"

He kissed her thumbs as they came close to his mouth. "Anything for you, Lady de Shera," he said. "I shall find the finest inn in all of London and feed you a meal fit for a queen."

Douglass laughed softly. "I would settle for bread and cheese and wine at the moment," she said. "Any meal is the finest in all of London as long as you are sharing it with me, my husband."

My husband. Tiberius had never heard such sweet words. He never imagined he would even like them, but he found that he did. He loved them. Kissing her yet again, he led her out of the dark, smelly church and into the moonlit night beyond, in search of a meal fit for newlyweds.

CHAPTER SIXTEEN

T IBERIUS MADE IT as far as he could that night, moving through the dwindling suburbs of London, looking for a decent place to spend the night with his new wife. Contrary to his habits in the past, where he was willing to take a woman any time or any place so long as his sexual urges were satisfied, he wanted his wedding night with Douglass to be as special as he could make it. Already, it meant something to him.

From the White Friars section, he made it up to Holborn Street and headed west, away from the smelly, dark city, traveling through the boroughs with their small homes, all nestled together along the avenue, like berries clinging to a vine. Holborn turned north and he traveled up to the main road of Westway, which took them out of the city.

Soon, the structures thinned out and they continued along a stretch of road, plodding along beneath the full moon, until they came to another group of structures that were situated along a crossroads. There was a two-storied tavern on the northeast corner of the crossroads and the sign that was hung from an iron rod announced The Hummingbird and the Rose.

Tiberius didn't want to travel any more tonight and he hoped that the tavern had an empty room. If not, he wasn't beyond throwing someone out so he could take the bed. Wearily dismounting Storm, he led the beast around the side of the tavern, with

Douglass still on the horse, until he came to a small yard behind the building with an equally small stable. There was a boy just inside the door, sleeping on the straw, and Tiberius kicked the lad's foot to awaken him.

The boy, with straw in his hair, leapt up and rubbed his eyes at the sight of the knight and lady. He approached the big, gray charger to take him but the horse snapped its teeth at him and the boy jumped back, eyes wide. With a smirk, Tiberius muzzled the beast before turning him over to the lad.

"Make sure he has a manger of feed in front of him before you unmuzzle him," he told the boy. "He'll be distracted by the food and less apt to take your arm off. Do you have any cold porridge?"

The lad blinked his eyes in confusion. "Porridge, m'lord?"

Tiberius pointed at the horse. "He loves it," he said. "Give him some porridge and he will consider you his friend."

The lad seemed to think that was a very good idea and, confident his horse would be well tended, Tiberius pulled Douglass off of the saddle and set her on her feet. Collecting his saddlebags, he took his wife by the hand and led her into the tavern by the back door.

The inn was crowded inside, which was odd because it clearly hadn't looked crowded from the outside. Smoke floated in a thin mist along the ceiling and Tiberius had to duck his head to keep from hitting it as they passed through the narrow doorway that connected the kitchens to the common room.

The common room was full of drunk, loud people; several soldiers near the door at the far end with a few wenches between them, the occasional traveling merchant, and other travelers and visitors. The tavern keeper and his employees were very busy keeping everyone full of food and alcohol but when the man spied Tiberius standing at the edge of the room, he quickly made his way towards him through the rabble.

"M'lord," he greeted, wiping his hands on his dirty, stained tunic. "What'll it be?"

Tiberius kept a tight grip on Douglass in this room full of men with little self-control. "A room for my wife and me," he told the man. "The best room in the place."

The tavern keeper lifted his eyebrows. "I only have the master's room available," he said. "It will cost you."

"I will take it."

"Let me see your coin first."

Under normal circumstances, Tiberius would have been grossly insulted by that comment, but with Douglass at his side he found he couldn't become too angry about it. He didn't want to upset her, especially on the night of their wedding. Therefore, he dug into his purse and produced a gold crown, more than enough to pay for a room and meal. The tavern keeper took it gladly.

"Up the stairs and go to the right," he told them. "It is the last door on the right. I will send food up to you."

Tiberius didn't even thank the man, still miffed by a demand to show coin. There was little trust in doing business these days. Grasping Douglass by the hand, he pulled her up the stairs with him, following the tavern keeper's directions until they reached the master's room.

Douglass entered first, observing the room they had paid so handsomely for. It was dark, with a cold fire and no illumination anywhere. As Tiberius came in behind her, carrying their possessions, she stumbled into the very big bed, feeling around for a flint on the table next to it. There was a small taper and, as Tiberius bumped into something in the darkness behind her and grunted in pain, Douglass found the flint and lit the taper.

"Did you hurt yourself?" she asked, holding up the taper to illuminate the chamber.

Tiberius set their possessions down on the bed, rubbing his knee. "Not much," he said. "Usually, I hit my head, not a knee."

Douglass grinned, setting the taper down. "You *are* the tallest man I've ever seen," she said. "Our children will probably be giants."

He gave her a half-grin. "Let us hope the girls are not," he said. "It would be difficult finding them husbands."

She gasped in mock outrage. "My daughters have not yet been born and already you are marrying them off," she said. "Allow me to spend the first few months of their lives with them, at least."

Tiberius snorted at her, humorously, as he moved to the hearth to start the fire. "What about the boys?" he asked. "Do you want to spend the first few months of their lives with them before I send them off to foster?"

Douglass sat on the bed, which was rather comfortable and surprisingly clean, watching as Tiberius lit the kindling in the hearth. "Of course," she said. Her gaze lingered on him as she grew serious. "I look at you and I can still hardly believe we are married. After everything that has happened, it does not seem possible."

Tiberius stacked more peat onto the new blaze, watching it catch fire. "You have me for life, lady," he said, turning to grin at her. "I will tell you about some things now that it is too late for you to change your mind. I snore, I like to eat and drink to excess, and I forget to bathe. I have gone months without bathing until my brothers force me into water so I will not offend their wives."

Douglass bit her lip to keep from grinning. "I will do the same," she said. "Have no fear that I will make sure you bathe once a week whether you want to or not. You will not offend me with your smell, either, or I will kick out of our bed and force you to sleep with the pigs."

He laughed, standing up and brushing his hands off. "So you think to kick me from our bed, do you?" he said thoughtfully, but it was all a ruse. Suddenly, he flopped onto the bed beside her, pulling her down with him. "Think again, Lady de Shera."

Douglass shrieked with surprise as Tiberius pushed her to the mattress and partially covered her with his big body. The man was easily twice her size and she found great comfort and great excitement in that knowledge. But she was also quite virginal, having never even been kissed by a man before she met Tiberius, so his intimate closeness, so suddenly, rattled her. She was having trouble forming a coherent thought as Tiberius began to nibble her tender earlobe.

"Ty?" she gasped. "What… what are you doing?"

Tiberius, vastly experienced in lovemaking, could hear the apprehension in her voice. He was very careful with her, his hand on her face as he gently kissed and suckled her neck and ear.

"What does it look like?" he asked. "I am tasting my wife for the first time. You knew I would, did you not?"

"You did not marry me simply to bed me, did you?"

"Nay," he murmured, his lips on her neck. "I married you because I love you."

Douglass didn't know what to say to that. She was staring up at the ceiling, becoming acquainted with the feel of Tiberius next to her, his lips on her flesh. It *was* rather pleasurable. In fact, it was more than pleasurable. She liked it a great deal. As the fire in the hearth crackled and popped, gaining speed, Tiberius' hands began to move.

As his lips nibbled on the tender skin of her shoulder, his big hand moved up her arm, to her neck and face, and finally to her hair. He pulled all of that glorious golden-red hair over his face, smelling its delicate scent, acquainting himself with the texture. It was one of the most erotic experiences of his life, already finding great pleasure in even the simplest of things. Her hair was glorious and he ran his fingers through it, rubbing it against his stubbled cheeks and thinking that it felt like silk.

"I can hardly believe you actually belong to me," he whispered. "When I first met you, marriage to anyone was the furthest thing from my mind. But with both of my brothers married, I knew there would be a time when I would have to prepare for it. That day you smacked me over the head as I tried to save you was the best day of my life."

Douglass, utterly breathless over his attentions, giggled at the remark. "Will you ever forgive me?"

Tiberius growled suggestively. "I am sure I will," he said. "There is much that you can do to convince me to forgive and forget."

Douglass knew he meant something intimate, sexual even, but beyond that she had no idea what he truly meant or how to respond. She started to giggle, nervously. "I am sure you will tell me what you want from me."

Tiberius growled again, this time more gently. "Better still," he murmured. "Let me show you."

With that, his mouth slanted over hers, hungrily. Off-guard, Douglass simply lay there, having no idea what more she should do. His lips were hot, insistent, and delicious, and before long, she was responding to him, kissing him as he was kissing her. It was easy to mimic and she soon realized that she liked kissing him very much. Her hands came up, timidly, and held his face, her heated flesh against his. It was all Tiberius needed to drive him mad.

Swiftly, he pulled away from her, lifting himself off the bed and pulling off his mail coat. It came off quickly, landing in a heap, and the padded tunic came off next. Once his tunic came off, he pulled Douglass into a sitting position and deftly released the fastens on the back of her dress. Once they were loose enough, he pulled the garment off of her, sliding it off of her body and pulling it free of her legs. As Douglass sat on the bed clad only in her shift and hose, looking rather uncomfortable, Tiberius proceeded to strip off the rest of his clothing.

He kicked his clothes aside, as naked as the day he was born as he leaned over the bed and pulled back the coverlet. He had absolutely no problem with parading around naked but Douglass was immediately embarrassed by it. As he pulled back the coverlet and made sure the fire was stoked, all of this with a semi-arousal, she turned her head away and tried not to look. She'd never seen a naked man in her life so this was all rather sudden and rather shocking.

"Douglass?" Tiberius said. "Are you not going to finish undressing?"

Douglass pushed herself to the end of the bed so she could unfasten the ties on her hose. "I will," she said, uneasy as she pulled off the hose and carefully folded them. "Did... didn't the tavern keeper say he was sending a meal to us?"

Tiberius nodded, coming to realize now that she wouldn't look at him. Her modesty made him grin. "He did," he replied. "The door is unlocked. They can simply let themselves in to leave the food. They will not bother us."

Douglass gasped, looking at him in horror before realizing he was teasing her. He stood next to the bed, silently laughing at her and she quickly turned her head away.

"You are a devil," she muttered.

Still grinning, Tiberius went over to the door to make sure it was bolted. Then, he turned back to his wife, who had already yanked her shift off and was now under the coverlet. It happened that fast. She was laying there, coverlet pulled up to her neck, staring at the ceiling, and he could no longer hold back the laughter.

"Douglass," he said softly, in that sweet purring voice he was so capable of. "Look at me, sweetheart. There is nothing to be ashamed over."

Douglass didn't move. She remained focused on the ceiling. "I know," she said, forcing her bravery. "It is just that I have never seen a... a nude man before."

"And you will not ever see one if you do not turn to look at me," he said. "If you do not look at me, it will severely damage my confidence. Aren't I worth looking at?"

She turned to him, then, although it was slowly. She kept her eyes fixed on his face. "You are handsome and charming and lovely," she said. "I am sure I will come to like seeing you in the nude."

He shrugged and moved to the bed, tossing back the coverlet and climbing onto the mattress beside her. "You had better," he said, snuggling his naked body up against her naked body. "Because I go without clothes every chance I get. I will do it more if I realize it embarrasses you so the sooner you get used to it, the better."

Douglass looked at him, laughing softly. "You really *are* a devil, Ty," she said. "But you are my devil."

Lust such as he had never known filled Tiberius' veins as he looked at her. "Aye," he whispered, cupping her face in one big hand and kissing her cheek gently. "I am your devil and yours alone. You will always be my forever, Douglass. Remember that."

Douglass couldn't even speak. His mouth claimed hers once again and this time, she gave herself over to him completely. His big, warm body covered her, his weight bearing down on her, but she hardly cared. He was with her, on her, the way it was always meant to be. She was eager to know all of it.

Tiberius didn't keep her waiting. As his lips feasted on hers, a big hand closed gently over a breast, feeling the silken texture against his palm. The action startled Douglass but she didn't pull away from him. She even came to like it when he began tugging at her nipple, toying with the hard, little pellet, and when his mouth left hers and began nursing against that nipple, she gasped in both surprise and ecstasy. Every suckle sent bolts of excitement shooting through her body and between her legs, a flame ignited that she'd never known before. It was something that sent her pelvis rocking, thrusting and twisting slowly, seeking a satisfaction that she had never experienced.

Tiberius could feel her squirming and he knew exactly what she needed. As he worked her breasts hungrily, his fingers sought out the red curls between her legs. She was already wet and swollen down there, her body preparing itself for his entry, and he pushed a finger into her tight, wet passage, slowly moving in and out of her, mimicking the thrusting that would soon be taking place. Douglass groaned and opened her legs to him, instinctively, and Tiberius could wait no longer.

Carefully, he positioned his heavy phallus at her threshold, pushing into her slick and waiting body. He was so big that Douglass gasped with the shock of his sensual intrusion, wriggling her hips as she tried to fight him off, tried to ease the sting of possession. But a sting was all it was as he thrust again, breaking her maiden's barrier, claiming this woman for his wife as he'd never claimed another. She was his now, body and soul, and he would die before relinquishing her.

She belonged to him, forever.

Carefully, he began to thrust, his arms going around her as he gathered her up tightly against him, her chest to his, the feel of her soft breasts against his flesh feeding his lust. Beneath him, Douglass groaned and gasped at the new sensations, her legs opening wider for him, begging him to plunge deeper, as her nails dug crescent-shaped wounds into his shoulders. Whether or not she consciously realized it, her body was responding to his, the primal mating ritual taking hold between them.

Tiberius had never experienced anything so sweet in his entire life. His body pounded into hers and she accepted him, all of him, and began moving with him, her pelvis thrusting up against his. It was purely magical, his manhood burying itself in her wet folds as her body tried to coax forth his seed. The de Shera seed that would grow within her, producing a proud de Shera son. She wanted it. She wanted all of it. Her hands moved from his shoulders to his buttocks as if to force him to give up his seed. She squeezed his smooth buttocks and Tiberius surrendered without a fight.

His hot, thick seed exploded into her womb and Douglass felt him shudder as he released. He kept moving within her, however, his hand moving to the junction between her legs, stroking her until she, too, experienced her release. Gasping as wave after wave of pleasure rolled over her, Douglass had little idea what had just happened. All she knew was that Tiberius had worked magic on her.

As the ripples of pleasure died down, Tiberius remained buried in her, kissing her gently, showing her without words of his love for her. A woman he had fought for, and won, was now his wife and come what may, he would never leave her side. He adored her more than words could express and the power of this moment, where the two became one, had overwhelmed him. He'd never been over-whelmed like this before.

The food came later and the servant knocked and knocked but received no answer. Finally, he was forced to go away as Tiberius and Douglass slept deeply in each other's arms, the moment of a love finally achieved having enveloped and sated them both. There was no need for food at the moment. They were content where they were, sleeping with the one who loved them best, each with the other.

For the first time in his life, The Thunder Knight finally knew what it was like to finally be a man.

Isenhall

THE SUN WAS fairly warm this day as Maximus and Gallus stood in the bailey, watching a scene they never thought they'd see. To the side of the gatehouse where the knights and soldiers often trained in the soft, dark earth, Stefan was mock sword fighting Cassius as Scott and Troy stood by, offering instruction and encouragement to Cassius.

The lad was uncertain with the feel of a sword in his hand. He much preferred a smithy's hammer, but Scott and Troy were being very patient with him as Stefan pretended to fight him. *It's all about the weight of the weapon, young de Shera,* Scott would say. *Use the weight to your advantage. Be one with the sword, boy.* Well, Cassius was surely trying to be one with the sword but almost three weeks after his arrival at Isenhall and only a few days after meeting his father, he still wasn't sure he was cut out to be a knight. It all seemed rather complicated to him.

At one point, Stefan clipped Cassius on the arm, drawing blood. Cassius wasn't quick to temper, which was quite different from his father. He had patience that Maximus didn't. That had been evident all morning. He was also a very hard worker. Even though it was clear that he was uncertain about what he was doing, he tried to do everything that Scott and Troy told him. He listened well.

"Already, I see skill in him," Gallus said confidently as he watched Cassius take a rather strong swing at Stefan. "He will make a fine knight."

Maximus, arms crossed as he observed the scene, shrugged. "If it is something he wants to do," he said. "Unfortunately, the boy has not grown up around knights. It is not something he has been privy to his entire life. He is very uncomfortable swinging a sword."

Gallus could see that, too. He grunted in agreement. "He will improve," he said. "Already, he has a very good grip and a good deal of strength. He is most definitely your son."

Maximus watched as Stefan clipped the boy again with the sharp edge of the sword and he could tell that Cassius was trying not to become upset about it. Already, he had several little bloodied nicks on his arms, adding to the humiliation of the session.

"He is much calmer than I am," Maximus finally said. "By now, I would have clobbered Stefan with my fist."

Gallus chuckled. "Stefan is trying to get him to fight back."

Maximus nodded. "I know he is," he said. "But having never used a weapon before, Cassius does not yet know how to. However, maybe if...."

He trailed off and Gallus looked at him curiously. Maximus appeared very thoughtful before emitting a sharp whistle between his teeth. Everyone came to a halt, turning to look at him. Maximus pointed to the men with swords.

"Drop the weapons," he commanded. When Stefan and Cassius immediately set the swords on the ground, Maximus continued. "Cassius, Stefan has cut you quite a bit this morning. I cannot imagine that pleases you."

Cassius was trying not to appear disgruntled, wiping at his bloodied arms. "N-Nay, m'lord."

"He is doing it to help you."

Cassius simply nodded, although he had no idea what Maximus meant. Help him do what? Bleed to death? As he looked at his scratched arms, Maximus continued.

"Cassius," he said. "Since Stefan is no longer holding a sword, what would you do to a man who repeatedly hurt you?"

Cassius wasn't sure what Maximus meant. He looked at Stefan, who was a very large man, but Cassius was also a very large man. He didn't have the muscle structure yet that Stefan did, but pound for pound, they were nearly equal in mass.

"I... I-I would not let him d-do it again," he finally said.

Maximus was driving at something. He was trying to bring out the boy's inner beast, the one who would fight for his very life. So far, Cassius had never had cause to do that. It was time for him to learn.

"How?" Maximus asked.

Cassius was eyeing Stefan, who was gazing back at him quite unemotionally. "I-I would fight him."

"With what?"

"My f-fists."

Maximus took a few steps in Cassius and Stefan's direction. "He's trying to kill you, boy," he suddenly boomed, causing Cassius to jump at the sheer volume of the man's voice. "He's trying to kill you and you just stand there and let him. Kill him before he kills you! *Kill him!*"

He was yelling quite aggressively and Cassius, spurred on by his voice and the sight of all those bloody nicks on his arms, realized he had been made a fool of and he launched himself at Stefan, ramming his head right into the knight's midsection and wrapping his arms around his torso. Before Stefan realized what had hit him, he was lying on his back with the wind knocked out of him as Cassius came down on top of him, fists flying. It was all Stefan could do to get his arms up so he could protect his head.

Gallus grinned as Scott and Troy rushed to break up the fight. Maximus, however, yelled to his knights.

"Nay," he bellowed. "Better to let the boy work through it. Stefan, if you can hear me, you are permitted to fight back!"

Stefan did indeed hear him and soon, Stefan and Cassius were rolling around on the ground, throwing serious punches at each other, while Gallus stood back and laughed at the whole thing. It was attracting quite a crowd as soldiers began to gather, watching the two men go at one another. Scott and Troy simply kept the crowd back, watching Cassius land a fairly serious blow on Stefan's mouth. Maximus, however, couldn't have been prouder of the boy. Finally, the de Shera compulsion was coming forth.

"Max," Gallus said from behind him. "He has that killer instinct you do. All you needed to do was bring it out in him. If I were you, I'd stop him before he hurts Stefan or even himself."

Maximus, smiling, glanced at his brother. "I will," he said. "I just wanted to see if he had the de Shera fighting instinct. I am proud to see that he does. Mayhap it is not with a sword yet, but it is definitely with his fists."

Gallus chuckled as Maximus caught Scott and Troy's attention, directing them to stop the fight. Troy reached in to grasp Cassius but Cassius, infuriated and in fighting mode, threw a punch that sent Troy onto his arse. Shaking the bells off, Troy pushed himself up and tried again while Scott took hold of Stefan and dragged the man out from under Cassius. But in doing so, he bumped into a soldier, who in turn fell into a group of men standing there watching the fight. Someone shoved, another man threw a punch, and soon there was a full-scale brawl going on, now amongst the de Shera soldiers.

Gallus stopped laughing long enough to move towards the roiling mass of fighting men, yelling for them to stand down. Out-of-control fighting was never a good thing. Maximus was already there, tossing men aside, concentrating on stopping the brawl until he realized that Cassius was right in the middle of it, dropping men with a powerful right-handed blow. Maximus couldn't help but chuckle at his son, who was indeed at home in the middle of a fight whether or not he realized it. It was in his blood. He was, indeed, a de Shera.

"Max!"

Maximus could hear Courtly screaming at him and he immediately scrambled away from the mass of men, spying his wife standing on the stairs of the keep. He made his way towards her, seeing from her expression that she was quite distressed. She pointed to the fight as he made his way up the steps.

"What on earth his happening there?" she demanded. "We could see it from the top of the keep!"

Maximus gave her a lazy grin, turning to look at the fight, which was mostly breaking up now with Scott, Troy, Gallus and even Stefan pushing men apart and attempting to calm the situation.

"It all started with Cassius and Stefan engaging in some sword play," he said. "Cassius is very timid and Stefan kept trying to draw the lad out. Finally, I had them drop the swords and provoked Cassius to the point where he attacked Stefan with his fists. I am very proud to say that he took on a much more skilled knight and held his own in a fist fight."

Courtly looked at her husband, an expression of exasperation on her face. "God's Bones," she exclaimed softly, shaking her head. She pointed to Cassius, now standing on the outskirts of the battle zone, watching what was going on. "Look at him. He is a mess!"

Maximus was as puffed up as a prideful peacock. "He is a de Shera."

Courtly couldn't hold her exasperation for long. The inevitable smile crept onto her lips at her husband's prideful boasting. Resigned, she shook her head.

"Aye, he is," she said. "I knew that without having to watch him in a fist fight. Look at him, Max. He's a bloodied mess. Send him to me and I will clean him up."

Maximus shook his head. "He will clean himself up," he said. "Let the boy become a man."

Her eyebrows lifted. "If you get in a fight, I clean *you* up," she said. "Does that make you any less of a man to have your wife help you?"

He reached out, pulling her to him, lifting her off the stairs and nuzzling her cheek. "I am *all* man," he growled in her ear, "as you well know. Now, go back inside. I will come in shortly. It should be close to the nooning meal by now."

Courtly squealed weakly in protest as Maximus nibbled on her sensitive earlobes before setting her to her feet.

"What about Cassius?" she asked, flushed at her husband's attentions. "Will you bring him with you or will you leave him with the knights?"

Maximus' gaze trailed out to Cassius once again, watching as Stefan approached the boy and affectionately slapped him on the side of the head. Cassius grinned and all was right in the world again between him and Stefan, who had quickly grown close in the past few days. Being that they were only a few years apart, Cassius seemed to identify with the silent, young knight, and Stefan didn't mind having Maximus' son tagging along after him. In all, the past few days had seen Cassius quickly assimilate into life at Isenhall. But one thing he hadn't taken swiftly to were the women.

"I am not certain yet," he said, turning to look at Courtly. "He seems so uncomfortable around you and Jeniver. It may be best simply to let him be with Stefan and Scott and Troy right now. A great deal has happened in his young life in the past few weeks. Better to let him settle down first."

Courtly's gaze lingered on the big lad standing in the bailey. "It seems that he has not been around women very much," she said. "It has only been Cassius and his grandfather all of these years. Given time, he will become accustomed to us but not if you keep him away. He must become accustomed to women sooner or later."

Maximus shrugged. "That is true," he said. "But give him a few days still. Then we shall see if he can stand in front of you and not break into a cold sweat."

Courtly grinned, thinking of the first time she had been introduced to Cassius on the evening that Maximus had first met the boy. He'd hardly been able to speak a word to her or to Jeniver, his face flushed and his hands shaking. It was clear that he had been very nervous, so since that night, Maximus had kept the lad with the men because that was where he seemed most comfortable. Still, he would have to become accustomed to his step-mother and aunt at some point.

"Mayhap I shall make him something special to eat," she finally said. "Mayhap I can win his confidence through his stomach. In that respect, he is not much different than Tiberius. Both Tiberius and Cassius seemed to be easily won over with food."

Maximus gave her a half-grin. "That is true," he agreed, his focus lingering on Cassius. "I am anxious for Tiberius to meet him. If anyone can bring Cassius out of his shell, Tiberius can."

The focus shifted from Cassius to Tiberius and Courtly eyed her husband. The subject of Tiberius had come up and that wasn't something they had spoken of much since Gallus and Maximus returned from London. Any mention of Tiberius was quickly diverted. Both Courtly and Jeniver had noticed. But now, Maximus was speaking of his younger brother and Courtly followed his lead.

"Max," she said hesitantly. "The last I saw of Tiberius, he was riding with you and Gallus to escort Sir Bose and Lady Douglass to London and when you returned, it was without him. When the subject of Tiberius has come up, you have told me that he is remaining in London but you will not tell me why. We have hardly spoken of him, which is very unlike you and Gallus. You speak of Tiberius constantly. Has… has something happened to him and you are afraid to tell us?"

Maximus shook his head. "Nothing has happened to him," he said. "He is of good health."

"Then why did he remain in London?" she pressed. "Is it because of Lady Douglass? She told Jeniver and me that she was traveling to London because the king had selected a potential husband for her. Did Tiberius remain in London to vie for her hand also?"

Maximus' good mood fled. The day Gallus had told him about Tiberius swearing fealty to de Moray was the same day that Maximus had received word about his son. It had been a very difficult day, indeed, with thoughts of Cassius and Rose at the forefront, but now that the days had passed and he was coming to know Cassius, thoughts of Tiberius were weighing heavily upon him. He still could hardly believe what Gallus had told him... *Tiberius is sworn to de Moray now because of Lady Douglass.* God, it just didn't seem real. Every day that passed saw him feel worse and worse about it.

But they hadn't told the women yet. It just wasn't something they wanted to discuss, even among themselves. None of the knights knew, either. Maximus was simply hoping that Tiberius' behavior was just a phase he would grow out of, something he would get over and then return to Isenhall to beg forgiveness, but Gallus seemed to think that it wasn't a phase at all. He thought that Tiberius was quite serious. Therefore, no one said a word about it. It was still too fresh and painful and confusing to think on.

"Aye," he said simply. "He is vying for Douglass' hand."

Courtly thought his answer sounded odd. "Then I am happy for him," she said, watching the expression on her husband's face. "He seems to like her a great deal."

Maximus sighed heavily. "Ty likes every woman a great deal," he muttered, but he didn't want to speak of Tiberius any longer so he changed the subject. "Return to the keep and prepare something you believe a growing young lad would like. What will you cook?"

Courtly could see that, once again, he didn't wish to discuss Tiberius, which concerned her a great deal. But Maximus had said that Tiberius was well, so she didn't worry over his health. Still, something was amiss. She could sense it, but she graciously allowed her husband to change the subject. He would speak on his brother when he was ready.

"Let me think," she said thoughtfully. "We have a good deal of cherries left from the summer harvest. I could make cherry pudding."

Maximus frowned. "Cherries are my favorite," he said. "I eat them every day with cream. You will not use all of them."

He sounded like a petulant child and Courtly fought off a grin. "God's Bones, Max," she scolded softly. "We have baskets and baskets of those things. Making Cassius a cherry pudding will not take away from your private store of cherries. You are going to have to learn to share."

Maximus scowled at her but it was without force. Then, he pulled her into his arms again and kissed her. Down below in the bailey, men were resuming their posts, nursing swollen lips and scratches from the impromptu fight. As Courtly kissed her husband one last time and turned for the keep, the sentries on the wall let out a cry of approaching horses.

Gallus, who was still in the bailey making sure the fight was, indeed, finished, was the closest to the gatehouse when the call went up. He called up to the sentries.

"Who is it?"

The sentries were trying to gain a better view. Even though it was a clear day, the riders were still fairly far out. Time passed. No one was completely sure until one man finally waved down to Gallus.

"De Montfort, my lord," he called. "I see the white and blue banners!"

Gallus immediately turned to Maximus, who was coming down off the keep steps, approaching him. "Did you hear?" he said to his brother, loudly, as the man came near. "De Montfort approaches. God's Bones, we are in for a scolding for not having gone to Kenilworth when we were summoned. We did not go to him and, therefore, he has come to us."

Maximus wasn't particularly thrilled to hear any of this. "Damnation," he muttered. "I have not thought of Simon in several days. In fact, I'd forgotten about our summons to Kenilworth."

Gallus ordered the twin portcullises open before answering his brother. "I have not but, frankly, I did not want to deal with the man at this time," he said, sighing. "When we explain to him about Cassius, he will understand. He will want to meet the boy, of course."

Maximus nodded. "And he shall."

"He will also wonder where Tiberius is," Gallus said, a sense of dread in his tone. "Inevitably, he will ask."

Maximus was feeling sickened and saddened all over again. He had successfully dodged the subject of Tiberius whilst speaking with Courtly but now, the subject was back again. He emitted a heavy sigh.

"What will you tell him?" he asked quietly.

Gallus pondered the question seriously. "I have been thinking on that question since leaving Tiberius back in London," he said. "I will be honest when I tell you that I do not wish to tell de Montfort the truth. I feel as if somehow… somehow that will taint Tiberius. I am not sure I can explain it any better than that, but suffice it to say that our baby brother is prone to whims. If Lady Douglass was another whim, Tiberius will soon realize that, as I hope he does, then I do not want de Montfort or any of the other barons to know that Tiberius has momentarily defected to the enemy because of a woman. It makes him look so very foolish."

Maximus thought on that for a moment. "Do *you* think it is a whim?" he asked. "Do you truly believe it is only a passing fancy?"

Gallus looked at him and, for the first time, Maximus saw a flash of pain for Tiberius' absence. "I pray it is," he muttered. "I hope it is but I am not entirely sure. You know I cannot face him in battle."

"Nor I."

"Then we tell de Montfort that Tiberius is in London securing a betrothal and nothing more."

"Agreed," Maximus said. "As it is, de Montfort is going to be angry with us for not answering his summons to Kenilworth. Any news of Tiberius defecting is likely to send the man into madness."

Gallus couldn't disagree. When the riders bearing de Montfort's white and blue standards began to fill the bailey of Isenhall, Gallus and Maximus were there to greet them. It was loud and chaotic, with dust flying from the horses' hooves, as the de Shera soldiers coordinated the traffic.

Eventually, de Montfort himself entered the bailey in the middle of the escort and his focus went directly on the Lords of Thunder. He did not look pleased. But Gallus and Maximus didn't notice, at least not right away. They found themselves looking at the man who had ridden in beside Simon. It was a historic day when the bloodlines of the king entered the fortified walls of Isenhall.

Prince Edward, in the flesh, had arrived.

CHAPTER SEVENTEEN

"**G**ALLUS!" SIMON CALLED as he dismounted his enormous blond, Belgian warmblood. "I am surprised to find you here!"

Gallus took a deep breath to brace himself and made his way over to Simon de Montfort. A big man with dark, graying hair and piercing eyes, de Montfort was the heart of the movement against King Henry. De Montfort had many barons, some more powerful than others, but he had very few people that he permitted close to him. The de Shera brothers were some of the very few. Therefore, de Montfort's relationship with them was more on a personal level than a business level, but even that friendship could be tested. As Gallus approached the man, he wondered if today would be one of those days that would see it fall to the test.

"Why would you be surprised to find us in our own home, my lord?" Gallus said, grasping the man's outstretched hand.

Simon squeezed Gallus' hand, studying the man a moment. There was something in his eyes as he looked at Gallus, something cold and judging. It was typical de Montfort.

"Because I told Edward the only way you would not immediately answer a summons is if you were in some manner of trouble or if you were dead," he replied, the warmth fading from his expression. "You are not dead, so what manner of trouble are you in?"

It was more than a question. It was a command that instructed

Gallus that some manner of trouble must be descending upon the House of de Shera. It was the only excuse Simon would accept for the refusal to answer the summons. Gallus kept his expression impassive but as Maximus walked up behind him to greet Simon, Gallus spoke softly.

"We have received some news about a relation of Max's," he said quietly. "It has kept us at Isenhall. Will you come inside so that we may speak of it?"

Simon's expression went from suspicion to concern. "A relation of Max's?" he repeated. "What does that mean?"

Maximus was catching up on the conversation and immediately realized what his brother was speaking of. Evidently, Simon had demanded the reasons behind ignoring the summons sooner than they had expected. It was clear that explanations were immediately in order or they would find themselves in a good deal of trouble very quickly.

"Come inside, my lord," Maximus said softly. "I will tell you."

Simon put his hand on Maximus' arm. "Is it serious, Max?"

Maximus shook his head. "I will say that it has changed my life," he said honestly, for the introduction of Cassius certainly had. "I am sorry we have not sent word to you yet but this… this situation has taken all of our time and focus."

By now, Simon was very concerned and very serious, but he caught sight of movement out of the corner of his eye and noted that Prince Edward was rounding the horses and heading in his direction. He held out a hand to indicate the prince.

"Let us make all introductions first and then we shall retreat into the keep," he said, lifting his voice when Edward came near. "Your Grace, this is Gallus de Shera, Earl of Coventry, and his brother, Maximus de Shera, Baron Allesley. My lords, meet His Grace, Edward, the next king of England."

Both Gallus and Maximus had spent a good deal of time with de

Montfort in his struggles against the king and they had, on many occasions, seen Edward. They had never been formally introduced to him, however, so this was a first. It was an awkward moment but they tried to overlook that, instead, focusing on Edward. He was a tall man, thin but powerfully built, and his blond hair had a reddish tint to it. He wasn't particularly handsome in feature, especially with one eye that drooped, but his dark eyes were intense. There was fire behind them. Gallus remembered once that he had heard the man described as a "leopard". He could see, looking at him at close range, where that might be a reasonable description. There was something about him, even at his young age, that was intimidating.

"Your Grace," Gallus greeted him. "Welcome to Isenhall."

Edward's piercing gaze lingered on Gallus a moment before turning to look at the fortress around him. "It is rather small," he said. "I have heard tale of Isenhall and had built it up so much in my mind that I expected golden walls and great pillars."

Gallus' eyes twinkled. "And I had built you up so much in my mind that I expected fire from your eyes and doom from your lips," he said. "Although that still may happen. The day is young."

Edward looked at him, suspecting an insult, but he ended up breaking down in a grin. "It is," he said. "Watch, now, I still may shoot fire from my eyes and burn you to cinder simply to amuse myself."

Gallus chuckled, glancing at Maximus, who was not grinning in the least. Maximus had never had any love for Edward or the man's reputation so Gallus put himself between Edward and Maximus to avoid any immediately conflict, pointing to the keep.

"Let us go inside and speak," he said. "Allow us to show you Isenhall's hospitality."

Edward and Simon moved for the keep with Gallus as Maximus moved a few feet behind them, and Edward began to look around as they mounted the steps to the keep.

"I seem to recall that there are three de Shera brothers," he said. "Where is the third brother?"

"In London, Your Grace," Maximus said before Gallus could speak. "He has business there."

Simon turned to look at him curiously. "Oh?" he asked. "What business?"

"Tiberius hopes to secure a betrothal," Gallus said, hoping he could cleave this line of conversation quickly with a simple explanation. "My youngest brother has decided he no longer wishes to remain unmarried now that Max and I have taken wives. He should be joining us very soon, so not to worry."

Simon nodded although Edward didn't care at all. Betrothals were not his concern. Still, Simon wanted more information.

"Tiberius? Married?" he snorted. "I never thought I would live to see the day. I hope he is not marrying into a good family. I would hate to explain away his behavior when he shames the woman by being unfaithful. I do not want to lose an ally because of him."

Gallus lifted his eyebrows, a helpless gesture. "If he does, then I suppose I will be the one doing the explaining," he said. They were just coming off the stairs and the entry door loomed ahead. "Please come inside, now. We will have refreshments brought out. I am sure you are weary from your ride."

Maximus entered the building first with Simon behind him. Gallus and Edward brought up the rear and Gallus graciously allowed the prince to pass into the keep before him. As Edward entered, Gallus turned to the bailey and spotted Scott. He caught the man's attention with a sharp whistled and indicated for the man and his brother to join them. With Scott and Troy moving towards the keep as a second set of ears to the meeting with Edward, and leaving Stefan now in charge of the bailey, Gallus followed Edward inside.

It was cool and dark inside as the men moved into the small, vaulted-ceilinged solar just off the entry. It was their most common gathering place, the place where they conducted their most important business or perhaps shared a family meal. Those old walls had seen much over the years and now they were about to see a prince.

Maximus had already sent a servant running for Jeniver and Courtly so as the servant went off, the men began to settle around the table and fine wine, imported from Spain, was brought to the table. It was sweet and dark and red, and Edward smacked his lips with satisfaction at the first pleasurable taste.

"Excellent wine," he commented. "I would expect no less from the House of de Shera."

Gallus dipped his head in thanks. The truth was that he was on-guard with the prince, both he and Maximus were. For years, Edward was the right hand of Henry and now, he was here, pledging his loyalty to de Montfort. Both Gallus and Maximus knew it was because he wanted something from Simon and they were equally sure that Simon knew that as well. The man was no fool. Therefore, it was with absolutely no trust that they sat down with the prince to discuss whatever it was Simon was here to discuss. The mood of the room was one of caution and doubt.

Simon wasn't oblivious to that. He took a seat next to Edward as Gallus and Maximus sat across the table from them both. The lines, invisibly, were drawn – it was Simon and Edward facing off against Gallus and Maximus. When Scott and Troy entered the chamber, Simon indicated the twin brothers to Edward simply to divert the sense of suspicion that was filling the room. Already, the meeting was unpleasant and he didn't want things to grow worse.

"Sons of the mighty William de Wolfe," de Montfort said to Edward. "The blond beast is Scott and his dark counterpart is Troy. They have their father's skill and cunning. I have tried many times to convince them to swear fealty to me but, alas, they are attached to the de Shera brothers. There is no accounting for their taste."

It was meant as a joke. Gallus smiled weakly as he indicated for Scott and Troy to sit, which they did on the opposite side of Maximus. Now, it was four men against two. If Edward sensed that, which he surely must have, he didn't acknowledge it. He was regarding the big de Wolfe brothers.

"William de Wolfe," the prince said pensively. "I was raised on stories of the man's valor. He and my father were quite close, years ago, but things have since changed. It is unfortunate."

Gallus wasn't sure if that was a statement directed at Scott or Troy, so he spoke for them. "Men change, Your Grace," he said politely, his gaze fixed steadily on Edward. "Loyalties change, of which you are evidently living proof."

The tension and suspicion was now acknowledged. Edward nodded faintly, looking across the table at Gallus de Shera and knowing the man was formidable. *The Thunder Lord*, they called him. Aye, he knew of the man and his brothers. Everyone in England did. The man was known to bring down the thunder with him in a battle, unleashing hell, and Edward knew this personally because he had attended battles where the de Shera presence had been heavily felt. At this moment, he was having difficulty seeing the man as an ally and he knew Gallus was having the same issue. It was obvious in everything about him. More than that, the very big and very mean Maximus de Shera was seated next to his brother, glaring, even if he didn't realize he was doing it. Edward braced himself for what was to come.

"Loyalty is a complex issue," he finally said. "Loyalty can be a hindrance or it can be an asset."

"Depending on how it suits one's purpose," Gallus supplied. "What is *your* purpose, Your Grace? I am interested to know."

Simon cleared his throat softly. "Gallus," he admonished. "He has declared allegiance to me. That is all you need know for now."

Gallus turned to de Montfort. "Then why did you bring him here if I am not allowed to question him?" he asked. "As with all of your allies, if we are to support the prince as we support you, then I would know why we are doing it. That is only fair."

Simon didn't like Gallus' attitude because, in a sense, the man was questioning him as well. He opened his mouth to reply but Edward cut him off.

"It is all right," he said, holding up a hand to Simon. His eyes, however, never left Gallus' face. "My reasons are many fold, de Shera. My father has all but handed over England to his Savoyard relatives. The English barons are resistant to that and the resistance grows. I fear that when it is time for me to assume my father's place, England will be a province of France. That is one of the reasons."

Gallus wasn't convinced. "What else?" he asked. "You have wars raging in France yourself. I have heard you are running out of manpower to supply them. Have you come to de Montfort seeking some of his allies to fight your wars for you?"

Simon was becoming increasingly upset over Gallus' blunt questioning but Edward didn't seem to mind. "It is possible," he said. "That has not come up in conversation yet. But I also bring a good deal to de Montfort's cause."

"Like what?"

"Manpower."

Gallus cocked his head, confused. "How much manpower?" he asked. "Most of your assets are in France."

Edward shook his head. "I bring men and material with me," he replied. "I have relations that are eager to support de Montfort against my father."

Now Gallus looked at Maximus, his bewilderment growing, before returning his attention to Edward. "What relations?"

"Lusignan support."

Gallus' jaw dropped. "Lusignan?" he repeated. "You bring your

French relatives to fight for de Montfort when it is the French faction we are trying to remove from England? That is utter madness."

Simon had to speak. He could no longer remain silent. "Gallus, the Lusignans hate Henry's Savoyard contingent deeply," he said. "Lest you forget that the Savoyards are deeply entrenched in Henry's court. They have all but taken it over."

Gallus was growing more outraged by the moment. "I know that all too well," he said, his gaze moving back and forth between Edward and Simon. "But the Lusignans are the queen's relatives and that is most certainly not an element we need or want in England. This will only make matters worse if the de Montfort cause takes on French support. Simon, you will have your barons leaving you in droves."

Simon's jaw ticked faintly. "Including you?"

Gallus backed off a bit, but not enough. He had always been a truthful man. "Including me," he said quietly. "Unless you give me a reason as to why taking on Lusignan support is a good idea, I will leave and I will take the de Shera allies with me."

The threat hung heavily in the air, a brittle point of contention that was simply waiting to be shattered with the anger that was sure to follow. But no anger came as Edward spoke softly.

"You have the queen's support as well," he said. "My mother wants my father's faction out of England as well. Eleanor gives her full support over to me and over to Simon."

Gallus went from outraged to stunned. His mouth actually popped open. "The *queen* supports a rebellion against her husband?"

"She does indeed."

That fact would change the tides of the war. Gallus looked at Maximus, who seemed equally stunned. A glance to Scott and Troy showed their surprised reaction as well. As Gallus gathered his wits to form a reply, they were distracted with Jeniver and Courtly entering the room.

Beautiful women in beautiful clothing filled the solar with their light and grace, pushing aside the tension that had been so heavy only seconds before. Happy to have the distraction, Gallus stood up and held his hand out to his wife as Maximus rose to collect his.

"Your Grace," Gallus said to Edward. "Please meet my wife, the Lady Jeniver ferch Gaerwen de Shera. Jeniver is the hereditary princess of Anglesey. Jeni, we are honored to welcome Prince Edward to Isenhall."

Edward rose to his feet. "Lady de Shera," he greeted. "It is an honor. Your family is an old and prestigious one."

Jeniver smiled thinly at the man who was a great enemy of all Welsh people. "Your Grace," she greeted evenly, although there was instant hatred in her heart. "Welcome to Isenhall."

Edward bowed politely, sensing something cold from the woman. But he didn't much care, to be truthful. Women were inferior and he gave them little regard, even hereditary princesses. He looked to Maximus and the lovely blond woman on the big knight's arm.

"My wife, Lady Courtly de Shera," Maximus introduced her.

Edward nodded in acknowledgement. "Lady de Shera."

Quickly, Edward reclaimed his seat and his wine chalice, no longer interested in the wives of the de Shera brothers, as Simon rose and made his way around the table to Jeniver, who was heavily pregnant. He smiled at the woman.

"Lady de Shera," he said, indicating her big belly. "When is Gallus' son to be born and how long will it be before I can count on his sword?"

It was meant as a joke, to lighten the mood, and Jeniver politely smiled. "Give him at least a year or two, my lord," she said. "At least until he can walk."

Simon grunted. "If he is a de Shera, then he will be born with a sword already in his hand."

Jeniver rubbed her belly. "I thought I felt such a thing," she said, teasing. "Rather poking me, but I could not be sure."

Simon laughed politely, turning his attention to Courtly. "And you, Lady de Shera?" he asked. "When can I expect a son from you?"

Courtly appeared thoughtful. "In April, my lord," she said. "At least, I believe so. I am sure it will be a boy."

Standing next to her, Maximus' eyes widened. "What is this?" he demanded. "What did you just….?"

Courtly turned to him, grinning. "I was trying to find the right moment to tell you," she said, making a face as if she had just said something quite shocking. "Lord de Montfort asked and… well, it just came out. I am sorry I did not tell you in private."

Maximus just stared at her as Gallus and Simon started laughing. "It just came *out*?" Maximus repeated, stunned. "How can such a thing just come out?"

Courtly could see that he was torn between outrage and glee. "I just told you… he asked."

That didn't help Maximus' sense of shock. "We… we are to have a son?"

"Hopefully."

"You are certain?"

"I am."

Maximus didn't know what else to say or do. All he could think to do was wrap his arms around his wife, which he did, while Gallus clapped him on the back and Simon laughed with delight at Maximus' shock. It wasn't often that the great Thunder Warrior was rattled, but he was rattled now. Simon clapped his hands together.

"We must celebrate this joyful news," he said, moving over to the pitcher of fine wine and pouring more for himself and Edward. "I congratulate Baron and Lady Allesley for the coming addition to their family. It is a happy event!"

Simon and Edward drank as Gallus hugged Maximus, and then Courtly, and Jeniver hugged them both as well. It was truly wonderful news although, in truth, Jeniver already knew, as Courtly had confided in her about the pregnancy days earlier. It would seem that Courtly's only symptom had been missed menses and she was eating like a horse, feeling fine and energetic in contrast to Jeniver's very delicate pregnancy.

Therefore, there was truly no way Maximus could have known any differently about his wife's condition unless she told him, and now she finally had. Maximus had never been happier about anything in his life but the mention of a baby brought about thoughts of Cassius. *Another son.* As Maximus reluctantly sent Courtly and Jeniver out of the solar so they could continue with their meeting, he brought up the subject of the reason behind their delay in answering de Montfort's summons.

"So now you know my good news when I do," Maximus quipped softly. "Truly, she could have picked a better time."

Gallus laughed at him. "It does not matter in the grand scheme of things," he said. "I am wildly happy for you, brother. A new generation of de Sheras are to be born."

"Indeed," Maximus said, still rather stunned by the news. As he reclaimed his seat, he looked to Simon, who was halfway through another cup of fine wine. "In fact, a new generation of de Sheras is the reason we were delayed in answering your summons, my lord. As Gallus told you, our delay had to do with a relative of mine. A son, in fact. It would seem that I fathered a child fifteen years ago and he has only just come to Isenhall to claim his de Shera birthright."

Simon's eyebrows lifted in surprise. "*You* fathered a bastard?" he repeated, astonished. "I can hardly believe my ears."

Maximus nodded. "It is true," he said. "Years ago, when I fostered at Kenilworth, I fell in love with the daughter of a smithy. When my father found out, he sent the girl and her father away, but she was pregnant with my son when she left. I did not know this, of course, but she has since died and my son has come to Isenhall."

Simon was listening with great seriousness. "I do seem to recall something like that," he said. "Antoninus de Shera was quite upset about the affair, as I recall. He had me send away one of the best smithies I have ever had. A big man who stammered, as I recall."

Maximus nodded. "The same man," he said. "He and my son are now living at Isenhall."

Simon absorbed the news. "And that is why you did not immediately answer my summons? Because of your bastard?"

Maximus didn't like Cassius being referred to in such a way. "His name is Cassius," he said quietly. "I would appreciate it if you addressed him as such. Being called a bastard is so… cold. He is a de Shera to the bone and I embrace him completely."

Simon was rather amused at Maximus' defensive stance. "And your wife?" he asked. "Does she embrace him completely?"

"She does."

Simon held up his cup to Maximus. "Then I congratulate you," he said. "I would like to meet this lad."

"You will."

Simon drank from his cup and poured himself more. As Gallus and Maximus continued to speak on the coming babies, Edward sat silently and observed. He seemed to be taking it all in, digesting it, studying the men who were once his enemy. Perhaps they still were. As he poured himself a third cup of wine and prepared to re-enter the brittle subject of his support, the queen's support, and the Lusignan contingent now behind de Montfort's rebellion, Stefan sudden appeared in the solar entry.

"My lord," he said to Gallus, sounding rather breathless. "We have sighted a lone rider approaching Isenhall."

Gallus' brow furrowed. "A lone rider?" he repeated. "Why is that of concern?"

A hint of a smile flickered on Stefan's bruised lips. "It is Tiberius, my lord," he said. "I recognize his big, gray stallion. I thought you would want to know that Tiberius is coming home."

Tiberius is coming home.

Gallus and Maximus were up and running for the keep entry before anyone could draw another breath.

TIBERIUS COULD SEE the great portcullises of Isenhall lifting, the chains creaking and the smell of scorched hemp in the air from the heavy ropes that also secured it. He knew the sentries recognized him because Storm was so distinctive. In certain light, he appeared silver, and with his black mane and tail, the horse was quite recognizable. He was not hard to spot, even at a distance.

The truth was that the sight of Isenhall caused a lump in Tiberius' throat. *Home*, he thought. *I have come home.* Truthfully, he wasn't sure when he would ever see his beloved Isenhall again after swearing fealty to de Moray. It was possible that it was something he would never see again except in the wrong end of a battle, so this moment was particularly sweet for him. Four days after leaving Wintercroft, he and Douglass had finally arrived, and Tiberius was both relieved and thankful. He thanked God that he had made it.

But he began to grow concerned when he passed through the gatehouse to the cheers of the de Shera soldiers and saw a collection of de Montfort horses and men inside the small bailey. It was quite crowded, in fact. He had to shove another horse out of the way so he could actually enter the ward.

"God's Bones," Douglass said as Tiberius dismounted and held up his hands to help her off the horse. "Who is here? Look at all of these horses."

Tiberius glanced over at the escort bearing the blue and white of de Montfort. "Simon de Montfort is here," he said with some trepidation in his tone. "Undoubtedly to berate Gallus for not obeying his summons."

Douglass slid down into her husband's arms and even when she was on her feet, she remained pressed against him, uncertain in the crowded conditions. "What summons?" she asked.

Tiberius kissed her on the forehead and took her hand, smacking a big horse's arse to move it out of his way as he moved through the crowd towards the keep.

"The summons de Montfort sent us before we escorted you and your father to London," he replied. "We were supposed to go to Kenilworth but instead I convinced my brothers to ride escort for de Moray. If de Montfort is here to chastise them, then I must take the full blame. They did it because of me."

Douglass held on to Tiberius' hand tightly as he made his way through the sea of men and animals towards the keep. She was forced to admit that the thought of Tiberius in trouble with de Montfort frightened her. Anything that was a threat to her husband's welfare frightened her.

The past four days, traveling from Wintercroft to Isenhall, had seen the two of them bond in ways she never knew was possible. The days of riding had been hard and fast, with little time for rest or conversation, but at night he always made sure she had a comfortable bed to rest in. The nights had become their time together, to talk of all things serious or trivial, and to discover the intimacies of being a husband and wife. Tiberius wasn't shy about letting his naïve wife know what pleased him and she was coming to discover what pleased her as well. She'd never felt so close to anyone in her life and her love for him knew no bounds. Therefore, the thought of him in trouble with de Montfort was terrifying.

"What will de Montfort do?" she asked, apprehension in her voice. "Will he punish you?"

Tiberius could hear her fear. "Nay, sweetheart," he assured her. "He will yell and he will threaten, but he will not punish. He never has before."

Douglass felt a little better with his reassurance but she was still anxious. As they approached the steps of the keep, the door opened and men were flying out at them. It took Douglass a moment to realize it was Gallus and Maximus.

"Ty!" Gallus exclaimed, throwing his arms around his youngest brother. "You have returned!"

Tiberius grunted when Gallus hugged him too tightly. "I have," he said as Maximus grabbed his head and kissed him on each cheek. "Great Bleeding Christ! You act as if I have come back from the dead."

"You nearly have," Gallus said, immediately seeing Douglass at Tiberius' side. He wasn't quite sure how to react so he decided to be blunt in his questions. No need for tact at that moment. "Can I expect de Moray to lay siege to Isenhall now?"

Tiberius started to laugh. "Nay, brother," he said assuredly. "She is mine, legally and morally. De Moray gave her to me but it was not an easy task. I will tell you about it sometime, but for now, you will tell me what de Montfort is doing here?"

Gallus sighed heavily, with great relief. "In a minute," he said, pointing at Douglass. "Is she my sister now?"

"She is."

Gallus went to the woman and put his arms around her. "Thank God," he said, hugging her. "I cannot tell you how glad I am to hear that."

Douglass grinned as she accepted Gallus' somewhat enthusiastic hug. "It was most definitely a battle," she said as Gallus let her go and she accepted Maximus' kiss on her cheek. "Tallis d'Vant and your brother had quite a battle. I was there. I saw the whole thing."

Gallus and Maximus looked at Tiberius, greatly concerned and greatly interested. "Is that so?" Gallus wanted to know. "Can I now expect all of Cornwall to lay siege to Isenhall because you defeated one of her sons?"

Tiberius chuckled. "Not at this time," he said. "I will tell you all about it, but first let me go inside and explain everything to de Montfort. I am sure he will want to know why I pledged my fealty to de Moray."

Maximus put out a hand to stop him as he started to mount the steps. "He does not know," Maximus said quietly. "We did not tell him. We did not tell anyone, in fact. No one knows. For all they are aware, everything is as it should be and you have simply returned home with a new wife. Leave it at that."

Tiberius' brow furrowed. "You did not tell anyone that I swore allegiance to de Moray?" he asked, both perplexed and oddly relieved. "Why not?"

Gallus answered. "I could not bring myself to do it," he said honestly. "Ty, we are the de Shera brothers, the Lords of Thunder. It is always the three of us and the loss of one diminishes the other two greatly. I suppose... I suppose I could not accept that you were no longer with me. I could not bring myself to face it."

Tiberius put a hand on Gallus' shoulder. "I will always be with you," he said softly, warmly. "I suppose I could not face being away from you, either. You are where my heart and soul lies. In fact, that is why I have returned. I had to fight d'Vant and nearly the entire de Moray contingent to get here, but I am here. I have come across some information that you must know. I am glad de Montfort is at Isenhall for he can hear it as well."

Gallus and Maximus were deeply concerned. "God's Bones," Maximus exclaimed. "What has happened?"

Douglass had been listening to the brothers speak and the way Tiberius had glossed over the real struggles he had faced to make it back to Isenhall. As arrogant as he was, she could see that, as a warrior, he was quite humble when it came to the true scope of things he had faced. She admired him a great deal for his sense of modesty in that respect.

"He would not tell me what it was," she said, watching the men look at her. "He kept it to himself, for my safety, I am sure, but I will say this. Tiberius has fought very hard to return home to Isenhall to tell you what he knows. He is evidently too modest to tell you the struggles he went through, but they were great. I know, for I saw everything. He is noble and true, and he is deeply devoted to you both. Before my father permitted us to wed, he was going to return to Isenhall without me in the hopes that whenever these troubles were over, he could return to claim me. He only thought of you two before all else and I am very proud of him for it. Understand that he risked his life to return to you."

Tiberius appeared rather embarrassed while Gallus and Maximus looked at their brother with a mixture of awe and concern. "Then I am anxious to hear it, Ty," Gallus said, putting his hand on his brother's cheek. "Let us go inside and tell de Montfort."

Tiberius nodded, escorting his wife up the stairs as they headed for the keep entry. "He must know most of all," Tiberius said. "It involves one of his holdings."

The dark, cool innards of Isenhall's big keep swallowed Douglass up first and squeals of joy could be heard as Jeniver and Courtly, having seen the arrival from their rooms at the top of the keep, welcomed yet another de Shera wife into the fold. As the woman chatted and hugged happily, Maximus put his big body in the doorway and prevented his brothers from entering. He focused intently on Tiberius.

"Now that your wife is not within earshot, what in the hell has happened?" he demanded, his voice low. "Tell us quickly. What is so important that you had to fight and struggle so that you could reach us?"

Tiberius didn't hesitate. "Henry has ten thousand French mercenaries to support him," he said quietly. "I overheard d'Vant tell de Moray and de Winter that Henry no longer plans to fulfill the provisions he promised to uphold back in May when the councils met in London. He wants to take control of his country and he plans to start by confiscating Erith Castle in Cumbria. He wants to use the castle as his base while he secures the north. His orders to de Moray and de Winter were to rally their troops and move north to the town of Ingleton, whereupon the rest of Henry's allies would amass and move on Erith. Had you not known this and were called to help defend Erith against attack because it is de Montfort's holding, you could have walked into a slaughter. This I could not have allowed. I nearly killed d'Vant so that I could come home and tell you."

Maximus and Gallus had the same look Tiberius had when he first heard the news; sickened and tinged with dread. Gallus finally hissed. "Ten *thousand* French mercenaries?" he repeated, astonished. "Is it really true?"

Tiberius nodded. "That is what d'Vant said," he replied. "This is purely confidential information, you understand. I heard it purely by accident. When I was discovered, d'Vant wanted to execute me as a spy but de Moray and de Winter would not let him. It finally came down to a rather brutal fight and when d'Vant was incapacitated, de Moray let me go. He wanted me to warn you as well."

As Gallus shook his head, overwhelmed by the entire circumstance, Maximus grunted in disbelief. "So you fled," he said. "But you fled with de Moray's daughter."

"That is because de Moray let me. I have his blessing."

"You would not lie about this?"

"Of course not. Ask Douglass if you do not believe me."

Gallus put up a hand to stop the conversation between them. "Whether or not he married Douglass without de Moray's blessing is not at issue," he snapped softly. "What is at issue is the fact that Henry is moving thousands of French scum into England to do battle for him and his first target is Erith Castle. De Montfort must know immediately."

Tiberius nodded firmly. "Indeed, he must," he said. "But there is one more thing – de Moray told de Winter and d'Vant that Edward is siding with de Montfort. He did not divulge who told him the information, of course, but if Henry does not yet know that his son has betrayed him, he soon will."

Gallus and Maximus processed that bit of information. It seemed as if both sides knew something quite serious about the other. The situation, the struggle within the greatest hierarchies of English power, was growing in magnitude. But instead of moving into the keep to inform de Montfort, as Tiberius expected, Gallus' gaze continued to linger on his younger brother. There was curiosity there and perhaps even suspicion. There was a great deal he wanted to say.

"It seems there is much that has happened since you have been away," Gallus said quietly. "Now that you have delivered this information to us, what does this mean for me and Maximus and you? Will you now return to de Moray to fight with him or will you remain with us?"

Tiberius smiled sheepishly. "My loyalty was never truly with de Moray," he said. "Surely you knew that. I was honest in my intentions when I pledged to the man, but even he knew that my heart and soul are with you. I am not sorry I went with de Moray for I have what I set out to acquire; his daughter. But I am sorry that I withdrew my fealty from you as if it were an easily breakable bond. It's not, you know. Will you accept my oath, brother? I swear to you

I shall never withdraw it again."

Gallus gave him a lopsided grin. "I knew your loyalty was never with de Moray, either," he said. "I knew you would come back someday. I prayed you would."

All was right in the world again now that the de Shera brothers were reunited. Gallus hugged Tiberius and Maximus kissed the man on the cheek again. All was forgiven, as if nothing had ever happened. As if Tiberius had not strayed. With nothing more to say, the three of them continued on into the dim interior of Isenhall Castle where de Montfort had just been introduced to Lady Douglass de Moray de Shera by Lady Jeniver.

De Montfort lifted an eyebrow at the fact that Tiberius' new wife was a daughter of a supporter of the king, but he said nothing. Nor did Edward when he was introduced to the woman a few minutes later. Politics and loyalties, these days, made for oddly arranged marriages.

When the de Shera women were settled in another room and Tiberius told de Montfort and the prince what he had heard at Wintercroft, they were rather glad Tiberius had evidently been consorting with the enemy for if he hadn't been, he would not have been in a position to collect vital intelligence. De Montfort was about to lose a strategic property if they didn't move quickly and as much as the de Sheras did not want support from the Lusignans, de Montfort did and it was his property they were defending. The French were in.

As the afternoon waned and turned into the evening, a war council met in the solar of Isenhall, men planning to make their way north to Erith Castle and circumvent King Henry from taking what did not belong to him and use it for a launching point in his attempts to subdue the north from de Montfort's influence. By midnight, the de Shera army was mobilizing for a dawn departure as the de Shera brothers, along with de Montfort and Prince Edward, attempted to get a few hours of sleep before departing. Already, things were in motion because there was no time to waste. They had to make it to Erith Castle quickly or all would be lost.

A storm rolled in just before dawn and the thunder began to roll, with pounding rain and strong winds, but Gallus, Maximus, and Tiberius didn't mind a bit. It was a good omen as far as they were concerned.

The Thunder was about to storm.

CHAPTER EIGHTEEN

"**D**O YOU HAVE everything, then?" Douglass asked, securing the leather tie on one of his saddlebags. "I have never seen you off to battle before so please tell me if there is anything more you need."

Tiberius was dressed from head to toe in full armor. He was wearing a padded tunic, a full mail coat, the heavy woolen de Shera tunic over the top of that, heavy leather breeches, boots, and a full regalia of weapons placed strategically around his body. As tall as he was, the addition of full armor made him appear infinitely more imposing. The man was ready for war.

But he wasn't so focused on what lay ahead that he couldn't sense his wife's apprehension. He had made love to her three times during the course of the night simply because he couldn't bear the thought of leaving her or, worse yet, not returning to her. He'd never experienced any feeling like that, ever, so he was having a difficult time reconciling it. Douglass' nerves at his departure only made it worse.

Tiberius was nearly packed and the bailey was jammed with de Shera men, ready to ride to battle, and only a moment ago he heard Maximus bellowing at the men. It was true that the rain was pounding and the thunder rolled, but it was never a good sign when Maximus started to bellow, even if it was to be heard over the elements, so Tiberius knew he had to get moving. It was time to bid his wife farewell.

"I have everything," he told her, stilling her hands when they continued to fuss with the leather tie. "Come and sit with me a moment, please."

Clasping Douglass' hands between his very big ones, he pulled her over to the messy bed and sat down on the end, forcing her to sit next to him. Douglass was looking at her hands, enfolded in his, until Tiberius forced her chin up so he could look her in the eye.

"Sweetheart, I know you are anxious," he said softly. "I realize this entire circumstance is a bit of a shock, having been quickly married and then your husband departing so swiftly afterwards, but you are in very good hands with Jeniver and Courtly. You needn't worry."

Douglass gazed into his eyes, feeling as if her heart was about to burst from her chest with sorrow. She could hardly breathe for it. "I am not worried about life at Isenhall after you depart," she said, struggling not to weep. "As I said, I have never had to send anyone I love off to battle before. Papa has gone, of course, but this… this is different."

Tiberius could see how she was struggling with her emotions and he pulled her head to him, his lips against her forehead in a comforting gesture.

"I know," he murmured, his lips against her flesh. "I have never left anyone behind before that I have cared about. But I know that everything will work out in the end. We will do our duty and I will return to you, I swear it."

She was silent a moment, resting her head against his. "You still have not told me what it is you are going to do," she complained. "I know that it is serious and I know that it is something that involves my father. Will… will you at least tell me if you are going to face him in battle?"

He stroked her glorious reddish-gold hair. "I truly do not know," he said honestly. "There is every chance that I will, but I cannot be sure. If I do, however, I promise you this – I will not raise my sword against him. He saved Maximus' life and is therefore someone my brothers and I will go out of our way to protect, even on the field of battle."

That gave Douglass a huge amount of comfort. Her head came up, her dark eyes glittering with emotion. "And you?" she whispered. "Who will protect you?"

Tiberius kissed her, deeply and sweetly. "My brothers and I all watch out for one another," he told her, kissing her cheek as he released her. "You needn't worry about me, wife. I can take care of myself."

Douglass had no choice but to agree. To dispute him would make it look as if she had no confidence in him. Therefore, she did the only thing she could – she nodded and squared her shoulders bravely, determined not to be an emotional mess, at least not until after he had left.

"I know you can," she said with forced confidence. "Where are you going once you leave Isenhall? Are you going straight to your destination?"

He shook his head. "We are going to Kenilworth to collect de Montfort's men," he said. "De Montfort sent missives out last night to our allies, so at some point, we will be converging with them. It should be a mighty army we field."

A mighty army for battle, she thought to herself but she didn't comment on it. She kept her thoughts to herself. "I am sure it will be," she said as evenly as she could. "Please let me help you take your things outside now. I am sure your men will be waiting."

He shook his head, standing up. "Nay, sweet," he said. "It is wet and miserable out there. I will go alone. I would rather remember you sitting here, warm and sweet, rather than out in that drench of water. Will you say farewell to me now? I must go before Maximus comes looking for me. He will try to punch me if he is mad enough."

Douglass stood up next to him, craning her neck back to look at him because he was so tall. She forced a smile, the best one she could produce under the circumstances. All she really wanted was to roll into a ball and sob.

"I will save you from your brother," she said, teasing. "But I know you must go now. Everyone is waiting for you. I will therefore say something simple by way of a farewell – I will tell you that I love you madly. You have become my heart, Tiberius de Shera, and you will always be my forever. Please remember that."

Tiberius smiled, touching her soft cheek. "You will always be my forever, too," he whispered, bending down to kiss her. "I love you very much. I will come back, I promise."

"I believe you."

He wasn't entirely sure if she did or not but he didn't force the issue. He merely smiled again as he collected his saddlebags and sword. His shield and other weapons would already be loaded onto his horse by the squires. Throwing open the door with the intention of heading out, he was hit in the knees by squealing girls as Violet and Lily charged in, giggling and shouting at their favorite uncle. The dogs, Taranis and Henry, were right behind them and Tiberius was nearly knocked over as the girls and the dogs rushed into his chamber.

Douglass, laughing, stood out of the way as the children and animals created instant chaos. They were jumping on the bed now, demanding Tiberius join them and, after a moment's indecision, he set his possessions down and lay across the bed so the girls could jump on him. They did, gleefully, pretending to conquer him. Tiberius dutifully pretended to weep. It was their usual game and he would take a few moments to play it with them. He had missed it.

"Violet!" Jeniver gasped, abruptly in the doorway. "Lily! Off of your uncle with you! He must leave!"

Tiberius lifted his head, putting a hand up to prevent Lily from kicking him in the face. "It is all right," he assured his sister-in-law. As he pushed himself off the bed, the girls clung to him, and he found himself carrying them both to the open door. "One game before I leave will not change the fate of a nation."

Jeniver smiled contritely. "They have been swarming by your closed door for an hour waiting for you to come out," she said. "I am sorry if they disturbed you."

Tiberius shook his head. "They did not," he replied, kissing Lily on the cheek before he set her down but being thwarted from kissing Violet, as she did not like kisses. He simply put the girl to her feet. "But I really must leave now before Max comes looking for me."

Jeniver nodded firmly, taking the little girls by their hands and pulling them out of the way as Tiberius collected his possessions once more and quit the room. He was almost to the end of the corridor when Courtly emerged from the bedchamber she shared with Maximus.

"There you are!" she said to Tiberius. "I can hear Max raging all the way up here. You'd better hurry!"

Tiberius waved her off as he took the stairs quickly. "I am hurrying," he assured her. "Take care of my wife!"

"Godspeed, Ty!" Courtly called after him. "We will take great care of Douglass!"

He was gone, out of earshot, and Courtly and Jeniver instinctively turned to Douglass, who was standing in the chamber doorway. Douglass' expression was taut with longing, with worry, but it was clear she was attempting to be brave. They were all trying to be brave, as all of their husbands were leaving this morning, heading into battle. That was all the women knew. No one knew the details. There was no reason to. All that mattered to them was that the men return safe.

Douglass forced a smile when she realized her two new sisters were watching her, each lady with a good deal of sympathy. Although Jeniver and Courtly knew her bravery was forced, they didn't comment. They didn't try to ask her of her feelings or force her to speak of them. They simply went into Jeniver and Gallus' chamber, the one that faced out over the bailey, to watch their husbands depart. Once the men left the safety of Isenhall's enclosure, the rest was up to God.

As Douglass watched the de Shera and de Montfort banners pass through the gatehouse in the pouring rain, she found herself praying harder than she had ever prayed in her life. Praying for the husband who had very quickly become her entire life.

Be safe, my love, she prayed. *God grant you the strength and skill and luck to return to me.*

Hopefully, God was listening.

Somewhere south of Erith Castle, Cumbria
Ten Days Later

THAT LAD IS *Maximus' son.*

Tiberius couldn't help but watch the very big youth as the lad rode a big, brown rouncey on the battle march north. Tiberius had only been informed about the boy the day they left Isenhall for Kenilworth and now, ten days into their march northward, Tiberius was still having difficulty accepting the fact that Maximus had a bastard. For years, the rumors of such things had always been about Tiberius, so for the grandson of a smithy to have been declared Maximus' bastard was still something of a shock. Tiberius always imagined he would be the one meeting his bastard child someday, not Maximus.

Not strangely, however, he took to the awkward, young man right away and for the past several days, Cassius had been following Tiberius around and Tiberius had been imparting his knowledge on the boy. Tiberius had a wonderful way of communicating, a skill that was not lost on Cassius. Additionally, Cassius seemed very attached to Stefan, and the son of Maximus with the skip in his speech was finding acceptance among the greatest knights that England had to offer. For a young man who had known little acceptance or even friendship in his life because of his speech impediment, it was a wonderful, new world for him. Finally, he felt as if he belonged.

"Have you ever been this far north, Cassius?" Tiberius asked the lad.

Cassius shook his head. "N-Nay, m'lord," he replied. "I-I have spent all of my t-time with my grandfather at Ogmore. We d-did not travel much at all."

Tiberius slanted the boy a long look. "You do not have to address me formally," he told him patiently. "Did I not tell you that before?"

Embarrassed, the boy shrugged. "I c-cannot help it," he said. "I f-feel as if I must."

Tiberius gave him a wry expression. "Every time you address me formally, I am going to throw something at you," he said. "It may be a tiny pebble or it may be a giant rock. You will not know so the fear of not knowing will cause you to think twice before addressing me as 'my lord'. Is that understood?"

Cassius laughed although he was trying not to, not entirely convinced that Tiberius was serious about the threat. "I will try," he said. "P-Please do not throw rocks at me."

"Then do not address me as 'my lord'."

"W-What should I call you?"

Tiberius puffed up proudly. "I am your Uncle Tiberius," he said. "Does that not sound grand? Not many people can claim to have an Uncle Tiberius."

Cassius nodded and chuckled. But he soon sobered up, his dark green gaze looking north. "A-Are we soon to reach our d-destination?"

Tiberius nodded. "Soon," he said, looking around at the green, rolling hills of the north. The scenery at times was quite dramatic. "Possibly tomorrow. But if we happen to see any action before that time, I will tell you what I have told you before. You will go back with the provisions wagons and remain. I do not want you anywhere near any fighting. Is that clear."

"A-Aye."

"Good."

Cassius felt rather scolded but he knew it was for a purpose. No one wanted to see him hurt and, since he had not yet mastered the skill of a sword, he understood. His gaze traveled to the front of the column they were riding in, to the multiple banners they were flying. It looked quite crowded, and quite impressive, up there. He pointed up to the front.

"Where is Hugh B-Bigod's seat?" he asked.

Tiberius could see the blue and yellow Bigod banner up ahead. "He is from Norfolk."

"A-And de Clare?"

"He is a marcher lord, so he stays to the Welsh borders."

"These are very g-great men."

"Indeed they are."

"D-De Montfort has gathered a mighty army, then."

Tiberius shrugged. "As great as he could gather at such short notice," he replied. "We were lucky that Bigod and his men were still gathered at Kenilworth and we were able to join with de Clare as we marched north. It takes time to assemble a great army and since we are moving so quickly, there has not been much time."

Cassius looked around him. "S-Sir S-Scott said that his f-father had returned home," he said. "S-Stefan said that as well. Do you think their f-fathers will be joining us?"

Tiberius shrugged. "It is possible," he said. "De Wolfe is much closer to Cumbria than du Bois is, so it is possible you will be able to experience battle with the mighty William de Wolfe. It would be something to tell your grandchildren."

Cassius grinned at the impressive thought. Even he had heard the legends surrounding the Wolfe of the North, William de Wolfe. He looked over his shoulder at all of the infantry following them.

"H-How many men do you t-think there are?" he asked.

Tiberius looked around, too, at the variety of different factions gathered under the de Montfort battle march, all moving northward.

"I would say well over two thousand men," he said. "Mayhap even more than that."

That was a lot of men having gathered for de Montfort's cause. "Are more c-coming?" Cassius asked.

Tiberius cocked his head thoughtfully, thinking on what he had heard from d'Vant – *ten thousand French mercenaries*. If that was really the case, then two thousand men would not stand much of a chance, but he didn't voice his concerns.

"Mayhap they are," he said steadily. "Word has gone out to most of the major barons so it is possible that more of them are moving for Erith as we speak. We will not know until they actually arrive."

It was an overwhelming thought for a young man who had hardly seen such things. It seemed to him that all of England was moving and his father and uncles were right in the middle of it. Now, he was right in the middle of it. For a lad who had only been introduced to the knighthood recently, he was coming to think that he might indeed like to have it as his profession. As difficult as it was sparring with Stefan, and working from dawn until dusk with the de Wolfe brothers hanging over him, he still found it something worth doing. In spite of everything, he was coming to like it. He wanted to fight, too.

To the west, dark clouds were forming and as the de Montfort army traveled norward, they could hear the thunder rolling in the distance. A storm would soon be upon them. As most men were looking to the west, Cassius was looking to the east. He was seeing something dark as well, only it wasn't clouds. It looked like a dark line on the horizon, on the crest of a distant hill. He stared at it awhile before pointing it out to Tiberius.

"L-Look over there," he said. "W-What do you suppose that is?"

Tiberius looked to where the lad was pointing and it didn't take him long to realize exactly what it was. He was suddenly furious that the scouts and sentries, men who were supposed to be on watch, hadn't seen it sooner.

"Get back to the provisions wagon," he told Cassius. "Go now and do not argue."

Startled, and also fearful, Cassius did as he was told as Tiberius spurred Storm through the ranks of men, charging to the front of the column where the great barons were riding, including de Montfort and Prince Edward. Tiberius charged right up in front of them, nearly cutting off the entire group.

"Look!" he shouted, pointing.

All heads turned to the east, seeing the thin dark line that was moving, shifting, and undulating. Like a line of ants, the dark mass was moving and everyone who saw it knew what it was, just as Tiberius had. The cry began to go up and men began to move.

"We form lines here!" de Montfort bellowed. "Move the men off the road and form lines! Form them now!"

Gallus, Maximus, and Tiberius were moving with the de Shera men, eight hundred of the best men England had ever seen. They had around two hundred archers with them, men skilled at the long bow, and then every infantry man was armed with a crossbow. The de Shera contingent usually went to the front of any fighting line and this battle line was no exception. As the storm rolled in from the west and big, fat droplets of rain began to fall, the de Montfort army positioned itself against an army of men approaching from the southeast.

"We are hours away from Erith Castle," Gallus said to de Montfort as the two of them watched the incoming black tide of men take form. "If we take a stand now, then mayhap we can prevent them from reaching Erith altogether."

Simon was watching the incoming army with great concern. "I have already sent messengers ahead to Erith announcing our arrival and telling my garrison commander, my son Richard, to be vigilant," he said, agitated. "I want to know why none of our scouts returned to tell us that the army was coming at us from the southeast."

Gallus adjusted the straps on his helm. "I want to know that as well," he muttered. "The only reason I can think of is that they were spotted by Henry's army and killed before they could reach us. That is the only explanation."

As the two of them pondered that scenario, Hugh Bigod, a powerful blob of a man, rode up on his great, white charger. Gallus and Hugh had a good deal of history together, most of it bad. Months ago, before Gallus had married Jeniver, Hugh had wanted Gallus for his own daughter and Gallus' marriage to Jeniver had caused a great rift between them. These days, the peace between them was very brittle but they were able to work together when necessary. As Hugh came to a halt, he looked directly at Gallus.

"Why was Henry's army able to come up behind us?" he demanded. "Your men were scouting, were they not?"

Gallus' eyes narrowed dangerously at the man as de Montfort spoke. "We were just discussing that issue," he said steadily. "We believe that Henry might have killed them in order to prevent them from warning us. That is, in fact, the only explanation. Gallus' scouts are beyond reproach. Go back to your men, Hugh. You are covering my left flank. I suggest you get back there."

Rebuked and infuriated, Hugh slapped his visor down and charged back to where his men were gathering. He only had a few hundred with him, a far cry from the thousands he commanded. He'd sent word to his properties in Norfolk but reinforcements would take time, and time was something they did not have. Therefore, the barons that usually remained to the back of any battle, watching it rather than participating, now had to actively fight. This included Bigod.

As Hugh rode away in a huff, Tiberius took his place. The knight had his crossbow in hand, something he usually did at the commencement of a battle. He would join the infantry in launching arrows at the opposing infantry.

"The men are positioned, Gallus," he told his brother, struggling to contain his excited horse. "We will await your signal."

Gallus lifted a hand, indicating he understood him, and Tiberius thundered off to resume his post, which was traditionally directly behind the archers. As Tiberius assumed his position, he kept one eye on the incoming army and the other eye on Maximus, who would generally deliver the command to release the arrows. Now that everyone was in position, it was time to fight and the anticipation grew.

In tense silence they waited, watching the army in the distance as it grew steadily closer. They were flying standards but as the clouds gathered and the rain began to fall more steadily, it was difficult to see the colors. In fact, de Montfort's army began to notice that the incoming army was no longer advancing. They were forming loose blocks but certainly nothing that seemed threatening. It was confusing. Tiberius broke ranks and made his way over to Maximus.

"They are slowing down," he said to his brother. "In fact, it looks to me that they have stopped altogether. Moreover, that does not look to me like ten thousand men. Does it look like that to you?"

Maximus was fixed on the enemy in the distance, wiping the rain out of his eyes so he could see more clearly. "It does not," he said. "It looks like a few thousand men at the very most. But why have they stopped?"

Tiberius shook his head. "That is a very good question," he said. "Mayhap we should take advantage of it and rush them while we can. Catch them off-guard, as it were. Mayhap if we can break them and scatter them, we can make our way to Erith and reinforce her ranks before they regroup and charge."

Maximus nodded. "It sounds like a reasonable idea," he said. "I will relay it to de Montfort. If he wishes to charge, I will give you the signal. Resume your post and wait for me."

Tiberius returned to his position, struggling with his frenzied horse, who sensed the approaching battle. The truth was that he was excited, too. Excited to charge into battle and excited to scatter Henry's gathered forces. He was both relieved and confused to realize it wasn't the ten thousand men d'Vant had spoken of. He wanted to scatter this army, to crush it, and to send them back where they came from. It was what Tiberius was born to do, something he'd done a dozens of times in his service as a knight, and the rush of battle was something he fed off of. Therefore he waited, impatiently, for Maximus to give the signal.

The thunder rolled and the rain began to pound in earnest as the red standards that de Montfort used to signal an attack were raised. The red standards indicated the infantry and knights while the yellow standards indicated the archers. The yellow standards weren't raised at all, leading Tiberius to believed that they were to keep the archers out of it and conserve their arrows for possible use at Erith when, and if, they moved on to the castle. As the lightning flashed, the red standards were waved, and the rush of horses and infantry began in earnest as they charged towards the distant army.

Tiberius was at the head of the charge. He was leading hundreds of men, setting an example for them, and the crossbow was secured to his saddle in favor of his sword. With his weapon in hand and shield slung over his left knee, he drew closer and closer to the opposing army who, so far, was simply standing there. They weren't moving at all. But that didn't matter to Tiberius. He plunged into their lines, swinging his sword, cutting down a standard bearer and trampling on the standard.

He realized too late that it was a de Winter standard.

CHAPTER NINETEEN

"**N**AY," TIBERIUS GASPED when he saw the de Winter emblem, pounded into the muddy earth. "Dear God... *nay!*"

He screamed to the de Shera men to call them off but they couldn't hear him over the rush of the wind and the pounding of the rain. They were feeding on bloodlust, determined to eradicate the enemy, and they didn't hear his frantic yelling. Maximus however, did hear him, and he saw with horror the muddy standard that declared de Winter's army. He was the first one to see the de Moray standard, too, sopping with wet with the colors running. The weather had been so bad that they hadn't seen either of these banners until they were on top of them. Horrified, Maximus looked around to see that his men were slaughtering the de Winter men, who seemed to be in some disarray. The de Moray men were fighting back a bit more, an effort that increased when a big knight rushed into the skirmish.

Tiberius and Maximus recognized Garran's horse right away. Kicking aside men, shoving and pushing, they made their way towards Garran, who seemed to be the lone knight in a sea of infantry. It seemed odd, so very odd, and Tiberius began shouting to Garran as soon as he drew near.

"Garran!" he roared. "Garran, hear me!"

Garran saw Tiberius and Maximus as they made their way to-wards him. He, too, began to kick through the mass of fighting men as he struggled to make his way to them.

"Stop!" Garran shouted. "The men have been instructed not to fight! Stop it or you will slaughter them all!"

Bewildered, Maximus and Tiberius began to shout to the men to stand down. More of de Montfort's knights heard their cries and, without question, they also began to call for the men to stand down and back off. The storm was now wild overhead, dumping rain in buckets and creating a great swamp that men were slugging around in. Even the chargers were getting stuck in certain spots. As the cry to cease fighting rolled through the ranks, Gallus came riding up, utter confusion and outrage on his features.

"What in the name of Great Bleeding Christ is happening?" he demanded. "Why are you calling for a cessation?"

Tiberius pointed to the mashed de Winter standard. "This is a de Moray and de Winter army," he said, feeling sickened. "The men have been ordered not to fight, Gallus. We are simply slaughtering them where they stand!"

Gallus was livid. "What do you mean they have been ordered not to fight?" he demanded, looking to Garran, in the slop a few feet away. "What is happening?"

Garran motioned for the de Shera brothers to follow. "Come with me," he said. "You must come with me."

Tiberius started to follow but Gallus was not so easy. "Why?" he bellowed across the storm. "Why must we come?"

Garran didn't have time to explain. "You *must* come!" he begged. "Please!"

With that, he spurred his charger towards the east, back where the provisions wagons and surgeon were gathered. Horses were corralled and tethered, and someone had hastily erected a tent. Because of the random copse of trees throughout the field they were fighting on, the de Montfort army coming in from the east hadn't been able to see the tent and the gathered wagons near the crest of the hill. Moreover, the blinding rain had fairly well obscured everything, including all other identifying standards.

With the fighting dying down, Gallus, Maximus, and Tiberius spurred their animals after Garran. The man came to a halt near the half-erected tent, bailing from his charger. He bolted into the tent and the de Shera brothers followed.

The tent was dark and cold but it provided some shelter from the storm. There were two lit tapers throwing weak light into the darkness and as Gallus, Maximus, and Tiberius entered the tent, the first thing they saw was Grayson de Winter on his back. Davyss and Bose were next to him, and Grayson's youngest son, Hugh, stood at his father's feet and openly wept. Stricken, Gallus pushed forward, getting water all over the bedroll that Grayson was laying on.

"God's Bones," he said, stricken by the sight. "What has happened? Uncle Grayson, what is wrong?"

Bose looked up at him. "I heard the fighting," he said. "You attacked, did you not?"

Gallus looked at the man, baffled. "We did," he said simply. "We did not know it was you. We assumed it was Henry's forces, and correctly so, but we did not know it was only de Winter and de Moray men. Bose, what in the hell is happening?"

Bose sighed heavily. He looked as if he had aged ten years since the last time Gallus had seen him. Rather than answer the question, however, Bose moved his attention to Tiberius. In fact, it seemed as if Tiberius was all he could focus on for the moment.

"Douglass," he said, his voice hoarse. "Is she well?"

Tiberius nodded. "She is, my lord. Healthy and happy."

Bose closed his eyes briefly in thanks. "Have you married her?"

"I have."

Bose accepted that information "Excellent," he muttered. "Her mother will be delighted."

Tiberius was comforted that Bose was pleased with his marriage to Douglass but he was also rather edgy as he looked about the tent, peering into dark corners.

"Where is d'Vant?" he asked. "Is he here also?"

Bose shook his head. "Nay," he said quietly. "He went back to London to inform Henry of Edward's defection to de Montfort. They should be a few days behind us."

Tiberius was relieved to hear that but it did nothing to ease his sense of confusion at the entire circumstance. He looked from Bose to Grayson to Davyss and Hugh.

"I see," he said. "But what is happening? Why was your army ordered to stand down? We charged into them before we saw any standards and I am sorry to say that you have lost men. What in the hell is going on?"

Bose lifted his head, drawing in a deep breath. Exhausted, he scratched his dark head. "We left Wintercroft and headed north to Erith Castle shortly after you left for Isenhall," he said. He sounded so very weary. "We were outside of Cambridge when we picked up about two thousand French mercenaries who had recently landed to the north of Canvey Island, at the mouth of the Thames. They were traveling east on the orders of Henry. They attacked us at first until we were able to convince them that we are allies of Henry, but we suffered some injury, the results of which you see with Grayson."

Gallus, Maximus, and Tiberius were listening carefully. "Where are the French?" Gallus wanted to know. "They did not come with you?"

Bose shook his head, throwing a thumb in a southerly direction. "Nottingham," he said. "We convinced them to wait there for the bulk of Henry's army coming up from the south. But we knew that de Montfort would be riding hard for Erith and we had to come ahead to tell you that d'Vant's information was wrong. It is not only the ten thousand French he spoke of. We were told, by the mercenary commanders, that there will be thousands of Teutonic and Irish mercenaries as well, more mercenaries than we believed possible. They are coming soon, Gallus. We cannot stop them."

Gallus felt rather sickened by the news. "So why are you telling me?" he asked. "You are allied with Henry. He will not like that you have told me this."

"Is de Montfort with you?"

"He is."

"Then we will tell him together," Bose said, sounding defeated. "The truth of the matter is this, de Shera. I owe Henry my very life. I have supported the man under any circumstance, even to the point of being pit against my friends and former allies. But what he is doing is encouraging an invasion of England by foreign forces and this I cannot support. There will soon be more French and Irish and Teutonic men on these shores than Englishmen and it is not something I will tolerate. If only to give England back to the English, I will no longer support Henry and Grayson feels the same way. We are therefore here to join you, Gallus. Will you accept our support?"

Gallus was stunned. He never thought he would hear such words coming from de Moray and the realization was overwhelming. But one thing was abundantly clear. Even though de Moray and de Winter were staunch supporters of the king, and ever had been, he believed de Moray without question. This was not a trap or a ruse. This was a man realizing that England as a country was more important than a king and his foolish whims.

Bose was English and he wanted to protect his country. That fact was as clear as the rain that was falling from the sky. As the wind howled and the thunder rolled, Gallus could only think of one answer.

"With the greatest of pleasure I will accept your fealty, my lord," he said softly. Then, his gaze moved to Grayson. "Both of you, in fact. Now, tell me what is wrong with Uncle Grayson? How can we help?"

Grayson, hearing his name, rolled his eyes open. He was extremely pale, his skin the color of paste, and his lips had a sickly, blue tinge to them. The man looked like death.

"Where is Maximus?" Grayson asked softly.

Maximus, who had been standing back with Tiberius and absorbing the stunning turn of events, took a few steps forward into the weak light of the taper.

"I am here, Uncle Grayson," he said. "What may I do for you?"

Grayson's gaze fell upon the big de Shera knight and his features seemed to relax a bit. "I am glad you are here," he muttered. Then he groaned a bit, shifting, as if something greatly pained him. "I took a mercenary sword to the back. The wound itself was not terribly bad but a day later, my chest began to hurt terribly. Now, I can hardly draw a breath and it feels as if my entire chest is in a vise. I have had pains in my chest since I was a young man but never like this. This time, it is different and I fear I shall not survive long. I asked de Moray to find you and that is why we are here. I would not let him leave me behind with the rest of the wounded because this is too important. We are here to support de Montfort in the hopes he can give England back to the English but we are also here because I need to speak with all of you. Particularly, I need to speak with you, Maximus."

Maximus' brow furrowed. "Why?" he asked. "What may I do for you? Whatever it is, I shall do it."

Grayson reached out a hand to Maximus and the man took it, holding it tightly. "You can listen to me," Grayson said, his words soft and nearly slurred. "All I ask is that you listen."

Maximus nodded, glancing at Davyss as he did. The eldest de Winter son was pale with sorrow. Davyss idolized his father and was undoubtedly crushed by what had happened. When he met Maximus' gaze, the man could feel the impact of sorrow. He had to look away or be caught up in it.

"I am listening," Maximus said softly.

Grayson tried to draw in a deep breath but it was nearly impossible. He ended up coughing and causing himself tremendous pain. When the coughing spasms died down, he spoke in raspy tones.

"You are aware that your father, Antoninus, and I were the best of friends," he said. "We grew up together and we fostered together. Antoninus met your mother, Honey, at a banquet. I was at the same banquet but I did not meet her until hours later and by that time, she was already smitten with your father. Unfortunately, I was smitten with *her*."

Maximus glanced at Gallus. They both knew this story. They had heard it before. They had discovered right after Honey's death that Grayson had always been in love with the woman. He'd said as much. This information was nothing new and they did not want him to distress himself.

"We know," Maximus said, squeezing Grayson's hand. "It does not matter to us. You are still Uncle Grayson, a treasured member of our family."

Grayson looked at Maximus, his old eyes glimmering dully. "Mayhap that his true," he murmured. "But there is something more you should know, something only your mother and I knew. Maximus, your father was a good man. The best. But, much like Tiberius, he had a wandering eye. In his younger years, there were rumors about him and other women, rumors that your mother chose to ignore. I do not believe she ever told you that about Antoninus. She wanted his sons to view him with the worship of a son. She did not want to taint your view of him with the humiliation of a wife. I am sorry to tell you this, but the rumors of him were true. I saw evidence of it with my own eyes."

Maximus glanced at Gallus again before looking over his shoulder at Tiberius to see what their reactions were and, as he had suspected, they had none. He returned his attention to Grayson.

"I will not dispute you if you say it is true," he said, "but I fail to see why you are telling us this now. Our father has been dead for nearly ten years."

Grayson nodded faintly, closing his eyes because his chest hurt terribly and talking made it worse. But he had to finish what he was about to say. If he died, then the truth died with him. He did not want that to happen. It was selfish of him and he knew it, but he had to speak. The truth had to be known to those it would affect.

"Right after Gallus was born, your father fancied a woman from London, the daughter of a wealthy merchant," he muttered. "Although he loved Honey a great deal and was very proud of his first son, he could not resist this woman's charms. He swore that she would be the last mistress in a long line of them, but as time passed and he spent more time in London, Honey became quite distressed about it, enough so that she wrote to her father. Christopher de Lohr, as you know, is not a warlord one would want as an enemy. Christopher told Honey that he would go to London and settle the situation with Antoninus once and for all and while he was in London, I went to Isenhall to comfort Honey. I will admit that it was purely for my own selfish reasons. I was also quite bitter that Antoninus had married the woman I loved yet he treated her very poorly. Your mother was distraught and I comforted her. I also seduced her. She was weak and I took advantage of it. I bedded her and I am not sorry I did it, not in the least. I loved her, Maximus. I loved her very much."

By this time, Maximus was looking at the man with a mixture of loathing and shock. He was still holding Grayson's hand and he dropped it, struggling not to become enraged.

"Why do you tell us this?" he demanded. "Is it a death bed confession you give? Do you seek our absolution for your sins against our mother? I will tell you now that I will not forgive you for that, not in the least."

Gallus wasn't in control of himself much more than Maximus was but he put his hands on his brother to settle the man down. Maximus tended to get violent when angered and now was not the time. Gallus, too, was looking at Grayson with a good deal of shock and loathing, but he also sensed there was something more to this. He didn't imagine the man was telling them simply to clear his conscience. There was something more to this confession and that suspicion had him on edge.

"Quiet, Max," he hissed, settling his brother down. He returned his attention to Grayson. "Why are you telling us this, Grayson? What *is* your purpose?"

Grayson could see that Gallus and Maximus were outraged by what they'd been told. Behind them, Tiberius simply hung his head and it was difficult to see what his reaction was other than deep sorrow. Saddened to burden these men he loved with such knowledge but spurred onward by an innate need to spill the truth, Grayson continued.

"Hate me if you will," he said. "I do not blame you. But my purpose in telling you is this. Maximus, you were born nine months after I bedded your mother. Although she is not sure I am your father because she and Antoninus reconciled shortly after my time with her, she long suspected that you are a de Winter and not a de Shera. Look around you, boy. Look at Davyss and Hugh. See how you favor them? Gallus and Tiberius are fair whilst you are darker and meatier. You also carry the supreme de Winter trait of a temper. Davyss has it, as does Hugh. It is entirely possible that you are my son, Maximus, and I wanted you to know that. Before I die, I had to tell you that I have loved you since the moment you were born as *my* son. Antoninus loved you as his own and he never knew what had happened between Honey and me. You were a de Shera in his eyes and he was proud of you as such, but I was proud of you for another reason. I believe you are my first born son, Maximus. I am sorry to tell you this now, but I must. I pray you do not hate me overly for it."

Maximus rocked back onto his heels as if he'd been struck. His mouth popped open and he slapped a hand over it as if to keep the scream that was rising in his throat from bursting forth. He was utterly overcome with emotion; shock, dismay, disbelief, sorrow, and grief. Everything he could possibly feel was raining down over him and he bolted up, rushing blindly from the tent before anyone could stop him.

Maximus staggered out into the storm but he didn't get far. Gallus and Tiberius were behind him, grabbing hold of him, preventing him from running off. Maximus tried to pull away from them but he was unable to. He hadn't the strength. The shock running through his veins had sapped all of his energy. He could only stand there and hang his head and quiver.

"Max, listen to me," Gallus said urgently. "He is not sure it is the truth. Even if it is the truth and you are his son, it does not matter. Do you hear? It does not matter in the least!"

Maximus was nearly in tears. "It *does* matter," he bellowed. "Did you hear him? I am not a de Shera. I am a de Winter. God, so many things make sense now. I never looked like either of you. I never acted like either of you. It never occurred to me that there was a reason behind the fact that I am different from you and Tiberius. I am and you know it."

Gallus shook him, gently, but Tiberius pushed Gallus out of the way and grabbed hold of his middle brother. There was so much grief swirling around them, grief mixed up with the wind and the storm, and they were all trying to make sense out of it. Too much had happened on this night, too much to process. But they were trying. God help them, they were trying.

"Max," Tiberius said. "It does not matter what he said. It does not matter if you have de Winter blood or de Shera blood because we *are* brothers, do you hear? We are brothers in the heart and in the mind and in the soul, and the words of a dying old man cannot take that away from us. I look at you and I see a man I have admired my entire life. You are The Thunder Warrior, the fighter that all men hope to be. I was born five years after you, enough of an age gap that I was just far enough behind you to be an annoying little brother who worshiped you. I still do. Whatever Grayson said in there can never take that away. Regardless of who your real father is, you are my brother. You are a de Shera and our bond, our brotherhood, is unbreakable. That will never change."

By this time, Maximus was looking at Tiberius, digesting his words, letting them stop the bleeding of the wound that Grayson had so recently inflicted upon him. Gazing at Gallus and Tiberius as the rain poured and the lightning flashed, he struggled to calm himself.

"Nay," he finally said. "It will never change. I do not want a dying man's words to destroy my entire life but I cannot un-hear what I have heard. I cannot erase those words from my head."

Tiberius still had his hands on him. "If you discovered that I had another father, would it make you feel differently towards me?" he asked. "Would you cease to think of me as your brother?"

Maximus shook his head. "Of course not," he said. "We are bound by our bonds of love and loyalty. Nothing can ever change that."

Tiberius shook him gently. "Exactly," he said quietly. "Nothing can ever change our brotherhood, Max. We are bound for eternity by the de Shera name and our love for one another. As long as we have that, we are invincible."

Maximus took a deep breath, laboring for calm, laboring to settle

Grayson's words in his mind and the words of Tiberius. His younger brother, the man who was at times so glib and so annoying, was also infinitely wise in his view of the world. His words made so much sense, quenching the sorrow that had filled Maximus. There was still a shadow of sorrow there, a phantom of grief, but Tiberius had managed to tame them. At least, somewhat. Maximus was grateful for that. After a moment, he smiled weakly.

"I have never given you much credit for being so wise," he said to Tiberius. "You surprise me sometimes."

Tiberius grinned. "That is a good thing, is it not?" he said. Then, he grasped Maximus' hand and lifted it up, glove against glove. He held Maximus hand tightly. "We are unbreakable. You are a de Shera, Max, no matter what. Say it with me – *I am a de Shera*."

Maximus grunted, reluctantly, but he did as he was asked. "I am a de Shera."

"Say it louder."

Maximus grunted again. "I am a de Shera."

"Louder!"

Maximus lifted his face to the heavens, shouting it into the storm. "I am a de Shera!"

The words were drowned out by the storm but it didn't matter. Maximus felt better for having said them. He looked at Tiberius again, seeing the man through different eyes.

"You have grown up, Ty," he muttered, putting a big hand on Tiberius' cheek. "Somewhere in the past few weeks, you have grown up. I rather like this man you have become."

Tiberius chuckled, looking between Maximus and Gallus. "I have had the best examples in the world set for me," he said. Then, he sobered. "What Uncle Grayson said in there about father... mayhap the man had his unsavory traits. I think we all do at some point in our lives. But he is still my father and I still miss him every day."

Gallus nodded strongly, with feeling. "As do I," he said. "Nothing Grayson said has changed my mind about Father, or Honey for that matter. Sometimes... well, sometimes we do things in moments of weakness that we never do again. I would like to think that Honey was not a weak woman, at any point in her life. Whatever happened... it does not truly matter."

As they stood in the rain, pondering their mother's relationship with Grayson de Winter, they caught movement out of the corner of their eye and saw Davyss standing a few feet away. The knight appeared uneasy, nervous even, as he eyed the de Shera brothers.

"Maximus," he said, rain dripping off his dark lashes. "I just wanted to say that I am sorry for what my father said. I hope that does not change how you view the House of de Winter. I still view you all as my family. I would be shattered if that is now ruined."

Gallus shook his head. "It does not change anything," he said. "We are still strong, Davyss, mayhap now more than ever."

Davyss was visibly relieved. "Then I am grateful," he said. "Truly... thank you for your graciousness. But you must forgive me now, as I have also come at the request of my father. He has asked me to ask you if you will grant him a favor."

Gallus glanced at Maximus before replying. His brother had no discernable reaction so Gallus continued.

"What is it?" he asked.

Davyss appeared uncomfortable again but he responded. "My father wishes to be buried near your mother when he finally passes," he said. "He has asked if you will consider his request."

Gallus sighed heavily and looked at Maximus and Tiberius. His brothers were visibly dubious, a reflection of Gallus' own feelings on the request. It was clear what they all thought about it. Gallus returned his attention to Davyss.

"Although I understand that your father had feelings for my mother, I think it would be disrespectful to my father and your mother to allow it," Gallus said quietly. "Tell your father I will consider it, but know that, when the time comes, he will be buried in the de Winter crypt and your mother, when she passes, will be buried alongside him. I think you will agree that is the best thing to do."

Davyss nodded, rather ashamed that deep family secrets had come out this night. "I do," he said. Then, he hesitated a moment before continuing. "My mother and father have always been cordial to one another but it was not a true love match. Max, I am so sorry about all of this. I had no idea he was going to say what he did. To all of you, again, I am very sorry."

Gallus held out a hand to the man and he came close, taking the outstretched hand and holding it tightly.

"Davyss, you are not to blame for the passions and indiscretions of our parents in their youth," Gallus said. "What matters now is that we stay true and honorable to our family names. No matter what your father has said, Maximus is still a de Shera and you are still very close in our hearts. We will fight alongside you now that the winds of loyalty seem to be shifting and we are proud to do so. Now, if you will excuse us, we need to find de Montfort and tell him what de Moray told us. We will continue on to Erith and we will continue to fight to keep England for the English. That is all we can do."

With that, Gallus, Maximus, and Tiberius turned and headed for their horses as Garran, Bose, and finally Hugh wandered out of the haphazardly-pitched tent, watching as the de Shera brothers mounted their mighty steeds and rode off into the night, off to find de Montfort and off to plan the course of England's future. For them, family loyalty and the bonds of men who called themselves brothers were stronger than bloodlines. For them, nothing – not even the words of dying men or the mention of past infidelities – could break that bond.

For the men who tamed the lightning, the Lords of Thunder, their bond and their strength would live on into legend. With wives acquired, children to be born, and new children discovered, the House of de Shera was guaranteed to live on from generation to generation, but the greatest generation of the family came in the form of three brothers with an unbreakable connection to one another. Their lives, and their loves, were deeply entrenched in one another and would be forever more.

The de Shera Brotherhood would live on.

EPILOGUE

1271 A.D.
Isenhall Castle

"GRAB HIM!" MAXIMUS shouted. "Grab him or he will get away!"

Tiberius threw himself forward, grabbing at Cassius, but Cassius was stronger than a bull. He pulled his uncle along with him as he struggled across the hall but he was sent to his knees when his Uncle Gallus and his father leapt on top of him as well. Even though Cassius was pinned on the floor by three very big men, he was still struggling to break free. He was clawing at the floor of Isenhall's great hall, trying to pull himself out from under the pile of men.

"You made this... this d-deal," Cassius grunted. "I d-did not agree to it!"

Maximus was trying very hard not to laugh. Tiberius, who had Cassius around the shoulders, was losing the battle against the giggles, and they couldn't see Gallus' face because he was lying on Cassius' legs.

"Great Bleeding Christ," Gallus groaned. "He is cutting off the circulation in my arm. He has *me* pinned!"

Tiberius started to giggle and he lost his hold. Sensing his uncle's weakness, Cassius tried to break free but the three de Shera brothers tightened their grip. Maximus reached over his son's head and hooked his fingers in the man's nostrils, pulling his head up. With his arms pinned, Cassius howled.

"Let me go!" he demanded. "Cease your torture!"

Maximus wasn't pulling hard enough to hurt but hard enough so that it must have been uncomfortable. "Swear to me you will not run if we let you go," he said calmly.

Cassius squeezed his eyes shut, defiant and in pain. "I will not!"

"Then we are going to be here a very long time, Cassius," Maximus said. "You are making an arse out of yourself. Turn around and see your brothers and sisters and cousins laughing at you."

Maximus looked over his shoulder to see a gaggle of children standing in the entry to the great hall. When they saw Maximus looking at them, grinning, they started to giggle and squeal. Maximus laughed at his sons, daughter, nieces, and nephews.

"Come in, everyone," he said. "Come and sit on Cassius. He is being quite foolish, you know. He deserves to be sat upon."

The dam burst and children rushed in. The first to pounce on Cassius were his younger brothers – Augustus, who had seen twelve years, and Kellen, who had seen ten years. They were both back from fostering at Kenilworth Castle, big and strong boys for their age. They were followed by their younger cousins, Magnus and Bose, sons of their uncle, Tiberius, and after those four, the very young children piled on after them – three and four-year old Lucius and Justus, who looked just like their father, Maximus, and then the girls came – eight-year-old Elizabetha, daughter of Maximus, and twins Thomasina and Josephine, three-year-old daughters of Tiberius. All of the children piled on to Cassius, who was by now simply laying there and trying to cover his head because Thomasina and Josephine seemed to think it was a very good idea to sit on it. He wasn't fighting back in the least now.

The only child left was not really a child at all, but a lad bordering on manhood. Bhrodi de Shera, the oldest of the children at thirteen years of age, stood in the entry to the great hall and watched the frolicking with distaste in his expression. His father, who had since pushed himself off Cassius to allow the children to pile on, went to his son.

"Why do you not jump on Cassius like the rest of them?" Gallus wanted to know. "He deserves the punishment."

Bhrodi frowned. He was a very serious young man recently returned from spending a couple of years in Wales with his grandfather, Gaerwen, who was old and feeble these days and did not travel. Bhrodi had been spending time with the old man, learning the ways of his Welsh heritage because his mother wished it. He had also been training with Welsh fighters and had learned the Welsh way of battle, something his father had been trying to work out of him. Bhrodi would one day hold the lands of Coventry and it was important he understand his English heritage as well. But the result, at this age, was a lad who was torn between two cultures and didn't really fit in either of them. He watched his cousins and uncles roll about on the ground.

"It all seems rather silly to me," Bhrodi finally said. "The man does not want to be married, Father. Why must he be forced?"

Gallus smiled faintly at his only child, his beloved son. "This marriage was brokered many years ago by your Uncle Maximus," he said. "Cassius is to wed the daughter of a great de Shera ally. He is simply nervous because has had not yet met her."

Bhrodi looked at his father. "Who is the ally?"

Gallus glanced over at the pile on the floor, noting that Maximus and Tiberius were now standing by, watching as their children beat up on Cassius.

"Bose de Moray," he said. "Cassius is to marry your Aunt Douglass' youngest sister, Lady Sable. She should be here very soon. In fact, that is why we are all here, to witness the marriage of Cassius to Sable. It is a joyous occasion."

Bhrodi doubted that by the way his older cousin was resisting the union. "If it is, then someone forgot to tell Cassius," he said. "He wants to leave."

Gallus shook his head. "He cannot leave," he said flatly. "There will be more guests arriving, including your Aunt Courtly's sister and her husband."

Bhrodi thought on the aunt he'd seen fairly frequently while he had been in Wales because she didn't live far from his grandfather's castle. "Aunt Isadora is coming?" he asked, watching his father nod. "I... I do like her husband, Kirk. He has come to Rhydilian Castle to sup with Grandfather and me. He has also taught me some skill with a sword. He is very good."

Gallus smiled. "St. Héver is quite talented with a blade," he agreed. "They are bringing their son, Keenan, whom your Aunt Courtly has not yet seen. She is most anxious to see her nephew."

Bhrodi didn't much care about his new cousin. He was still looking at Cassius, who was now trying to sit up but the toddlers wouldn't let him. As Cassius finally gave up his struggles to escape his family and began tickling little ribs, a de Shera soldier entered the hall looking for Gallus.

"My lord," the soldier addressed the earl when he finally spied him. "We have spotted two incoming parties, one from the north and one from the south."

Gallus nodded in acknowledgement, looking to his son. "What should you ask the soldier, Bhrodi?"

The question was all part of the training Gallus had been trying to give the boy since his return from Wales. He was trying to force the boy to think, to assume some of the authority that the earldom he would inherit someday would require. Bhrodi, knowing he was being tested, gave his question serious thought.

"Do you see any standards?" he asked the soldier.

The soldier fought off a grin at the young lad, trying very hard to be cool and in command. "Black and red de Moray colors from the south, my lord," he said. "They should be here very shortly. As for the group coming in from the north, we cannot say yet but we believe it to be de Winter. I am sending out scouts to make sure."

Bhrodi nodded and thanked the soldier, looking at his father to make sure he should not have asked more questions. Gallus smiled proudly and Bhrodi let out a sigh of relief. As the soldier headed out of the hall, Cassius, who had heard the man's report, climbed to his feet.

"So she is here," he said even as children were hanging on him. "I suppose I c-cannot escape now even if I tried. They will see me and they will pursue."

Maximus came to stand next to his disgruntled son, now twenty-eight years of age and a very big and very powerful knight in his own right. Cassius de Shera rode with the de Shera armies, with his father and uncles, and he was well-respected and well-liked by the men. He had Maximus' fighting ability, Gallus' cunning, and Tiberius' intelligence all rolled into one. The stammer he had been born with was now hardly mentionable and he could bellow clear and determined orders better than his father could. More than that, he was quite pursued by women demanding their fathers make marital contracts with him but de Moray had been smart enough those years ago to lay his claim first for his youngest daughter. Now, Lady Sable de Moray was of age and the wedding mass was planned for the morrow if the groom didn't escape.

"If I were you, I would not try to run from Bose de Moray," Maximus said to his son. "If he catches you, I will not be able to help or defend you. You are on your own."

Cassius frowned at his father, noting that his Uncle Tiberius was now standing next to him. Knowing he was cornered, defeated, he put his hands on his head and groaned.

"No offense to Aunt Douglass, for she is a lovely woman," Cassius said, "but I have not even seen her sister. What if the female beauty in the family is not consistent? No one has even seen Lady Sable for years because she has been fostering. What if she is a horror? Must I still marry her?"

Maximus was sincerely trying not to grin at his desperate son. "Look at your Aunt Douglass," he admonished. "Can you truly believe a full-blooded sister would be a horror?"

Cassius couldn't, in truth, but he still wasn't excited about this marriage. Therefore, he avoided the question.

"I am simply too young to be m-married," he said, frowning. "I still want to travel the world."

Tiberius, standing next to him, cocked a wry eyebrow. "So take your wife with you."

"I want to go places where women are not welcome!"

Tiberius burst into laughter while Maximus spoke, incredulous. "Where in God's Good Name would that be?" he demanded. "A harem of a great sheik? A Roman bath meant entirely for men?"

Tiberius was still laughing at Cassius, who knew that weeks and months and even years of protests were all in vain. Therefore, he simply shut his mouth. When he didn't answer, his father poked him in the arm.

"Look around you," Maximus said quietly. He was pointing to the array of younger brothers and cousins standing around him. "You are frightening your brothers with your fear of marriage. If you have imparted your feelings onto them, your mother will have your head. You had better watch what you say. Already, the younger ones are suspicious."

Cassius looked at Augustus and Kellen, standing a few feet away from him. "Would you want to marry someone you have never met?" he demanded, pointing to Augustus. "Well?"

As Maximus rolled his eyes, Augustus responded. "I will choose my own wife," he said in a tone that sounded very much like Maximus. "I will not let Papa choose her for me."

Maximus cocked an eyebrow at his son who had much the same personality as his mother; frank, honest, and forceful at times. "Is that so?" he said. "We shall see about that, lad."

Augustus looked to his younger brothers for their reaction, hoping he hadn't said anything that would greatly provoke their father. Maximus was a very loving father but a strict disciplinarian. With five sons and a daughter, he had to be. Uncle Tiberius was considered the peacemaker among all of the offspring. He was the one his nieces and nephews ran to when Maximus or Gallus was enraged. He'd been known to hide children from angry parents until the parents had the opportunity to cool down. With five young children and his wife pregnant with their sixth, he was much adored by all of the de Shera progeny.

As Augustus backed off of a confrontation with his father and Cassius stood among the men and fumed, Gallus returned his attention to Bhrodi.

"You will not be reluctant to marry, will you?" he asked his son.

Bhrodi, like most boys his age, hadn't truly thought on the idea of marriage. He lifted his shoulders. "If she is beautiful and smart, I suppose not," he said, rather arrogantly. Then, he shifted the subject because, like Augustus, he really had nothing much to say about it. "Papa, are Violet and Lily coming home for the wedding?"

Gallus shook his head. "Nay," he replied. "There is some great feast or festival going on in London right now and they begged to remain. Evidently, being part of Edward's court is more important than coming home, but do not be insulted – the men I sent to London with your sisters to watch over them and guard them have told me that they both have their eye on young men there. They are both of marriageable age now and I suppose that is what is most important to them."

Bhrodi shrugged. He didn't know women's minds and didn't pretend to. As he made his way over to Cassius to perhaps offer some condolences for his coming wedding, there was a commotion in the entry. Everyone turned to see Jeniver and Courtly enter the hall.

Jeniver was carrying a layer of clothing across her arms as Courtly followed, carrying her year-old son, Pollux, on her hip. Courtly began waving the children over to her.

"Joey and Tommie!" she called to Tiberius' twin daughters. "Aunt Jeni must put you in a clean tunic. Hurry, now. Lucius and Justus, come here. Elizabetha, help me, please."

The children were beginning to scramble, rushing to their mother and aunt. "What's amiss?" Maximus asked as he went to his wife and took his toddler son from her arms. "Why the rush to put clean clothing on the children?"

Courtly had her three-year-old son by the arms, pulling his dirty tunic over his head as the child whined. "Because the de Morays are arriving," she said. "Douglass has gone to meet them with Charlotte by her side. Ty, you should as well. I promised her we would put the younger children in clean clothing for the introduction to her parents so it does not look as if we have all raised a pack of dirty, wild animals."

Tiberius left the hall with his older sons Magnus and Bose in tow as Courtly tended his youngest child. But she and Jeniver had their hands full tending all of the children, putting clean clothing on them and wiping off dirty faces. Gallus, Maximus, Bhrodi, and the reluctant bridegroom stood by, watching, waiting for the de Moray family to make an appearance. Cassius thought it was all a lot of fuss over nothing, fuming, as Gallus and Maximus watched the man for signs that he was going to try and bolt again.

"Hugh de Winter was married two months ago," Gallus said to Maximus as they watched Cassius twitch. "I went to the wedding, if you recall."

Maximus nodded. "I do," he replied. "Hugh married Roger Mortimer's daughter, didn't he?"

Gallus nodded. "He did, indeed," he said, speaking loudly with the sole purpose of Cassius overhearing his conversation. "He inherited a baronetcy from her. Baron Audley, you know. Quite prestigious, you know. And his wife is lovely. He was reluctant to marry, too, but it worked out in his favor."

Maximus glanced at his son to see if he was listening to them. "Davyss is bringing his wife, Devereux, and their four children," he said, returning his attention to Gallus. "He seems to have changed a good deal since marriage. Often, it settles a man. Fills a need in him. I know it did with me."

They were trying to make marriage sound wonderful and happy but Cassius wasn't buying what they were attempting to sell. He simply rolled his eyes and looked away, wondering just how horrible his bride was going to be. All he knew was that she had been fostering for the past several years in Lincolnshire, or so he thought, and that her name was Sable. That was essentially all he'd ever been told, ever since his father had bartered the contract those years ago. Grossly unhappy as Jeniver and Courtly finished cleaning up the children, he plopped down onto a bench next to the feasting table and brooded.

It was a move that didn't go unnoticed by Gallus or Tiberius. Cassius was looking at the entire situation as one that would ruin his entire life and there wasn't anything more they could say about it. As Cassius sat with his chin in his hand, Maximus handed his year-old son back over to Courtly and then turned his attention to Gallus.

"God help us all if that girl is homely," he muttered. "At least I saw my wife before I married her. I had a choice."

Gallus nodded. "As did I," he whispered. "In any case, Cassius has no choice and neither does Lady Sable. I will admit that I am anxious to see her myself."

Maximus grinned. He could hear commotion outside of the hall entry and he turned his attention in that direction, as did Gallus. In fact, everyone turned their attention towards the entry, enabling Cassius to move away from his family and towards the small service entrance that the servants used. He was fully prepared to run. As he casually made his way in that direction, slowly as not to attract attention, Gallus and Maximus remained focused on the great entry.

"Speaking of Davyss and Hugh has reminded me of something," Maximus said. "You do not think that Davyss will bring up burying his father here again with Honey, do you?"

Gallus shook his head. "He stopped asking years ago," he replied. "I was particularly shocked when Lady Katherine de Winter sent a missive asking if I would consider burying her husband next to our mother. Lady Katherine is a woman with balls of steel to ask such a question. I have never met a more brazen and determined woman."

Maximus chuckled. "How cozy," he commented dryly. "Burying Uncle Grayson here would create a sweet little threesome with Grayson and Father on either side with Honey in between. What happens when Lady Katherine dies? Do we bury her on top of Honey?"

Gallus started to laugh but his chuckles were cut short as people began to enter the hall. The first one through the door was Tiberius followed closely by a very pregnant Douglass, who looked positively radiant. Following Douglass was Bose, his dark hair now almost completely white, and a small, lovely older woman in a delicate, white wimple and fine gown. Gallus and Maximus immediately moved forward.

"Gallus," Tiberius called out to him. "Greet Lord de Moray. He has come a very long way to beat you at a game of cards."

Gallus laughed, extending a hand to Bose, who took it strongly. De Moray had aged a great deal over the past thirteen years but he was still as sharp and as powerful as ever. His black eyes were warm on Gallus and Maximus.

"You do not age, my lord," he said to Gallus. His gaze then moved to Maximus. "But you look terrible, Baron Allesley. How fortunate you married such a beautiful woman that she can overlook such things."

Everyone chuckled at Maximus' expense. "I cannot insult you because you have your womenfolk about you," he said to Bose. "But, rest assured, when we are alone I will have no such restraint. I will verbally beat you into the ground."

Bose grinned. He was very glad to be with Gallus and Maximus and Tiberius again. He reached out to the small woman standing beside him. "I shall try to prepare myself," he said wryly. "But until that time, let us move on with pleasantries. I should like to introduce you to my wife, Lady Summer du Bonne de Moray, whom you have not yet met. Summer, this is Maximus, Baron Allesley, and Gallus, the Earl of Coventry."

Summer de Moray was a lovely woman with beautiful, pale green eyes. Her hair was covered by her wimple but they could see tendrils of blond peeking out. She greeted Gallus and Maximus politely. "I have heard so m-much about you, my lords," she said, a slight stammer in her speech. "I am t-truly honored."

Gallus took her outstretched hand gently in greeting. "It is our pleasure, Lady de Moray," he said. "To finally meet Douglass' mother is truly delightful. Welcome to Isenhall."

Summer smiled, a gesture that looked exactly like Douglass. "You are soon to have another daughter of m-mine," she said, her gaze turning to Maximus. "Baron Allesley, it is your son that my youngest daughter is pledged to. I will be honest when I say she did not want to come at all. We had to practically tie her to the wagon. She is young and stubborn, but I assure you that she is a kind and obedient girl."

Maximus had to laugh. "We have had much the same issue with Cassius today," he said. "Arranged marriages are very difficult when the couple has not seen one another, so let us get on with the introductions. I am looking forward to meeting Lady Sable."

Summer and Bose turned to look at the rear of the group of people that had accompanied them and Bose held out his hand, obviously focused on one of the persons back in the pack. As he did so, Maximus turned to bring Cassius forward and was stricken when he saw that his son was almost to the servant's door, preparing to escape. He boomed.

"Cassius!" he shouted. "Come here this instant!"

Cassius had his hand on the iron latch, cringing when he heard his father shout. He was at the door, very nearly to freedom at that point, and it would have been so easy to run. But run to where? He truly had nowhere to go and his father would only catch him. Nay, if he ran now with everyone watching, it would only make a bad situation worse. Frustrated, angry, he took his hand off the latch and turned to look at the group of people standing over near the hall entry. He prepared to meet his doom.

As he watched, a young woman emerged on Bose de Moray's arm. She was petite, with long, shiny hair the color of polished copper, and skin as pale as cream. Cassius could see her as she stiffly greeted his father and uncle, and he could clearly see when she looked in his direction because Maximus was pointing at him. Intrigued just the slightest, Cassius began to make his way back to the gathering, his gaze never leaving the small, beautiful woman with the copper-colored hair. It was so very shiny and as he came closer, he could see that she was dressed in a broadcloth gown that was dark brown in color, a gown that seem to emphasize a deliciously curvaceous figure.

God's Bones, Cassius thought. *Is it possible that this is Lady Sable?* There was only one way to find out. Cassius went to stand beside his father, no longer the petulant bridegroom but the seemingly very interested betrothed of a stunningly lovely young woman. The glorious words that came out of de Moray's mouth confirmed that she was, indeed, Lady Sable, and at that moment, Cassius couldn't even remember a time when he was reluctant about this marriage. For all he could remember, he had always been looking forward to it. His father spoke to him at some point and even nudged him to get his attention, but Cassius couldn't take his eyes off of Lady Sable. He couldn't believe his good fortune.

More guests arrived later in the day and early the next morning, including the House of de Winter and Courtly's sister, Isadora, but Cassius was hardly aware. He had been sitting with Sable and her parents since the moment they'd been introduced, hanging on Sable's every word, coming to know a young lady who also had a bit of a stutter in her voice just as her mother did and just as Cassius did. He felt drawn to her as he'd never felt drawn to anyone in his life, a kindred spirit in their similar speech patterns, and when the marriage took place the next day at Vespers in Isenhall's tiny chapel with not only the living as witnesses, but generations of de Sheras in their crypts, Cassius took his vows with the greatest sincerity and soon enough, Lady Sable de Moray became Lady Sable de Moray de Shera. Cassius was thrilled.

At the wedding feast, Gallus, Maximus, and Tiberius stood back and watched the festivities. They watched Cassius and Sable's joy as well as Bose and Summer's bittersweet happiness as they married off their youngest daughter. They watched Davyss de Winter tell wild stories to an enraptured audience of his lovely wife as well as Courtly's sister, Isadora, and her husband, Kirk St. Héver, who rolled his eyes periodically at Davyss' very tall tales. The de Wolfe brothers were no longer with the House of de Shera, having returned north to serve with their father, William de Wolfe, but Stefan du Bois was still with the House of de Shera these days, in charge of a new stable of fine young knights. All of them were feasting in the hall this night, enjoying the fine food and celebrating a good life.

For all of them, especially the Lords of Thunder, it had been hard-fought to get to this moment. For once, there was peace in the land with a new king and new ideas, but even so, there had always been joy within the walls Isenhall no matter what. On this night of nights, the joy knew no bounds.

"I feel her here, you know," Gallus murmured softly.

Maximus turned to look at him. "Who?"

Gallus smiled faintly. "Honey," he said confidently. "Can't you feel her? She is everywhere."

Tiberius, standing on the other side of Maximus with a cup of fine wine in his hand, nodded in agreement. "She is sitting in her chair near the hearth," he said, pointing over to the snapping, sparking hearth and a small, cushioned chair that was positioned there. "I can see her as clear as day. She is sitting there, watching all of us with great approval."

Maximus could see his mother, too, as he'd seen her sitting in that same chair, in that same position, for many years. "No matter what we have done in life and no matter how hard we have fought or what we have done to survive, a night like this is our reward," he said quietly. "It makes all of the trials and tribulations worthwhile. Although I wish Honey had lived to see all of this, it is enough to know that she lived as long as she did. But tonight… tonight, I miss her very much. I wish I could tell her that."

Gallus could feel himself becoming very emotional. "She knows, Max," he whispered. "Her presence is here, in this hall, in every child we have and every breath we take. She knows you miss her. She knows we all miss her."

Maximus could feel himself growing emotional as well. "If there was one more thing you could say to her, Gal," he wondered, "just one more thing… what would you say?"

Gallus took a deep, thoughtful breath as he contemplated the question. "One thing only?" he asked rhetorically. "I suppose I would tell her that I loved her."

"And I would thank her."

It was Tiberius who spoke. Gallus and Maximus turned to look at him. "Thank her, Ty?" Maximus said. "Why?"

Tiberius smiled. "Look at what we have," he said, indicating Jeniver, Courtly, and Douglass as they sat talking to their guests. They were three of the most beautiful, smart, and passionate women in all of England. "Look how fortunate we are. We owe it all to Honey. She made us what we are, don't you see? Without her, there would be no 'us'. There would be no Lords of Thunder."

Gallus grinned. "How right you are," he said. "I would thank her, too."

Inevitably, their attention turned towards the chair still next to the hearth, the chair that their mother had favored, the one they'd never had the heart to move. She was still there, watching them, proud of her sons as only a mother could be. Proud of the men they had become and the families they had raised.

Aye, she would have been very proud. And she would have been very happy that the legend of the Lords of Thunder, for one and for all, would live on.

THE END

Children of the Lords of Thunder

Children of Gallus and Jeniver

Violet (Gallus' first marriage to Catheryn)b. 1253

Lily (Gallus' first marriage to Catheryn) b. 1255

Bhrodi ap Gaerwen de Shera b. 1258

Tacey ferch Gaerwen de Shera b. 1279

Grandchildren of Gallus and Jeniver (through Bhrodi's marriage to Penelope de Wolfe)

William

Perri

Bowen

Dai

Tacey (g)

Morgana (g)

Maddock

Anthea (g)

Talan

Gallus

Children of Maximus and Courtly

Cassius (son of Maximus and Rose) b. 1243

Augustus b. 1259

Kellen b. 1261

Elizabetha (g) b. 1263

Lucius b. 1267

Justus b. 1268

Titus b. 1270

Children of Tiberius and Douglass

Charlotte (Charlie) b. 1260

Magnus b. 1261

Bose b. 1265

Thomasina (Tommie) (g) b. 1268

Josephine (Joey)(g) b. 1268

Antoninus b. 1271

Marcus b. 1273

TIBERIUS' APPLIS PYE

(Since Lady Courtly would have had her cooks prepare a pie crust to pour the ingredients into, you can use a store-bought 9' pie shell to save time. However, for the Lady of the Castle who wishes to make her own crust, a Medieval recipe for pie crust is at the bottom)

5 medium apples

6 figs, chopped

¼ cup raisins

½ cup honey

1 ½ tsp. (equal parts ginger, cinnamon, cloves, and nutmeg)

¼ tsp. salt

pinch saffron

Preheat oven to 350°. Peel, core, and grate apples. Add figs, raisins, honey, and spices. Mix well and put into tart crust. Bake until done – about 40 minutes. Serve warm or cold.

PYE CRUSTE

This 16th century recipe is one of the earliest that is strictly for making pie crust pastry.

1 ½ cups flour
4 Tbsp. butter
2 egg yolks
½ tsp. salt
pinch saffron
about 3/8 cup water

Mix flour, salt, and saffron together in a large bowl. Cut or rub the butter and eggs into the flour mixture until it forms fine crumbs. Add water a little at a time until it just sticks together – too much water will make the dough too soft and sticky. Cover with a towel and allow to rest for 30 minutes. Roll out on a well-floured surface and place in pie pan.

The Lords of Thunder, the de Shera Brotherhood Trilogy, contains the following novels:

The Thunder Lord, the story of Tiberius's brother, Gallus:

The Thunder Lord

The Thunder Warrior, the story of Tiberius' brother Maximus:

The Thunder Warrior

The heroine of this novel, Douglass de Moray, is Bose de Moray's daughter. Bose is the hero of The Gorgon:

The Gorgon

For more information on other series and family groups, as well as a list of all of Kathryn's novels, please visit her website at www. kathrynleveque.com.

344

ABOUT KATHRYN LE VEQUE

Medieval Just Got Real.

KATHRYN LE VEQUE is a USA TODAY Bestselling author, an Amazon All-Star author, and a #1 bestselling, award-winning, multi-published author in Medieval Historical Romance and Historical Fiction. She has been featured in the NEW YORK TIMES and on USA TODAY's HEA blog. In March 2015, Kathryn was the featured cover story for the March issue of InD'Tale Magazine, the premier Indie author magazine. She was also a quadruple nominee (a record!) for the prestigious RONE awards for 2015.

Kathryn's Medieval Romance novels have been called 'detailed', 'highly romantic', and 'character-rich'. She crafts great adventures of love, battles, passion, and romance in the High Middle Ages. More than that, she writes for both women AND men – an unusual crossover for a romance author – and Kathryn has many male readers who enjoy her stories because of the male perspective, the action, and the adventure.

On October 29, 2015, Amazon launched Kathryn's Kindle

Worlds Fan Fiction site WORLD OF DE WOLFE PACK. Please visit Kindle Worlds for Kathryn Le Veque's World of de Wolfe Pack and find many action-packed adventures written by some of the top authors in their genre using Kathryn's characters from the de Wolfe Pack series. As Kindle World's FIRST Historical Romance fan fiction world, Kathryn Le Veque's World of de Wolfe Pack will contain all of the great story-telling you have come to expect.

Kathryn loves to hear from her readers. Please find Kathryn on Facebook at Kathryn Le Veque, Author, or join her on Twitter @kathrynleveque, and don't forget to visit her website at www. kathrynleveque.com.

Made in the USA
Middletown, DE
25 September 2017